Praise for the novels of Nicholas Nicastro

"By turns comic, gruesome, beautiful and devastating. Certain images are unforgettable . . . others laugh-aloud funny . . . a clean, swift, luscious read."
—*The Ithaca Journal* (NY)

"Nuanced, insightful, and thoroughly believable. . . . Nicastro does what the artist can do and the historian cannot: probe the inner mind of the historical [figure]. . . . Carefully researched, accurate in tone and detail."
—James L. Nelson, author of the *Revolution at Sea Saga*

EMPIRE OF ASHES

A NOVEL OF ALEXANDER THE GREAT

Nicholas Nicastro

A SIGNET BOOK

SIGNET
Published by New American Library, a division of
Penguin Group (USA) Inc., 375 Hudson Street,
New York, New York 10014, USA
Penguin Group (Canada), 10 Alcorn Avenue, Toronto,
Ontario M4V 3B2, Canada (a division of Pearson Penguin Canada Inc.)
Penguin Books Ltd., 80 Strand, London WC2R 0RL, England
Penguin Ireland, 25 St. Stephen's Green, Dublin 2,
Ireland (a division of Penguin Books Ltd.)
Penguin Group (Australia), 250 Camberwell Road, Camberwell, Victoria 3124,
Australia (a division of Pearson Australia Group Pty. Ltd.)
Penguin Books India Pvt. Ltd., 11 Community Centre, Panchsheel Park,
New Delhi - 110 017, India
Penguin Group (NZ), Cnr Airborne and Rosedale Roads, Albany,
Auckland 1310, New Zealand (a division of Pearson New Zealand Ltd.)
Penguin Books (South Africa) (Pty.) Ltd., 24 Sturdee Avenue,
Rosebank, Johannesburg 2196, South Africa

Penguin Books Ltd., Registered Offices:
80 Strand, London WC2R 0RL, England

First published by Signet, an imprint of New American Library,
a division of Penguin Group (USA) Inc.

First Printing, December 2004
10 9 8 7 6 5 4 3 2 1

Dedicated with love to my wife, Maryanne:

sine qua non.

Legend

- - - Alexander's route 334–323 BCE
- City
- ✕ *Battlefield*
- ◆ Sanctuary or other feature
- ⤨ Mountain pass

Aral Sea

Oxus R.

Maracanda

BACTRIA · SOGDIA

Sogdian Rock

Bactra

Caspian Sea

HYRCANIA

ARIA · Paropamiscus Mtns.

Taxila

PARTHIA

ARACHOSIA

✕ *Hydaspes*

PERSIA

Kandahar

The Altars

Pasargadae

Multan

Persepolis

Indus R.

Persian Gulf

GEDROSIA

INDIA

Patala

Indian Ocean

© 2004 Jeffrey L. Ward

A NOTE ON UNITS OF MEASURE

This book includes a mixture of ancient and modern units of measure. For the sake of convenience, modern units are used when they were more or less similar to their ancient counterparts (e.g., feet, hours, months). Verisimilitude has been served by including a number of antique units that are common in the relevant historical sources. Most prominent here are the *stade*, a Greek unit of distance approximately equivalent to six hundred modern feet (and from which our word *stadium* is derived), and the parasang, a Persian unit equivalent to the distance a person could walk in an hour. On average the latter equaled thirty Greek stadia or three-and-a-quarter modern miles. An army of the time could cover about six parasangs in a day.

The common monetary unit is the Athenian drachma, which is equivalent in value to six obols. The superordinate units are the mina, worth one hundred drachmas, and the talent, equaling six thousand drachmas. The *daric* is a common non-Greek unit of currency—a gold coin minted by the Persians worth about twenty-six drachmas.

We know that a decent house in a suburb of Athens in the fourth century B.C. would set the buyer back five hundred to one thousand drachmas (or five to ten minas); a gallon of olive oil, more than three drachmas; a good pair of shoes, about 10 drachmas; a healthy slave, three to five hundred drachmas. Still, for various reasons, expressing the value of a drachma in today's currency is not as straightforward as finding modern equivalents for, say, distance. According to an oft-cited rule of thumb, the wage for the average skilled laborer in classical Athens was one or two drachmas a day. A talent, therefore, works out to the equivalent of almost twenty years of work, or in modern terms something like one million dollars. The treasury of one hundred twenty thousand talents Alexander is said to have plundered at Persepolis was therefore equivalent to some seven hundred twenty million man-days of labor. This amounts to "real money" even in U.S. government terms.

As for the calendar, the reader will notice there are no absolute dates given for the events depicted here. This is due to the simple fact that no universal calendar existed until recent times (and arguably, does not exist even today, given that the Chinese, Muslim, and Jewish calendars are still in use). Instead, years were designated either by counting the years since some important event, or on the basis of who held important magistracies at that time (in Athens, years were named for the so-called "eponymous" archons; Alexander, for instance, was born in the year of Elpines's archonship, known otherwise as July 356–June 355 B.C.). The court case described here takes place in the month of Pyanopsion (the Attic equivalent of October), in the year of Kephisodoros (323 B.C.); the events recounted in the trial of Machon occur in the years immediately before and during the campaign of Alexander, spring 334 through spring 323.

PROLOGUE

Olympias examined the face in her bronze mirror. "Such dull features," she thought, frowning at her saffron-tinted reflection, believing she saw in it the trial of every Epirote winter suffered by her forebears. She narrowed her examination to her eyes, tracing a flicker of interest in them as they regarded themselves. "Yes, those are fine," she said. "But the rest—hopeless!"

Before her, laid out like military assets on a battlefield, were the tools of a despised but lucrative trade: depilatories, astringents, demulcents, emollients, pomades, perfumes, balms. Next to a jar filled with a Syrian unguent of beef fat, thyme, and seagull droppings, she had a flask of Corinthian warming ointment made from sesame oil and turpentine. There was an Egyptian face powder that smelled of oleander and was milled so fine it flowed like liquid between her fingers; though its color was perfectly white, it rouged her cheek when she applied it. She also tried a curious device invented by a Syracusan that, with a single click, cut all the hairs of the eyebrow to a uniform length.

These were in addition to the usual natron powder, foundation of metallic mercury, kohl for the eyes, chervil for the breath—all the attributes of an expensive courtesan. No respectable woman, installed in domestic glory within her walls, would need to create a seductively wan complexion by daubing her skin with lead, or fake a blush with ochre pencils. Such freedom was the gift of ignorance.

And so that afternoon, Olympias, consort of the King of Macedonia, daughter of the royal house of Epirus, initiate advanced grade in the holy mysteries of Demeter, the Kabeiroi and the Great Mother, painted herself like a lowly flute-girl.

This wasn't necessary in past years. From the moment of their first meeting Philip had shown himself vulnerable to her attraction. They had encountered each other on Samothrace, confronting the celebrated Mysteries, but Olympias presented herself to him as a very solvable enigma. When they first married he would interrupt his endless campaigns and sieges to steal nights with her. An heir was eagerly anticipated—and yet, strangely, had not come.

This delay she first attributed to her tendency to climax early, often several times before her partner could lumber up his own (and relatively brief) contribution. Her pleasure may have acted to drive off the male humors necessary to the process of conception, her doctors told her. So she held herself back.

Yet something still seemed to go awry, something that impinged or intruded upon the process. Too often the king left her bed at the earliest courteous instance, lips moving silently, a slash of annoyance across his face. "Too much muttering, not enough mothering," she said as she mixed the kohl with its little spoon. The result was a maddeningly empty cradle.

Philip came to her just as she finished her preparations. There was a faint look of irritation on his face—the kind he wore when state business pulled him away from dice games and drinking parties. He hardly looked at her until she turned to him, her face glazed dazzling white like a funeral jar, her cheeks like puddles of dried blood.

"You look like a streetwalker," he said.

"Shall I take it off?" she asked, rising.

Not quite by accident, her gown fell open. The look of gray distraction finally left Philip's face as he eyed what he saw there.

"No, I suppose not."

When he touched her, it was always the same, like a traveler always taking the identical route through a half-understood country. His first move was to denude her left shoulder and seize the breast. He did so. She kept her eyes on him, shifting her weight precisely in time with the force of his attentions.

Philip never had trouble spearing generals and envoys with his eyes. When he was alone with Olympias, though, he could never hold her gaze. She was never so shy, searching his full, square, deceptively kind face, taking the measure of him. This inevitably distracted him, until she found herself turned around. He was pushing her down from behind.

"The back is still your best side—and most affordable, I would think."

"Three obols a go, if that's all you've got," she replied, tight-lipped.

He yanked up her gown, regarding the cleaved

haunch as it swelled down from her hips and rounded off at that swale of lubricious womanhood. A mound of true sweetness, he thought, though with that cloying softness of her sex, that quicksand prospect of letting him sink slickly away until he could go no farther. But this was like sleeping on a too-soft pillow after weeks on campaign—an adjustment he was just too impatient to make. So he took the other road.

She started at this, turning to face him. Camp-style buggery was not the object of her afternoon's work.

"But if you prefer, we might have a special price on the 'racehorse' . . ." she said, coaxing him back onto the couch.

"Now here is something," he thought, as she settled in jockey position athwart him. The gown had been disposed of, and she was looking down at him through tumbling flutes of sweet-smelling hair, breasts standing forward and free, that same vaguely appraising look on her face. The latter annoyed him, but not much in that soft vise. She turned away as she commenced to rock, not in passion but to avoid his breath, which stank of sprats and whatever wine painted his throat.

"Don't I bounce lightly?" she asked him.

"Expertly, expertly."

It began pleasantly enough. The kind of friction between them, though, was rarely the right kind, and soon both became frustrated. She could easily have come and dared not. He wanted to have done with it but couldn't. The position was unique, yet impractical for him, since he needed to use his hips.

At last he half-rose from the cushions, bucking into her from below until he finished. Olympias grasped him with her thighs like a real rider, her body first hardening and then pouring herself out around him. Then she lay to his side, one leg still slung over him.

Monarchy's duty done, the king planted a preemptory kiss on the top of her head and moved to slip away. He was restrained by her rigid, cocked leg.

"Let me go," he said. "I have business."

"Tossing dice, no doubt."

"The worth of my pursuits is not for you to judge. Let me up."

"And what about *this* business?"

He opened his mouth to reply, but was distracted by the peculiar sight of her rubbing her cheek against the royal tool. Pulling back, she revealed a coat of white lead transferred from her face to the bulb. She was smiling with childish delight at this, her cheek now covered with a pink impasto of ochre, metal, and spunk.

"Damn you, woman, what are doing to me?"

She used her fingers to smear the rest of him with her paint. "So squeamish! See—I've made a statue of your best feature. . . ."

"Chamberlain! Pheredeipnos! Fetch water!" he cried.

She propped herself up on an elbow, like a drinker at a party. "O Philip, why do you have such contempt for me?"

The chamberlain opened the door and entered—but was frozen in his tracks by Olympias's withering stare. Then he retreated.

She turned back to Philip. "You are too proud, sir. Your serpent is pretty, but so is mine. . . ."

He felt her root beneath his head and pull something from under the pillow. She was now dangling a long, colorful object in front of his face. Looking closely, he met the beaded eyes of a small snake.

"Sisyphus, salute your king," she addressed the snake.

Sisyphus opened his mouth, revealing a blue interior and a pair of needle-thin fangs.

Philip shot to his feet, dumping Olympias on the floor. "By the gods, you should live in a cage! I should send you back to that tree in Dodona you fell from!"

"My love, wait," she laughed. "He's harmless, just a little baby. . . ."

He slammed the bedroom door behind him.

An hour later, Philip was slouching beside his general Parmenion on a drinking couch. The room was small and deliberately hard to find, adjoining the back of the portico that overlooked the flats of the King's burgeoning capital. Now deep in his cups, Philip was imagining what it would take to fill Pella's lagoon with his very own navy.

"The Athenian contractors pay a talent and a half for each vessel, not counting pay and supplies," Parmenion told him.

"Perhaps we might shave a little off the pay. . . ." The prospect of cheap, boundless military capability made Philip's eyes shine like an impatient bridegroom's.

"Dangerous. The Athenians have motivated men at the oars, even citizens—"

Parmenion broke off. Lowering his cup, Philip saw why: Olympias had found them.

His wife was standing there clearly and unabashedly naked. She had done nothing to clean herself after their labors, her eyes caked with mineral black, her cheek still smeared with the royal seed. Philip glanced at Parmenion—the officer's eyes were prudently lowered, but a smile played on his lips.

Philip could think of nothing to say, until he finally sighed, "Woman, you are an affliction."

Olympias was looking up and away from them, her arms raised.

"Rejoice, O Macedon!" she cried.

The king opened his mouth to call the chamberlain, but the words died in his throat. Small objects were cascading down from between Olympias's thighs. They were hard, round. Each was propelled from her in force, bouncing and rolling on the tiles.

"I am an oak! I have conceived in Zeus!"

Stunned, Philip could only watch as the shining, growing heap of acorns collected at the feet of his Queen.

I

What soon gets old? Gratitude.
—Aristotle

The day broke cold on the empty square. Lying in the shadow of Hymettus, Swallow watched the autumn sun rise over the ridge. A shining wedge descended to light the plumes of stoking smoke from the factories, then the bronzed encrustations of the Acropolis. As the market stalls opened, a mantle of haze kicked up by thousands of feet settled over the town, warming him with its familiarity. Filing past him on their way into the market, his fellow Athenians (bless them!) looked down with contempt upon his prone body.

He got up when the first beams reached the pavement. Shucking his blanket, he rose to empty his bladder through his morning semirigidity. The market girls grimaced, turning away from his baggy, tufted nakedness, but he was long past caring if he impressed those snoots.

"Pay attention to the shoes, sister!" he yelled at one of them. "These aren't cheap shoes!"

Relieved at last, he took up the blanket again and dressed himself. Since it was a court-day, he arranged it in what he considered formal style, wrapping it around full-length and with the fringe thrown statesmanlike over his left shoulder. That done (and looking quite philosophic, he thought), he reached back and stuck his left forefinger into his anus.

Rooting about, he found the silver tetradrachm he kept there for safekeeping.

"Good morning, little owl," he hailed the coin. Let the slave girls turn their noses up at that!

True, he favored the northwest corner of the market to spend the night because it caught the first sunshine of the morning, and the crossroad altar gave some privacy from the road. Equally important, though, was that it was a good spot from which to tell the mood of the day. After years of observation, he could read much from the atmosphere in the very first moments of the morning. The speed and disposition of human bodies, their numbers, the presence of magistrates— all were clues.

By the throngs that were already pouring in, momentous events seemed afoot. Macedonians, notable for their capes and their taste for vulgar display of gold in public, were much in evidence. Cadets were filing from their barracks on the slope of the Acropolis, fanning out toward the gates of the city. Shoppers seemed weighted down with more than one day's burden of groceries. Their demeanor, he saw, was very anxious.

There was a wine seller's stall east of the Sacred Way that opened early. The place sold most of its good product—the Chian dry whites and Thasian blacks—in bulk to provisioners coming in from far places. The proprietor would also mix up a three-measure jug of local stuff for an obol, which was good enough to take the edge off the morning chill. The only thing to beware was his use of dirty water—Swallow had once tucked into a cup of sweet Attic that had been mixed with effluvia from the tannery next door.

He was on his second cup when his friend Deuteros saluted him.

"Swallow! Have you heard the news?"

"Antipater is banging your wife?"

Deuteros gave a weak smile and pulled out the little cup he kept under his clothes. Swallow poured out two fingers' worth for him.

"Big trial today. It's listed right in the middle of the dias. And it's not just some crappy inheritance case. . . ."

Deuteros downed the wine, looked around nervously. Swallow had been going to the courts with him for years, had shared the cup with him countless times, and yet never known him to show the slightest effect of drink. He was always sober, always with that subtly hunted look. The reason may have had to do with marrying a girl far too personable and pretty. While this seemed enviable to Swallow (and, indeed, would to most men), Deuteros had contrived to be out of the house virtually all the time since his marriage. Even then, he still seemed to be keeping a permanent watch on the streets, as if expecting to see his wife humiliate him by going out in public.

Swallow poured out another two fingers. "Tell me why I'm buying you drinks, Deuteros, when you live in a nice house up on the hill?"

"The defendant is Machon."

"Alexander's boy?"

"The same. And the prosecutor is Aeschines."

"What, he's back?"

"Apparently. The charges are 'betrayal of the public trust' and 'impiety'—or something."

"Sounds like Aeschines. But he must be very long in the tooth by now. And to come back from such a long way . . ."

As his friend was standing and thinking and not drinking, Deuteros tipped more wine from Swallow's cup into his own.

"A trial like that has big stakes. What, to try somebody

from Alexander's staff, with his regent's army breathing down our necks? It's stupid if you ask me, dear Deuteros. Antipater could bring his rabble right down here. What can the old man have in his mind?"

The other issued a resonant snort through his nose as he drank.

"Or maybe that's the whole point," Swallow went on. "If Machon ran afoul of 'the Boy,' maybe Aeschines thinks his indictment will keep us in Antipater's good graces. It seems like a big risk to me, anyway. Nothing can stop those Macedonian dogs! Just to be safe, we should probably vote 'guilty' if we get on the jury, right?"

Deuteros looked around furtively. "You asking me?"

"Who else is standing here?"

"Sure, guilty—I guess."

"There he stands, an adept of Themis herself!" Swallow laughed, clapping his friend on the shoulder. "Athenian justice is safe with men like you, Deuteros!"

They made their way across to the courthouse. There already seemed to be a throng of men milling outside, though only a few could have been eligible for service. The spectators' box would be filled today.

"Good luck!" said Swallow loudly, and then leaning in to Deuteros's ear, whispered, "Remember the verdict."

They parted, each proceeding to the entryway designated for his tribe: Swallow to KEKROPS, Deuteros to ERECHTHEUS. Just inside, the former dropped his juryman's tag in the box. The archon's assistant immediately fished the tag out, scrutinizing the name.

"You again! The state can't afford your civic-mindedness— unless we start charging you to fumigate the place!"

"I resent that," Swallow replied, adjusting his blanket in

a manner reminiscent of one of Demosthenes's dramatic pauses. This got a big laugh from the other jury candidates.

"Get out of my sight!" the secretary cried, dropping the tag back in the box.

Before the allotment began, Swallow encountered someone he'd find less welcome on the jury than little Deuteros. Eteocles of Kikynna saw him at the same moment, registering his recognition with a scowl. At that, of course, Swallow had to go over to welcome him.

"My dear Eteocles! It's no surprise to see you here for this event. And not alone, it seems!"

Eteocles was standing with two other well-kitted nobles, all sweetly redolent of leather and horseflesh. Neither of them would even look at Swallow. With proper reverse snobbery, Swallow despised anyone who rode in on a horse—the conveyance of the old-guard, tyranny-loving, fish-feasting, sympotic, leisured prickocracy.

"It is a surprise to see you," Eteocles sneered, "when your beloved Demosthenes is not party to the case."

"But your beloved Aeschines is—and after so many years away! Don't we all enjoy the sweet ooze of his oratory, like some unglued beehive! I can hardly wait."

"May you enjoy the spectacle, dear Swallow! Who knows how long such events will be open to persons like yourself?"

"And may I return your sentiment! I, for one, would miss the charming futility of your ambitions."

Before their exchange could begin its usual descent into undisguised insult, the jury selection began. The magistrate at the door forwarded the box of juror tags to the junior archon in charge of the allotment. The tags went into the rows of slots in the face of the machine, and the mixed black and white cubes poured down the metal tube mounted on its side. As the secretary drew tokens from the bottom of the tube, their color either nominated or rejected the respective row of tags.

The drawing was repeated ten times. That made fifty citizens randomly chosen from each tribe, so the jury would have, alas, only five hundred members. Swallow was hoping for a one-thousand- or even a two-thousand-man allotment, as the really big juries tended to have a far more refreshingly democratic rowdiness.

After the last name was read out, Swallow couldn't restrain his impulse to tease Eteocles.

"It seems the gods favored me today, my dear friend! And you, I presume, will return to your barn?"

"I will be with the spectators. Respect your good fortune, Swallow!"

This was an unexpectedly gracious response, and it made Swallow ashamed he had gloated.

II

The trial was held in the courthouse chamber with the most room for spectators. The jurors were knotted outside, each holding a short wooden staff painted the same red color as the door lintel. Swallow had just turned in his token to the clerk when he looked back and saw his friend waving a red staff at him from the back of the crowd. Both had made the jury.

Swallow saved a spot on a front-row bench for Deuteros. Since the benches were covered only with straw, naive jurors expended the precious minutes before the session began fetching cushions to sit on. But Swallow knew the key to comfort in the courtroom was to forget the rear and tend to the stomach. The hour was already late to complete such an important trial; most likely the verdict would be delivered after sundown and all would be going home in the dark (though to his "home," fortunately, Swallow did not have far to go). In anticipation of the inevitable longeurs, he carried in the fold of his blanket a hunk of white cheese and a handful of olives. Seeing this bounty, Deuteros nodded his appreciation, then opened his cloak to flash a loaf of good bread.

"Now if they only allowed wine!"

The clerk tried to gavel the room to order. Since this was an Athenian court, the task took several attempts. Some bumpkin had sneaked a sick lamb to the proceedings, no doubt hidden under his cloak, which bucked free and scampered under the benches. There was some commotion as the baying animal was cornered; the uproar gave the Scythian bailiffs, who looked like vain bears in their animal skins and city jewelry, a relished opportunity to shove people. The lamb was ejected over the vigorous objections of its owner, who also insisted on leaving despite the fact that the doors were sealed, with no one permitted to enter or exit. The dispute was resolved by the application of a club to the juror's head. Out cold, the man was returned to his seat—hopefully to revive in time to cast his ballot.

All this time Swallow kept his eye on Aeschines, who was seated on the prosecutor's bench to the right of the magistrate's dais. The old master was sitting very straight, eyes moving over some scribblings before him, lips moving slightly, as if in final rehearsal of a prepared speech.

He seemed fit for a man of nearly seventy years. His skin glowed like a ploughman's in summer—a consequence, no doubt, of a recent sea voyage from his academic posting on Rhodes. His tanned skin set off his abundance of snowy hair and a gleaming white chiton adorned by a purple-fringed girdle. Sitting there, serenely indifferent to the plight of the loose lamb, he seemed to be playing the role of a character who slept very well at night, yet had very important matters weighing on his silver-crested brow. Or at least that's how it seemed to Swallow, who was old enough to remember Aeschines's former career on the stage, specializing in kings, gods descendant, and honored corpses lying in state.

The gavel sounded again, this time swung by the presiding judge. The seat was filled, surprisingly, not by a junior functionary but the king archon himself. The only trials he presided over were supposed to involve special heinousness, such as parricide and profanation of the Mysteries.

"Isn't that Polycleitus?" Deuteros whispered, noting the same irregularity.

"It is. So they've brought Aeschines back, and put Polycleitus in charge. Somebody has a great interest in seeing this Machon put down. Maybe we should change our verdict. . . ."

"Silence in the courtroom!" Polycleitus commanded. "The clerk will read the indictment."

"Hear, O Athens! This court is convened according to all proper custom, under the due supervision of those so charged and here present, before a jury properly appointed, and in the names of Themis-bearer-of-scales and Athena-may-she-protect-us, and of Aglauros, Hestia, Enyo, Ares Enyalios, Thallo, Auxo, Hegemone, Heracles, and the spirits of wheat, barley, vines, and figs, and of the boundaries of Attica. We gather here now, on this second day of Pyanopsion, under the archonship of Ciphisodorus, to hear and judge the citizen, Machon, son of Agathon, of the deme Scambonidae, on the charges so listed. . . ."

The clerk had to rustle through his notes, which seemed to be out of order. There was silence in the room now, and a general pricking up of ears and lightening of backsides, with the sole exception of the man who brought the lamb, who slumped down from the bench and hit the floor with a thud. No one helped him.

"The charges are, first, that he did contravene the instructions given him by the Assembly twelve years ago when he set out on campaign with the god, known in his human guise as Alexander III of Macedon; and second, that he did commit impiety before said god, who was deified by *decree of the Assembly of the People on the sixteenth Metageitnion of last year. These are the charges."*

"Who brings the indictment?" asked Polycleitus.

"By the gods, I bring it," said Aeschines, rising to his cue. His voice had a depth typical of actors, but with an orator's urgency. It broke on the audience like the crash of a falling boulder—abrupt, inescapable.

"Begin your statement. Start the water."

The clerk pulled the stopper out of the water clock. At the outset, the prosecution had the floor for twenty minutes, with additional time at the discretion of the archon. Blatherers and incompetents were given little indulgence; Aeschines, to be sure, would be given all the time he wanted.

Athenians, I stand before you today after a long time away. In those years among foreigners I had much opportunity to observe the ways of other people, and to weigh their respective features in light of what I know as a citizen of this city. And in that time I never lost faith in the basic superiority of our arrangements, no matter how sadly abused, and in the inherent repugnance to our people of indecency and injustice, no matter how ubiquitous those vices may now seem. And I appear today with complete confidence that you will again judge rightly as I offer you the facts. Please understand that I make such charges with reluctance, and have so only sparingly in the past, because I do not believe our city is well served by frivolous or malign actions. These procedures, on the contrary, should be reserved only for cases of the utmost seriousness, and on the clearest evidence, as I know you will agree is the case with our friend Machon.

I know this, because it is understood throughout

this city that verdicts on trials of this type—that is, of impiety—have grave implications not only for the accused but for every citizen, as the gods do not discriminate between the impious man and those who abet him. In this sense, it is our entire city that is on trial. You do not need to be reminded that there is dangerous talk afoot, and that those who have led us into disaster in the past have raised their heads again since the death of Alexander. And given that a foreign army is but a few days' march from Attica, and that the emissaries of that foreign power are present here today, I am bound by my duty and love of my native city to remind her that her responsibilities are to herself first. As I present these truths to you, your job will be merely to perceive—for to perceive what Machon has done, you will also judge him correctly.

As Aeschines referred to Antipater's emissaries, his eyes flicked toward the spectators' gallery. Swallow could easily pick the Macedonians out of the crowd: they were the beardless ones, real Alexander-style buzz cuts, with the expressions of mulish superiority on their rustic faces. Doubtless they were thinking there would be no reason for such cumbersome litigation in Pella. Just a secret order passed to an underling, and thence to some eager, doe-eyed thugs just in from the hinterlands. They did things differently there.

The first charge I will address is of Machon's impiety. I am certain you recall the resolution of the Assembly not long ago, in response to a message from Alexander requesting divine honors. I am also told—for I was not there—that debate on this measure was as uncontentious as any ever put before that body. Even Demosthenes supported it, albeit with his usual contempt for men of quality, saying "Let Alexander be

Zeus's boy. And Poseidon's too, for good measure."
The measure passed by simple acclamation. Read the
resolution, please.

*The timekeeper stopped the clock, and the clerk read the
city's conferral of divine honors on Alexander. Swallow well
remembered the day that resolution passed. It was indeed
uncontentious, though not due to any particular love for
Alexander, whom city democrats had taken to calling "the
Boy." Many of them had spent the last decade hoping with
every fiber of their beings that he go down in defeat in Persia. Clouds of birds and herds of sheep and goats were sacrificed to enlist the gods on behalf of the Persian king, Darius.
Faced with the Boy's demand for godhood, with the army of
his lackey Antipater poised, as it was that very day, to en-
force his adolescent whims, there seemed to be little choice
but to indulge him. As it was, most members of the Assembly considered the request something of a joke—a cry for respect Alexander couldn't earn from the Greeks with a
thousand victories. Swallow did not oppose it.*

As I have said, I was not in the city when this measure passed. I cannot speak to whether the motives
behind its approval were sincere or cynical. I can only
say that by any measure, whether in glory under arms,
or in patronage of the arts, or by that basic virtue of
character to which all men should orient like sailors to
the pole star, Alexander deserved such honors. Athenians, do we not owe our very city to his magnanimity? Twice the Macedonians could have laid waste to
Athens—first, after Chaeronea, when the disaster I
long warned of finally came to pass—and Demosthenes, incidentally, was high-tailing it from the battlefield. Recall that Philip could have continued south
and exacted our annihilation. But instead of invasion,

we received our prisoners back without claim of ransom, and the ashes of our fallen soldiers. Prince Alexander himself came to us as an emissary of peace. The second time was after Philip was assassinated, and some in the Assembly argued the time was ripe to throw off the Macedonian yoke, though to my limited knowledge of husbandry, no yoke has ever worn so lightly as the one Philip fashioned for us. To be sure, it is our eagerness for action that marks us as deeply as our democracy; as Herodotus wrote, it is easier to incite thirty thousand Athenians to war than a single Spartan. Thus it has been, and thus it probably shall always be.

Alexander, no longer Prince but King, appeared in Boeotia with his army, and besieged Thebes. As is all too typical of reprobates and cowards, the nerve of the anti-Macedonian rabble broke in the face of determined force. Thebes was destroyed—it cannot be denied. But Alexander shared his father's distaste for vengeance against Athens. He invaded Persia instead, and upon his subjugation of that kingdom he returned to us the figures of the Tyrannicides stolen by Xerxes. Many of you passed those statues on your way to this chamber this morning, though I wonder how many of you paused to consider to whom we owe such relics of our patrimony. Did Alexander deserve divinity? For Athens's sake, who deserved it more?

I remember Alexander's embassy after Chaeronea. Though I had met the Prince before, as a boy in his father's court in Pella, that occasion did not prepare me for the full splendor of his person. At eighteen years old, his beauty made slaves of men and women. His hair was fair and bright like the mane of a lion, sweeping up and back from his fine brow. Though he was short of stature, his spirit towered over every man in the room, not least over the political hacks sent to greet him, including, as it happened, Machon. Nor was that all that was leonine about the Prince. When he laughed, as he did freely, he showed a set of sharp teeth, like that of a young lion.

In Alexander's eyes was the real gleam of genius. I particularly recall their different colors, blue on the right, black on the left. The meaning of this feature was never obvious, but seemed to promise a unique destiny, which the Prince did easily fulfill. Yet not even this body could contain the noble spirit within it. That spirit was manifest in a sweetness of odor that seemed to emanate from him wherever he went, bathing his clothes, everything he touched, all around him, even poor Machon, in its perfume.

For the first time, Swallow took notice of the figure seated on the defendant's bench. His posture there did not show the theatrical flair of his opponent; he was bent over, shut off, as if he wished to disappear. In that position it was impossible to tell if he was short or tall, though from seeing Machon in the Assembly years before Swallow remembered he was of modest height, with curly black hair kept long in the Lacedaemonian style, so it would flow down from beneath his soldier's helmet. He had a coarse face, with a nose broken to the right. His eyes were also black but not dull. Instead, they shined in that way only the darkest eyes could, from some combustion of personality within. Or rather, they shined a dozen years earlier, before he left for Asia with Alexander.

As Aeschines spoke, Machon stared at the floorboards immediately before him, showing no reaction. He was so passive, in fact, that Swallow wondered if the magnitude of the event had overwhelmed him. The stakes were very high: conviction on a charge of impiety carried a mandatory sentence of death, while violation of the Assembly's trust carried an indeterminate penalty, but would at least include confiscation of his ancestral property. For Aeschines the risk was only to his career—failure to get at least one fifth of the vote for conviction would earn him a fine of ten minas and permanent forfeiture of his right to bring prosecutions in the future. He went on.

But we may well ask, who is this Machon, son of Agathon? Many of you may believe you know him from his role in public life. You know him as a wealthy man who discharged his liturgies with fair distinction, such as financing a tragedy by Kantharos for the City Dionysia fifteen years ago, for which he earned third place. He has rarely spoken in the Assembly or the Council, and when he has it has been exclusively about military affairs. He has served no magistracies, although you might recall one event in which he figured: As a member of the selectmen some years ago, he was chairman on the day a fire broke out in a warehouse at the Piraeus. While the flames were confined on land, Machon dithered, failing to call out the cadets in sufficient numbers, until the fire spread to the fleet offshore. Eight hulls were burned, with damages exceeding twenty talents. Here was an instance where our friend, who affects to have some expertise in the mobilization of men, had an opportunity to display his ability—and failed. Perhaps that is why, when he stood for the post of general from his tribe that year, he was rejected overwhelmingly.

But knowing Machon as I have come to know him,

you would not be surprised at his incapacity. His father, Agathon, was more successful as a public servant, acting twice as naval contractor, yet the source of his wealth was none too clear. There were persistent stories of vast sums hoarded in the house, to avoid additional liturgies. Agathon doled out loans with as little effort as most men put out the condiments at dinner, and exacted interest with ruthless efficiency—yet where is that fortune now? For certain, Machon has inherited it. So, are third-rate theatrical productions all your legacy can muster, Machon? The people want to know.

Of his mother's background the less said, the better. To claim she was a woman of questionable repute would be an exaggeration. It would be more accurate to call her a common whore; her face—or, shall I say, several other choice aspects of her anatomy, were nightly spectacles at the Sacred Gate. After enjoying her with his friends at some low establishment, Agathon further amused himself by purchasing her freedom. This was not to actually set her free, of course, but to increase his pleasure by placing her in debt to him. That he debased himself by proceeding to marry her was only the final act of a long, sad farce.

The sequel was our friend, the defendant. As I have shown you, he cuts a far diminished figure on the public stage than his father, but in one sense he is a chip off the old block. Shortly before departing for Asia, Machon threw a party for his friends in the city that, to this day, remains infamous. The evening started innocently enough, they say, but by the cracking of the fifth crater Machon brought in a very pretty freeborn Corinthian boy, ostensibly to play the harp. The skill of the boy's play, it is said, made the guests very excited at his talent, and there were demands for kisses from every quarter. The boy was respectable, however—a musician only. At this, Machon flew into a rage. Screaming that he had been cheated, he struck the boy across the face and threw him to the floor. There was, alas, nothing the poor creature could do to escape, as the servants had barred the doors, and to face drunken Machon is a frightful thing indeed.

Nor did the defendant's accomplices object to this behavior. On the contrary, they might best be likened to a pack of ravening jackals, surrounding the prone boy, lasciviously stripping him of his tunic. Machon ordered his footmen to the barn to fetch horsewhips, and for the rest, well, you can imagine it. Together the host and his guests amused themselves defiling the boy's tender skin, making their own kind of music out of his screams. Of this episode I will say nothing more. Search your memories and you will recall rumors of it.

Swallow looked inquisitively to Deuteros, who tossed his head in the negative. Neither had heard such a story involving Machon, though tales of similar incidents would circulate in Athens every few years. Whether Aeschines's recitation of it did any harm to the defendant's cause was not clear: its effect seemed merely to pique the jury's interest, sending amused murmurs through the room. Machon, for his part, gave only a single response, looking up with raised brow as Aeschines called his mother a whore. Then he went back to examining the floor.

You see, therefore, that the substance of the charges are not without foundation in the defendant's dissipated past. Even so, I declare that Machon deserves to indulge his cynicism, his hateful politics, and his vices, as any man should be free to keep his gluttonies in private. Where I object—where I *strenuously* object—is where such men are placed in positions where their foolishness may endanger the welfare of the city, and indeed in this case the welfare of all the Greeks. That Machon was insinuated in just such a position was not the choice of any man in this room, but was foisted upon us by a faction of dangerous fanatics who gave little thought to the consequences of their designs. Their motive was hatred only, and the result may yet be disaster. I am pledged to expose them, by the gods, but to do so I will require more time, and this I humbly request.

Polycleitus made a mark on the wax tablet before him. "Your request is recognized, and is so granted—if the prosecution agrees to adhere to the relevant charges only."

Aeschines put his hand on his heart. "To that, I do swear."

"Reset the clock, please."

III

Has the world ever seen the like of Alexander? Was there ever a man whose endeavors were more certainly blessed by the gods? For have the Greeks not lived in fear of another Persian invasion since Xerxes was driven from our shores? Did the Greeks in Ionia, in Ephesus, Miletus, Assos, Priene, not groan under tyrants installed by Persia? Did we all not grow up, age, and die under the shadow of the monstrosity we called the Great King?

No more. The Persian Empire, the client satrapies, the danger they represented to Athens—all have been swept aside. Alexander accomplished it, and indeed did it in about the time it took our ancestors to reduce the single city of Troy. Before Alexander, such a feat was not something any of us would have dared dream. How long did Greeks speak of uniting at last to remove this threat? How many fine speeches were made, how many eloquent pamphlets were published? But we have seen that speeches and pamphlets cannot accomplish such labors—only men like Alexander can.

Remember that Athens fought his leadership, and

in her jealousy remained an open sewer of plots and schemes while he was in Asia fighting for the Greeks. Yet we have all derived the benefits of his conquest. Never again will the Great King connive with Lacedaemonians and Illyrians and Scythians against us. Never again will the Ionian ports be closed to our trade. Never again will our grain supplies from the Black Sea be threatened from the flank. Proud Athens, can you not accept a boon so unexpectedly but so graciously delivered? Can you not rejoice?

There never was a better champion of mankind, never a brighter light among the barbarians. With Alexander, anything was possible. India trembled at his approach, and would have fallen into his hands, as no doubt would Carthage, Italy, Sicily. His empire would have stretched to both shores of the boundless Ocean, a vast common home for the Greeks that would have made our city the Queen of the World.

I say "would have," because Alexander is dead. Having understood what he accomplished, and the promise of his coming reign, you might well ask how this hero, this young god, who was so favored in Heaven, could have died in a manner so untimely, at the age of thirty-two. You might wonder whether the hand of weak, petty Man was implicated in the murder of the future. And you might ask, what does all this have to do with our friend Machon? What, exactly, was the nature of his impiety? Listen, then, and I will tell you.

Machon was present at Chaeronea. Of his conduct there, I have no independent report, except that he was captured and, at the mercy of Philip, was returned to Athens along with two thousand other prisoners. Upon his release, an inquiry was conducted on the reasons for the defeat. As one of the most senior officers to survive that sad day, Machon appeared before the subcommittee of the Assembly. His testimony was most remarkable. We have his whole speech here—it is a tedious document, too long to read today, which is unfortunate because it says much about the character of the man. At its essence it is a tissue of rancorous, unsubstantiated accusations, blaming the disaster on our generals, our soldiers, our equipment, our allies—in short, on everything and everyone except Machon himself. There is one section, however, that is most relevant to the charges under consideration. Please read it.

The clerk took up the transcript. "*For the reasons I have described, it will be most difficult to defeat this enemy. Our city cannot make the changes necessary to meet the Macedonians on equal terms, such as foundation of a permanent, professional army, as this would require changes in our system of government that would be repugnant to the citizenry. In the future, more subtle methods than direct confrontation will have to be employed, if this chronic threat to Athens is to be removed. I pledge myself ready to assist in this project in any way I can.*"

Aeschines turned to address Machon directly.

It is a continual wonder how some men roar with courage in peacetime, but bleat with pessimism at the first reverse. What do you mean, Machon, that Athens cannot meet the enemy on equal terms? Do you impugn the courage of our fallen comrades? Can the sons of Erechtheus fight only with fennel stalks? Do they bleed breast milk? This claim of Athens's inferiority should embarrass you, as it did the committee, which rejected your outburst.

Note the key phrase. He says "more subtle methods than direct confrontation will have to be employed, if this threat to Athens is to be removed." What can he mean? What other method, other than the clash of arms on the battlefield, would be worthy of men? Are we to resort to womanish scheming at every setback? To be sure, I doubt that anyone took his words seriously—they could not, in fact, because Machon was not punished for his foolishness.

The inspiration for Machon's brave call for subterfuge is not hard to guess. Shortly after, Demosthenes went around the city boasting that he had a vision directly from Zeus that Philip had died. Such a partisan invocation of a god would have seemed merely typical of the man's inveterate selfishness, and would have been dismissed as such—until word reached Athens that, indeed, Philip had been assassinated. As the King entered the theater at Aigai on the occasion of his daughter's wedding, he was stabbed by a retainer. All Greece was stunned by the news. Leaving aside the proposition that Zeus signals his intentions to Demosthenes alone, how he happened to learn of this event before anyone else in the city—even before mounted messengers could reach Attica—is a mystery. But in light of Machon's call for underhanded tactics against Philip, Demosthenes's connivance in his murder makes perfect sense.

On the death of his father, Alexander was bequeathed a kingdom whose rule would have challenged the powers of any mortal man. It stretched from the banks of the Danube to Thessaly, and from the Balkans to Byzantium. Thinking the new King, a mere youth of twenty, could not match the skill and determination of the old, opportunists incited rebellions among the tribes of Illyria, in Greece proper, and among the Thebans and here in Attica. What shame will ever adhere to this cynical enterprise—that civilized men of Thebes and Athens, who had duly sworn to respect the leadership of the King in Pella, would attach the fate of Athens to skin-clad barbarians! For had we not agreed, as did all the cities of Greece except Sparta, to aid Philip in his plan to humble the Great King? The pact was made in Corinth, shortly after Chaeronea, the terms of which I hold right here in my hand.

Take note of the parties stipulated in the agreement. It says, "the Greeks will respect the captaincy of Philip *and his descendants*." Could anything be more clear? Could any perfidy be more obvious than the course urged by the anti-Macedonians, who managed again to put Athens on a war footing, on course for another disaster? Note that the purpose of the Corinth alliance was to avenge Greece against the Persians. It demanded nothing of Athens—no booty, no levies, no garrison in our city. Philip expected only our trustworthiness, which one would think would be the least onerous demand on honest men. But instead, Demosthenes, Hypereides, Charidemos and their rabble seduced the Assembly with talk of overthrowing "the Boy," of marching all the way to Pella! What hubris! What rubbish! And with what dismay did these cowards watch as Alexander wasted no time in reducing the Illyrians: not only did he defeat their forces within the boundaries of his kingdom, but he contrived to float his army across the Danube on skin boats and exact the pledges of the tribes beyond. Was this not impressive campaigning for a mere boy?

And then, even more shockingly, Alexander marched south, through Thermopylae, and put Thebes to the torch before Demosthenes could even clear his golden throat. "Demosthenes called me 'a mere child' when we marched on Illyria," Alexander said to his troops, "and 'just a youth' when I came through Thessaly. I guarantee that when he sees me beneath the walls of Athens, it will be as a man!"

Naturally, plans for our glorious march on Pella were forgotten. Instead of an army, the anti-Macedonians sent out pledges of eternal fealty. Demosthenes himself volunteered to lead the peace delegation to Alexander's camp. He was hailed for his bravery, and after accepting these encomiums—for when has he ever refused cheap acclaim?—he rode out of the city in triumph . . . and then slunk away.

We had every reason to expect the worst from Alexander. From the slopes of Hymettus we could see the glow of Thebes burning. There was talk of gathering the fleet, of evacuating the people, of refounding the city elsewhere. This talk, too, was rubbish, because it took no account of the divine character of this new King, who never made a move toward Attica. Instead, he only asked for a recommitment to the Corinth pact, and for the detention of the worst of the demogogues. The latter stipulation was not even pressed—Demosthenes was spared. At this, even the most rabid of Alexander's enemies were taken aback. Was this the leader against which Athens had so treacherously plotted? When had Athens herself ever showed such mercy to a rebellious subject of her empire?

Yet the contrition of these zealots lasted only as long as the Macedonian army was in Boeotia. Having disposed of the father, they turned against the son. Unfortunately for them, Alexander was too quick a target, moving with his army the length and breadth of his kingdom, as I have already described to you. Thereafter, the young King took up his father's project of invading Asia. This campaign alone should have refuted the absurd claims of Demosthenes and his faction, as Alexander did not linger long enough in Greece to tax, oppress, enslave, or otherwise afflict anybody. But instead of at last putting aside their hatred of Alexander, they merely hatched an even more subtle plan to, as Machon demanded, "remove this chronic threat."

It is obvious now their solution was a kind of Trojan horse. Athens, like most of the other big cities, sent ships and troops to support the expedition to Persia. A ground force of one thousand landless citizens, outfitted by emergency decree from the Theoric fund, was organized. Machon, at the instigation of Demosthenes, was placed in command of this force. I was not present in the Assembly when this decision was made. All I can say about it is that it is a prime example of the burden under which our democracy labors, when strong personalities can undo a manifestly correct policy, and in this case subvert it utterly. How else may we understand the appointment of Machon to this command, when his prejudice had been made so very clear in his Chaeronea testimony? We may forgive the more honorable among us for their naivete, believing perhaps that this was an instance of mere cronyism on Demosthenes's part, when in fact the design was still more sinister. Machon even had the audacity to raise his hand and lie in the face of the Assembly when his orders were laid out.

At every point, the intent of his orders was clear: Machon was to support Alexander in "any way within his power"; the effect of the deployment was "to bring honor on Athens by any means practicable." Obviously these orders applied as much to Machon as to any hoplite in the ranks—Machon himself was responsible for their commission. Yet we all know the end of Alexander's story, of his premature death in Babylon under such suspicious circumstances. We likewise know that Machon's master, Demosthenes, was not above accomplishing by conspiracy what he could not on the battlefield. And so I must pose the questions: Did Machon support Alexander by "any way within his power"? Did his conduct bring honor to Athens? If your answers to these questions comport at all with the truth laid before you, then you already have your verdict on the second charge, of violating the sacred trust of his orders.

The Athenian expeditionary force was presented to Alexander at his camp. With some justification, considering the legacy of Athenian deceit cultivated by the anti-Macedonians, the King declined to accept our contingent into his army. What a stunning dishonor for Athenian arms, to be left on the shore at the outset of the greatest campaign ever to leave Greece! But all was not lost for Machon and his scheming sponsors: Alexander, the ever-mindful, salvaged the honor of our city by accepting one Athenian—Machon—into his inner circle of Companions. It was his fatal misfortune that his magnanimity was wasted on such a man.

It seems that Machon did not owe his position on Alexander's staff to his knowledge of military matters, but to his pen. This is curious. I am aware of no one who can attest to the defendant's competence as a historian; Machon has neither recited nor published anything of consequence. We may well imagine, then, the torrent of lies he must have told Alexander to convince him of his talent. On this point in particular, more than any vain protestations of his innocence, I am most interested to hear the defendant's statement!

The invasion began. Alexander was the first to leap ashore on the Asian side, claiming it all as his spear-won territory, and proceeding thence to the ruins of Troy. Wits back home chuckled at the story that he honored his ancestor Achilles with sacrifices under the ravaged battlements; they laughed when they heard that Alexander and his favorite, Hephaestion, stripped naked, annointed each other with oil, and ran around the citadel seven times. They ridiculed him outright for his presumption to borrow the armor of Achilles from the Temple of Athena. Sophisticates far and wide scorned the King's reverence for history—but sophisticates don't win wars. The effect of these rites on his troops was inspirational. Would that more Greeks today be a bit more reverent and a bit less sophisticated!

What the gods thought of Alexander's obsequies was evident in his first encounter with troops in Darius's employ. I say 'in his employ,' rather than 'Persian troops' because the greater part of the enemy was composed of Greek mercenaries. And here again, we see evidence of the decline of honor of our race, that matters have come to such a pass that Greeks would take gold to defend a barbarian kingdom. By all evidence Alexander understood this as well as Darius: in the end, Persians alone could never carry the field against him. Only Greeks can ever defeat Greeks.

The first battle was joined beneath Mount Ida's lowering hills. On the far side of the Granicus river, the Greeks faced an army almost as large as theirs, barring their way on high banks as strong and secure as a castle. In front were the Persian horsemen on their baleful steeds, cased in armored skins that shone in the afternoon sun, scimitars and javelins solemnly crossed upon their chests. Behind crowded the upturned pikes of twenty thousand Greek mercenaries.

At this sight, a pall of misgiving spread over Alexander's army, for they would not only have to defeat the arrayed host of their enemy, but the swift current of the river. Parmenion, a veteran general, counseled the King to delay his attack until morning. The position of the enemy, he said, was impregnable; the banks of the river, he warned, were treacherous, so that even if a crossing could be managed in the stream, the Greeks would never find purchase on the muddy slopes as they fought uphill against mounted foes. These were wise words, to be heeded by any leader of merely mortal stature; Philip himself might have accepted them.

All looked to Alexander, who said nothing at first, but seemed lost in thought, as if unable to make a decision. But when he finally spoke, it was the words of the Poet that came out. He sang—

And the silvered fish did swirl and bite
The tender flesh of newly-dead Lycaon.
You Trojans will die to a man as I fight
To far Ilium's hallowed towers.
Run you might, my swift blade will try your backs.
No escape for those who cower
Beneath the whirling surge of Scamander!
No sacrifice, no blooded bull on cobbled bank
Or fair-maned horse cast in the river
Will save them now, dressed in pain
Until the price in blood is settled
For Patroclus and the Greeks slain
Beside the beaked ships
While I was away. . . .

The Greeks' response to this was, at first, nothing. The words were familiar enough to them, of course, but only as part of a story. Alexander would use the words to write his own epic, studying them at night from the school copy of *The Iliad* he always kept under his pillow. He deployed Homer's lines like files of soldiers, crying: 'As Achilles fought the wide Scamander, may we churn this stream with our greaves!'

And with that, they say, he was gone, charging down the near bank.

IV

Several hours later, and with the exhaustion of Swallow's entire supply of cheese, Aeschines at last seemed to be winding down his presentation.

With Alexander's passage, the world paused. They say that a shadow passed over Babylon that day, and with it the sound of great wings rustling. Far away to the west, over Siwah, an eagle was seen wheeling over the Ammon temple. The very same hour, the priests attest, another eagle flew into the Zeus sanctuary at Dodona, coming to rest in the great oak of the oracle there. The bird stayed there for some time—calling plaintively, as if for a lost brother—until it took wing again into the mountains. Finally, and again on the same day, the keepers of the Zeus altar at Dion saw a great eagle come out of the east. Swooping down to the altar, it dropped a laurel wreath from its talons, circled seven times, then ascended home to the aerie of divine Olympus. For it was on that spring day, during the archonship of Hegesais in Athens, just shy of the thirty-third year of his age, that the great Alexander died.

Aeschines paused, but not to wet his throat. He just stood there for several moments, his head bowed, shoulders slumped. Just as the jury became restless, he resumed speaking again, in a voice that was very small, yet somehow carried to the very back of the courtroom.

That the King died of poison I take as granted. After his second and third marriages, his first wife Rohjane had reason to want him dead, and ample opportunity to make him so. You recall that the Babylonians had a taster sample the water she brought in to him. While it is true that this man did not die after he drank, he did suffer later from acute pains of the abdomen. Whatever caused these pains might not have been fatal to a healthy man, but could easily have been deadly to someone who was already weak with sickness. For as we all know, wise poisoners do not strike out of the blue, but wait for some natural illness to cover their handiwork.

You may judge this woman's motives and character by what happened the very day Alexander died: Rohjane forged a letter in the King's name to his second wife, Barsine, ordering her to attend him in Babylon. This letter reached Susa before news of his death was known there. When Barsine trustingly submitted to the royal escort, which was really a gang of thugs in Rohjane's employ, she was murdered. Like Rohjane, she was carrying a child of Alexander's. Please understand that I do not mean to play the partisan in the current dispute over the succession. With regard to her motives, and Machon's, it need only be said that Rohjane has since delivered a boy, and that the child now figures in this matter in a way he never would have, had Barsine lived.

Of Alexander himself I will say no more. I have eulogized him enough for the purposes of this prosecution. Suffice it to say that the world will never again see his like, and that he was too soon taken from us. Jealous men say he was flawed, and in that they are surely right, for whatever was divine in him, as in us all, was inevitably mixed with that which makes us mortal. I never said he was perfect—I only said he was a god.

Machon will surely attempt some sophistic assault on the charges we make against him. He will argue that it is impossible for a mortal man like himself to corrupt a divine being. For the record, I will say that I believe Machon to be a devious weakling who could not, by himself, have destroyed Alexander. My claim, rather, is that he was a corrupting influence who consistently worked to undermine that which was good in the man, and encourage that which was destructive. I remind you that Machon does not stand charged with killing Alexander. Rather, the good people of Athens accuse him of impiety before a god, and of violating his orders to support Alexander in a manner that would bring honor to this city. Athenians, tell me: having heard his story, do you feel yourselves covered with honor?

With all that I have placed in evidence, it is perhaps worth recounting the many ways Machon betrayed your trust. At Sardis, he lied about his association with Demosthenes, who was a known enemy of Macedon. At Gordium, he encouraged Alexander's ambition to untie the celebrated Knot, provoking him to take a risk that only the King's subtlety overcame. After Issus, he encouraged Alexander to abuse his captive, Stateira. Before the siege of Tyre, he was defeatist. In Egypt, we know by his own words that he plotted against Alexander's "defect." At the Susian Gates, he baited the King into what he believed was a foolish mistake, only to be confounded when Alexander succeeded in forcing the Gates anyway. At Maracanda, he goaded the King into killing his friend Cleitus, and boasted that he encouraged Alexander to believe that any offense would be considered just in the eyes of Heaven. In that same letter to Demosthenes, he further rejoices at Alexander's breakdown. We know, based on a letter that Machon wrote from Sogdia, that he intended to use Rohjane to further his designs. We also have material evidence that he received money from the thief, Harpalus, payable in Persian currency. Lastly, and most fatefully, we know that he actively encouraged Rohjane to fear Alexander's intentions. In this, he as good as encouraged her to act against him.

Aeschines struck up a rhythm that became almost a dance, shifting from one foot to the other as he ran through these points. Swallow and the rest of the jury rocked with him, very entertained, until he brought them up short with a final, dramatic indictment.

In the life of our democracy, so much of our time seems consumed by trivialities. And it might seem that our dispute with Machon is over little more than minor matters—words said at the wrong time, in the wrong place, or left unsaid; the petty boasts of a small man, temporarily enlarged by circumstances he neither deserved nor comprehended. Of Alexander's vices and virtues, you may believe what you wish, as he is not on trial here. It is this man, Machon, we gather to judge, in the light of the responsibilities he solemnly accepted as an agent of this city. And I say that in the discharge of such responsibilities none of us here—magistrate, juror, prosecutor, or defendant—is entitled to judge which are the important charges to keep, and which are trivialities. Our forefathers have made those decisions for us. I would expect the same standard to be applied to myself, if I were in Machon's position.

You will shortly hear from the defendant himself. Though he plays the laconic soldier, don't be fooled: he is as subtle as any con artist in the stoa, as skilled with words as he is useless with the tools of war. He has his work cut out for him, however. Considering that Alexander is untimely dead, and Machon was sworn to serve Athens by serving Alexander, it seems he has but two choices: he must either admit his malice, or plead utter incompetence. In neither case does he escape his guilt. I therefore beg that you hear his plea and judge it with the wisdom that is worthy of our legacy as Athenians. That done, I cannot doubt that justice, which is our only purpose today, will be served.

Aeschines finished exactly as the last drop of water ran through the clock. This impressed sophisticated jurors as much as anything he said, for it was difficult to accomplish this feat without making one's speech detectibly stretched or truncated. Turning to look at his colleagues, Swallow could see in their eyes that the verdict on Aeschines was already in: his was a most impressive return.

"The clock is set for a quarter-hour recess!" *the clerk announced.*

The jurymen used a latrine reserved for them in the alley behind the courthouse. This was a blind wall with a stone-cut channel flushed by running water. As he took his place in the line, Swallow always found himself contemplating the nooks and chinks knocked into the masonry, wondering at the generations of jurors who had thus pissed their way to a kind of immortality. The deeper the impressions, he gathered, the more long-winded the advocates. For his part, Swallow preferred style to power, attempting to write his name on the wall as he listened to the reviews of the trial so far.

"I'd hate to be that Machon right now, poor bastard!" someone said.

"Serves him right with that haircut!"

"But he stayed quiet for most of it . . . that's more than I would have stood for!"

"Aeschines handed him acquittal with that crap. There was not a bit of substance to it!"

"That's what makes it so good—it was delivered for the courtroom, not the schoolroom!"

"This is more about politics than the law."

"That was more about that prick Alexander than anything else."

". . . an overuse of enthymemes . . ."

"I've never seen them so liberal with the clock."

"Somebody wants this guy dead."

"If his speech takes more than two hours I'll want him dead!"

"I give top honors to the lamb!"

HAR HAR HAR HAR. . . !

Deuteros was standing at Swallow's elbow as he wrapped himself, sucking his lower lip. "I guess I don't see any reason to change our vote," *he said.*

"Why would we?" *replied Swallow.* "The defense hasn't spoken yet."

"Do you think it'll matter?"

"It will to me. Gimme that bread."

"So what does Swallow say about the trial?" someone asked. Others seconded the question, until every face was turned toward Swallow. As one of the most experienced jurymen, he was presumed to have seen and heard it all since the dictatorship of the Thirty. Swallow knew this was an exaggeration—he wasn't that old!—but didn't exactly discourage their esteem either.

"I am surprised at nothing from Aeschines," he said. "Except perhaps the timing of his prosecution. Why does he bring the charges now, so soon after Machon has come back? Why did he not wait until more witnesses returned from the east, so he could present live testimony? I am never comfortable with indicting a man on the basis of something in a letter."

The jurors stood pensively at their trough. Swallow continued, "I think that what we were expected to understand was not in the speech at all. And the winner, if the verdict is guilty, will not be Aeschines."

The silence lasted a bit longer as his fellow citizens took his meaning, or realized they never would. The argument then resumed as to which school of rhetorical style Aeschines's speech was best classified.

When they returned to their seats, the man who brought the lamb was still unconscious on the floor. He had missed the entire prosecution, and looked comfortable enough lying there to miss the defense too. There was a certain fairness in this, it seemed.

Aeschines was sitting now with a plate of figs and myrtle berries. He ate with his eyes glued to Machon, who likewise had not moved, but sat staring narrowly at his feet, as if refusing to gratify his opponent by glaring back. As the clerk gaveled the courtroom to order the defendant finally *looked up, his eyes sweeping over the mob that would decide his fate. Though Swallow believed Aeschines's case was a tissue of presumption and innuendo, he'd said one thing that was clearly true: Machon had his work cut out for him.*

"Having considered the case for the indictment," said Polycleitus, "the court will now hear the defense. Does the defendant wish to speak?"

"I claim that privilege," said Machon, rising. He turned out to be short—so short, in fact, many of the jurors in the back of the room would not see him at all. His voice also had a much higher pitch than one would imagine from his martial appearance.

"Very well. You have the usual measure of time."

For a moment Machon did not speak, but just stood there with his palms turned upward, as if to beseech Heaven, or to express his wonderment at the mess Aeschines had placed before them all. There were a few titters from the left side of the room, toward which Machon, in a clever gesture of confidence, actually winked. Swallow glanced at the Macedonians in the spectator's box: they were scowling. All this suddenly filled Swallow with anticipation—he leaned over to Deuteros.

"This might be something," he whispered.

•

V

*Alexander dead? Impossible! His corpse would fill
the world with its stink.*
— Demades, Athenian orator

Well then, what a performance! This prosecution was
well worth the wait for Aeschines's return from
abroad. I don't know about anybody else, but I'm excited to vote. Let's convict this Machon! Let's grab the
lout and string him up!

*Machon paused as the jury gave him a good laugh. As
much as Swallow enjoyed routine trials, he enjoyed innova-
tive defenses even more. For the speaker was treading dangerous ground with this flip tone—if he misstepped, if he
alienated enough jurors, it could cost him dearly. The last
person to take such a risk was Socrates when, upon his conviction, he suggested the "penalty" of receiving free dinners
from the state for the rest of his life. This piece of wit, such
as it was, so irked his jury that it earned him a lopsided vote
for death. This was not a promising legal precedent for Machon. Whether or not he could pull it off, no one could deny
his tack was most entertaining, like an acrobat working
without a net.*

Unfortunately, I don't think I can help you find
Aeschines's Machon, because I don't know him. *That*
Machon is a scheming scoundrel. *This* Machon is noth-

ing more than a simple soldier who, like many of the men in this room—but not you, Aeschines!—fought for his country at Chaeronea. Aeschines describes a man full of hubris. This Machon lives as modestly as his weakness may allow, pays his taxes, and contributes to the governance of his city, like all of you. Aeschines invents someone who is hip-deep in political faction. This Machon belongs to no faction at all. He has no ambition to matter more than he does. True, he rarely takes the myrtle wreath in the Assembly, and only when speaking on military affairs. But it is only because this Machon restricts his public statements to things he knows something about—unlike, apparently, the celebrated Aeschines! Indeed, the orator left out what may be considered the defendant's proudest achievement in politics: a decree of the Assembly, passed by unanimous voice vote, that all used equipment from broken-up naval vessels should be offered first to the public contractors, before it is claimed by fishermen and other private interests. This motion has saved the taxpayers thousands of drachmae in replacement costs. So while Aeschines may demand to know where my father's money is, I remind him that I have helped keep the public's money where it belongs!

So the first question is: why are we here, really? Why was this action brought against so insignificant a figure? There are at least two easy answers to the question. The first, I suggest, is fear. The death of Alexander has raised the hopes of those who would resist Macedonian power. Others are afraid that Athens will meet the same end as Thebes, if it comes to armed conflict. No point in Greece is more than two weeks' march away for Antipater's army. There is a need for an example to be made here, a sacrifice of someone supposed to be connected to the anti-Macedonian faction, to prove that Athens is not a threat.

The second reason is simple revenge. Of Aeschines's antagonism toward Demosthenes, I need not elaborate. He has stooped before to attacking Demosthenes's friends in lieu of the man himself. You may prove it to yourself: when Aeschines publishes his prosecution, as he always does, count how many times he makes reference to Demosthenes. The exercise will be very revealing. It might move you to ask who is really on trial here, though it is my neck that is in the noose!

But there is a larger, less obvious reason. It is this, O Athens: there is something wrong with our city. We can all sense it. We feel the pull of events and feel we must do something, but every way we turn raises howls of protest, or grave danger, or unpredictable consequences. It is as if we are at the top of a tall mountain, with a chasm all around us, and higher peaks beyond. We want to go higher, but we fear to take the steep path on the way. So we cling to where we are. And we admire men like Alexander, whom we, in our childish faith, believe would defy all limits.

I don't say these things to prove I am cleverer than anyone else. I observe them as a man who has been too long away from home, and spent at least a part of every day thinking about how he would get back. Sometimes fresh eyes give the clearest view. I wonder if my opponent agrees with me, so soon back from his own exile. Does this feel like the same city you left, Aeschines? Be honest! I understand that the hegemony of Alexander is not remembered as a time of glory here, but of hunger, of shortage. Yet how quickly some are willing to overlook the misery caused by his wars! Early in your statement, you said something about Alexander's good looks making slaves of men. I agree with you that slaves were made in Athens—I'm just not sure it was his beauty that did the trick.

I will pass over in silence the bulk of my opponent's calumnies, except to say that, his sensibilities notwithstanding, my mother was indeed a freedwoman, and my father's love for her was not a farce. Of wild parties and whipping boys, he lets me off easily, as he presents not the slightest shred of evidence. Not that he has ever let that small problem get in the way of a rousing argument! Such lies are therefore nothing to me—the wise man, as they say, is content to let asses bray. I trust members of the jury have been around this barnyard enough to know where to step.

As I see it, all that matters are the charges. Aeschines and his sponsors accuse me of impiety, because they have gotten wind of some alleged acts of mine in the east that suggest that I treated Alexander like a man, not a god. They also charge me with violating my oath to the Assembly, because I pledged to help Alexander, and he ended up . . . well . . . closer to the gods than when he began. Imagine that, a soldier dying on campaign!

More laughter—and more nervous shuffling by Polycleitus and the Macedonians. Aeschines, for his part, was drawing his cloak around him like a tortoise taking to his shell.

In any case, Aeschines says that I must either confess to malice, or to incompetence. But he forgets a third alternative—failure in good faith. Yes, I did fail to flatter Alexander's pretensions to divinity! And yes, I did fail to save him from the consequences of his own contradictions! If these be actionable crimes, then I accept my guilt without further contest. But I would also point out that if simple failure were grounds for prosecution of our magistrates, then courts like this would never adjourn!

Now the jury was expecting Machon to be funny, erupting before he could finish his punch lines. Polycleitus made a flicking gesture at the clerk, who banged the floor with his staff until order was restored.

"The defendant is directed to refrain from mocking these proceedings. This is not a burlesque!"

My apologies. I also ask the jury to forgive me, for I get ahead of myself. My point is only that my conduct was appropriate to the circumstances of the campaign, and that I did serve the King in the best way I could. Athens need not fear for her honor, for in those times there was dishonor enough to go around for all. But to show this I must tell you what really happened on campaign with Alexander. Some of you will be surprised at what you will hear of this; most likely you have never heard the truth, and never will again, for my history is not as felicitous as that of poor Callisthenes, or of the other second-rate scribblers who have sprouted from the gore and ash Alexander spread from here to India.

My story begins at Chaeronea. Like many of you, I traveled to the battle with all the joy of a groom about to see his bride unwrapped. To have all the tension of those years—all the uncertainty in our confrontation with Macedon—suddenly cast aside, filled all of us with a love for our city that was all-sustaining. Patriotism, we believed, would be our food on the march—

and for dessert, victory! Recall the sight: twenty thousand Athenians in the rusty armor of their grandfathers. Hayseeds and city boys streaming into the crossroads, greeting each other like reunited kin. The old men mustered for the last time, with steely gaze and hands trembling on the pikes, taking the kisses of young women on the roadsides. We were off to Boeotia, the theater of so many other battles that Theban Epaminondas rightly called it "the dancing floor of war." And like the Thebans facing down Spartan power at Leuctra, the Athenians were coming at last to dance with King Philip and his detested Macedonians.

Our campfires spread for miles up the road by night. We bivouacked without sentries, without order, and without care. There were rumors that a man named Stratocles was in charge. He was a strategical genius, they said, and he had a plan to rout the Macedonians, who were much due for a humbling. A drink to victory! And another to Stratocles! And more after that, until the fires were superfluous, and we danced away whatever energy the march had left to us.

The joy division reached Thebes, and streamed around her walls, thinking the Theban army would come out to embrace their new allies. But the gates stayed shut, and the guards in the towers looked down on us warily. On the far side of the city we saw a neat square of armored men waiting on the road. It was not the whole Theban army, but the best part of it: we had the Theban Sacred Band on our side, three hundred strong. Since the days of Pelopidas this Band had never lost a battle. They fought as couples, each man consecrated to his lover in the ranks. It was a coup for Demosthenes, to have convinced the Thebans to plight this, their most cherished unit, in our cause. What need, then, of strategy, tactics, security? On to victory! And then on to Macedon, to smash the half-barbarian upstarts who presumed to enslave true Greeks! The only sour note was struck by the Thebans: though undefeated in more than a generation, they marched diffidently, without joy or confidence on their faces. Some thought they felt dishonored to share the road with us. We might have suspected that they had a better idea of the quality of the opposition.

Our scouts sighted the enemy in a narrow valley in the north of Boeotia. From that moment the events of the day became a blur to me. Stratocles, it turned out, had no strategy in mind. Officers from different units came scurrying up to organize us into phalanxes eight shields deep, then sixteen, then back to eight. First we stood here, then we stood there. An order went out to march forward onto the plain—but the command went to only half the army, leaving big gaps in our lines. The mood passed from happiness to frenzy, as everyone wanted something done, but no one was clearly in charge, and the gaps infuriated the officers, who yelled at the gallant but frustrated boys and old men. With these annoyances we became aware that we were footsore and, though we had feasted on patriotism, hungry. The good times on the road gave way to squabbling as men were crushed against each other. The only cool heads were on the shoulders of the Thebans, who marched in precise order to our right flank and settled there, resting their peculiar crimped shields on the ground against their legs.

The Macedonians, meanwhile, were collected in their neat ranks, watching us struggle to form our lines. Of the Companion cavalry and Philip and Alexander, there was yet no sign. Somebody in the vanguard observed that the enemy had just tiny shields hanging from the shoulders, and that they wore only leather armor. A rumor was passed back through the ranks that the Macedonians had no protection at all, and for a moment all discomfort was forgotten, for the enemy had left their shields at Pella, and it would be an easy day of killing for the Greeks!

At last they had us all organized and pointed the right direction. I was on the right, adjacent to the Sacred Band, in the sixth row of a phalanx eight shields deep. I recall it was already late in the day to begin a battle; the sun beat down so mercilessly on my helmet that I could smell the liner cooking within it. To keep their hands dry on their spears, men up and down the line were wiping their sweaty palms on their breastplates, or struggling to bend over for some dirt.

At the sounding of the pipes, we marched forward in more or less good order. We were a loud army, clanking with every step, raising the paean; the Macedonians, on the other hand, moved over the battlefield in almost complete silence. The mood became very tense as the armies closed on each other. From many yards away we could see that the Macedonian pikes, their *sarissas*, were at least twice as long as the ones we carried. The whooping and hollering on the Greek side subsided; our lines contracted as each soldier pressed against his comrade to the right, trying to nestle behind his shield. This forced each shieldbearer to move to his right, until our whole line began to drift north, angling obliquely toward the enemy. Lacking true shields, our enemies could not hunker behind their fellows, but marched straight and true. Watching them between the shoulders of my comrades, I could see their faces: the Macedonians looked serene, even bored.

The enemy halted their advance as our first three ranks leveled their spears. Our boys kept on coming, giving throat to the cry that terrified the Persians at Marathon and Plataea—*eleleu eleleu*! With that, the Macedonians all turned around and withdrew on the double. There didn't seem to be any signal given for them to do this. They just did it, as calmly as if they were drilling on the parade ground.

Unlike at Marathon, our front ranks were not taken up by our toughest hoplites, but by our most enthusiastic. The Macedonian withdrawal confirmed what they had long imagined—that the barbarians had no stomach for fighting the free citizens of a civilized city! Our ranks dissolved as we tried to reach the retreating enemy; weighted down with ancient panoplies, the Greeks exhausted themselves trying to run after the lightly clad Macedonians. Our officers were screaming at their men, trying to organize an orderly advance. Yet our glorious commander Stratocles, who was very probably drunk, was off celebrating the rout, riding with sword aloft, crying "We've got 'em on the run, boys! Now on to Pella!"

With the sole exception of our Theban allies, who anchored our right with no trace of emotion, all semblance of organization among the Greeks was gone. Our army opened up like a boiled onion, the ranks peeling away from the phalanx one by one. Some of the hoplites, half-blind with sweat under ill-fitting helmets, tripped on rocks and clumps of soil; as they struggled to rise, they were trampled in the dust by their jubilant comrades. This was in chilling contrast to the Macedonians, who wheeled around in their thousands without a single man going down. Not a single one!

You know what followed. At the sounding of a trumpet, the enemy retreat suddenly seemed to halt. What had really happened, of course, was that the Macedonians didn't run away at all, but had only performed a withdrawal behind a new line formed by their best men. Having fooled many of the Greeks with this sham, they grasped their pikes underhand and leveled the tips. The Macedonian pike is long enough for men four and five shields deep in their phalanx to reach the enemy. Many of the Athenians were propelled by pure momentum into this swarm of spear points. Hemmed in by their comrades around them, hundreds were struck full in the face, noses or jawbones split. This was when I learned that the entrance of a metal point into the unprotected face of a man makes a peculiar noise—a certain combination of a *crunch* and a *thud*. I had much opportunity to hear it as the survivors tried to come about, colliding with the oncoming ranks, until we were all a helpless jumble of exhausted, blind men and boys, so terrified that we shat ourselves with fear, or cried for our mothers.

It was at this point that the enemy broke their silence. They let loose a cry that I cannot imitate for you—it was made in that strange dialect of theirs—a cry so concertedly made it rose over the ongoing din of shields and armor, freezing the blood of every Greek on the field. The Macedonians then started forward again, walking right over the Greek casualties, finishing off the fallen with downward thrusts of the iron points on the butts of their pikes. I remember seeing a face I recognized among the wounded: he was the teacher who taught me my letters decades before. I had not seen him since, and never did again, but only in that instant. He lay uncomplaining at the feet of the Macedonians, the contents of his testicles spilled on his groin flaps, his gray head annointed with the dust of sacrifice.

There was at that point still some distance between the enemy and what remained of the Athenian line. To the eternal credit of my fellow citizens, most of them stood firm as the enemy approached. Others, foreseeing only their imminent death, and finding themselves hemmed in on all sides by the phalanx, gave themselves over to panic. Just a few of these cowards, flailing to free themselves, was enough to disrupt huge swaths of our formation. And all the while the Macedonians were coming on, those damnable cocksure smiles on their faces—smiles like those right there!

Machon leveled a finger at the Macedonian observers in the courtroom, who were indeed grinning as they listened to one of the storied moments in their nation's history. Their smiles withered as five hundred pairs of resentful eyes bore down on them.

You may be thinking that I paint too dark a picture of the events that day. To those who were not there, it should be pointed out that the battle seemed far from over to us. There was still the opportunity for the Greeks to turn the tables on the enemy: to settle in, dig the butts of our spears into the earth, and impale the dogs as they charged.

We were confident we could do this, and prepared

for it, for we all understood exactly what was at stake. We had already learned, after all, that there was no defensive strategy against the likes of Philip—no resort to Long Walls and hope for bad weather. Can you remember when our grandfathers told us of the war with Sparta—when those half-hick stiffs would come every year at the same time, shake their fists at our Long Walls, burn a few haystacks, and go home? Remember how formidable those Lacedaemonians sounded to us, as children? Yet we all knew we were in for much worse if Philip's hordes poured into Attica. To Philip, walled cities were unshucked oysters, and the war never stopped for harvest, weather or any other reason under Heaven. His troops were neither part-time nor rented soldiers, but professionals who made a craft of intimidation, rape, and massacre.

There was nothing for us to do, then, but to put shoulder to shield and push hard against the line. We would accept the hours of exhaustion in our old panoplies, the heat, the terror of suffocation and the panicky spray of our neighbors' urine. We would push, and push some more, until the Macedonians broke for their mountains at last, and we would bury our spears in the backs of many as we could.

But it was not to be. The battle was not over in hours, but minutes, as the Macedonian cavalry somehow broke into our rear guard. Through one of the great gaps in our line, Philip's so-called Companions had ridden and commenced to slash at our back rank. The Greek army, it seems, had come that day without any cavalry at all, and so our flanks had no defense.

With that, the entire right wing of the Greeks crumpled. Hoplites dropped their spears, tore off their armor, and ran for their lives. The horsemen made them pay for their indiscipline: the deserters were chased down and butchered from behind by the Macedonian aristocrats. These were, incidentally, quite gaily turned out in their purple cloaks trimmed with gold. And how they seemed to enjoy the work of slaughtering fathers and grandfathers who came to fight for their children's freedom! As fate would have it, this was not the last time I would watch the Macedonians go about this, their favorite business.

Trapped in the center of the disintegrating phalanx, I was being propelled this way and that by waves of flailing, terrified men. Those who have been there know the danger: in the crush of armored bodies, it was difficult just to get a breath. Keeping upright was also a challenge, lest I suffer the fate of those trampled under the feet of their comrades. It was at that moment, when I was thus engaged, that I first glimpsed Prince Alexander.

I'm not sure how I knew it was him, as I was too far away to see his face. I might have guessed his identity because he was riding at the head of a retinue, or because his cloak had a reversed color scheme, gold trimmed with purple, or from the fact that he alone wore the Gorgon's-head device on his breastplate. Or it might have been for the same reason that the sheepdog always stands out from the rest of the flock—the princely way he rode a horse, cantering here and there, directing his forces, pounding his fist for emphasis, gesturing his displeasure over some unfulfilled command.

I watched him until I lost sight of him behind an obstacle—an obstacle that I belatedly realized was the Sacred Band, which was surrounded. The Thebans had formed themselves into a defensive square, with their spears presented at every side. Against them the enemy pikemen were forming up in columns thirty-two shields deep. When they were ready, the Macedonians charged at a run into the Thebans, with the soldiers in their back ranks pushing the ones in front. This kind of attack generated powerful momentum—the kind that drove leveled pikes straight through the armor of stationary men. The Macedonians did this over and over, giving each fresh regiment a crack at the Thebans; the defenders, who had locked shields, were able to hold their own for a while, but they lacked the force of forward movement, and their lances were too short to strike back. Inevitably, when their armor was holed or split, the Thebans began to fall. As each died, his comrade protected his body with his shield, or with his own body, as the case may be. The square gave way as the Macedonians kept up the attack; we Greeks watched with tears in our eyes as this glorious Band, its history unblemished by defeat, was ground into the dust.

At last, when there was only one stubborn pair left on what had become their funeral mound, Prince Alexander rode forward on his fabled mount, Bucephalus. Taking aim with his thrusting spear, and in a remarkable bit of horsemanship, he drove right into the morass of dead flesh and speared one of the Thebans straight through his breastplate. With the other resigned to do nothing more than watch, Alexander extracted the spearhead from the body of his companion, backed off a bit, then simply rode the last Theban down. The Macedonians roared as Bucephalus leapt free of the mound, and Alexander unfurled his tawny tresses and raised his bloodied spear in triumph.

This was not the end of the day's slaughter. In defiance of custom, Philip's troops massacred retreating Athenians for the rest of the afternoon, chasing them into the hills, into cornfields and granaries, up roofs and down into caves. Yes, the King made a gallant gesture of burning the bodies that were left on the battlefield and delivering the collected ashes to us here. But the bodies of hundreds of others—those who fled—were never recovered or given the proper rites. They were left to rot where they fell. We Athenians, for our part, did not ask awkward questions of the victors, but merely thanked the gods for what we were given.

Like many of you, I was at Chaeronea to save my country. But at the risk of encouraging Aeschines's bizarre speculations, I grant I did have an ulterior motive. It had always been my ambition to write a history. You may recall that Thucydides and Xenophon were soldiers, and commenced their histories because they foresaw that future generations might learn from an account of the conflicts of their time. I believed—and still do believe—that the same is true of our wars. Where Thucydides had his Pericles, Cleon, and Alcibiades, in our time we have Demosthenes, Philip, and, yes, Aeschines! So while my opponent attempts to make my ambition in this regard appear something dubious, he only shows his own contempt for the craft of history. How many of the men here would take up the pen too, if they had the means and the opportunity. . . ? To your shame, Aeschines, see how many hands are raised!

"The defendant may not pose questions to the jury," the judge objected.

"Your honor, would that rule apply to questions one might characterize as rhetorical?"

"You may ask rhetorical questions only if you clearly indicate that you don't want your questions to be answered."

"Eminence, am I to understand that if I ask a rhetorical question, and the jury elects to answer, I am to be held responsible for a transgression that I myself have not committed?"

The jurors broke into heated discussion. Polycleitus, glowing red with anger, called for order. It took several moments for the room to quiet again.

"The defendant will not ask questions, and the jury will not answer. Is that clear enough to you all?"

"Perfectly. I also request additional time due to the interruption."

"So granted! Go on, please."

To resume, I went to Boeotia as a soldier, but also with the eye of a chronicler, as I judged this to be a unique moment in the affairs of men. Fortunately for my project, I was not killed during the battle, but taken prisoner. Along with several thousand other Athenians and allies, I was placed in a stockade not far from the Macedonian camp. The pen was just an offhand thing, a corral built of thin sticks and brush, with ditch water to drink. Philip fed us with rotten onions collected from the haversacks of the dead; so famished were the Athenians that they fought over these meager rations. It is a fortunate thing for the men of Asia that Alexander did not inherit his father's cheapness.

Having foreseen the advantage of taking notes in the field, I had brought with me several lead tablets and a stylus, which I stored in the cave of my shield. It was at that point, when I had been in detention for two days without food, when the stench of the open-pit toilets rose to new heights, and rumors flew that we would all be sent to short, miserable careers as slaves in the mines at Mt. Pangaeus, that I believed I was sufficiently immersed in my subject to begin composing.

I had not gotten far along in recording my impressions of the battle, when a peculiar voice addressed me, asking, "Ye scribe, what dost thou?"

Perceiving that the question came from the Macedonian side of the fence, and in the archaic dialect of those backward northerners, I ignored it. A pair of booted feet came into my line of sight as I peered down at my tablet, and the voice resumed.

"Be ye poet or prosifier, o son of Theseus, I will own thine answer!"

Bowing to the inevitable, I looked up, and was confronted with none other than Prince Alexander himself.

VI

Anyone listening to Aeschines's description of this teenager would be severely misled. He spoke of fine long hair, which was accurate enough, but neglected the stringy, oily quality of it, which gave the impression of being perpetually wet. I still hear tales of Alexander's "blond" or "fair" hair when it was clearly brown and nothing more. It fell in unrestrained sweeps down around his face—a face that was not without a certain dignity, but coarse, big-boned, and full of pimples. His eyes were not blue or blue on one side but again, plain brown. At that distance I assure you I smelled nothing of the natural perfume that was supposed to permeate his body. His most remarkable features were a set of full, almost feminine lips, and a pair of wide-set eyes that focused on their object with a remarkable intensity.

He was but eighteen years old that day, flush from his first victory in battle. For the first time he was confronted with great numbers of Athenians, who despite their political rivalry with Macedon retained a certain stature in that primitive kingdom. To this day, the people of Pella still speak with pride of how Euripides spent his last days there, producing his *Bacchae* at the sanctuary at Dion, in the very shadow of Mount Olympus. It was therefore with an uneasy mixture of superiority and awe that he addressed me, a bona fide Athenian sophisticate.

"Did thy mother bear ye a tongue along with thy fingers?"

"She did," I replied. "But I cannot see how my affairs are any concern of yours, stranger."

The pimply Prince drew himself up to his full height, all of five feet and no inches.

"Mark me as a man who bested thee in battle, friend, for you cavil with the Crown Prince of Macedon!"

Having rendered for you how Alexander sounded in those days, for clarity's sake I will now translate his archaic Greek into our modern idiom. To be sure, beyond a certain awkwardness at first, communication was never a problem between us. He did come to take on a less backward mode as time passed, and my ear for his northern dialect improved. But despite the elocution lessons, despite Aristotle's tutoring, to the sophisticated Greek there was always something of the highland yokel in him, even when he was donning the diadem of the Great King at Susa.

"Well, your highness, I will say that you 'cavil' with no one, for I am just plain Machon of Athens, son of Agathon."

"And do you profess the craft of writer, Machon son of Agathon? Tell me, do you know these lines?"

> *The word "moderation" when spoken*
> *Is better than renown, and mortals*

> *Who practice it find it superior.*
> *For renown, when taken to extremes,*
> *Is not an advantage to men . . .*

"You insult me, sir, for what Athenian would admit he does not recognize the words of Euripides, from the prologue of *Medea*?"

"I mean no insult, sir, but to my mind there are too many poseurs carrying the attributes of your noble calling. If I were not Alexander, I would be a poet!"

"There are many in Athens," I replied, "who would urge both you and your father to pursue that ambition!"

Alexander laughed with what seemed like genuine ease, without a trace of adolescent self-consciousness. On a certain level, I found myself liking him immediately, which was not an unusual reaction to him in those early years. He was not without charm.

"Did you know that your Euripides found sanctuary at the court of Macedon?"

"I have heard it said."

"I saw you on the field. You fought well."

"Not well enough, it seems."

At the time I thought it impossible that the Prince could have recalled glimpsing me among thousands of others through the melee of Chaeronea. He has since gained the reputation of remembering an astonishing number of faces and names—Aeschines himself has repeated this claim. The truth is somewhat more complicated, as I will tell you presently. But again, I could not help being pleased by his flattery.

"You should know that I am not writing poetry. It is a history of this war."

"Whose style do you favor, then—Herodotus or Thucydides?"

"Herodotus is for children."

"Exactly right. Soon I will need men like yourself, Machon. Serious historians."

With that, he turned and walked back to his horse, which was held by a strikingly handsome youth that I later knew to be Hephaestion. The Prince seemed to give his friend an order, and the latter shot a measuring glance at me. Then, before he rode off, Alexander shouted back in my direction.

"I can only hope that I am not a villain in your story!"

He was smiling, but there was also a dark edge in his voice that was unmistakable.

Soon I learned what Alexander had instructed Hephaestion to do for me: I was moved from the stockade to a small officer's field tent nearby. Inside was a cot, a chair, a writing desk, and a sheath of Egyptian papyrus—truly an extravagant gift!

In truth, it was perhaps too generous. After days living outside, and having never before been confronted with such fine materials, the comfortable surroundings became a distraction. In the short time before I was sent home I got no serious writing done at all.

Contrary to what Aeschines has told you, I was not among those who attended the Prince during his peace embassy to Athens. Indeed, Aeschines's associates Phocion and Demades were among that party, though I will not descend to my opponent's level of scurrility in calling them "hacks." Suffice it to say that I was too closely connected to those who opposed Macedonian power before Chaeronea to merit an invitation. I understand that he mentioned my name on several occasions, much to the embarrassment of his hosts. Attending a sacrifice at the altar of Athena Parthenos, he was heard to ask, "Is Machon in the crowd? Who will point him out to me?"

Later, on his inspection of the Painted Stoa, he said "I think the paintings very fine, though I wonder what my friend Machon would say of them!"

I understand that he referred to me so often Demades made serious inquiries on whether he was simpleminded! In fact, Demades had no understanding of the Macedonian mind—Alexander asked for me not because he was simple, but out of custom on a visit to my city. Indeed, I received a note from him communicating his disappointment that I would not be joining the festivities, and his hope that work on my history was proceeding well. These testaments to his goodwill, and of my vocation as historian, I hereby place in evidence.

"They are so accepted," responded the clerk.

I next saw Alexander more than two years later. It was after his ascension to the throne of Macedon, following the murder of his father, and a short time after the destruction of Thebes. He was assembling his forces for his invasion of the Persian Empire; in deference to his position as the Captain of the Greeks, our Assembly resolved to send one thousand men to support his cause. Aeschines is quite correct to note that Demosthenes was the primary sponsor of my leadership of this force. He could not be more incorrect, though, in ascribing evil motives to my assignment. Rather, I was recommended by the simple fact that Alexander had shown a partiality for me, and these feelings might be of some use in pursuading him to overcome his mistrust of the Athenians. That, and the fact that Phocion, who was far more qualified, didn't want the job!

I came up to attend him at Dion, the Macedonian sanctuary of Zeus. At the time I arrived he was feasting with his officers under a great tent not far from the theater. It was a grand affair, in the style of all his celebrations: the tent covered an area larger than this building, and was lined with row upon row of gilded couches arranged around a royal loggia, where King Alexander reclined. Surpassing all other symposiasts, he served his guests the finest Chian wine from craters lined with snow fetched down from Olympus; the toasts were made with golden cups studded with jewels. One side of the tent was given over to trophies from his recent expedition against the Danubian Triballi—heaped pelts of bears and oxen, shields hewn from single enormous logs, belts dripping with amber beads. There was no loot from the sack of Thebes, however. Nor to my knowledge was this event ever mentioned.

"Machon, my friend! Come here and embrace me!"

He greeted me like an old comrade, commanding me to sit beside him. His enthusiasm was unique in that company. When they bothered to look to me at all, the rest of the Macedonians cast their eyes on me with obvious suspicion. Hephaestion regarded me unflinchingly from a nearby couch, his hostility unconcealed.

"So tell me of your book! Have you completed it?"

"Honestly, no. All I have so far is a prologue."

"You lack a protagonist!"

He looked at me with some sort of great significance in his eyes, rolling his cup between his hands. The years since Chaeronea had improved his appearance: his face, though still beardless, had lost its adolescent softness, and the spots were gone. His waxy hair shined in the lamplight in a way I saw could be taken for blond.

"Perhaps we can help each other in our projects, you and I."

He was distracted by a servant who whispered something in his ear. I was just able to hear the message: his mother, Olympias, had requested to see him. With a sigh that indicated more than simple weariness, he rose to go to her.

"We'll talk together later," he promised.

I didn't see him again for some time, after the third round of craters had been brought in. In the interim I sat alone, attracting stares more frigid than the ice used to cool the wine. As a precaution against the Evil Eye, I clenched the fingers of my right hand around my thumb and spat on the ground. The Macedonians around me responded by spitting on the ground too. This set off the revelers around them, in a wide concentric ring of spitting, until men all over the great tent wet the floor.

A man, gray-haired and heavily scarred in his face, finally approached me. Without introducing himself, and listing with drink, he set his feet and pointed an accusing finger at me.

"I saw you in Boeotia! You held a line of hoplites against three wedges of horse!"

Not knowing what to say, I shrugged. The drunk

then leaned forward, an expression of surprised gratification spreading over him.

"You know how to fight!"

He raised his cup, drank to me, and staggered off. Much later, I learned that I had been addressed by Cleitus, son of Dropidas—so-called "Black Cleitus"—and that praise from him was a rare honor.

Alexander returned. Taking his place on the couch again, he resumed our conversation as if there had been no interruption.

"I already have an historian for the trip to Asia. Have you heard of Callisthenes of Olynthus?"

"The son of Aristotle?"

"The nephew."

"I know nothing of him except his name."

"I will tell you that the Queen Mother doesn't like him. I will not bore you with the reasons . . . except to say that he is no soldier. . . . Give it here, son!"

He intercepted a servant with a wine pitcher, taking it from him to fill his cup. As anachronistic as the Macedonian court seemed to Athenian eyes, it was informal enough to oblige the King to chase after his own drinks. By comparison, Darius of Persia probably had three flunkies dedicated to the management of his potations.

We sat together, watching his officers carouse. Here and there, cups were drained down throats or down chins, and the cithara players swayed in their pleated costumes, and the blouses of the female entertainment were peeled away in happy, innocent debauch. The King tapped my cup with his own, asking "Don't you feel like a demigod among savages, when you sit with these Macedonians?"

How could I answer this peculiar question? It sounded like an invitation to insult him. Instead, I kept my silence.

"So tell me, Machon, if you might join our party."

"That is why I was sent."

"Not as a commander. I have enough of those! I need officers along who can carry a pack, but who can also marshal ranks and files of a different kind—the kind that go on scrolls. Do you favor my metaphor?"

It took me a moment to realize that he was asking this question in all seriousness. I said I admired his metaphor very much, of course, which clearly pleased him.

"How long a campaign do you envision?"

"To free the Ionian cities for good, no more than two years. Can you ride a horse? No? Shall we make you an officer of the Shield Bearers? Ptolemy, is he tall enough for First Company?"

"No!"

"Then it's Second Company! Fetch him a helmet!"

The order was passed from couch to couch and out the door, and drew back a peaked Phrygian helmet from the armory, which was likewise handed toward me from man to man.

"My lord Alexander, while I appreciate that you want my services, I have seen too much fighting in the ranks to be made a retainer."

"Our Shield Bearers are not retainers," Hephaestion said with some impatience. "In our army, they are the light infantry that keeps the cavalry in touch with the phalanx. You are being honored."

Alexander dumped the helmet in my lap and clapped me on the back.

"Welcome to the King's Hypaspists, Machon, son of Agathon!"

I sat through the rest of the party with only the helmet for company. It was old, with enough chips and dents to tell the story of Philip's seventeen years of unrelenting raids, battles, and sieges. And now it seemed the pattern would be repeated with the son. As to many of you, it came as a relief to me that the Macedonian juggernaut would at last be directed east, against the barbarians. In the meantime, while the post of expedition historian was not the role I came to play, it would give me ample opportunity to observe and report to the Assembly.

My decision to accept this offer was vindicated when all the Athenians but me were sent home. While he had the greatest esteem for the artists and philosophers of Athens, he held the soldiers of our city to be in a kind of bad odor. Aeschines suggests that he feared betrayal, but I don't agree: there were contingents from plenty of Greek allies, such as the Thessalians, whom he kept at his back without any such concern. Instead, I think he and his comrades dreaded the air of defeat they perceived around Athenian arms. The Macedonians had known nothing but victory for a good many years, and standing at the opening of a difficult campaign, and of provincial and superstitious minds, they simply wanted nothing but winners around them.

The chronicler's post turned out to have enormous advantages. Alexander, desperate as he was for acclaim, put few limits on where I could go, or to whom I might talk. By this he did not intend that I would write embarrassing things about him. There would be an official version of every major event on the march. However, the enforcement of his legend was accomplished most through immersing the writer so completely in the affairs of the King, his trials and his joys, the day-to-day substance of his great endeavor, that the historian could not help but sympathize with his subject. There was power in being allowed within the charmed circle of Companions—a power that Alexander used well. As evidence, I point to the manuscripts of Callisthenes that had already appeared at the bookstalls. Yes, even Callisthenes, who was eventually murdered by Alexander, casts his subject as history's finest hero.

My first sampling of this privilege came just before the army left for Asia, as I became aware of troubling reports from the inner court. Alexander had only recently finished erecting a splendid tomb for his father, which he accomplished at the cost of much time and money. Though father and son had been estranged in recent years, the young King discharged his duty with great devotion, showing the reverence for custom that marked his conduct in the years to come. I was at the royal cemetery in Aigai before the tomb's fine painted façade was closed forever and buried under the hill. Having retrieved Philip's bones from the pyre and bathed them in wine, Alexander installed them in their gold box and sealed the inner chamber. With his own hands, Alexander placed a pair of Philip's greaves at the door to his resting place, leaning them there as if his father had just stepped inside for a nap.

Cynics may do their best to impugn his motives. They may say that he made such a lavish dedication to his father's memory not out of genuine feeling, but to prove to the Macedonian nobles that the estates and privileges they gained under Philip were safe. It still cannot have been easy for any son to face the premature death of his father. Add to this the suspicion that Philip was seeking, by the end, to delegitimize Alexander's claim to the throne by marrying again, and we might begin to understand the welter of feelings in the young man. Yet it seems that Olympias only added to his troubles with a solemn announcement: Philip was not Alexander's father after all!

Of this scene I have only rumors, but they have the ring of truth. The Queen, who was still beautiful, had claimed for herself a new visibility with the ascension of her son. She was no longer Olympias at all, it seems, but Athena-of-the-flashing-eyes, striding around the palace in boots, perfumed helmet, and a cuirass made of crane feathers. Alexander's legitimacy, she declared, did not stem from her marriage to Philip, who was just a mortal after all, but from her union with the very King of the Gods. She then attempted to justify her account with inexcusable details. Zeus's cock, she reported, was as thick as a man's forearm, and hung slightly sinister. With mortal women he fucked like Pan, from behind. When he came the oak trees swayed, and thunder rolled along the mountaintops, and a feeling like the touch of lightning struck deep inside her. His mother went on like this until Alexander, covering his ears, ran groaning from the room. He never saw her again, and to my knowledge he spent not a moment regretting that fact.

No doubt Olympias meant in this way to aggrandize her son on the eve of his expedition. But the woman knew more about the genitals of gods and demons than about the feelings of the human beings who shared her world. Certainly, in the abstract, a god's paternity might seem flattering. Taken along with the Queen's taste for Bacchic excess, however, her story seemed nothing more than a euphemism for Alexander's bastardy. Just as we might soften the death of a loved one by saying "the gods took him," some women put the best face on illegitimacy by saying "a god fathered him." I say this without ever speaking with Alexander about it—this was never a matter he would discuss. But if you had seen his face after receiving this news, as I did, you would not say that he seemed gladdened by it.

This incident is also important because the episode at the Sanctuary of Ammon in Egypt cannot be understood without it. Having clashed with his father, as every adolescent does at some point as he attains his manhood, tales of some true, divine origin must have had some appeal to him. As a man, it is likely that Alexander knew his mother was insane. Yet as he puzzled over why he went from success to success, far exceeding Philip in the range of his conquests, her story ceased to be an embarrassment, and came to make some sense. By "sense" I mean more than propaganda value—I mean relief from the questions that disturbed his sleep. When he went to Siwah, then, he was much gratified, for although the Oracle told him exactly what Olympias had, it came without her excess, and her self-absorption. Surely it must be more than mere propaganda value that drove him, as his final wish, to want to be buried in Egypt, next to the Oracle, and not delivered home to his mother.

At this time Alexander gave every indication to me

that the war on Persia had been his own idea. But this pretense rang hollow. He had, in fact, inherited this war from Philip, who had already landed troops in Asia some time before, under the command of Attalus, son of Cleochares. Attalus had lately been suffering defeats at the hands of the Great King's Greek hireling, Memnon. The Macedonians were on the brink of being driven into the sea. Alexander's expedition was therefore something of a rescue operation.

The Macedonians made a virtue of necessity by turning Alexander's arrival on Asian soil into a theatrical event. While the real army crossed elsewhere under Parmenion's command, the King sailed to the shores of Ilion in a party boat hung with garlands and listing with the weight of officers and allied dignitaries. The historians were given a privileged place in the bows so they might witness the climax of the day's program: Alexander's landing. This was, incidentally, the first time I met Callisthenes. He had styled himself, it seemed, as a miniature version of his uncle, Aristotle, right down to the curly beard. I would have liked to speak with him, but the presence of what he took to be a rival historian seemed to have stopped his tongue. I will say more about him later, and about Aeschines's accusations that I was responsible for his sad fate. For now, let it be said that I had nothing but comradely feelings for him, as a devotee of our mutual muse, Clio. Any resentment between us was entirely on his side.

The plan was for the vessel to come into water shallow enough for the King to wade ashore. Just before he hit the water he would hurl his javelin onto the beach, whereupon the entire Asian landmass was supposed to become his spear-won territory. When we reached the spot that had been scouted out for the landing, Alexander stood ready with his spotless leather cuirass and his repoussé bronze greaves, hair blowing out long and thin in the spring breeze. At the captain's nod, the King lofted his spear, which arced ashore and stood up perfectly in the sand. As he dropped into the surf, however, he stumbled, dousing his hair. As no one had imagined he would take possession of his continent wet-headed, he climbed back on the ship for another attempt.

After taking some time to dry himself, he stood at the bows as the ship came into position. The captain nodded, and Alexander threw again. This time he didn't need to go into the water, because his spear did not stick in the sand. The collected officers and emissaries grumbled; the King gave a sharp look at the two historians, who turned away from the fallen spear as if they'd never seen it thrown. I cannot speak for Callisthenes, but I had the uncomfortable feeling that all this effort was being mounted for the benefit of the two of us, as the eyes and ears of future generations.

The third try did the trick. The javelin flew truly and stuck perfectly, and Alexander kept his balance despite the loose footing in the surf. Climbing out of the water, he strode manfully to the spear, and pulled it out with a confident, purposive expression on his face. Hephaestion shouted to him that all was well, and Alexander relaxed, sitting in the sand to wait for his crew to debark.

Ptolemy, son of Lagus, then appeared behind Callisthenes and me. Upon my first glimpse of this beetle-browed, block-chinned character, I didn't trust him.

Even today, as he styles himself for the throne of Egypt, he has all the charm of a jackal, and fewer manners. He seemed to have a similar effect on Callisthenes, who stood up awkwardly, then sat down, not knowing what he should do. Ptolemy smiled.

"What an event for our two little scribblers to witness! And for it to go so perfectly on the very first try!"

"Yes, remarkable," said Callisthenes.

I said nothing. He stared at me hard, perhaps not knowing that a man who had faced enemy spears in battle would never wither at a sharp glance. Yet I also knew that my silence had already earned Ptolemy's undying enmity—

The last drop of water ran out of the clock.

"The defendant has run out of time," declared Polycleitus.

"So I have. According to the usual custom, I request the favor of an extension."

"I see no reason for a substantial grant of time," the king archon said with his eyes shut, "if you go on about matters that have little to do with your defense."

"It was not my doing, your honor, that the entire course of my career with Alexander has been placed in evidence against me. I am obligated to refute the prosecution's version of these events."

"Your obligations are not material here. . . ." said Polycleitus, his eyes again flitting toward the two Macedonian spectators. Very clearly, Swallow saw the shorter of the two give a discreet toss of his head. Polycleitus continued, ". . . and the court will not be bound by them. You have a single measure of time to wrap up your statement."

"Your honor, I really must protest!"

"Fill the clock. Proceed with the defense."

Machon was about to resume his objection when Swallow gave a single, loud clap of his hands, and then another a few seconds later. Deuteros joined in, and then all of those around them.

"Men of the jury will be silent."

At that, all five hundred men in the jury gave the judge a slow ovation. He stared out at them for a moment, as if thinking of some way to punish them, but decided to scream instead.

"Stop that clapping! My decision is final! STOP THAT CLAPPING!"

Finally the king archon looked back at the Macedonians. Both of them shrugged, turning their faces to the floor.

"Very well, then," Polycleitus relented. "As it is customary to be liberal in these cases, you have the same amount of time the prosecution had . . . but not one second more!"

"For your fairness, I thank you," said Machon with a tight smile. His eyes rested on Swallow, who took his meaning and waved his hand, is if to decline any credit.

VII

As the Macedonian army formed up and began the march up-country, I was puzzled by the lack of organized resistance to the invasion. The Persian navy, after all, was made up of very capable Phoenician and Sidonese levies, together at twice the numbers Alexander could gather. It should have been a straightforward matter for this force to bottle up the Hellespont, intercept the Macedonian troop carriers, or execute whatever plan the enemy would have conceived. Or at least that's how it seemed to an Athenian used to thinking in terms of sea power.

No satrap was waiting on the shore for us with his hooded troops and mailed cavalry. Nor were the farms and towns of this rich country burned before our path, to prevent stores from falling into our hands; the granaries, instead, were bursting with last year's harvest. To the young Macedonian grunts, the invasion went as easily as their childish dreams made it. But to anybody who knew anything, the stillness suggested there was something very deeply wrong.

It was only much later, upon speaking with Persian courtiers who had been at Susa at that time, that I learned the truth: though the Persian Empire was vast, it was riddled with problems. The Great King, Artashata, otherwise known as Daryavaush III, or Darius, was a weakling who had alienated most of the nobility by poisoning his competitors for the throne. Egypt was in the midst of a revolt that had only just been put down by the Persian fleet when Alexander tossed his spear on the beach at Ilium. We might therefore say that Alexander had been lucky to arrive when he did, or cunning, in that he landed with most of Persia looking the other way. We cannot say, however, that his mere arrival represented much of a victory.

I might as well take the opportunity now, as I have Alexander on his way toward the Granicus, to correct an impression you might have gotten from our friend Aeschines. Judging from his account, only Alexander—along with a few other minor players and a faceless army—was present at his battles. But it takes more than one extraordinary man to make an army. Some of the others who went with Alexander had a lot to do with his victories.

I'm thinking of Parmenion, the old stalwart who served Philip too. True, he was not the kind of flashy performer who plays to the gallery by taking foolish risks. He was, in fact, too fat to mount a horse. But he knew how to hold a line against superior foe, which is something Alexander never had to accomplish. I've already mentioned Ptolemy, and Cleitus. These are unsavory characters—thugs, really—but they were loyal and ruthless, and such men can accomplish a lot. I would count in their company Peithon, son of Crateuas, though to look at him you would say he seemed more scholar than warrior. His area of knowledge, I came to learn, was the infliction of lethal force on those too weak to defend themselves. I will describe some of his notable works as the occasion arises.

To my recollection Aeschines mentions Perdiccas son of Orestes only once, which is strange because he now sits on Alexander's throne in Babylon! In most ways he was cut from the same cloth as Alexander: face full of curl-lipped arrogance, born to make war, hunt frequently, and drink his wine neat. He even took care to cut his hair just like Alexander. To his credit, he was a decent phalanx commander in the early years, and scaled the ladder of influence with hardly a misstep. Perdiccas never seemed ambitious, but events always seemed to go his way. For all his resemblance to the King, however, he lacked one important element: Alexander's impulse to understand the world he was destroying.

There were many others who had their moments on the stage over the next twelve years—Peucestas, Coenus, Nearchus, Craterus, Aristander the soothsayer . . . and Philotas, whom Aeschines mentions only in relation to the ridiculous charges that led to his death! If you and I were sharing a drink, I would tell you about them all—from their best moments to their worst, and how they shaped the success that has come to compose the legend of Alexander. But we have time today to speak only of Machon—a minor figure indeed! If I say to you, though, that Alexander was more a corporation than a man, and his myth a work of many authors, it is because I was there. Let only those who marched with me dispute my words!

Hephaestion is another bit player in Aeschines's story. Alexander would never have countenanced this.

They were friends since boyhood, and lovers for almost as long. Alexander was the "bottom," and Hephaestion, who was bigger and stronger, the "top."
Olympias begged her son to produce an heir before he
left for Asia, but he was too much in love with Hephaestion even to function as a man. Of the pair, Hephaestion was the more ambitious. It was he who
encouraged Alexander to march on after Issus, to take
on the entire Persian Empire, and it was he who argued the strongest for an invasion of India, though no
one else would agree with him. So great was his influence with the King, he almost succeeded in cajoling
him onto the Gangetic Plain.

But foremost among the forgotten characters is Arridaeus, Alexander's half-brother. I see your faces—
you don't believe it! Bear with me, then, and you will
see.

You have been given a rousing account of the battle
at the Granicus. I congratulate my opponent on his
powers of description. Listening to him evoke the
scene, it was as if I was there—until I realized I had
been there, and it was nothing like he described!

Imagine this: the Macedonians on one side of a river
swollen with spring melt, the mounted Persians high
on the other, backed up by a Greek army. Alexander,
after a spirited invocation of Homer, single-handedly
charges the entire Persian line—and lives! The Macedonians follow, and striking "like Hephaestus's ham-
mer," they smash the enemy. Thousands of Persians
die, and the Greek mercenaries, astounded by this
wonder, stand around and wait for the Macedonians
to cross the river in force, organize themselves, and
surround them. Thousands of the mercenaries are

slaughtered too. And the toll for Alexander's army?
Just twenty-five dead, says Aeschines.

Most of us are veterans of war here . . . do we not
smell a rat? Do single riders charge entire armies and
survive? How could it be that the Macedonians could
cross a torrent, proceed uphill against their enemy,
slash their way through the Persian lines, and lose
only twenty-five men? Having seen cavalry cross
muddy, miserable spring rivers, I would expect more
than twenty-five to die just falling off their horses! To
doubt this is not to engage in what Aeschines calls "so-
phistication." It is to use common sense.

What really happened was this: our scouts reported
that the Persians were gathered at the Granicus river,
and Alexander proceeded with his officers to inspect
their position. They observed that the enemy was
blocking the only fording place, and that the manner
of their deployment, on a bluff above the far bank,
would result in horrific casaulties among the Macedonians. Parmenion therefore recommended a subtler
strategy. The Persians, the old general explained, were
anxious to secure their horses against theft at night,
and so made a practice of tethering them by both bri-
dle and the feet. As these precautions made it hard for
them to saddle and mount in an emergency, they were
obliged to make their camps far away from their enemies. In this case the Persians would bivouac
overnight well out of touch with their scouts on the
river. Why not wait until before dawn the next morning, asked Parmenion, cross the river in secret, and
take them all by surprise?

Alexander carped, complaining that he hadn't
crossed the mighty Hellespont just to be stopped at a

mere trickle. Hephaestion declared that strategizing was for weaklings, and that the barbarians would scatter at the first flash of steel. But there was no denying that the river flowed fast and deep, the Persian armor was blindingly numerous, and that the Macedonian infantrymen were spooked. Even if they managed to break through the horses, at least twenty thousand Greek mercenary pikemen waited behind them, each one no doubt desperate to redeem the reputation of Greek arms against Macedon. Perhaps most important, a defeat or a costly victory there, at the very outset of the invasion, would doom the entire enterprise.

The King took Parmenion's advice. Overnight, swimmers were sent across to silence the Persian watchmen. And as the first blush of dawn appeared in the sky behind the enemy camp, Alexander got his Cavalry Companions across the river, and most of the pikemen, before they were observed by the Persians. A melee ensued in the twilight; Alexander led his horsemen forward to meet the enemy, who had been roused before their time and wore only half their armor. Marching with the Hypaspists, I reached the enemy camp in time to see Alexander sitting on the ground, being ministered to by a doctor after he was struck in the helmet with an axe. Cleitus, who had saved Alexander at the last second, crouched with his hands on his knees, looking down at the King.

That was when I noticed something curious. Alexander was out of the action, barely conscious, but someone very much like him, with the same build, same stature, and virtually the same voice, was still directing the attack on the Persian camp. With unerring perception of the flow of forces around the battlefield, he directed cavalry and footmen into flying columns that cut the disorganized enemy to pieces. As the sun broke over the horizon, we could see scattered remnants of the Persian cavalry fleeing, and many of Darius's Greek hirelings still in their camp clothes, surrounded.

Who was the commander who accomplished all this? Sighting him again, I followed some distance behind. His resemblance to Alexander in both movement and voice was striking, yet he wore far more armor than the King, including a muscle cuirass and greaves. Coming closer, I could see that he wore a lot of armor, but nothing else—no cloak, no tunic, no groin-flaps. His ass was bare for the world to see!

This spectacle intrigued me, to say the least, for this half-naked apparition was directing the relentless slaughter of virtually all the Greek mercenaries. By midday more than fifteen thousand bodies formed an enormous mountain of fly-strewn flesh. But in the time it took me to glance at the dead and then look back, the mysterious commander was gone. In his place was Alexander, discussing with his officers the enormity of incinerating such a mass.

To be sure, I made many inquiries into what I had seen. The Macedonians were aggressively reluctant to discuss it; Callisthenes acknowledged that he had seen the figure I described, but would not elaborate. In the months to come, using every method I could think of, including bribery, I was finally able to learn the truth.

We know of him now as Philip Arridaeus. He was Alexander's half-brother—a bastard produced by the union of Philip and a Thessalian concubine. The official historians are loathe to speak of him, because from a young age he was an idiot, barely able to speak or take care of himself. He had other odd problems, such as an inability to tolerate the touch of other people, and a deep aversion to the wearing of clothes. Instead, he preferred the feel of metal against his skin. For this reason he wore either armor or nothing for his entire life.

Yet he did have certain talents. His memory, for instance, was prodigious. By the age of three he could recognize and name all the different units of Philip's army. By eight he memorized the entire text of *The Iliad*. He knew thousands of men by name, and the names of their fathers, and could recount their deeds in battle with precise detail. Alexander, on the other hand, was a charmer, but had no head for the common man. When he was forced to interact with them, he never knew their names. Arridaeus remembered everything.

The man was in every way fascinated by war. From a young age he liked nothing better than to pore over maps, planning for his fanciful campaigns. As I will recount, he was also invincible on the battlefield, with talents as a strategist that turned out to be more than imaginary. But I shouldn't get ahead of myself. Suffice it to say that you will never read of Arridaeus in any official history, because the combination of martial virtue and complete idiocy was incomprehensible to the Macedonians. They were, and are, deeply embarrassed by what they owe to him.

The origins of his illness are obscure. Some say he was born that way, others that Olympias, fearing competition for Alexander's future throne, had the infant Arridaeus fed poison with his breast milk. Her intent was not to kill him, which would have been too obvious a crime, but to destroy his mind. I am told that there are preparations of mercury or arsenic that might have such effects if used in small quantities. But bear in mind that I have no proof that he was poisoned. I know only that, wherever he came from, and however he did it, he became the secret weapon of the Macedonians.

Arridaeus's skills were discovered by accident during the assault on Thebes. Alexander didn't expect to take the city, but instead wished no more than to teach the Thebans a lesson. Arridaeus, who was dressed in his usual armor when he appeared on the field, was mistaken for Alexander when he began to issue commands. Sizing up the situation in an instant, he dispatched troops to the weakest part of the Theban wall. The city fell.

This victory caught Alexander by surprise. In his confusion, he didn't know what he wanted to do with the prize, so instead turned the decision over to Thebes's petty and resentful neighbors. They, of course, wanted the city razed. Alexander acceded to their selfishness—a decision he regretted for the rest of his life.

For later battles, Arridaeus was brought out on a horse, with an escort of mounted Companions around him to conceal his presence from the rest of the army. From this cocoon the simpleton sent orders around the battlefield. With each victory of Arridaeus, Alexander's reputation for invincibility grew. Ever resourceful, Arridaeus added his brother's renown to his arsenal, deploying Alexander like a psychological weapon. "Send Panic over there," he would say, or,

"More Terror on the right." The only thing that was more remarkable than his generalship was the Macedonians' refusal to acknowledge it.

Machon paused as the jury turned in a body to the Macedonian spectators. They just stood, shaking their heads in a vaguely menacing way, as if the defendant had sealed his fate with this testimony.

In any case, the Macedonians had their victory at the Granicus, and also managed to kill most of the Greeks fighting in the service of the Great King. Notice that, unlike Aeschines, I make a distinction between the two peoples. We kept hearing from him about the Greeks at Issus, the Greeks at Gaugamela. I assure you there were very few Greeks on campaign with Alexander in Asia, except for myself, and some Thessalian cavalry, who were held mostly in reserve anyway. The Macedonians have little use for Greeks except to kill them. Outrageous, you say? You would agree if you counted the Greek casualties among the enemy at the Granicus and Issus. It is a fact that Alexander's army killed more Greeks than anyone in history. By that I include Xerxes, Darius, or any other foreign king!

As I have said, I will not revisit every word Aeschines has said, except to note that he has flattened the character of Alexander, who was a man in full, into something close to bas relief. Because he admired Athens and history so much, the King accepted me into his company as if I had always been there with him, in the opulent but cold palace in which he was born. His candor was astonishing. For example, when I asked him privately about the serious manner in which he drank, he told me it didn't matter, since he expected to be dead by the age of thirty. Pressing him further on this,

I learned that assassination was the acknowledged lot of Macedonian kings, with not a single one of his predecessors having died of old age. When he was somewhat deeper in his cups, I asked him why he bothered to go on campaign, if his future was so clouded.

"But that is exactly why I do go, my dear Machon! If I am killed in battle, I will deprive them of a king to murder!"

His replies on these matters were not always consistent. Sometimes he expressed the outright desire to die; others he aspired only to deprive his officers of the pleasure of killing him. Still others he showed an overwhelming sense of grief for the destruction of Thebes, which he believed was a sin that the gods would never forgive. He carried this fatalism to the battlefield with him, letting it drive him to acts of reckless valor. His enemies perceived this desperation in him, this assurance of his own death, and stepped aside. It was the unique combination of Arridaeus's madness and Alexander's despair that drove the success of the Macedonians. No army could cope with them both.

What I learned about him gives a different meaning to the old story about Alexander and his doctor. According to the legend, Alexander was suffering from sickness when he received a written warning from Parmenion that the royal doctor, Lycius, had been bribed by Darius to kill him. At the same moment Alexander read the letter Lycius was handing him an emetic to drink. The King, they say, cheerfully handed Parmenion's warning to the doctor. Lycius read the accusation, and was preparing to deny it, when he saw that Alexander had already swallowed the drug! And although the stuff was foul, and was meant to sicken him to his stomach, the King did nothing more than soothe Lycius's consternation, so sure was this innocent fellow that he would be executed.

This tale, which I have no idea is true, is supposed to show Alexander's implicit trust in his men. What it may show instead is his faith in his own destruction. Recall these lines from *Alcestis:* "My mother was accursed the night she bore me, and I am faint with envy of all the dead." Euripides, by the way, was always Alexander's favorite poet; that he favored Homer is an outright lie perpetuated by Ptolemy.

Alexander approached the unraveling of the Gordion knot as something of a stunt. The episode ended up as a fiasco that has somehow has been transformed into a triumph. Aeschines says that I encouraged him to attempt the puzzle in order to see him fail. The truth is that I argued with him not to offend the gods by presuming he could solve it. He replied that the challenge would teach him something about himself. We argued in his tent as he prepared to go, and our quarrel continued outside in front of witnesses, where I could not speak freely. At last I threw up my hands.

"Go ahead then! Bring the fury of Heaven down on our heads!"

He posed with one hand behind the crown of his head, fingers wagging, like the wavering aura of some divinity.

"You forget who I am, my friend!"

Then he laughed, and was off to the Zeus temple where Gordius's wagon was kept. I anticipated disaster, but somehow couldn't stay away from the spectacle. The relic was in the shadow of Midas's great funeral mound, in the Temple of Zeus: an oxcart of

very common appearance, very much like the rude
wains Alexander must have seen on his youthful maneuvers in the fields around Pella. It was said this was
the very vehicle that had carried Midas's father from
his farmhouse in Macedonia to the throne of Phrygia.
The Knot, a great ball of stripped bark, fastened the
heavy double-yoke to the shaft. The man who untied
it was destined to seize the throne of the Great King.

Standing in the back, I watched as he circled the
cart, quite possibly realizing the magnitude of the
trouble he had taken upon himself. Generations of ad-
venturers had tried and failed to untie the Knot. The
entire population of Gordion seemed to be waiting
outside the temple; the Macedonian officers were there
too, their childish faith in their King yet unspoiled.

The Knot was so long untouched that spider webs
hung from it. Alexander began to pick at it, as if trying
to find some loose end to work free. But public challenges go unmet for centuries for a reason: in this case,
the Knot was as tight as a drumhead, and seemed held
together by some kind of glue. He tried to get a fin-
gertip under one of the leather strands but slipped,
ripping off part of a nail. He cursed. The priests sucked
in their breaths at this blasphemy in their sanctuary.
Alexander ignored them, taking out his sword. Working the tip between two strands, he struggled to widen
the opening, but the Knot moved too much, and he
could not grip the blade tightly enough. The King became frustrated, stabbing at the wobbly thing until he
went red in the face and everyone became embarrassed for him. The nervous whispers of the onlookers
became louder, and Hephaestion looked as if he was
ready to intercede. That was when Alexander raised

his sword and commenced hacking at the Knot as if he
were chopping wood.

It was a big sword, and though he was short,
Alexander had a strong arm. Yet it still took more than
twenty blows to cut through the leather mass, and by
the end the King was wide-eyed and sweaty and
oblivious to the expressions of horror on the faces of
the natives. With a look of accomplishment on his face
that was as absurd as it was childish, he held up the
two severed halves of the Knot. At that, the senior
members of his staff clapped their hands, and with
their glances made sure the junior officers followed,
until all the Macedonians were applauding him.

It was an anxious moment, in fact, because the natives' and foreigners' attitudes to this sad spectacle
were so different. But in the end the ones with the
weapons prevailed, and the King basked in an ovation
that seemed to go on forever. The celebration paused
as a peal of thunder was heard above the temple. All at
once the nervousness returned, and some even proceeded suddenly to jeer the King, believing that the
gods had expressed their disapproval of what he had
done. But Perdiccas leapt on a plinth and settled the
issue.

"Zeus has thrown his thunderbolt! The new King of
Asia is crowned!"

All at once the pendulum swung from uncertainty
back to servility. The soldiers ripped the ancient cart
from its moorings, lifted Alexander inside, and rolled
him around the sanctuary in triumph. As the temple
emptied, I stayed behind to watch the head priest. The
man knelt before the discarded halves of the Knot,
threw the folds of his cloak over his head, and wept.

In the wake of Alexander's "triumph" there seemed
an urgency to clear out of Gordion as soon as possible.
The army prepared to move on to Ancyra, about
twenty parasangs to the east. As we decamped, I noticed a tiny figure atop the great mound of King
Midas. Coming closer, I saw it was Alexander, sitting
up there with a wine jug and his sword stuck in the
mound beside him. He hailed me as I came up to join
him.

"Machon! Have you nothing better to do than climb
hills?"

"It is a remarkable hill that we both have climbed."

And it was. The mound, which they say is heaped
atop a fabulous hoard of undiscovered treasure, commanded the plateau for miles around. Around the city
stretched a patchwork of farms, split by the winding
ribbon of the river Sangarius. The Macedonian camp
was a constellation of torches by the river. From that
distance, and as the twilight came on, no figures could
be seen in the town or the camp below. We seemed to
be alone—the monarch and his memoirist, or in his
mind, the King and History itself.

"I wonder if anyone would have done it."

"It?"

"Loosened the Knot for real. And don't look so
shocked, my friend! The storyteller need not believe
his own stories."

He held out his cup. I sat down next to him, and together we finished the jug as the sun sank into the
plain. I turned east, in the direction of Ancyra; the sky
there was the darkest—a soiled indigo with the dying
light and the smoke of hearth fires. Alexander climbed
to his feet.

"Tomorrow, we go there. Let's see what it brings us!"

As we entered the town we learned that Ptolemy and Craterus were desperate to learn where the King had gone. Soldiers filled the streets, breaking down the doors of every wine shop in the city. With a wink, the King hid his head under his cloak and disappeared into an alley. He was not seen again until late the following morning, when he was found sleeping in his bed.

With the fall of Persian resistance throughout the western half of Asia Minor Alexander's promise to liberate the Ionians was accomplished. While it is true that the ease of their victory tempted the Macedonians to take all of the Persian lands, it was equally true that the invasion had gathered its own momentum, and that other forces were then at work to keep it in motion. Cities in Alexander's path insisted on surrendering before he had even arrived, forcing him to march east to preserve them from anarchy. The pattern repeated many times, until it seemed that the Macedonians were being sucked inevitably eastward, farther from their homes, their families, and in some sense, from themselves.

So we reach Issus. Aren't we all tired of descriptions of battles? The hero is always fearless, the enemy is always in hordes. While the Greeks do exceed all other people in the arts of war, the bravery of the Persians, as men, should never be doubted. The fact was that our enemies were indifferently led. The Great King could more easily find one hundred thousand soldiers than one decent company commander. Darius, who showed up at last to defend his kingdom, was compe-

tent only at setting up troops for battle. The more essential skill, that of leading them through the adjust-
ments that are inevitable in any fight, was completely
beyond him.

Darius disposed his forces in a defile along the
banks of the river Pinarus, from the foothills of Mount
Amanus on his left to the sea. His center was again
held by his Greek hirelings, who burned to avenge the
humiliation of the Granicus. The banks of this river
were even steeper at the Persian center than at the last
battle; Darius increased his odds of success by using
gangs of slaves to mound up even more earth there, so
that his mercenaries would look down on us from a
great height. On his right Darius massed a multitude
of armored cavalry. Arrayed behind this narrow front
was a horde of crack archers, slingers, and native infantry.

Aeschines was most expansive on this matter, so I
won't expend my time on the details. The fact is that
Alexander was late showing up on the morning of the
battle because he was hungover. The more he drank
the previous evening, the more he became assured that
he was fated to die, either at the hands of the Persians
or of his own men. His drinking companions, Hephaestion, Parmenion, and Cleitus, indulged this fan-
tasy by asking him how he would dispose of his new
kingdom. He replied that he cared only of disposing of
himself, for his preferences would not matter the
slightest bit after he was gone.

Of course, he didn't die at Issus. But his words
proved prophetic, as the present circumstances surrounding the royal succession show.

That Darius would offer battle in such a narrow valley was unexpected. The Macedonians, who had been prepared to face a large cavalry force on open ground, were confounded that the Great King would negate his own best advantage. They suspected some hidden strategy was at work.

The armies stood staring at each other for some time until Arridaeus could be brought to the field. In a glance the fool discerned the weakness in the Persian battle-order: a body of lightly armored infantry on the enemy left that he somehow felt to be wavering. There Terror should go, he said, and with it the battle.

So Alexander went where he was told. And just as Arridaeus had predicted, the Persian left broke. The King exceeded his mandate, however, by wheeling to his left and charging the enemy center, where Darius's retinue stood. From their respective places around the battlefield the Macedonian generals watched helplessly as Alexander risked turning victory into defeat.

I try to imagine what the Great King must have seen as he stood in his garlanded chariot. Set in the center, he would have had a view of his forces breaking the advance of the vaunted phalanxes, while the very mass of his cavalry on the right promised to break Parmenion's line. In the confusion, in the dust churned by hundreds of thousands of feet, he would scarcely have noticed a disturbance far to the north. Over the din of crashing shields before him, he might have heard a thin chorus of screams. Perhaps one of his retainers would have told him his left wing had broken; perhaps he even expected it, having planted weak troops there in order to bait Alexander away from what he expected would be the main action. He still might have looked forward to turning the Macedonian left, flanking the Foot Companions, and having his antagonist, that bald-cheeked upstart, brought to him in chains by sunset.

He might have thought these things, and at that very moment may have glimpsed the Companion cav alry through the dust, sweeping his forces aside as they headed straight for the Persian royal guard. Alexander would have been unmistakable in their van, white plumes flying on his helmet, his thrusting spear pointed right at Darius.

There must have been very little time to think as the Macedonians closed and the fate of a continent hung on an instant. The golden figure of Alexander pressed his attack, weaving his way through the flailing scimitars like a rider avoiding the overhanging branches on a trail. Darius would have seen the fear in his retainers' eyes—those fearful, flashing whites—as they failed to stop this onslaught. The Great King would have held his breath as another figure on horseback, in the panoply of his royal house, finally detained Alexander. There was a brief struggle as the flanks of their horses met, a crunch of metal plates buckling under the weight as well-trained mounts turned around each other. Someone gasped as Alexander's spear point found a gap in his opponent's armor. Down went the Great King's defender—but there would be little time for Darius to mourn the death of his own brother. He would have seen his tormentor turn to face him at last.

The Persian royal guard, the Immortals, had been taken by surprise by Alexander's lightning maneuver. As they gave ground, Darius was exposed with astonishing ease—a development no one would have expected. But the surprises did not all work to the Macedonians' advantage: at that time no one knew that Darius was renowned for his skill in single combat. From Cleitus, I learned that Alexander made straight for the royal chariot, made a pass with his stabbing spear . . . and missed. Darius, who towered above the rest of the battlefield in his high-peaked leather warbonnet, had a javelin ready. With a barbarous cry, he let loose as Alexander rode by, striking him in the leg just above the knee.

Everything on the battlefield seemed to come to a halt when Alexander was wounded. It was as if when he fell everyone believed the war would instantly end—that the combatants, their reason for fighting gone, would simply disengage, shake hands, and go home. Only Darius was still in a frenzy, screaming for another javelin. We did yet know at that point that the Great King took haoma before the battle—an extract of the ephedra plant that is taken with milk. This drug is said to instill feelings of euphoria, and in greater quantities, ecstatic awareness of the hidden secrets of the universe. It also gives great strength, though at the cost of a disordered mind. It was what the Persians used in their worship of their gods, just as the Greeks use wine in our rites of Dionysus. In this sense both Kings came to the battle in a very devout state!

It might have been the haoma that allowed the Great King to make such a remarkable throw. However, when Alexander proved able to pull the javelin out of his leg, the drug's disadvantage showed: all at once, without even being touched, Darius panicked. Before the Macedonians could organize themselves, we were looking at the back of his chariot. The entire mass of the Persian army immediately broke in retreat. Alexander, still looking for a spectacular exit from this life, was stabbing and slashing at anyone in reach.

The day ended much as it had at the Granicus, with the field in the hands of the Macedonians and the ground littered with the bodies of Persians and Greek mercenaries. Alexander, who regretted that his injury was superficial, was restrained by his doctors from giving chase to Darius. The fact that he was wounded at all was judged to be a disaster by the Macedonians, particularly Ptolemy and Hephaestion; they would have preferred to lose five thousand men than brook any hint of the young conqueror's mortality. So you can see that they were already thinking in these terms, that the legend must emerge that Alexander was unstoppable because he was a god.

To his shame, Darius abandoned not only his troops but his household to the enemy. By now you have all heard of the luxury Alexander saw in the camp of Darius. The Great King's field tent was more resplendent than Philip's royal tomb in Aigai. Darius touched nothing that was not precious—golden cups, golden plates, golden bathtub with working taps, a golden commode for his backside. His nostrils were caressed by golden braziers burning aromatic woods from Arabia; his feet trod on carpets spun of golden thread and as soft as a woman's thighs. For official functions, he sat on a chryselephantine throne with as many precious gems as stars in the night sky. The Macedonians stood in quiet awe, never having imagined such splendor.

All this gold had an effect on the Macedonians' willingness to go all the way to Persia. Not to put too fine a point on it, but the question arose of what wonders awaited the enterprising conqueror who took the royal palaces at Susa, Persepolis, or Ecbatana, given that Darius's field camp was so resplendent. That the Macedonians went so far east because of strategic considerations is at best only a half-truth; the simple promise of loot loomed at least as large for the mid-level officers, without whom Alexander could never have convinced his army to go anywhere.

I cannot pass over in silence how my opponent portrays my remark upon seeing Darius's tent: "At last we see what it means to be a king." Again, there is an insinuation here of sinister intent that is more cynical than convincing. Those who were present took it as it was meant, as a jest. Shame on you for making it more than that, Aeschines! As far as I am aware, having a sense of humor is not yet an actionable offense in the courts of the Athenians.

VIII

Among the captured treasures were the dependents of Darius's house, including his wives, concubines, and four-year-old son. The Great King's mother, dark-eyed Sisygambis, came to make entreaties to Alexander. She was the first woman of the Persian court the Macedonians had seen—a handsome, proud figure of sixty, bejeweled and besilked in a splendor of which Olympias could only dream. She put an impassive face on the fate she expected for herself and her grandchild. She entered the bedchamber and touched her forehead to the carpet not before Alexander, who was still on the bed, but to Hephaestion.

There was a gasp at this faux pas. Hephaestion, who was indeed the taller man, gently bid her rise and led her to Alexander, who watched her repeat her submission. Her consternation at her error must have showed on her face, because Alexander was moved to reassure her, saying "It hardly matters. Hephaestion is Alexander too." Then he embraced her as his very own mother, pledging his full protection of her and her family; he even promised to send messengers after the fleeing Darius to tell him that his loved ones would not be insulted. It must have seemed an incomprehensible act to old Sisygambis, who must have been expecting the ravages of a barbarian.

Aeschines's portrait of Sisygambis is fair—perhaps it is the actor in him that affords him such a sensitive understanding of old women. But I fear he makes too much of Alexander's gallant treatment of Stateira, Darius's principal wife. I ask you, why should anyone be surprised at this? Of course Alexander protected the royal household—every soul in it was his property!

Alexander was usually abstemious in his dealings with women. Slanderers have misrepresented his gallantry as evidence of certain defects of character with respect to the pleasures taken by men with men. The presence of Hephaestion, his best companion, is offered as evidence of Alexander's intemperance in this regard. Yet the very opposite might as well be argued, that the King kept but one true favorite through those long years. True, a man is expected to grow out of such affairs in the fullness of time. There are other attributes of seniority, such as a wife and children, that Alexander was likewise late in taking up—yet these have never been the object of so much cheap gossip. By the gods, I will have many other matters on which to criticize him! On the flavor of his loves, though, I think a man like Alexander, who sacrificed more sensual pleasure than we will ever know for a short life spent in army camps, can be granted this single indulgence.

I did witness an incident that suggests that Stateira was not so virtuously treated after all. It was some time after the initial meeting. The King and his cronies were passing the evening in their usual positions—

horizontal on the wine couch. This was still early in Alexander's campaign to change the world, before the weight of events soured the wine. Don't revolutions always start off that way, with everyone together in a merry band of brothers—until the sport starts? And doesn't the sport always start?

It began this time when Craterus had the idea of inviting the most beautiful woman of Asia to their party. Alexander, having delivered himself into intoxication as quickly as possible, agreed. The order went out, and the servants ran to retrieve her.

This call was made quite late at night—she was probably roused from her bed on this whim. As you might think, the woman imagined the worst, and attempted to stall. But this only gave the symposiasts time to get drunker still. Their anticipation heightened, they repeated the summons—this time more insistently.

Every pair of eyes paid her homage as she appeared at the tent flap. Stateira's veil had been stripped away by the guard, revealing a face of such sublimity that the men were awed in the same way as they would be before eclipses, volcanoes, or other wonders. Her skin was a sunny shade of golden untroubled by flaw; her hair was black and shining like the cloudless night that follows the day. She was clothed in a linen gown that revealed nothing except the shapes of her limbs. This only seemed to magnify her appeal, as the Macedonians knew little of the nude female form, but instead liked to fill their houses with statues of half-draped nymphs and disheveled maenads.

If you have not seen a noble woman of Persia, you cannot know that there is a kind of doleful beauty that belongs solely to them. In all the countries I have traveled, I have never seen women so good looking look so wretched. Stateira's only imperfection, I would say, was the fact of her perfection, which left her somewhat characterless. This did not seem to be the kind of woman any mortal could love.

For her part, Stateira was entirely impassive, looking at no one and taking no notice of her surroundings except to reach the couch next to Alexander. There she sat, as straight as an infantry pike, accepting no food or drink and saying nothing. The shape of her nostrils expressed resentment of the very air she breathed. There seemed an old woman's share of desolation hidden behind her eyes.

The mood Stateira brought with her, the lure of both her beauty and her forlornness, reduced all the men around her to stupefaction. It was Cleitus who finally broke the silence, asking how any man could abandon such a prize, or even bring her so close to the battle that such a loss could be contemplated.

"I must say I am disappointed," replied Peithon, "for I expected her to be younger."

"In her case it doesn't matter."

"Oh, it always matters with women! Here is the secret to escape becoming a slave to a pretty maid, boys: tell yourself that in five or ten years she'll droop. It's inevitable. It is the curse of the sex."

"And boys don't grow up? Men don't droop?"

"Oh, who's talking about men?"

With that, Peithon gave a glance at Alexander, and then to Hephaestion, who was unique in the group for his lack of enthusiasm for calling out Stateira, or for her presence. Cleitus had no such reticence, however.

"To me there's no comparison. I've had it all, done it all from here to Kerkyra, and for my money it's women."

"Women have their uses," countered Peithon, "but not for inspiring true desire. That cannot be denied."

"I deny it—it is possible to have passion for females."

Cleitus and Peithon went back and forth, debating the respective virtues of each sex until Perdiccas looked to the King. "And what does Alexander say of this?"

The King lowered his cup, smiled. "Diogenes recommended neither women nor boys, but masturbation. It's like satisfying your hunger just by rubbing your stomach!"

During this exchange Stateira was there to look at, and as the looking was good, nothing more was demanded of her. But by the cracking of the fifth crater the men weren't seeing so well, and some more lively form of entertainment seemed in order. Do you sing? they asked her. Dance? Recite the epic poems of your people? To each of these she gave a small toss of the head that we were given to understand meant "no."

"Well then, what can you do?"

Craterus asked this question with the downward direction of his glance making clear his true meaning. The company, including Alexander but not Hephaestion, gave a laugh; Philotas, ever the jolly comrade, picked up the theme.

"But surely you play *the flute?* Don't all women play the *flute?*"

More chortling, more drinks all around. As the merriment rolled on, Stateira's eyes began to moisten in the torchlight, until she hid her face behind her hands. Philotas slammed his cup to the table.

"Oh spare us this phony propiety, woman! Barbarian marriage isn't like ours . . . you're nothing but a fancy concubine."

"You may count yourself lucky not to be passed among the guards," warned Cleitus.

Darius's wife began to to sob through her hennaed fingers, and with the first teardrop Alexander's nobler instincts were aroused.

"Of course she plays the flute! That privilege, however, is for kings only. Now all of you, out!"

There was a moment of hesitation as everyone wondered if he was serious.

"*Out*, I said!"

The celebrants rose as best they could, topping off their wine cups on the way. Hephaestion was in the lead until Alexander called him back.

"Not you, my friend."

"There is something I must attend. I—"

"Come here! Remember, you too are Alexander!"

Hephaestion obeyed, his face glowing red with rage and humiliation, as the rest of the party cheered and slapped him on the shoulder. From that moment it was clear to me just how unpopular Hephaestion was among his own people. His relationship with Alexander was so resented that it was a wonder that in all his battles he never ended up with a Macedonian arrow in his back. The last I saw was Hephaestion from behind, standing at awkward attention just inside the tent, as Stateira stared at him with fear rising in her eyes. The tent flap fell shut.

I am reminded here that Aristotle once told Alexander to be a leader to the Greeks, but a master to the barbarians. Of this particular incident Stateira, of course, said nothing. But when she died nearly two years later, it was not due to the rigors of living on the road, as Aeschines has said. After all, the Persian court was always on the road! Instead, I have it on good authority that she died in childbirth. Of the fate of her baby I have nothing to report—not even Sisygambis knew, or if she did, she never divulged anything. So was Stateira's honor respected? You be the judge.

I was much entertained by Aeschines's account of the siege of Tyre. The problem, of course, was that the Persian fleet was still sailing unopposed in the Aegean, free to foment resistance and harass Macedonian garrisons. To deal with this fleet, Arridaeus suggested a novel strategy: Alexander would not assault it directly, as his navy was small and the enemy employed vessels manned by seasoned Phoenician and Cypriot seamen. Instead, he would wear down the Great King's navy by depriving it of safe harbor. This would require not only the closure of all the ports in Asia Minor, but also the subjugation of the Phoenician cities on the Levantine coast. Old Parmenion disagreed, urging a fight at sea that would, in any case, be less expensive and time-consuming than conquering every harbor. Alexander heard his advice, weighed it, and ordered his fleet disbanded. He would gamble all on Arridaeus's land strategy.

As fast as Alexander's army marched, news of his victories spread faster. Marathus, Byblos, and Sidon opened their gates to him, and emissaries from Tyre, the richest of the ports, made pledges of neutrality. Alexander accepted the Tyrians' goodwill gifts of provender, and a golden crown, asking only that he be allowed into their city to make a sacrifice to Heracles.

"That, alas, we cannot allow," said the head emissary, heaving a thespian sigh. "The Great King would no doubt see that as a violation of our neutrality."

"Perhaps he would see it that way—but I will not accept a refusal. There is no neutrality possible now." He left unsaid the obvious concern that any port not in his allegiance after he marched east could be used by the enemy's navy to support operations against his rearguard.

"May we suggest an alternative for your observance, O King? The Temple of Heracles Palaeotyros, for instance?"

"Is it within the town?"

"Your eminence, it is within our territory, but a short distance outside the city proper."

"I think," said the King, "that the only alternative to a sacrifice within your gates will be an unpleasant one for you."

At this the haughty Tyrians, whose city stood on an offshore island ringed with high walls, dropped all pretense of humility. They laughed in Alexander's face.

"Unless you Greeks have gills, Tyre can never be taken!"

At that, Alexander told them to prepare to defend themselves.

IX

The King called a war council to hear the advice of his generals. Tyre, he was told, stood on an island half a mile off a windswept coast. She was protected by massive fortifications one hundred fifty feet high on the landward side, only somewhat lower to seaward. As Alexander had sent away his only ships, taking the city from the water would be impossible. "Then it must be from the land," he concluded. Constructing a mole across the strait was likewise impractical, said his admiral Nearchus, as the channel was deep there. "How deep?" Alexander demanded. No one knew.

At this point Nearchus argued that the Persian fleet was still at large and might appear at any moment to support the Tyrians—which was true—and that the city might be safely bypassed anyway—which was not. But his objections only confirmed Alexander in his course: he would take the impregnable island city from the land.

The Macedonians seized the mainland coast across the Tyrian strait. Battalions of Foot Companions and mercenaries were ordered to take off their armor and don workshirts. Whole forests were cut down for pilings, and all movable boulders in the vicinity roped, dragged, and dropped into the channel to support the construction of the greatest artificial causeway ever conceived.

While these preparations were under way, the Macedonian camp was shaken by an ominous sign: as the army's bakers removed their bread from the ovens, they found drops of human blood in the loaves. Panic spread among the Greeks in a way it had not before the battles at the Granicus or Issus. The campaign was saved by Alexander's personal seer, the Telmessian Aristander. Instead of disaster, Aristander interpreted the bloody bread as a promising sign: since the blood flowed on the inside of the bread, it must mean that the force *within* the city was doomed, not the attackers. As this seemed reasonable to most of the Macedonians, work resumed in earnest.

Alexander searched his army for strong swimmers who might survey the underwater course of his mole. As this was dangerous work, he promised each survivor a talent for his trouble. So confident were the Tyrians that the seige would fail, however, that they declined to shoot at these scouts as they appeared under their walls. Instead they laughed, asking them whether their King thought himself Poseidon's master.

The causeway was supposed to be wide enough for an eight-man front of Foot Companions to march across, and high enough for the top of it to be above the winter swells. Working in day and night shifts, the Macedonians quickly finished the section over the shallows. As his men worked, the enemy sent out boats with crack archers in them. Thinking perhaps that Alexander was bluffing, at first they resorted only to insults, jeering at the workmen, telling them they were a race of mules, not warriors. When this failed to stop the work, the archers brandished their bows. Finally, they commenced shooting at the workers, forcing them off the mole. Alexander brought up Cretan bowmen equipped with flaming arrows, driving the boats away. To protect his men, he altered the design of the mole, equipping it with a pair of wheeled towers, topped with rock-throwers, that could be rolled forth as the work proceeded.

Unable to approach the causeway from the water, the Tyrians sent boats filled with cutthroats down the coast to attack the work crews inland. Alexander detailed his Illyrian auxiliaries to protect the workers. The enemy turned to diplomacy, paying the Arab tribes of Mount Lebanon to harry the Illyrians. In response, Alexander launched a land campaign, bringing the Arabs to heel in just ten days.

The work proceeded into greater depths. The magnitude of the task seemed to grow more and more absurd, like burying the ocean, as we watched tons of stones and trees disappear into the water. The head of the mole, meanwhile, was now in range of archers on the city walls, a proximity they used with telling effect. Alexander countered the Tyrian bowmen by erecting sheets of canvas around the head of the mole to conceal his men as they worked their way closer. Poseidon made his allegiance known by sending strong winds through the channel to rip away the canvas, leaving the workers exposed to enemy fire. Alexander replaced the canvas with heavy skins, weighted down at the bottom with shorn logs, which had the additional dividend of breaking the high waves. Poseidon grumbled and bided his time.

Alexander was often out on the mole, exposing himself to danger, always ready with words of encouragement for his men. At last his faith seemed to bear results, as the Macedonians looked down to see the mole's foundation inch toward the surface. Morale surged; it seemed as if the task was possible after all.

Understanding that this was a key moment, the Tyrians launched their counterstroke: a sulfur-caked merchant vessel, stripped of everything that would not burn, filled to the gunwales with fuel and choice accelerants. To insure that the fireship would ground herself on the mole, they shifted its ballast aft, so that its prow was pitched free of the water. The next windy day their best oarsmen towed it into the channel and, with spirited war cries, propelled it toward the enemy.

The ship struck home and exploded in an enormous conflagration. With particular ingenuity, the Tyrians suspended cauldrons of boiling pitch between the ship's masts, so that when these collapsed, additional fuel poured onto the blaze. Mounds of unused timber, cordage, canvas, and idle catapaults went up. The fire spread so quickly that the guards in Alexander's towers were forced to dive into the sea. Enemy triremes swarmed around the helpless Macedonians, beating them senseless with clubs before taking them all as hostages. The Tyrian archers, meanwhile, drove back anyone coming out to fight the fire. The entire mole burned to the waterline.

That was when Poseidon seized his chance. Sending forth a storm, he punished the very foundation of the mole until it gave way, collapsing in a heap on the seafloor. So completely was the structure destroyed that when Alexander came out to view the damage from this attack, all signs of his months of work, wet or dry, were erased. I was there during the episode Aeschines described, when the Tyrians gathered on their wall to jeer at Alexander as he stood on the denuded shore.

These developments provoked fresh carpings from Nearchus, who complained that the city would never be taken if the Tyrians were left in command of the sea. This was no doubt intented to dissuade Alexander, since the enemy had a strong fleet and the Macedonians had none. Alexander nevertheless ordered the mole rebuilt at twice the width and with double the number of towers. His men, weary and discouraged, stripped an even greater area around the country for materials. Alexander, meanwhile, rode north with his personal guard. He was away for seven days.

The gods alone must know what the Tyrians thought of Alexander's disappearance. We may suppose, though, that they believed he had given up and that the seige was finished; Poseidon himself must have assumed as much, since the winter storms ceased and the sea settled down for some time. It was on one of these calm days that their lookouts sighted a fleet approaching from the north. They cheered again, for they thought it surely must be the Persians coming to drive the beseigers away for good, or perhaps a relieving force from Tyre's daughter city of Carthage, riding to the rescue of their ancestral temples.

These illusions were shattered as the devices painted on the fleet's sails came into view. The fleet, two hundred ships strong, was a mixed force from

Sidon and Cyprus; at the prow of the very first ship stood Alexander.

Now it was the Macedonians' turn to cheer and their adversaries' to groan. With such an overwhelming force against them, the Tyrians recalled their dispersed fleet, and took the additional defensive action of blocking their north and south harbor mouths with merchantmen. Alexander's Sidonese allies showed their value immediately by launching fireships against the obstructing vessels; several were burned, but the enemy replaced them. Alexander ordered a blockade on the city.

With the enemy fleet out of action, work on the second mole proceeded faster than on the first. The Tyrians responded by erecting wooden towers atop their walls to increase the range of their heavy artillery. With these engines they threw boulders into the sea, hoping to impede the movement of Alexander's ships. This strategy pleased Alexander, since the enemy was providing good material for his work crews. He sent out triremes to haul up the rocks and dump them at the head of the mole.

Perceiving their mistake, the Tyrians produced up a squadron of ram-ships to attack the triremes. The ram-ships were great armored vessels, with even their oar-shafts clad in bronze. Though they were slow and would easily have capsized in rougher seas, they caught the Macedonians by surprise, sinking several of their vessels and, in the process, further littering the landward channel with obstructions.

The Tyrians, having regained control of the waters under their city walls, came up to threaten the mole again. Fighting resumed along the causeway, as

Alexander's men took refuge in their towers. Bolts from the Macedonian artillery clanked harmlessly off the metal skins of the ram-ships. Alexander, furious, ordered the immediate construction of his own armored fleet. This was completed within days, and launched with selected crews from among his Sidonese and Cypriot allies. Outnumbered, the enemy withdrew.

The allied triremes resumed pulling up the stones. To frustrate them, the enemy sent out waves of divers to cut their cables from underwater. The Tyrian swimmers, who seemed able to hold their breaths for superhuman lengths of time, also assaulted the mole from below, using metal hooks to work the cobbles loose from the tree branches the Macedonians had sunk there. These attacks did real damage to Alexander's plan. Having no divers of like skill, he ordered the anchor ropes of his triremes replaced with iron chains, and boats with archers to patrol the channel and kill the Tyrians before they could submerge. The latter tactic met little success, but in any case the divers could do nothing against the chains, and gave up.

With the noose tightening around the town, the Tyrians tried to break the blockade by sallying out against the enemy ships at the north end of the island. A force of the city's best fighters gathered behind a canvas screen erected at the harbor mouth. Coming out in midafternoon, when the Macedonians were rotating their crews, thirteen Tyrian ships rowed out in complete silence and again caught their enemy by surprise. All the blockading ships were taken and either burned or cast adrift in the swift current, to founder on the rocks downstream.

Learning of this attack, Alexander rushed to the fleet blocking the southern harbor and ordered it to pull for the other side. So quickly was this order obeyed that the Macedonians caught the Tyrians still at their destructive work. Upon seeing the reinforcements, and Alexander conspicuous at their head, the Tyrians made frantic signals for their scattered force to retire. The Macedonians fell on most of these before they could find shelter in the north harbor; only a handful of the enemy escaped, making the overall losses even for both sides. It was a draw Alexander could afford more than the Tyrians, however.

A strange inactivity then came over the defenders; their artillery fell silent, and the archers just sat on the walls, watching the Macedonians come ever closer. To the workers on the causeway, this stillness was most ominous.

In fact, the defenders were preparing a new weapon. The slings of their torsion catapults were replaced with bronze shields, the missiles abandoned for something far more noxious. Just as the mole came up under the walls, the Macedonian workers were seen to cry out, tear off their clothing, and cast themselves into the sea. Mystified, Alexander came out to investigate. He soon learned that the Tyrians were using artillery to project loads of red-hot sand against his men. The effect of this weapon was to send down a spreading, molten cloud that destroyed anything it touched. Siegeworks were scorched, lungs seared, and skin burned as the sand worked into the seams of the men's armor.

There was no countermeasure against this horror. Work on the mole was abandoned. Alexander, in de-

spair, punished the Tyrians by using his biggest rock
throwers against the landward walls. Two full days of
constant pounding worked only a few cracks in the
fortifications, which the Tyrians quickly filled in from
behind. The bombardment was called off.

There seemed nothing more we could do. The winter and spring had been consumed by the siege, and
summer had begun; no doubt somewhere Darius was
using the time to strengthen his position. Alexander's
spies in Greece reported that the Lacedaemonians
were trying to enlist the Athenians in an alliance
against Macedon; accounts reached him that the Persian fleet was forcing open the port of Miletus. It
seemed as if Nearchus's advice was correct after all—
Tyre must be bypassed.

Then a most unusual sign appeared. The waters in
the channel began to churn. Onlookers gathered on
both sides and watched in wonder as the great, dark
back of an enormous sea monster parted the waves.
Given their reverses, there was great nervousness in
the Macedonian ranks at this apparition, and the be-
ginnings of outright panic among some of the more
ignorant Thracian and Illyrian allies.

Alexander came to the shore to view the creature in
the manner of a master inspecting a fine horse. Dismissing all talk of omens, he refused to consult Aristander on the matter, instead recounting what he had
learned about such creatures from his tutor, Aristotle
of Stageira.

"I was told he examined one of the monsters that
had washed up alive on the shores of the Thermaic
Gulf," recalled the King. "They are blooded animals,
and toothless. As he undertook a vivisection, a baby

sea monster beached itself on the shore next to the other. The bigger monster then laid a fin over its calf. At this, Aristotle broke off his investigations, leaving the harmless things to die in peace."

This account seemed to quiet his men. The Tyrians, by contrast, were in an uproar. As the monster circled the channel, they sought the favor of Poseidon, whom they called Yamm, by cutting the throats of their prisoners and casting them into the sea. They implored the monster to smash the enemy warships. Instead, it swam under the walls and paused at a place just off the south end of the island, on the seaward side. With its nose just out of the water, it seemed to be pointing to a place on the fortifications. Then it pulled itself back into the water and disappeared.

Alexander leapt on his chariot and, to everyone's surprise, proclaimed "It is a sign! That is where we attack!"

Of the truth of this episode I have nothing to tell you. I was not there to see it, but was away in the interior, attempting to learn something more about Arridaeus. I suspect it was he, and not some sea monster, who deserves the credit for identifying the weakest section of the Tyrian walls. Yet behind this tale hides an element of the truth, for it is exactly as a monster that the Macedonians saw Arridaeus—as a presence that was unexpected, inexplicable, and that filled them with dread. Curious about this, I plied Callisthenes with questions, but his indifference to this mystery was as fervent as my curiosity. There was nothing to learn from him.

To penetrate the conspiracy around the King's half-brother was dangerous. Yet there could be no pretending that I was a historian if I preferred childish fables to the complexities of real human affairs. I therefore decided to risk learning more, even if accusers like Aeschines would eventually crawl forth to impugn me, and to tell me that I had failed in my oath to the Assembly. To my knowledge, my oath never bound me to transmit lies to my fellow citizens, both live or yet to be born. I make no apologies for this decision.

With a few silver coins placed in the right hands it was not hard to find where Arridaeus was kept. He was installed some distance inland from the Levantine coast, and safely remote from the main encampment of the army, in a back room of the Temple of Herakles Palaeotyros. The place was well-guarded by Alexander's most trusted troops, which happened to be the first division of the King's Hypaspists. As my title in the Macedonian army was that of an officer in the second division, it was a straightforward matter to pull rank and get inside before the guards could scurry back to the main camp for instructions. Their resistance mounted the deeper I got into the temple, however, so that I became nervous that I would not reach my goal before someone of superior rank arrived to stop me.

It was only with a threat of flogging that I convinced the last sentry to step aside. My heart pounding, I pushed the door open, and then peeled aside a black curtain stretched behind it. Though it was midday outside, the room was obscured by a thick, sulfurous darkness. Peering within, I saw a corner of the room was heated with braziers, and lit by a single oil lamp. A stench like a latrine hit me full in the face.

The King's brother was sitting on the floor. He was

surrounded by miniature tin figures of soldiers, cavalry, and siege engines, which he had arranged in opposing phalanxes. His armor—the only kind of clothing he would allow to touch his skin—was stacked against the wall behind him. He was naked as he sat there, rocking with a slow rhythm as he hummed to himself, absently handling the head of his penis.

Just then something moved behind him, and I realized he wasn't alone: an old woman was there, sitting on a cushion with a bucket and mop. She was staring in my direction as the feeble light from the rest of the temple penetrated the sanctuary. When she spoke to me, the enclosed space made her voice seem as if she was speaking from beside me.

"He's not hungry. Leave it."

Arridaeus never looked up, never showed me his face, but continued to hum and rock, and would evidently continue until he soiled himself in whatever way and the old woman would clean him. And though I have no evidence that this was the totality of his life, apart from his brief appearances on the battlefield, it was not hard to believe it was so. If there were any other exits from his tomb, they were not obvious; if there were any other concessions to human companionship granted to him, I didn't see them.

There was a commotion behind me, and the sound of booted feet on marble. Not wishing to be arrested with my head inside the forbidden chamber, I withdrew.

Craterus met me at the foot of Heracles's statue. He had a bemused look on his face, as if he had bested me in some game. He had two guards with him, but instead of arresting me they straightened, saluted, and let me pass. As I walked away Craterus must have observed my attitude, obliging him to make a single justification to my back.

"Arridaeus is not unhappy, Machon. In fact, he thinks he is a god!"

There were no serious consequences to what I had done. Arridaeus was not moved for the rest of the time of the siege, and aside from a single long look at me from his couch that evening, Alexander never showed any awareness of the incident. Of this I can only speculate that the King, for reasons known only to him, decided to hold me immune from any penalties for this adventure.

There was a single consequence only: for the rest of my time on the campaign—almost eleven years—either Craterus or one of his junior officers kept a constant watch on me. I never learned whether Alexander had assigned him as my "minder," or whether Craterus had taken that responsibility upon himself. Considering that I could have been killed, imprisoned, or sent home for what I'd done, I thought it best not to ask.

On the coast, Alexander took a ship to the south end of the island to survey the weak point the "monster" had indicated. He noted that the topography of the shore made that portion of the Tyrian walls the lowest of all. When he returned, he put his carpenters to work constructing retractable gangways for his ships.

The next day dawned fair and calm. The catapults on the mole were reloaded. On the water, Alexander pressed every available man into service on every vessel in his fleet; his ships came out and anchored just out of range from the Tyrian rock-throwers. Fireships were loaded with fuel and positioned off the mouths of both harbors. In response, the enemy warmed up their sand weapon. There was a sense on both sides of the conflict that the issue would be fully and finally decided that day.

Alexander appeared on his flagship in Achilles's battle armor. Moving so that all could see, he took his position at the head of the gangway and took his lance. The cheers of his men drowned out the sound of the sea. Just as the uproar was at its loudest, he gave a nod, and the signal went up to attack.

The Macedonians made a furious assault on the city from every direction. Ships stood off the weaker, seaward side, using artillery to crack open the masonry there, forcing the Tyrians to expend manpower on repairs. Where there was room between the waterline and the wall, his men landed and began sapping operations against the foundations. The defenders dumped everything they could—rocks, sand, boiling water, anvils—down on the engineers. The Phoenician allies launched their fireships, setting the obstructions in the harbors ablaze, putting the Tyrians in a panic as they tried to save their fleet.

Just as the enemy was most overextended, the rock-throwers assailed the spot in the wall where the sea monster had pointed. It collapsed in short order. The first Macedonian vessel to drop its gangway was commanded by a man named Admetus, who led a column of Shield Bearers through the breach. They didn't get far, as the Tyrians massed their defense there, cutting all the invaders down. But Alexander was close behind, and when the enemy saw him coming, singing the paean as he leapt over the rubble, their nerve broke.

Soon the Macedonians broke through at several points. I went in from the city's north end, and saw more than I care to relate. The city was overwhelmed so rapidly that the Tyrians did not have time to organize a final defense; after its highly coordinated beginning, the day gave way to an afternoon of chaos as the Macedonians, stymied for months, having lost more men at Tyre than at the Granicus and Issus combined, worked their frustration against the people. The bodies piled up as the Tyrians continued their resistance from their doorways and rooftops and the Macedonians, equally determined, hacked their way into homes, shops, and temples. By sundown, I saw that the pipes bearing sewage from the streets to the sea were gushing red. The waters ran so thick that the seabirds, smeared with human blood, could not fly.

Having given his men their moment of revenge, Alexander commanded that all survivors be spared. The entire royal family was captured alive in the Temple of Heracles, along with a party of Carthaginian emissaries. The Tyrian king, Azemilcus, was released with his retinue, while the Carthaginians were packed off for home, with a message from Alexander that he now considered that city his enemy. The entire remaining population of Tyre, rich and poor, some thirty thousand souls, were given in chains to their rivals. It was said that the markets of Sidon were so glutted with product that a slave could be purchased for the equivalent of a few dozen drachmas. Even minor farmers could afford to buy themselves a former aristocrat or fashionable lady for whatever purpose they desired. Thus are the wages of resistance to the "Captain of the Greeks."

Machon allowed this grim imagery to sink into the minds of the jurors. Swallow glanced at the Macedonians in the spectators' box: there was such a transparency of pride on their hairless faces that he wanted to spit on them.

Before he left the empty streets, Alexander made a victory trophy of a Tyrian ship, mounting it in the sanctuary with the inscription he had written himself. It read, DEDICATED TO THE GOD BY ALEXANDER, SON OF PHILIP, FROM INSIDE THE CITY. He then did as he first requested seven long months before—he made sacrifice to Heracles at his temple within the walls.

If nothing else, Alexander hoped the siege and its aftermath would lessen future loss of life, as fewer cities would refuse to open their gates to him. Unaccountably, it seemed to have the opposite effect in the next big town he encountered on the way to Egypt. The satrap of the city of Gaza, an Arab named Batis, had watched the reduction of Tyre and took the opposite lesson: that Alexander could be defeated if he was denied the use of his artillery.

Gaza stood on a great hill, ringed by well-built walls, that was surrounded by loose sand too unstable to erect towers or heavy equipment upon. Siege trains bogged down to their axles. The city was situated in such a lofty spot that catapults could not hit the walls at an effective angle from anywhere around it. The defenders were well-supplied, and a besieging force would need to subsist in dry, difficult country. Batis made it more difficult still by burning all the fields in the surrounding area before Alexander arrived. As Gaza was not a port town, and therefore could not supply the Persian fleet, Batis may also have believed his enemy would content himself with a mere show of force.

Suffice it to say he was mistaken. As his campaign advanced, Alexander was even less willing to brook resistance. Nor was he inclined, he informed us, to expend another half a year reducing another recalcitrant city. His staff must find a way into the place in a matter of weeks, not months.

After much discussion, it was agreed that tunneling was the one tactic the soft soil around the city did afford. Accordingly, excavation began from a place out of sight of the Gazans, so Batis would not know what was coming. To further distract the enemy from taking an effective defense, Alexander had a ring of siege towers built from large trees dragged all the way from Lebanon. The trunks of these had to be sunk many yards into the ground to give support to his engines. The Gazans took the bait: they commenced raising the tops of their walls to match the works of the enemy. Alexander ordered his men to build higher—Batis also built higher, racing the Macedonians skyward until the extremities of both structures were so tall they could be seen from miles out at sea. It was all a splendid ruse, however, as the real attack was completely out of sight, under everyone's feet.

So it happened that one day Alexander was out among his engineers, helmetless in the great heat, when fate intervened again. A crow, flying out of the west, passed over him and dropped a heavy object on his head. The King was briefly stunned, and the bird, strangely, did not escape but landed on a siege tower. The object that hit Alexander was an abalone, which was closed when it fell from the bird's grasp but opened up after it hit the ground. Aristander the soothsayer was summoned to explain this event; making a quick examination of the evidence, he was concerned, saying that the fact that the abalone had opened meant the town would fall, but that Alexander could be killed in the assault if he was careless.

This omen caused some consternation in the Macedonian camp, as the life of Alexander was far more valuable than the submission of Gaza. Alexander would not be deterred, of course, promising only that he would stay away from the front lines.

Fate is not so easily changed. As Alexander was sitting far to the rear, watching unhappily from a distance, a Gazan soldier was presented to him as a deserter. This man was allowed to keep his shield for his interview with the King. Casting himself at Alexander's feet, he begged permission to join the Macedonian army; the King bid him to stand and be accepted into his service. At that instant the deserter, who was really an agent of Darius, pulled a hidden dagger from his shield and fell on Alexander. The attacker was cut down before he could harm the King, wounding him only lightly in the neck. Without a thought for the danger he had just barely escaped, Alexander directly called for Aristander: as the assassin's cut must qualify as the wound he had prophesied, could he now return to the front ranks? But Aristander shook his head, for the injury was too minor. Disappointed that the cut was not serious enough, Alexander sank, dejected, back on his throne.

Having seen their tormentor go down earlier that day, the Gazans saw an opportunity. Sallying forth that night, they took the Macedonian sentries by surprise and nearly reached the siegeworks with their torches. None were surprised when the King forgot his pledge and threw himself into the fight. Suffering great losses, the Gazans retreated, but not before Alexander was wounded in the shoulder by an arrow. Instead of worrying him, this injury filled him with delight: Aristander's prediction had at last come true, so the town must fall.

With redoubled energy, pushing his men to their limits, Alexander caused the siegeworks to rise and the mines sink deep into the earth. At last, near the end of the month of Maimakterion, all was ready: at their leader's signal, the miners removed the supports they had installed in the tunnels, and a wide section of the wall collapsed in a heap. The Macedonians stormed into the breach just as the last stone came down. The rest of the day saw bitter fighting, as the Gazans knew the fate of Tyre, and expected no better. Every one of the ten thousand men in the town was killed in the fight; the women and children went to the Sidon markets, where they sold even more cheaply than the Tyrians.

A single exception was made for Batis himself. Orders went around that the satrap was to be taken alive, and this was accomplished, though he did his best to achieve a soldier's death. When he was led before Alexander, he looked his conqueror straight in the eye, refusing to bend knee before him. Alexander threw up his hands, saying "What shall I do with this man? With just a word he could save himself, but he stands there mocking me on the field I have duly taken from him."

Instead of begging for his life, the Arab merely

smiled and made a cutting gesture across his own throat. Impatient, exhausted in body and spirit, Alexander exploded at this insolence. "You count on death, but by the gods your pride has earned you worse!"

With that, he summoned a chariot. Batis's ankles were pierced between the bone and the tendon (which broke his silence), and looped through with a rawhide strap. The ends of the strap were then attached to the back of the car. As the man writhed on the ground, Alexander stood over Batis, quoting Homer to him.

Hector's body lashed to the car, dragging the head
Mounted Achilles lofted his shining arms
Lashed the strong horses to flight, so they sped
Through the dust of Ilium he raised
By Hector's black hair spread upon the ground—

Unlike Achilles, Alexander did not mount the car, but just slapped the lead horse to start him on his way. All watched, curious, as the chariot raced off toward the sea, Batis's head carving a bloody furrow in the shell-strewn dust. Some time later riders went out to retrieve the chariot. The man's remains were not buried, but left for the crabs to devour.

The end of Batis may seem cruel to us. Alexander too was often given to merciful treatment of worthy enemies, as I will later relate. The one thing he could not abide, however, was the presumption of arrogance by beaten men. If nothing else, he would teach humility to all the Persians. Some critics, Demosthenes among them, have made much of Alexander's supposed descent into oriental despotism, pointing to

Batis's death as a notable example. But there is nothing about this execution that smacks of the barbarians. Indeed, I say the opposite: it was Homeric, which we may agree is as Greek as it gets!

It is one of the imponderables of this campaign that it was the fall of Gaza, not Tyre, that made Alexander's name throughout the world. That such a well-protected city was reduced so fast, in less than two months, at last established that mere walls were no defense against him. There were other sieges, to be sure, but in the years to come all the large cities just opened their gates to him. His name alone made walls moot.

Egypt agreed with the young King. Having millennia of experience in investing weak characters with the trappings of godhood, the Egyptians had become most accomplished in their sycophancy. Not that Alexander was the least worthy of their flattery—on the contrary, he was every inch the gallant conqueror, as young and winning as the old Persian satrap had been cowardly and rapacious. For the reasons I described earlier, when he left the oracle at Siwah he was as convinced of his divinity as I had ever seen him. Cash and favors poured from him like wet from the Nile. Emissaries from all over the world came to pay him homage, or to beg his indulgence in settling their petty disputes. In short, from the time he rejoined his army for the march to Damascus until he took possession of Babylon, he was much the hero that Aeschines described. This was a period of less than a year.

At the ancient capital of Memphis he held court, feasting the local nobles and regaling them with the finest poets and musicians from Athens. He sponsored a program of athletic contests on the plain of Giza. At the end of the day, he climbed up the highest pyramid, that of Cheops, and surveyed the sweep of his new province. To a mind determined to confront all obstacles, the linearity of Egypt, thrusting so grandly into the heart of Africa, was a tonic.

Sailing up to Egyptian Thebes, he was welcomed at Karnak like its long-lost master. Dressed in flawless white linen, he strode down the aisle of the great Hypostyle Hall between throngs of plaited, intoning priests. He entered the sanctum alone, to gaze at the very image of the god Ammon recumbent in His golden pavilion. The next day he took the double crown of Upper and Lower Egypt on his head, and was called Horus, Horus-of-gold, He-of-the-sedge-and-the-bee and the Son of Ra. By the end of the ceremony the Egyptians unveiled a likeness of their new pharaoh: a colossus in black basalt, enthroned with the crook and the flail. This impressed Alexander, as the carving of this statue must have begun well before he entered the country. It is in the nature of the Egyptians to think of everything.

Here I must turn aside from my story to dispute how Aeschines has portrayed my conduct in Egypt. He makes special reference to a report I sent to the archon Nicetes, and proceeds completely to misunderstand the substance of it. By the orders of the Assembly I was duty-bound to report what I saw in Alexander's company, whether it flattered him or not. Therefore, if I observe that the King's troops laughed at him behind his back when he put on Egyptian garb, it is because that is what I saw! Would Aeschines prefer that I mislead the Assembly? Likewise, I did write that Alexander's enthusiasm for barbarian finery was a weakness in his character, and that this weakness might someday lead him into trouble. Given subsequent events, was this anything less than the unvarnished truth?

Recall at this time that King Agis of Sparta approached this city with an offer of alliance against Macedon. The Athenians refused, which was fortunate for us, as Agis's revolt was defeated by Antipater on the plains of Megalopolis. To those who longed for an end to Macedonian hegemony, my reports of Alexander's defects gave the virtue of patience: if the young King would ultimately destroy himself, why risk the very existence of our state on Agis's hopeless cause? In this way, what I learned was of direct benefit to you all. Note that this doesn't mean I sought to destroy Alexander myself! If that was my object, I could have stuck a dagger in his heart on any of a thousand occasions. So I ask you again, how have I served my city wrongly?

Returning to the Delta, the new pharaoh turned west, toward the great oasis of Siwah. He announced that it was his intention to consult the god Ammon at his sanctuary, as his ancestors Heracles and Perseus had before him. Taking a small force of two hundred Hypaspists—Hephaestion, Aristander, and myself included—he started along the coast, skirting Lake Mareotis. On the way, he paused at a site he perceived to be an ideal spot for a new city, situated on sloping ground between the lake and the sea. Perhaps inspired by his experience at Tyre, he foresaw how a mole running out to the Pharos island would afford deep, calm anchorage. Anyone with a particle of ambition would already have exploited the site, declared Alexander, except that the pharaohs of old had never thought any other land worth conquering, and so never built a true seaport from which to rule.

He was so impatient to see his perfect foundation realized that he immediately began surveying the site. Marching ahead of his secretaries, he dictated the future locations of the temples, the marketplace, and the palace. To compensate for the lack of high landmarks in the area, he left instructions that a lighthouse exactly one stade tall be constructed on the island to guide ships into the port. To be sure, nothing of the kind had ever been built before, but none doubted that Alexander would see it done.

His clerks fretted that they had no surveying equipment with them, so they could not record the King's wisdom. Alexander commanded his men to use the flour in their packs to mark the boundaries. The Egyptians warned against this, as the flour would be necessary for the difficult journey across the desert to Siwah. Alexander ignored them, using every bit of grain to lay out the capital's walls and streets. When he was done, he looked with satisfaction at his design, until a great flock of seagulls arrived and began to eat his city. He deployed his troops to drive away the birds, but it was too late: the lines of flour were trampled by thousands of little feet. 'What can this mean?' Alexander turned to Aristander. The soothsayer had a ready answer.

"Fear not, O King! The splendor of your capital will attract men from abroad like gulls from the sea, and make it the Queen of Cities."

"The gods were so anxious to see the place built," added Hephaestion, "that they want you to mark the boundaries with something more permanent, like stones."

Both answers pleased Alexander.

The trip to Siwah took us into a waste so trackless that our guides had difficulty finding their bearings. Such desolation is unknown anywhere in Greece; rain was so rare there, in fact, that the natives of Siwah long ago stopped building roofs on their houses. Short of water, and with no flour for food, it seemed that the Macedonians were in trouble—until the gods intervened again. Zeus sent a great rainstorm. Then Hermes manifested out of the ground in the form of an asp, and led us directly to the oasis. The Egyptians were amazed at these events, as if they were used to only nominal divinity, not true miracles, from their god-kings.

Alexander's party was met in the outer courtyard of the temple by the high priest. The man's Greek was so poor that instead of referring to Alexander in the vocative case, as "O my son," he used the nominative, as in "*the* son," or "the son of Zeus." It was a trifling difference in the sounds of the words, a common mistake for barbarians, but it intrigued Alexander. The priest, in his turn, observed the expression on the King's face.

Alexander went alone into the Holy of Holies. He was there for some time, as if in long conversation with the god. While nothing is known of what Alexander asked of the Oracle, or the nature of the replies, what he learned there must have confirmed his new, and growing, sense of his unique destiny.

Returning to Memphis, Alexander installed his governors. In his wisdom, he understood that Egypt is too rich a land to trust to one man alone. He therefore divided its administration among two governors and three garrison commanders. Each was sworn not only to serve their King, but to respect the local governments and religious customs of the natives. He then led his army back to Phoenicia.

X

The army reached the river Euphrates via Damascus some weeks later, making an uncontested crossing near Thapsacus. While the King was in that vicinity he paid a visit upstream to Bambyce, where there is a temple to Atargatis. Beyond paying homage to the goddess, however, he had in mind to see a certain wonder he had learned about from Aristotle: namely, the collection of marvelous fish that lived in the lake of the sanctuary.

The lake is in the temple courtyard. At the center of it is an altar in the shape of a phallus, to which the acolytes swim out to decorate with flowers during the spring festival. In the water there are fish (some say carp, some say catfish) that are each as big as a man, and utterly tame. To visitors they swim up and roll themselves over to be scratched; some say the fish even have humanlike faces. The priests encourage this legend by adorning them with jewels and gold on their fins, and conversing with them as if they can speak. Very few had ever witnessed this miracle before Alexander came, however.

They say that when the King arrived the fish became agitated, churning at his feet as if caught in a net. Suddenly the biggest one leapt clear of the water. Lying on its belly at Alexander's feet, it raised itself on its bejeweled fins and said, in a clear voice so that all could hear: "With thanks, I consecrate myself to the table of the Great King." And with that it kissed Alexander's toe, and dropped dead.

I cannot vouch for the truth of this story, as I was not there. In any case, the event made a deep impression on the priests, who fell to their knees in wonder. Alexander, for his part, expected no less a gift for the son of Zeus-Ammon. "We must honor this old fellow's sacrifice," he said, speaking of the fish. "Cook! Peristalsis! Fetch a cauldron!"

What the King proposed to do was unprecedented. The Syrians never consume the fish in the goddess's lake, believing this to be a dire sin. Still, a desire to be eaten could not have been more clearly expressed by the fish. And so Alexander and his friends dined on a sacred carp of Atargatis that evening. In the long history of the temple, they were the only visitors to have been granted this exception.

It was at this time that Darius sent an envoy to Alexander. He was a Greek named Aegoscephalus. He had lived in Susa for most of his life, and declared (though for no clear reason) that he was equally proficient in Greek, Persian, Elamite, Akkadian and Aramaic. For his appearance before Alexander he wore the garb of a Persian dignitary, with layered, ankle-length robes and a flat-topped, fluted headdress. Receiving him, Alexander gave every indication of being more interested in this striking getup than in any message the man had to relate.

The envoy began by suggesting there was no reason why Darius and Alexander need be enemies. Had not peace obtained between their peoples for generations, until his father Philip sent an army into Asia? Why had Alexander never sent emissaries to his court to communicate his grievances, whatever those might be? Against Alexander's sudden aggression, Darius had risen to defend his people, as any king might. Even so, to reestablish peace required only goodwill on both sides. To this end, Alexander would find a willing partner in the Great King.

The ensuing offer was undeniably impressive. All the lands between the Euphrates river and the Aegean coast would henceforth be ruled by Alexander. Darius would pay the Macedonians any reasonable annual tribute they wished to name, in addition to a ransom of ten thousand gold talents for the release of his son, wife, and mother. To seal the alliance, Darius would hand over his eldest daughter to Alexander in marriage.

Everyone in the room found these terms most favorable—it was the widest conquest of territory and treasure ever accomplished with so few losses and in so short a time. Everyone was satisfied, that is, except Alexander, who yawned in the envoy's face.

The Greek was sent away so that the King could consider the offer. In reality, the offer was never considered, for Alexander's mind was already made up. Parmenion shook his head at the King.

"If I were you, I'd take what he's selling."

"And if I were Parmenion, I would take it too. Bring the man back."

Aegoscephalus was led in, perhaps sooner than he

expected. In making his reply to Darius, Alexander spoke to him in imperious, condescending tones, pointing his finger at the envoy. His reply went something like this:

"First, you shall address me as the Lord of All Asia, as is only fit. Your employer is not my equal, but mere leaseholder on the lands that remain to him. . . . They are not his to trade away, but mine if I wish to take them. The same applies to his money, and to his women, both of which I shall claim as my own in due course. If he wishes to reunite himself with his family, let him come to me and beg for this privilege! He need not be afraid, for Alexander is as fair to his supplicants as he is merciless to his enemies. . . . You say that there is no reason for war between us, but the Persian's memory serves only his vanity. His ancestors disfigured Greece with their invasions, having looted and burned her holiest sanctuaries. The kings of Persia have meddled in the affairs of Macedon since before the time of Philip. Your King has even boasted that he set the plan in motion that killed my predecessor. In truth, your employer is a pretender, for it is known here that he murdered by poison the legitimate heir to the Persian throne. No reason for war between us? How many more reasons do we need?"

At this point, Parmenion was so disgusted at this hubris that he left the room. For even as Alexander sat there insulting his opponent's manhood, he bore a scar from when, in single combat, Darius had sunk a javelin into his leg. Equally chilling to Macedonian ears was the way he evaded acknowledging Philip as his true father by calling him his "predecessor." But Alexander was not finished.

"If your employer takes himself for a man, he will take exception to what I say. If so, let him not flee from me, but stand and fight. Rest assured that I will give him every advantage. And if the day is his, he can expect that his enemy will not run, but welcome whatever fate the victor should decree. But until that day, let him know that the Lord of All Asia considers him little more than a criminal, and will pursue him to the ends of the earth until the day he appears where his servant does now, on bended knee, and begs my pardon. Now off with you!"

Soon enough, we learned the Great King's answer to these insults.

That night Alexander received reports from scouts sent to find Darius. They found neither the enemy nor significant resistance, but did learn that an urgent call had gone out to every corner of the empire for all native levies to gather near Babylon. Rumors held that Darius blamed his defeat at Issus not on Alexander's leadership, but on the tight topography, which restricted the movement of the superior Persian cavalry. Alexander smiled at this conceit, but must have burned inwardly; as you will hear, his desire to leave Darius no excuse for his defeat had more effect on his tactics at Gaugamela than any military consideration.

The Macedonians crossed the Tigris without the loss of a single man. After the army made camp on the easterly shore, two significant events occurred. First, there was a total eclipse of the moon, which appeared high in the sky at the change of the midnight watch. The Macedonians were not so much frightened by the apparition as uneasy about its meaning on the eve of such an important battle. Aristander interpreted the eclipse as evidence that a great contest was under way in Heaven, with the moon allied for Darius and Earth for Alexander. The spectacle portended the final victory of the Macedonians.

The second event was the eclipse of Stateira, Darius's wife. Despite Parmenion's advice that the Great King's family should have been left in Sidon or Damascus, Alexander had kept Sisygambis, Stateira, and the rest close to him. For him, it was nothing less than a guarantee of his honor as inheritor of the Achaemenid royal house. Despite his protection, however, the Queen was somehow gotten with child, and was far along in her pregnancy when the end came. Of the circumstances of her violation I know nothing but the fact of it—I saw her expectant form myself one evening, in silhouette against the fabric of her tent. When she fell ill she sank quickly, despite the best efforts of the King's personal doctor, Philip. Alexander grieved at her death, decreeing that her funeral be conducted in true Persian fashion.

I witnessed these curious rites. The body was placed under a white shroud and left exposed for three days beside lamps filled with aromatic oil. Instead of cremating her body in civilized fashion, the barbarians prepared a deep grave to house her bones. Believing that deities somehow care for the moral conduct of human beings, the priests of Zoroaster kept up a long series of chants in their native tongue, enjoining their gods to give the dead entrance to their heavenly paradise.

As dogs are sacred to the Persians, packs of yowling mutts kept up a constant din. They came off the leash for a particularly odd custom: the priest broke a loaf of bread into three parts, and placed the pieces on the body at the breast, stomach, and hipbone. Then a dog was invited to climb up on the bier and devour the bread. If this makes any sense at all, it is perhaps rooted in our myth of Kerberos, or in the purificatory use of dead dogs by fools and old women, though these rites are much distorted in the minds of the barbarians.

Alexander, remarkably, took part in these honors, donning the white funeral garb and mouthing some of the prayers in the Persian tongue. Instead of distributing portions of the sacrificed animals, he forbade the consumption of any meat in the Macedonian camp. These embarrassing extremities led some to speculate that Alexander bore some tender feeling for the dead Queen. None would have denied his right to avail himself of her. Yet in the letter he sent to Darius informing the latter of his wife's death, the King denied any such relationship. To my knowledge, none have attested to any contact between him and the Queen since their first meeting. Those of goodwill assume that Alexander's observance of the Persian rite was meant to discourage resistance to his rule. Those of illwill may believe what they wish.

On a plain east of the Tigris, not far from the little town of Gaugamela, Darius gathered the force that would decide his future. We've all heard of the host Xerxes brought to humble Greece in the time of Pericles—his army numbered five million men, claims Herodotus. But the number we use to ennoble ourselves in the eyes of our children need not deceive us now. Xerxes brought no more than four hundred thousand soldiers with him into Greece, and fewer than that were at last defeated by the allied cities at Plataea. Aeschines' claim that Darius brought a million or a half-million men to his last battle is likewise a fiction.

From every corner of the Persian Empire, arranged all around the Great King, the enemy numbered no more than two hundred thousand. I assure you that from where we stood, this seemed plenty. Looking out across the ground Darius had smoothed for the contest, we were confronted with a many-colored host that loomed like a mountain range and stretched to the horizon. There were Median spearmen in their belted tunics and trousers, waiting with daggers at their thighs and spears resting on their front feet. There were Scythian axemen in their pointed headgear, and Bactrian, Parthian and Massagetan cavalries that outnumbered the Macedonian levies five to one. There were Persian, Carian and Mardian bowmen, and Lycians in their crested felt caps, and foot soldiers and chariots of the Assyrian, Babylonian, and Susian satrapies, and contingents of Syrians, Albanians, Cappadocians, Machelonians, Armenians, Daae, Hyrcanians, Uxians and Sarangae with their knee-high boots, and Mycians, Utians, Paricanians, Chorasmians and Cissians in turbans, and Arachosians, Cadusians, Arians, Gandarians, Sacesinians, Gedrosians, Sogdians, Colchians, Sitacenians, and leopard-skin-covered Ethiopians and Arabs. There were two hundred scythed chariots, and fifteen war elephants with their breechclothed mahouts. And, of course, there were seasoned Greek mercenaries, all eager to avenge the deaths of their comrades at Issus and the Granicus, and in some cases at Chaeronea too.

Some of the enemy, such as the so-called "Apple

Bearer" battalion of Immortals who defended Darius, were clad in fine plate armor; others arrived at the field with wicker shields, or naked, or bearing only clubs. There was no chance for fancy strategy against such a motley force the Macedonians had no idea how these barbarians would fight. Instead, Alexander made good on his promise to Aegoscephalus and simply offered battle, with a double phalanx of Foot Companions in the center, Parmenion and the Thessalian cavalry on the left, and his Hypaspists and Cavalry Companions beside him on the right. He deployed the rest of his cavalry with their lines swept back, to resist envelopment.

To say that the Macedonians confronted the day's task with utter confidence would be a lie. With such overwhelming advantage in numbers, Darius did not need to prevail in the first clash, or even the second, third, or fourth. He needed only to hold his army together long enough to whittle the Macedonians down, then crush them with wave upon wave of fresh reserves. This was not a plan that required subtle generalship. Standing the ranks with the other Hypaspists, I could sense an unease that had not been there at Issus; many of those men expected to be dead by the afternoon. When I saw Alexander early that morning, there was no trace of the arrogance that marked his treatment of Darius's envoy. Instead, he was almost deliriously chipper, as if he would finally get his wish that day, and permanently avoid the assassin's knife. I also noticed that he did not risk besmirching Achilles's armor by wearing it at his likely defeat.

Now you will recall that when Aeschines told you of Gaugamela, I could not hold my peace at his lies. Of course, Aeschines was not there, so he may not know to what degree the story of this battle has been distorted. My rudeness was wrong, and I apologize for it. But be assured of these facts: the fighting at this battle was real, and it was terrible, and there are Macedonians walking around to this day who lose sleep over the horror of it.

Taking the initiative, Arridaeus directed the Macedonian line forward. This, he knew, was exactly what Darius hoped, that he would charge straight ahead and allow himself to be flanked on both sides. But this was only a bit of misdirection. At the opportune moment, he had the archers on his right wing spin on their heels and push south, making a dash for an area beyond where the Persians had leveled the ground for their chariots. His plan was to make the enemy extend his lines in an undisciplined manner, so that gaps would appear for Alexander to punch through.

It didn't work. Instead, the Bactrian cavalry on Darius's left covered the enemy in good order. On the contrary, the rightward extension of the Macedonian line caused a wide gap to form between the archers and the Hypaspists. Darius's Massagetan cavalry was through the hole in an instant, rampaging in the Macedonian rear. It was fortunate for the latter that they did not get through in enough numbers to end the battle right there. Instead, the back ranks of the Foot Companions did an about-face and presented their pikes, forcing the Massagetans to find easier prey among the baggage animals and camp followers.

Darius sent out his scythed chariots to soften up the enemy front. Contrary to what Aeschines has said, these terrible things were not defeated by just stepping aside as they passed. The phalangites tried to do this, but the Persians had changed their tactics: instead of coming on in scattered fashion, the chariots formed a flying wedge too wide to avoid. The chariots were met by a storm of missiles, but most of them got through. That was when the Macedonians suffered a further surprise: the Persians had modified the axles so the drivers could trigger a spring that extended the iron blades sideward. Hundreds of men were cut down at midbody. Though I was some distance from all this, for the rest of my days I will remember the screams of the Macedonians. Later, just after the battle, I saw the place where the scythed chariots had rolled through: for a distance of hundreds of yards, there was nothing but lopped extremities and their dying remainders. So suddenly were these men killed that some of their severed legs were left upright in the mud, still standing in the straight rows of the phalanx.

What stopped the chariots at last was the simple accumulation of dead bodies. The torrents of blood pouring on the ground destroyed the footing of the horses, while piles of armored corpses slowed the vehicles down. In time the Macedonian javelins and arrows did their work, and the last chariot was brought down. But never let it be said that this was easy work!

As all this went on, small groups of Persians and even individuals were showing their courage by running out onto the field, challenging the Macedonians. More often than not, if a phalangite or Hypaspist was foolish enough to meet them, the Persians won these duels. Yet each of these private victories was really a defeat, for when these impetuous Persians rushed out they opened gaps in their lines. Here, as at Marathon,

Plataea, Issus, and a hundred other battles, the Persians failed to understand the most important principle of modern war: to stay together, to keep the line, even at the cost of appearing cowardly.

Arridaeus was never fazed by minor reverses. Since I had trespassed on his hiding place, it seemed that further precautions were taken against discovery of his secret. Unlike the rest of the Macedonians, who wore Phrygian or Boeotian helmets that left the face exposed, Arridaeus's head was encased in an old-style Corinthian helmet, with a visor. The horsehair mane of his helmet had also been stripped off, to make him less conspicuous. Finally, the system of signals he used to command the troops was altered: instead of sending riders to communicate with the trumpeters, which risked attracting attention, the trumpeters were stationed right next to Arridaeus.

The time came when the idiot's unerring eye detected a significant weakness in the Persian line. The order was made, the trumpets sounded, and Alexander rode out at the apex of a cavalry wedge. He was, this time, dressed not in Achilles's panoply but the standard gold-fringed cape of Macedonian royalty, with a mailed corslet underneath that he had stripped from the corpse of a Persian noble at Issus. But even naked we all would have recognized that distinctive half-crouch in which he rode, his shoulders squared to the enemy, spear cocked far forward.

Arridaeus was right again: the light infantry in the King's path was too thin to stop him. Some among the enemy were ridden down; the others fled, opening up a gap in the enemy front. The gap was shallow, with thousands upon thousands of reserves drawn up beyond it. Yet, unaccountably, the Persian allies did not come up to plug the hole. Instead, they stayed rooted in their spots. They wouldn't fight.

More than anything Darius failed to do, it was this hesitation that lost the battle for the Persians. Fearless and terrible, Alexander tore through rank after rank of mostly unarmored troops, burying himself in the midst of the enemy. His voice, guttural and strange, could be heard back in among the Hypaspists.

"Kill me! Who among you will kill me?"

True to their pattern, the Asians wanted nothing to do with this mad, lethal apparition. Men ran from him in any direction they could, disrupting the entire Persian left wing. By the time Alexander made his turn to make for Darius, half the Great King's army had lapsed into frenzied, disorganized retreat.

There was heroism on the other end of the Macedonian line too. The Parthian and Median cavalry were bearing down hard on Parmenion. Outnumbered, his line began to crumble under the pressure. By his sheer determination, Parmenion willed his men to stand their ground, digging their pikes into the earth as the Thessalian horsemen charged to their rescue. It was a superb defense against overwhelming odds, and the old man accomplished it without Alexander's help. By that, I mean there was no headlong dash by the King's Companions to save Parmenion's skin. Anyone who had been there would know this is a fable—that line was miles long, strewn with obstacles like the wreckage of destroyed chariots and bodies and rampaging elephants! No, Alexander's rhapsodizers cannot have it both ways, cannot make him the hero of the right wing and the left. If you leave this trial knowing anything for certain, it must be this: Parmenion earned the victory at Gaugamela every bit as much as Alexander did.

The King's only object was a final showdown with Darius. He found him waiting in the center, standing tall and defiant in his chariot. Having long since lost his thrusting spear, Alexander held his sword aloft, making straight for the Great King. Darius was ready for him, his throwing arm cocked with a javelin.

"Wait for me, brother!" shouted Alexander, tears in his eyes.

"Come to me, dear boy!" answered hooded Darius.

But before they could clash for the last time, the Great King's charioteer turned his horses around and fled. This was not at Darius's order. On the contrary, Darius could be heard protesting very clearly, thrashing the driver with his flail. I don't know if Darius had taken haoma that day, but it seems the charioteer had. All the witnesses told of the devastated expressions on the faces of both kings as the distance increased between them. Although they perhaps had different reasons, each was disappointed at having been cheated of their final embrace.

My opponent has already expounded on the consequences of Gaugamela, and I will not dwell of those now. What is most relevant here is that Alexander was stunned at this victory. He fought as a man liberated from any thought of tomorrow, and when Darius was carried away, he was suddenly confronted by a universe of decisions. The empire of the Great King was finished. What would replace it was then largely in Alexander's hands. Yet how could a man with no purchase on the shape of his own future contemplate the dispensation of a continent?

When in doubt, Alexander made gifts. Along with the usual tithes to the major sanctuaries, he decided it was his obligation to honor anyone when had done anything brave in the last hundred and fifty years. Descendants of the fallen at Marathon got sacks of Persian cash; he sent pledges to rebuild the city of Plataea for its service against Xerxes. He honored even obscure figures, such as Phayllus of Croton, who had defied his countrymen to send a trireme to fight at Salamis. I don't know how this was perceived here, but it all seemed presumptuous to me. In this way Alexander sought to attach his name not only to his own victories, but to any victory—as if he had invented valor!

The departure of Darius's court had again left a swath of fancy detritus in its wake. Unique among these was Bagoas, the court eunuch Aeschines has spent so much of his precious breath railing against. That Bagoas sacrificed his balls is about the only true thing my opponent has said about him. Even on that score, I wonder how Aeschines comes by the extraordinary fact that Bagoas kept his dried testicles in a locket, or that they were the size of chickpeas! Why not the size of olives, Aeschines? Or lentils? For my part, I have no idea to which kind of garnish Bagoas's balls might best be compared. Unlike Aeschines, I will not testify about matters I know nothing about.

I see you all laugh . . . and that the archon again suspects I turn these proceedings into a burlesque! But let him see that I am not laughing, and indeed no one should, for this Bagoas was a troubling presence in

Alexander's court. For it is true that he replaced Hephaestion in the King's bed, and at a time when
Alexander's connection to his old life in Macedon was
growing tenuous. The source of his charm was difficult to describe. He was beautiful, yes, but with the
sleek-eyed slyness of a predator. He could no more be
mistaken for a woman than a gelding could be taken
for a mare. Yet to a man of Alexander's taste and experience, he may well have presented the best of womanhood without the disadvantages. I will not put too
fine a point on it; we all know that soft thighs are never
just soft thighs, but that there are a hundred differ-
ences in touch, smell, and consequence when we par-
take of the most womanly male or mannish female.
Alexander, as I have said, took the lower position with
Hephaestion. With Bagoas, he claimed his place in the
mount, and with that perhaps began to imagine wider
possibilities for himself—even atop women, if the
need arose.

The eunuch was an accomplished dancer and jug-
gler. He also became practiced at manipulating
Alexander. Whenever he wanted something, he would
need merely to say, "Darius gave it to me," and
Alexander gifted him too. He had merely to tell him
that Darius had done some foolish thing, and Alexander would emulate it. With eyes wide open, he became
a kind of slave to the eunuch. Having taken an oath to
aid the King, I therefore made it my business to keep a
close watch on this Bagoas, and if necessary to act
against his influence. So you see that Aeschines has
gotten the truth reversed: I was not conspiring with
Bagoas, but against him!

You may wonder what Hephaestion thought of

Alexander's new companion. The answer must have been, "Not much," though I believe that like most aspects of his relationship with Alexander this issue was complicated. The King had the prerogative to take whatever lovers he pleased; beyond that, Hephaestion's devotion to Alexander was so unqualified as to make sexual jealousy nearly beside the point. Still, there must have been some expectation, if only unspoken, that the King's preference for another meant Hephaestion had to be compensated with more independent responsibility. This is exactly what he got.

It was about this time that news from home reached us of Antipater's victory over the Spartan rebels at Megalopolis. The word came through it was a hard-won fight, with the combatants finally having at each other with bare hands. King Agis, we learned, found a glorius death in the line, while Antipater personally led forty thousand Foot Companions into battle though he was old enough to be Alexander's grandfather.

The response to this in Alexander's court was a puzzle. At first there was concern that some great disaster had been allowed to happen. When the fact that it was a victory sank in, however, there seemed to be great embarrassment all around, as if the next-worst thing had occurred. Alexander's jealousy was plain, and troubling. When the messenger finished reading his account, he waved his hand as if to dismiss the whole business from his mind.

"What concern of mine is this? These are the affairs of mice!"

Yet Antipater's victory over the Spartans was more impressive than any of Alexander's one-sided romps over the Persians. After all, it was a battle between Greeks, the antagonists each defending a brilliant tradition, both loath to fall short of their ancestors' legacy. Unlike Alexander, Antipater is a modest man—he made little celebration of his victory, professing only his subordination to his master. And unlike Darius, the Spartan king inspired ferocity in his men. It would have been a very long road to India if Alexander had faced a few more "mice" like Agis along the way!

Babylon surrendered without a fight. This was for the same reason Egypt did: as a place of consequence in former times whose glory had faded under the Great King, she saw no cost in trading one master for another. We approached the city at first along the Persian Royal Road, and thence directly across the well-watered plains of the Mesopotamians. Before long we glimpsed the ramparts of a massive conurbation, blue in the distance. The effect of seeing these fortifications was sobering to the Macedonians. Smashing the Persian line was one thing, but reducing a city with titanic brick walls hundreds of feet high, and thick enough for two chariots to drive abreast on their summits, was very much another.

The sight was still more humbling at night, as the towers were brightly illuminated; beyond them could also be seen the crown of a great ziggurat, blazing and stretching still higher. Some thought the city itself must be burning, for lamps of such power, producing such a luxury of artificial light, are unknown in Greece. The answer to the puzzle was soon presented to them, as emissaries from the town of Mennis arrived in camp with gifts of clay vessels filled with naphtha. This is a black liquid that flows from the ground in certain places in that country, including Mennis, which may be used like lamp oil, except that it is far more potent. The emissaries demonstrated its power by sprinkling the substance on the path to Alexander's tent. When the King appeared that night, at a signal, they struck a spark, and the path was lined with two great sheets of flame. Alexander, though delighted at the show, was not surprised by it, as his tutor Aristotle had once instructed him on naphtha's remarkable properties.

Not knowing in what mood the Babylonians would receive them, we approached the city in full battle order. The city gates opened, and disgorged not a hostile army, but a torrent of well-wishers. The sides of the road were heaped with flowers; a mass of citizens more numerous than the army itself surrounded the Macedonians, cheering and welcoming them. An official embassy, headed by the satrap Mazaeus, met Alexander under the gates. Under a blizzard of rose petals fluttering down from the city walls, the Persian disembarked from his jewel-encrusted chariot, placed his sword on the ground, and knelt before his new master. Alexander dismounted and invited Mazaeus to stand before him. The crowd roared its approval, the collared leopards snarled, and a chorus of magi chanted thanks to Marduk, whose worship the Persian kings had suppressed, but whom Alexander was destined to honor as he did all local deities.

The procession continued to the Ishtar Gate, ablaze with great enameled figures of kings and demons, and passed inside. Marching down to the Euphrates, Alexander beheld a stupendous stone bridge more than five stades in length. Every inch of this wonder was lined with ecstatic natives, each waving small cloth banners emblazoned with Alexander's profile. Indeed the Babylonians, whose notions of decorum differ from ours, thought nothing of presenting their wives and daughters to the Macedonian soldiers right there in the street. Not a few exposed a breast or two to sweeten their hospitality. The riches and temptations crowded so densely around the Macedonians that they staggered with the magnitude of what they possessed. Compared to Babylon, Athens was a provincial town, and Philip's capital of Pella a poor and piddling village. It is said that Hephaestion leaned toward Alexander and, echoing what he uttered upon seeing Darius's royal tent, remarked, "So *this* is a city."

This admiration was matched by the Babylonians' gratitude that the army had not sacked the place. Still, the occasion had its measure of anxiety, as some upstarts on the walls dropped heavier things than rose petals on the Macedonians; when the great bronze statue of Darius came down, a hush came over the crowd that betokened more fear than joy. Alexander, fearing his spear-won property would be looted at the first opportunity, forbade any Babylonian from entering the public buildings until further notice. This edict caused much puzzlement and anger among his new subjects, especially as the newcomers proceeded to take up residence in Hammurabi's old palace.

Alexander improved his position, however, when he promised to rebuild the ziggurat called Temple of the High Head, and all the temples of Bel that had been desecrated by the Persians. These measures earned him the support of the priestly classes, who bear an influence in eastern lands we can hardly imagine. In gratitude, the priests shared a vast bounty of knowledge with the newcomers—their secrets of chemistry, metalworking, agriculture, their thirty thousand years of astrological records. From the engineers of the ziggurat of Esagila our engineers gleaned much that would help them in the construction of the proposed lighthouse at Alexandria. The Babylonians revealed the secrets of the terraced forest known as the Hanging Garden, which, though it had seen better days, still exceeded in ingenuity and splendor anything made in the Greek world. The only question upon which they could not enlighten the Macedonians was the fate of Darius's money: the royal treasury, they suggested, must have been removed to Susa.

Perceiving that their rustic liberators were easily dazzled by cheap tricks, the Babylonian magi organized magic shows for their delight. This was harmless enough, until the Macedonians took it upon themselves to experiment with naphtha on their own. So it was that a young boy, a worker in the baggage train, cheerfully submitted to being doused and lit. It seems that neither the boy nor the rest of the Macedonians understood that this substance produced heat when burned. So great was his surprise that he had an astonished look on his face as he died—he gave a kind of shrug, and the spectators around him did the same, until there was nothing left of the boy but a blackened, shrugging husk.

As a tourist, Alexander seemed to enjoy the place. Its architectural wonders, and its geographical centrality in his future empire, recommended it as his capital. But in the end, as he learned firsthand of the burdens of administering such a stupendous city, with a walled area of more than one hundred eighty square miles, a population as great as all of Macedon, and hordes of priest-bureaucrats practiced at ankle-biting and boot-licking, his dominion lost its luster.

He stayed there a month for no other reason than he had little idea what to do next. On this question, Arridaeus could be of no help. Hephaestion then seized his opportunity to restore his position at Alexander's side, urging him to go on to conquer all of Asia. The King agreed to this for no more profound reason than that he wished neither to go back nor stay where he was. The farther he went from the throne at Pella, the more the memory of the place seemed redolent of Philip, whose fatherly command he grew to resent. Friendly god Ammon, after all, had never flogged him, nor banished his friends from the palace, nor begrudged him his overlordship of the universe. Nor did the prospect of a reunion with Olympias have much appeal.

And so, with Hephaestion, he drew up plans for a new war and reorganized the army. Which is to say, he gave Hephaestion free rein to take revenge on those who had disrespected him, dissolving units whose officers had joked at his expense, or spread unflattering rumors, or who had looked at him in some way that displeased him. At this same time, he welcomed more Persians into his service, for the simple reason that they knew how to administer what the Macedonians had conquered. In many cases Alexander simply took the oath of whatever satrap or native king he found in the lands he passed through. There is much talk of Alexander's "wisdom" in this regard, in his supposed respect for local custom and native ways. Yet in this he had innovated nothing, but only emulated the policies of the Great Kings, who, if nothing else, were masters of skimming off the cream and delegating away the rest.

And what cream it was! There was no precedent for the fortune that turned up on this march: ten thousand talents at Sardis, fifty thousand at Susa, one hundred twenty thousand in the royal treasury at Persepolis. These are magnitudes by the light of which the very preciousness of silver and gold becomes absurd. Although Alexander recognized its utility, unlike many of his fellow Macedonians he took no direct pleasure in the spectacle, smell, and touch of money. Its only use for him lay in giving it away, preferably by the talent. And so we hear of the king giving out rewards of one round talent for increasingly trivial attainments: a talent for each man in a nicely turned-out infantry rank; a talent for a skillful air on the cithara at dinner; a talent for a well-polished cuirass or for policing up the camel dung around camp. So aggressive was Alexander at this gift-giving that his men fell victim to outsized expectations. Ordinary soldiers came to expect a talent for their mere proximity to the King; if overlooked, an otherwise good man who once would have exulted in a bit of royal praise went away muttering, "What, no talent?" Someone should have told the King that gifting, like any pleasure, could become something of a vice if overindulged. Yet it is no surprise that, as they went around with their hands out, none of his friends got around to telling him this.

XI

Of the renowned "victory" at the Susian Gates, I can say no more than that it was a colossal waste of lives. Any commander with a shred of respect for his enemy would have anticipated that the Persians would block that pass. I warned Alexander of ambush myself. But the young King was in the grip of his own legend by then, and would not agree to the simple precaution of taking the coast route into Persia. That he managed to force the Gates I credit to Arridaeus's instincts and the stamina of the Macedonians. No one else deserves praise for surviving this stupidity.

The army passed out of Mesopotamia and into the enemy homeland. The Achaemenid royal seat at Persepolis beckoned, but first Alexander had to force a sheer pass through the Zagros mountains to the plateau of Persis. For this he took with him only his most mobile forces, elements of his Hypaspists, the Agrianian allies, his best scouts; the heavy troops were placed under the command of Parmenion and ordered to march the long way around by the coast.

We met no resistance all the way to the Gates, and then most of the way through the pass until he reached the narrowest part. At that point the march was stopped by a wall of rude blocks that the enemy had thrown up. The Macedonians were puzzled over how to attack this wall when an avalanche of rocks, arrows, and javelins fell on them from the heights: the Persians had sprung a trap on them. Alexander had his troops take cover, still imagining he would force his way through, when the enemy rolled boulders down on his men, so that their upturned shields were no longer any defense. Alexander's position was hopeless; the enemy was dug into positions on the hillsides where the Macedonians could not see them, much less mount a counterattack. Alexander ordered a general retreat. The great cheer went up from the Persians as they saw the young King's back for the first time.

With the Persian cheers echoing in his ears, Alexander led his men on the bitterest maneuver of the campaign. This was not only a matter of pride: the conquest of so large an empire would take decades if the Persians were emboldened to contest him in every place they could. To discourage this, Alexander was loath to accept anything less than instant, total annihilation of all resistance. But the Macedonians had already lost more men that day than during the fight at the Granicus, while the Persians had suffered not a single casualty.

Craterus and Ptolemy suggested that they avoid the obstacle by proceeding around by the coast route into Persia. But as the Macedonians had left unburied dead in the gorge, Alexander could not compound defeat with desecration. Moreover, he refused to give the Persians the glory of turning the tables on Thermopylae, where the Lacedaemonians had delayed Xerxes's invasion of Greece. He called for all the Persians captured in the area to be brought forward, and asked them if they knew of some hidden route by which the enemy might be outflanked. Under threat of torture, all these men swore that there was no way around the wall—with one exception. This fellow, a shepherd, suggested one possibility, but then seemed to withdraw it.

"The path is no more than a sheep-track," he told Alexander. "Your men will not manage it."

"Are you saying we cannot go where your sheep can?"

"You will be making the attempt in the dark, and there is snow," came the reply.

After such a challenge, Alexander could naturally accept no other course. "Prepare to lead us up," he told the prisoner, "and never doubt that we will follow, whatever the difficulty!"

Craterus was placed in command of the camp, and given a thousand men with which to make a diversionary attack on the wall. Then, after night fell, the Macedonians followed the shepherd up along a narrow ledge, onto the ridge above the gorge.

The prisoner had not exaggerated the meagerness of the path. No more than a few feet wide in places, it often disappeared under snow, just as he had warned. As we could not use torches, and the walls of the gorge prevented starlight from reaching us, we groped along in complete darkness, all the while trusting that our guide was not leading us into another trap, or over a cliff. For safety, the Macedonians used pikes to probe ahead of them, or to keep in touch with their companions grasping the other end; several men were thus saved from falling by their comrades, who used their *sarissas* to pull them back from the chasm. When one man did slip and fall over the side, the mishap was more felt than heard—as he plunged to his death, he bravely protected the army's position by keeping his silence. Nevertheless, despair laid hold of us as the path wound higher and higher, and the men were forced to abandon baggage on the way, and the shepherd turned back to Alexander, whispering, "See, I told you it was impossible!"

In time the path leveled, and then began to descend. Just as the first fingers of light touched the eastern sky, we were able to look down and see the smoke from the Persian camp below. A gasp went up among the Macedonians as they realized they had succeeded. Alexander bade them all to keep quiet, and issued his commands for the final assault: Ptolemy, with the Hypaspists, would fall on the enemy by the path the prisoner had showed them. Alexander and the Agrianians, meanwhile, would go to the far side of the pass and charge the enemy from that quarter. He trusted Craterus would hear the attack as it was under way, and make a frontal assault at the critical moment.

The battle unfolded exactly as he planned. Alexander charged into the Persian camp, taking them completely by surprise, as Ptolemy swooped on them from above. The troops by the wall were further pinned down by Craterus's attack, so that the Persians were beset from every direction. Thousands were killed before the sun mounted the hills and revealed the full extent of the rout. The day was not destined to rise on a Persian Thermopylae.

The way was open to Persepolis. This was a city

synonymous with the power of the Great King, where Greeks from the Ionian cities had been forced for generations to appear on bended knee, and where the accumulated loot of a continent waited for the victor of Gaugamela. With the fall of the Susian Gates, the capital of Cyrus, Darius, and Xerxes lay at the pleasure of the twenty-five-year-old King of a people despised by the Persian overlords as a servile race. But as the Thracian porter asked Hippias in Aristophanes's *The Crows*, is not the bended knee now on the other foot?

Rejoining his forces to those under Parmenion, Alexander marched in no great hurry toward the city. He was met on the way by two parties: first, emissaries from the royal chamberlain Tiridates, begging the Greeks to advance on the capital with all speed, as a mob was swarming to loot the treasury. Anxious that his property be protected, Alexander quickened the march—until a second party arrived that stopped him in his tracks.

To the Macedonians, it seemed that an army of corpses had come forth to meet them. But the suppliants were Greeks, four thousand of them, who had been freed from their imprisonment by the Persian nobles as they fled; moreover, they were not corpses but, like Alexander's soldiers, living men. That was where the resemblance ended, for no more pathetic husks of humanity were ever loosed to haunt the living. It was said that most of them suffered mutilation, removal of eyeballs and noses and ears and limbs. What was most apparent from the pattern of these outrages was the depraved humor behind many of them, such as the amputation of every finger except the small one on the left hand, or removal of the entire lower jaw. Still others bore the scars of repeated burnings, brandings, and scourgings, or of tattoos proclaiming that they were dogs attached to the houses of their Persian masters. Several of these wretches—the ones still capable of speech, that is—were brought before Alexander to tell their stories, which invariably involved years of deliberate torture, of casual brutality that so tore at the heart that the King wept openly, crying out that he could take no more.

The prisoners were given shelter and food, and promised that those who wished to would be free to return to their homes, along with enough money that they would suffer no discomfort for the rest of their lives. Those who had no families to go to, or who could not face the reactions of their countrymen to their injuries, were pledged land and slaves with which to settle in Alexander's empire.

Aeschines is right: if the Persians had applied half the ingenuity they showed in tormenting these poor men to perfecting their tactics in battle, Alexander would never had made it beyond the Granicus. What he did not say, however, is that a good number of these ex-slaves came from places that were destroyed by Alexander or his father. Many were from Thebes or Amphissa or Olynthus, and had been away for so long they did not know the fate of their cities. So when the poor wretches hobbled, crawled, or were carried into Alexander's presence, and thanked him for liberating them so they could again glimpse their beloved Cadmeia, the King could only turn away in his guilt, having himself been responsible for pulling down the Cadmeia stone by stone. Instead of the truth, the prisoners were given a travel allowance and an escort back to Greece.

We may only guess what they thought of their liberator when they saw the empty field where their city once stood. Did these homesick men rejoice when they saw that the Macedonians had spared the house of Pindar? Did they savor the irony, worthy of some tragedian's imagination, of preserving the house of a poet while leaving nothing of all the poet held dear? Or did they only weep?

We were the last generation of mankind to see in its glory the great citadel of Persepolis, or Parsa, as the barbarians called it. There was no sight elsewhere that I would compare it with, but can only say it resembled a mass of towering majesties arrayed on a great game board. I say "game board" because it stood on its artificial terrace with nothing around it but flat country, and because there was something of the architect's model about the place. Even when I had my eyes on it, it seemed like some grand but unlikely abstraction. When I saw it again, on the way home nearly ten years later, reality had imposed itself on the dream: dust was blowing into the great audience halls, the ornamental arbors were dead, and the local farmers were carrying away the scorched stones. Curious what he might say, I asked one of the farmers what had happened there.

"The Greeks came," he said.

As you might imagine, this answer made me angry, for only a single Greek had had a hand in that barbarity, and that one Greek was a courtesan. Yet not even she had thrown the fatal torch. The following was what really happened.

First, some clarification: when Aeschines recounted

the sack of Persepolis to you, he really meant the sack of the town adjacent to the citadel. This was a settlement built largely of mud brick, and contained the houses of the servants who ran the palace, and the artisans who continued to work on it up until the day it was destroyed. Parsa was, in fact, never a completed work, and was never truly lived in. Let it be a testament to its opulence that the greed of the Macedonian soldiers could be satisfied in this way. It was the richest sack many of them had seen in a lifetime of looting Greek cities, and they had seen only the servant's quarters!

No—the real treasures were looted by a quieter, more discriminating bunch. As the glow of the fires below the citadel began to rise, and screams of the raped and murdered Persians filtered through the tiled walls, Alexander and his friends embarked on a torchlight tour of Darius's palace with the Great King's chamberlain. It took all night to get through the maze of pylons and palaces, armories and stables. The gardens alone had no parallel in Greece or Macedon, with great reflecting pools flanked with pomegranate trees, jujube, willows, and tamarisk, and stocked with enormous carp that practically nuzzled one's hand to be fed. Peafowl and ibises strode the paths, and hidden among the topiaries, our guide said, there remained a single survivor from the Great King's collection of tame Indian tigers.

The greatest excitement was reserved, of course, for the treasuries. It was the big room, the vault of the great Darius, that contained the fortune in bullion I have mentioned—some one hundred twenty thousand talents' worth.

The chamber was too dark for the party's taste, so a brazier was lit with whatever fuel was at hand. By its light, they marveled at a spectacle of gleaming metal that inspired some, such as Ptolemy, to drop to their knees in a fit of pecuniary ecstasy. More braziers were ordered, and some old books heaped up to feed the flames, until the Persian guide lost his voice, his face having gone white.

"What is it?" asked Hephaestion, smiling.

"You are burning the original manuscript of the Avesta—twelve thousand leaves in letters of gold, dictated by Zarathustra himself. It is a thousand years old."

"How old is this?" asked Alexander, holding up a gilded drinking cup.

The King's taste, you see, was different: gold interested him more when it plated or gilded fancy things, such as the flatware made for his table, or the fine cedar beams that held up the tapestries that would soon cool his crowned head.

The impression that I got of the place from a distance, that it was a kind of royal dollhouse, was only strengthened when I got inside. The carved gateways and palmetted columns seemed to bear no distinctive style. Or shall I say they had a kind of corporate style that was at the same time Greek, Egyptian, and Babylonian, and therefore amounted to none of these. Though we understood construction of the citadel to have begun by the elder Darius well before the first invasion of Greece, the floors seemed unscraped by groveling retainers, the striding stone bulls unappreciated by human eyes. Not even the royal dinnerware seemed ever to have known use.

We were not prepared to find temples or sanctuaries of any kind in Persepolis, for Herodotus had written that the Persians abjured such things. We were fools to place any stock in Herodotus: there was a splendid fire temple there, reserved for the use of the Great King and his family. In design it was a windowless, orthogonal room, unadorned with any of the faux-Egyptian or -Babylonian frillery we saw elsewhere. The walls were caked in a fine, black, aromatic ash that both charmed the nose and devoured all light except the glow of the sacred flame. The atmosphere was both tomblike and intimate, like the private boudoir of Kore.

Unlike in our temples, there was no statue of their god, and the altar was inside the temple. The latter was a bed of glowing embers on an upraised platform. It is said that this fire, the Atash Bahram, had first been kindled in the days of Zarathustra himself, centuries before, and had been carried to Pars from the east in an earthenware pot during the reign of Cyrus the Great. At first I dismissed this as a mere story. In all the years since that time, after all the invasions and upheavals, did not this Atash Bahram go out at least once?

I began to believe the legend when Parmenion announced that his scouts had captured two Persian priests traveling away from the capital in different directions. Each of these priests bore an earthenware pot with burning embers from the sacred fire. As the Zoroastrians considered the number three to be sacred, I imagine a third messenger escaped Parmenion's screen. The embers he carried might already have kindled another Atash Bahram, safely hidden from the Macedonians, as it was from the invading As-syrians, Medes, Cimmerians, Scythians, and Babylonians in their time.

As it was, Alexander had no interest in extinguishing the altar. On the contrary, he declared that it looked unhealthily weak! On his orders, wooden chairs and tables were fetched from elsewhere in the palace, broken up, and tossed on the altar so that it flared up like a proper campfire. The priests dared show neither approval nor disapproval at this, but stood off to the side smiling tightly, shadows cast by the fire dancing on the bare walls behind them.

The climax of the tour was the royal throne room. It was known as the Hall of One Hundred Columns, which testified to the literal truth. Yet here again the combination of enormous expense and practical uselessness was striking, for at no place in the Hall was a view of the throne unobstructed by a column. This could only have been the work of a deliberate but perversely alien mind.

As Alexander faced the throne of the Great King, he saw that someone had toppled a large statue of Darius's ancestor, Xerxes. Then, as he was wont to do at dramatic moments, he mused conspicuously.

"Shall I set you back on your feet, Xerxes, because the heart of a lion beat in your chest? Or shall you lie there as a villain, because of your crimes against the Greeks?"

It seemed a good question, but not one Alexander cared to answer, for he was already distracted by the carved device of the winged disk over the throne. He pointed at the inscription underneath.

"What does that say?" he asked the chamberlain.

"It says that the Great King of Kings has built a

palace befitting Ahuramazda, Anahita, and Mithra, and that the gods approve of what he has done in the name of *asha*, or righteousness. It says that as Ahuramazda honors the King as his earthly counterpart in the great struggle against the daevas, his home will never suffer its degradation."

"The daevas?"

The chamberlain, looking uncomfortable, took a long time before answering.

"They are minions of the Hostile Spirit, Angra Mainyu. They are bringers of chaos and destruction."

At this, Alexander gave only a nod, and passed the throne by without sitting in it. It may have been the warning by Ahura Mazda that dissuaded him, but more likely he did not want to risk a repetition of his misadventure on the throne at Susa, where his legs were too short to reach the floor.

Alexander lingered at Persepolis for almost five months. As the exhilaration of this conquest wore off, the King's determination to keep going wavered. His mandate from the Greek cities, after all, had provided only for the freeing of the Ionians. His rant at the Persian envoy notwithstanding, he came to worry that everything else he had done, from the destruction of the Persian army three times over to the occupation of Babylon to the seizure of the royal seat, smacked of hubris. To change his mind, Hephaestion, Ptolemy, and the rest came at him from every side, arguing that to break off the offensive then would invite a counterattack. If Darius did not return this year, or next, he would in ten years, or twenty. And besides, of what concern to a god such as Alexander are the bleats of urban gossips back home? Even to a mortal king like Philip, those people counted for little.

The jury shuffled and muttered. Though Swallow was used to forensic hyperbole, even he was beginning to resent the constant belittling of Greeks by the Macedonians. On this point alone, if only half of what Machon claimed was true, Aeschines's prosecution was in deep trouble.

While these arguments raged behind closed doors, the Macedonians diverted themselves with contests. Actors, athletes, raconteurs, and musicians from home came in a procession down the Royal Road from Sardis. Among them was Thettalus the actor, who has appeared to great acclaim in the plays of Sophocles here and in the palace at Pella, where he first became familiar with Alexander. In the years before his ascension the Prince often used Thettalus as his unofficial envoy. With his military success he did not forget his friend. At Alexander's eager expense, Thettalus was given a free hand to produce Euripides's *Bacchae* anywhere he wished at Persepolis.

Thettalus chose a great processional staircase of Darius's palace as a backdrop. This represented the reception hall of Pentheus, King of Thebes. As you know, at the climax of the play Pentheus attempts to spy on the rites of Dionysus by dressing as a woman, but is unmasked by the crazed celebrants. In an inspired bit of stagecraft, Thettalus has Pentheus escape not into a fir tree, but atop one of the great carved statues of Darius. The audience roared with delight as the maenads toppled the statue to get at Pentheus, who was played with great skill by Thettalus himself. They sat in wonder as the actor playing Pentheus's mother, in ecstatic thrall to the god, foaming at the mouth, ignored her son's pathetic pleas and ripped his arm from its socket. Here again, Thettalus was an innovator, for the act is performed onstage as the Messenger describes it. Cleverly, Thettalus fashioned a costume with a sham arm, having subtly withdrawn his own arm under his cloak. This production bore the kind of spectacle we never see in the Theatre of Dionysus, but judging by the response of Macedonians and Persians alike, it may represent the future. Now there is a true master of the stage, unlike the mediocre arts of our friend Aeschines!

Other kinds of performers also made their way to Alexander. I am thinking in particular of a courtesan named Thais. She was quite well-known here in years past—I see by the reactions of some of the well-heeled gentlemen in the jury that they were familiar with her. In her time she had beauty, but please understand, she was the kind of woman who was beautiful no matter what she looked like.

Today you will find her preparing to join Ptolemy on the throne of Egypt. That she came into alliance with that character I take as no surprise—Ptolemy deserves her. For those who never purchased her services, you know the type: to strangers, impeccable, unapproachable, unimpeachable. Show her a few drachmas, and she is your best friend, bursting with a thousand ideas of how to spend your money so *you* don't appear a fool. Show her a few more, and she is brazen, guttermouthed, leaving you panting but with her legs firmly closed. The cost of unsticking those gams was never quite clear! But when you hammered at her gates, they say she earned her nickname, which was "the Handshake."

So it came to be that Thais talked her way through the palace doors and onto a couch in Alexander's drinking parlor. She was quiet at first, just sitting and showing off her white arms through her chiton, contenting herself just to keep up with all of us, all the hardened soldiers, cup for cup and crater for crater. The conversation touched on diverse topics, including politics, food, and the follies of certain mathematical cults. Thais was prepared to hold forth on all of them, taking Callisthenes's side in a debate with the King and myself over the existence of the so-called "irrational" numbers.

"It cannot be denied," proclaimed the historian, "that if we imagine a square with a side length of one unit, the diagonal of that square will be the square root of two. Try as we might, we cannot find a fixed unit of any length that will evenly divide both into the side length or the diagonal. They are, as the Pythagoreans call it, incommensurable."

"Short of trying every possible common unit, I cannot understand how you can know that," I told him.

"Your opinion is shared by others," Thais said. "The man who first proved the existence of irrational numbers was expelled from the order of the Pythagoreans. His colleagues gave him a funeral and a tomb, as if his suggestion amounted to intellectual suicide."

"And yet Hippasus was correct," added Callisthenes.

Alexander shook his head. "I take the soldier's part, and agree with Machon. No one can claim to know that no common factor exists unless he tries them all."

"Then why don't we try here, now?" asked Thais. With that, she untied her girdle and knelt on the floor. The mosaic in the center of the room had a pattern that seemed close to perfectly square. Folding the girdle into a length equivalent to the side of the figure, she first showed that the diagonal of the square was almost half again as long as the side. As she demonstrated this fact the men were not watching the girdle at all, but the casual exposure of a breast as firm and unshriveled as a virgin girl's.

No matter how many times she folded the girdle, from one-half to one-quarter to one-eighth the length of the side, no number of whole units fit into the diagonal. There was always some material left over. A dark aureole likewise insisted on presenting itself, standing free of her folds.

"So you see, they are incommensurable."

"A most revealing demonstration!" applauded Callisthenes.

"Revealing, yes, but no demonstration," said the King. "I can imagine units much smaller than Thais can make with a piece of cloth. How do we know none of these may factor evenly into both lines?"

"We know, because it is a matter of mathematical proof."

The argument went on for some time with neither side convincing the other. But as competent as Thais was on matters geometrical, she took over the room as the wine flowed and the men grew tongue-tied. She picked up the cithara and played a romantic air, then played it again with racy lyrics she made up on the spot. Verses from Homer, Hesiod, and Pindar tripped lightly from her tongue, but especially lines from Euripides, for she had done her homework. And she danced, creating music in the men's minds by the swaying of her hips, hiking up her gown to show her upper thighs.

By the climax of the evening all of us were gazing at her with our aspirations plain, including the King, who blushed like a lovesick boy with his pleasure of her. But before any propositions flew, she suddenly turned the conversation to matters of politics, and of history.

"Mine was a wealthy family," she said, "before the Persians came to Attica. We had farms near Dekeleia, and a townhouse. My ancestors drew liturgies—they ran at the battle of Marathon, commanded ships at Salamis. There was a tripod dedicated to a first-place finish at the Festival of Dionysus. It was destroyed when Mardonius burned the city on his second occupation. . . ."

As she said this, all hint of titillation went out of her manner. She was intimate, confessional, showing far more than just arms and thighs. Whom was she speaking to? We all thought it was to ourselves alone, her deference to Alexander notwithstanding. As she spoke of the fires of Mardonius, the flames of the braziers shone in her eyes. A stray lock of hair, so fetching as it came loose in her dance, fell across her cheek, like that of a windblown child standing at the foot of the burning Acropolis.

"My family never recovered from the Great King's predations. To survive, my mother was forced to board her children to different houses around the city. What 'boarding' meant was not hard to understand: for a fee, we were placed in the power of unscrupulous men with little regard for our age. I was sent into the service of a man named Bitto, who owned a house not far from the Whispering Hermes. On pain of beating, I was forced to cooperate with his criminal enterprise: having been blessed—or cursed—with a pretty face, I was obliged to show myself to the male passersby in the street. When the inevitable insults came, I was to let them into the house, and let them have their way with me. This would go on until Bitto contrived to 'surprise' us in the act. Pretending to fly into a rage over the insult of his only daughter, he would lock the men in the house and declare that he would return with others of his family, so that they could together seek the justice they had coming. Naturally, the dupes promised any sort of payment to avoid their fate.

"With this blackmail, and by my ruin, Bitto attained quite a high style of living. That none of the victims suspected that I was no longer innocent I put down to my age—just ten years old—and the foolishness of most men regarding the anatomy of women. With experience, I was able to fool most of them by offering my anus instead, or even a chance to rub themselves between my thighs, so ignorant were they! Yet as the months passed I fell more into despair, for there seemed no way for me to escape the power of this Bitto. And so with my hopelessness I lost my fear, and swore before the gods that I would live to turn the tables on him.

"My opportunity came when I took into my bed an older man named Evaces. This fellow was very pleasing to me, for he was courteous, and wore nice clothes, and seemed to have few vices except for a weakness for young girls. When Bitto sprung his trap, I therefore told Evaces not to concern himself with his rantings, but to trust me instead. When Bitto threatened to get his brothers, I instructed Evaces to call his bluff. Enraged, Bitto tore open the door and pointed a knife at Evaces. At that point, in front of many witnesses on the street, I proclaimed 'I am Evaces's daughter, not Bitto's.' Bitto sputtered and fumed, but could say nothing when the men in the crowd demanded he prove his relation to me; he barred the way for us to escape, but backed down when Evaces threatened to summon a deputy of the Eleven.

"And so I came into the house of Evaces, in which I lived as a concubine until my sixteenth year. When Evaces died of sickness, he made certain to leave three minas to his brother toward the cost of my maintenance. He honored his dying wish for several months, but reneged on his responsibility by claiming that as a freeborn woman I was the responsibility of my family, none of whom I had seen in many years. So instead of returning to the relatives who had sold me into disrepute in the first place, I took what I could from Evaces's house and went to Corinth. There I learned the finer arts of the only profession left to me.

"Sitting here with you, I know what you must think of me. Yet you should know that I would have had a different fate, had the gods been willing! I think of the girls of Athens today, safe in the strength of your protection, dear King. They will have no need for the arts of women like me. They will never know these depths...."

At this all the men, including myself, leapt to object to her self-professed degradation. We were lying, of course, well aware of the only real use to which she had availed herself. All of us, that is, with the possible exception of Ptolemy, whose depth of foresight we can only imagine. Did he see her as his Queen even then?

"No, it cannot be denied. My future has been sealed by my past—it is too late for me. But I did come here with a thought in my mind, O King, that would go some way toward healing what has been broken. I dare not utter it. . . ."

"Go on, speak," said Alexander, who could not help but adopt the humility in her tone.

"I look around me," she said, "and think of the majesty of those who built this place, and of their arrogance, believing that free Greeks would ever bend knee before them. I look, and I think, what an irony it would be, if one of the children they dispossessed took ultimate revenge on their works! A girl of Athens, for instance, with just a torch, could erase the mighty Xerxes from the memories of men. Is that not a thought?"

In an instant, her eyes were back to promising all sorts of diversions, and we men, whipped between desire and pity, were ready to grant her anything. Ptolemy rose from his couch and declared that the time had come to avenge the violation of the temples in Athens and Delphi. Why should it not be a woman that ignites the flames, added Craterus, igniting a gutteral belch to punctuate his question. And I must confess, as I looked at Thais sitting there, chewing her lip with girlish anticipation, her eyes softening as they peered through the smoky lamplight, that yes, her suggestion was a thought indeed.

But the only opinion that counted was Alexander's, and he said nothing. Seeing this, Thais sought to please him with a feat of entertainment even we experienced symposiasts had never seen before. For instead of delivering the usual show—frigging herself, for instance, or blowing a slave—she commenced her tour de force by approaching Bagoas.

The eunuch had been quiet so far. At her display of skill he seemed only to be taking mental notes; at her approach he looked bemused, as if she was wasting her time. That was my assumption, after all! But as she descended to put her lips on his, the act was done with such a tender deliberateness it was like the kiss given in the spring of new love. And it went on, her tongue drawing forth the tongue of Bagoas, her hands leading him to her breast, now miraculously exposed. As their clinch tightened, Bagoas responded as if he were a real man, pulling her chiton off her shoulders, clutching and clasping her. And when she felt the moment had arisen, Thais pulled herself off his lap, and pulling his tunic aside, showed the engorged fruit of her genius.

The rest of us cheered, exclaiming that yes, the divine Thais had indeed aroused a eunuch! And Bagoas, who seemed to see or hear nothing but her, seemed to be speaking to no one when he said, "The Palace of Darius must burn." Alexander, awed, drunk, nodded.

Our labor began in the Hall of One Hundred Columns. Torches appeared, and the party stood before the throne and gold-spun tapestries enclosing it. Alexander gave a brand to Thais, invited her to throw it on the cushions. Wisely, she declined.

"To the conqueror goes the honor," she declared.

The King, who was barely able to keep his feet, threw the first torch. It missed the throne, clattering on the marble floor. With that, Thais rushed forward, retrieved it, and set the tapestries alight. We all cheered again, raising our cups to the conflagration as it climbed the fabric, consumed the canopy, and bit into the painted cedar rafters.

The party had to move when the room filled with smoke. In the courtyard, we saw the Macedonian soldiers running up from their camp with bags of sand, thinking the place had caught fire by accident. But when they saw us standing there, laughing and toasting our handiwork, they rushed off to contribute more fuel. Soon the inferno reached an intensity that the entire terrace was uninhabitable. Darius's palace went up so fast that Alexander didn't have time to retrieve his own belongings from the room where he had been sleeping. This was among the many things Alexander regretted about that night, for he lost all his copies of Euripides' plays in the fire. The ancient armor of Achilles was, alas, saved. But ironically, this was not thanks to any Macedonian or Greek, but to the quick thinking of a Persian slave boy.

This, then, was how the most important city in Asia was destroyed.

XII

We saw two kinds of settlements on our march through Persia. Near the rivers we found villages built out of reeds, ringed with fields of grain, rice, and indigo. These places were often recently abandoned, though whether this was due to the army's approach or the seasonal travels of the people was difficult to say. In the arid places there were settlements of baked brick that appeared, from a distance, much the same ashen color as the land around them. On closer inspection, however, these villages were full of gardens, cooled by date palms and pipal, their walls shimmering with reflected light from half-shaded pools of sweet water.

Alexander's army had grown to such a size that it filled canyons and passes from end to end. It consumed the miles ahead of it and sloughed back remainders of feces, smoke, and Greek-speaking satraps. Anyone could see it coming days ahead, a plume of trail dust hanging over it, and watch it recede for days after, thousands of marching feet scouring the earth.

With each parasang beyond Persepolis, beyond Media and the high Zagros Mountains, the army had reached territories few Greeks or Macedonians—traveler, soldier or slave—had ever seen. Aristotle's geographies proved worthless. Ignorant and frightened, the Macedonians glimpsed surpassing weirdness in everything around them. They saw the natives bathing in cow urine and believing themselves clean. They saw men worshipping flame as they wore cloths before their faces, feeding dogs before their children, holding marriages by firelight that ended with eggs being tossed on roofs.

The Macedonians, understanding nothing, looked to Alexander for his example. In return he gave them a simple task: find Darius. Everything else, he seemed to say, was just details.

Ever since Darius had escaped from the battlefield, Alexander had maintained a network of spies to inform him of his enemy's movements. It was known that the latter still had the loyalty of some of his satraps, notably those from Bactria and Arachosia. He had reconstituted an army around him, small by Persian standards but approaching the numbers Alexander himself had possessed when he first landed in Asia. If, by some perversity of the gods, Darius learned to use his forces in a clever manner, he could still cause much trouble among the small garrisons and unsteady governors Alexander had left strung out behind him. Securing the long-term loyalty of Alexander's Persian subjects would be impossible as long as they believed the Great King would return. For this reason it was essential that Darius be retired, one way or another.

Alexander set about this task with characteristic vigor. Leaving his slower units behind—including myself, being no horseman!—he pushed north, skirting the eastern slopes of the Zagros on the way toward Darius's summer palace at Ecbatana. There he learned that Darius had retreated further, into the Elburz Mountains in Parthia. Lingering only a moment over the riches of the palace, Alexander struck northeast with his speediest cavalry, pausing for nothing but essential supplies. Many of the Thessalian horses died beneath their riders as they were pushed beyond their limits. These were replaced, and replaced again, as Alexander drove them on across the plateau and toward the Caspian Gates.

On the way, he encountered the overnight camps that Darius and his men had occupied first a week, then a few days, then mere hours before. He used these remains to spur his men, reigniting the campfires with the still-burning embers, showing them there was only a short distance to go. Soon they came upon further evidence of their quarry's desperation: the path was littered with armor and dead horses, as well as rich furniture, chests, plates, and gold utensils spirited from Persepolis, Susa, and Ecbatana. These were left where they lay in the dust.

Passing through the Caspian Gates, he heard disturbing news: the closeness of the pursuit had moved Darius's allies to panic. The Great King had been betrayed by his Bactrian satrap, a man called Bessus, and was very possibly already dead. This intelligence sent Alexander into a fit of indignation—after sitting on Darius's throne, taking his wife and mother into his house, and sleeping in his bed, he had come to imagine a kind of brotherhood between them. Coming so close upon his old adversary on the chase, seeing his campfires and the kind of tracks his horses left in the dirt, he imagined he was achieving some deep understanding of the man. Obsessed now with rescuing Darius from his captors, he stripped his force to a minimum—just one hundred and fifty mounted men—and rode all night toward the enemy's last known position, somewhere in the desert northwest of the Gates.

The local people were forced to show the Macedonians a shortcut that might end the pursuit. There was a steep and narrow defile through the hills that was unknown to the Persians; Alexander hurtled through first, and was off ahead of his escort as he sighted a mass of riders and carts in the remote distance ahead. We may well imagine what his quarry must have thought of his tiny galloping figure at it rushed toward them, virtually alone! Specialists in horsemanship, they would have recognized the King's mount as a Macedonian one before they perceived the rider to be Alexander himself. In any case, there was a tumult in the Persian retinue—a sword flashed in the sun, and the riders abandoned the carts as they put the crops to their horses's flanks. With the gleam of that sword, the second-darkest nightmare of any king, the murder of another king, was realized.

Alexander's men found him staring down into one of the carts. Some in his party rushed to pursue the murderers; Alexander forbade them, gathering them all around him as he settled into a deliberate reverie. Though this was the last time he lay eyes on Darius, it was the only occasion in which they were engaged in something like a common cause. Even in death, Darius was an impressive figure, taller than Hephaestion, with a vigor that belied his fifty years. He had been stabbed in the heart, and though unconscious he was not yet dead. Even then, bleeding and abandoned in a donkey cart, Darius cut the kind of noble figure that was ever beyond the tiny Alexander or his one-eyed, coarse-grained father. The Persians did not need to beg oracles to have their King taken as a god, but easily and unanimously saw him as the mortal axis of Ahura Mazda's worldly empire. For his life to end at the hands of a fool like Bessus invited the question of what low character would, in time, get his blade into Alexander, no matter how much of a god he styled himself.

The Macedonians watched their enemy expire, imbibing from both kings the gravity of the moment, and perhaps a new appreciation for what their army had accomplished in Asia, for this was the great Darius prone before them. They bore his corpse back to Persepolis in a cortege that steadily grew as Alexander gathered his scattered forces. The necropolis of the Persian kings had been expressly spared the sack; a grand funeral was staged there, with all the proper customs observed. I saw Sisygambis make her final appearance in public to grieve for her son, showing perhaps less sentimentality at his passing than Alexander did. We may imagine that even she understood Darius was a flawed man, possibly adequate for less momentous times, but entirely run down by history. Her gaze was fixed on his shroud, never glancing at the company of Persian nobles who had come to mourn the old King and ingratiate themselves with the new. Her contempt for Bagoas, who liked to tell stories of what he had seen in Darius's court that flattered

Macedonian prejudices, was obvious. She was destined to outlive her son for only a short time.

Gathered near the still-smoking ruins of Persepolis, Alexander's court swelled into an ungainly mass of Macedonians, Persians, and allied nobles, riven by mutual contempt and suspicion. With the death of Darius, Alexander was the acknowledged successor in form as well as substance, charged with the task of governing the whole without alienating the parts. He met this ascension with the public adoption of certain practices he had indulged before only in private audiences or drinking parties, such as wearing the Persian diadem, sleeved robes, and high-heeled shoes (which he took to quite readily, given his modest height). There were also a number of court rituals unknown to the Macedonians, such as taking state dinners behind a crepe curtain and flanking himself with servants bearing fly whisks and sunshades. The latter seemed particularly absurd to the Macedonians, who were quite used to seeing Alexander broiled red with sunburn as he shared his troops' discomfort on campaign. They were also disturbed by a custom among the Persians of keeping their hands hidden in the King's presence—a practice that would have been outright worrisome in the blade-strewn dining halls of Macedon.

The men were at least encouraged by the expectation that after more than four years in Asia they would all soon be going home. In due course Alexander called an assembly to make an announcement. He took care to revert to Greek dress for the occasion, for he did not expect his news to be welcome.

Alexander began by praising his troops' historic

achievement, telling them that no army, not even the storied Ten Thousand, had marched farther or overcome greater odds. When they did turn back for Greece, it would be as living legends, and as rich men, for Alexander would discharge every man with enough wealth to make him a figure of substance in his city.

"But the job is not finished!" he said. "I have received word from Bactria that Bessus, the betrayer of Darius, has taken the headdress of Persian kings and now styles himself Artaxerxes V, King of Asia. Can any of us doubt that he will soon gather an army around him, and if we do not seek him he will come west, to take away what we have so dearly earned? The Bactrians are tough soldiers, and cannot be trusted behind our backs. Can it be long, do you think, before Bessus spreads tales that the Greeks are afraid to confront a competent enemy, instead of the hapless Darius? For this reason, we march tomorrow, so that we may show 'Artaxerxes' the true depth of his folly."

Against a campaign to preserve Macedonian honor, there could be no argument. The army struck east across the eastern satrapies of Parthia and Aria. On the march, Alexander either accepted or exacted the submission of all the tribes. In cases of voluntary allegiance he showed great lenience, often confirming the suppliant in his current domains or enlarging them at the expense of those who refused him. Word of this policy of course spread ahead of him, so that actual resistance became more and more exceptional.

Bessus had probably expected that Alexander would proceed carefully, consolidating his hold over the lowlands and ensuring his lines of supply before forcing the passes into Bactria. In anticipating how his enemy would fight, Bessus proved as unsuccessful as old Darius, for the Macedonians came on as inexorably as winter itself.

The crossing of the Paropamisus mountains came at great cost, with Alexander's troops unprepared for the great cold and the fainting sickness often seen in high places; Bessus had furthermore torched all the villages and farms in the region, hoping that hunger would force the Macedonians to retreat. They froze, but most did not starve, having brought with them prized luxuries, such as honey, from the palaces of Darius. With the end of these, Alexander ordered the men to stalk as many of the wild, spiral-horned goats of the region as they could find, and after they were gone, to root underground for the native herbs, just as the goats had.

When grubbing in the dirt proved less than sustaining, he diverted the troops by showing them a great landmark of the area: the famous crag of Prometheus, high above the clouds, on a ridge at the crest of the Paropamisus. This was the very place where the Titan was bound in punishment for bringing fire to men, condemned for all eternity to have his liver devoured by an eagle. Alexander paused long enough to allow those who were interested in the crag to go up to it in small parties, where they marveled at the very spot where the victim suffered, his rusty shackles still in place. They were further cheered by the implication that Alexander's army would surely have freed Prometheus, had the King's ancestor, that underachiever Heracles, not been lucky enough to get there first.

It was in these mountains that I suffered my only

wound of the campaign. As you see here, I am marked by the experience in a way that is trifling, but permanent. . . .

Machon held up his right hand, revealing that the index and middle fingers had been severed at the last knuckle.

The fault is entirely mine that I didn't notice my fingers turning black. The handiest treatment—if I might put it that way!—would have been to warm my fingers in the snow, which was as warm as a blanket compared to that cutting wind. But I was lucky compared to others, who lost whole fingers, feet, or the ends of their noses.

Aeschines speaks of the crossing of the Paropamisus as a feat of logistics and a tribute to Alexander's leadership, which I suppose it was. But consider this question: how many people had to starve for each mile Alexander's army was provisioned in that country? In these matters I saw more than anyone in the Macedonian general staff did, including Alexander. The task of separating the native people from their food was left in the hands of low-level officers. When the Macedonians came to a place with a significant concentration of families, soldiers went out to demand that all their stores be deposited in a central place by a certain day. Crimes of opportunity were not uncommon during these visits, including murders of recalcitrant men and abductions of young women.

Alexander frowned on these practices. He even punished an inveterate rapist, a certain Hero, son of Alcaemon, with a run through the gauntlet. But as his comrades took turns punching Hero, the "punishment" took on the quality of a mass congratulation of the man. Nor was he removed from the duty that seemed to trouble him with so much temptation.

Some of the villages held back supplies and were destroyed. The rest submitted, though the "donation" of their winter stores would inevitably reduce them to starvation in the months to come. Like living reproofs of these outrages, women with stick-thin babes and shriveled breasts hung around the army's camp for the whole time the Macedonians campaigned in Bactria. The soldiers were not immune to pity—on several occasions I saw them toss a morsel or two out to these victims. The women fought over them like ravening dogs.

This was how Alexander's triumph in the mountains was supplied. I don't say that he was unique in this regard, or that the Persians didn't do the same in their marches through territories of the Greeks. In lands of wealthier people the Macedonians were content to buy their supplies, though such people were, ironically, far better able to survive outright theft than the mountaineers. What I am saying is that you should not believe that the burden of cold, hunger, or disease fell only on Alexander's gallant soldiers, as the current stories lead you to believe. For every hungry soldier who didn't get enough to eat there were three villagers who got nothing; for every cold soldier there was a family robbed of its bedclothes.

In this way, he crossed the mountains with a loss of only a twentieth of his army. Before the winter ended he descended from the highlands and, after setting beacon-fires to guide the rest of his men down from the mountains, raced to take the towns of Drapsaca and Bactra with whatever forces he had with him.

Bessus, hoping to find reinforcements in the lands of the Scythians, retreated north across the Oxus river. To forestall pursuit, he burned anything within a thousand stades that would float. The Macedonians followed by resurrecting a trick Alexander had used to cross the Danube years before, rafting across the river on sewn-shut tents stuffed with grass, leaves, and wood chips.

With his failure to stop Alexander at the Oxus, the Persians had seen enough of their new king. Riders delivered the message that Bessus was arrested and waiting for Alexander a short distance ahead of his army. Thus ended, as dishonorably as it had begun, the short reign of "Artaxerxes V."

Alexander had definite plans for disposing of the traitor. Ptolemy was sent ahead to secure the prisoner, strip him naked, and place him at the side of the road where the Greeks marched. As the troops went by, they saw him humiliated there, a dog collar around his neck. Riding in his chariot, Alexander turned to the prisoner with a sneer, as if confronted with a pile of dung.

"Why did you betray and murder your King?" asked Alexander.

Bessus responded with equal arrogance, asking "Alexander, why did you betray and murder your father, Philip?"

"I ask you again to account for yourself."

"What I did, I did for all the Persians, unlike the king of the Macedonians, who works only for his own glory."

Alexander put the question a third time, and Bessus, knowing that his death was certain, showed his contempt by indulging the part of a collared dog, growling and barking. This ended their interview, for surely any man who would bark at his conqueror was a fool. Bessus was seized and packed off to Bactra, where his treachery was dealt with in traditional Persian fashion, which I will not describe beyond saying that it involved disarticulation. That Alexander allowed such practices is perhaps not surprising, insofar that the Persians could not be expected to take up civilized ways immediately. But the episode did shock a good many of the Macedonians, who would just as soon put a sword through the neck of a traitor and have done with him. To allow such a deliberately sadistic death was unseemly.

With Darius gone and his betrayer most definitely dead, the rationale for continuing the war dwindled. Yet cities and kingdoms far ahead were sending emissaries to Alexander, capitulating in advance, promising their alliance and support against those who resisted him. With such ripe fruits demanding to be plucked, it would have been difficult for anyone to stop.

The campaign became ever more squalid and loathsome. Alexander's awareness that much of his success was due to Arridaeus increased his hunger to show he was a conqueror in more than name. From that point, he refused to call on his brother's help in certain minor campaigns where he believed his personal valor alone would carry him through. These wars were usually against primitive tribes short of everything but pride. Tapurians, Mardians, Ariaspians, Drangae, Gedrosians, Arachosians, Abian Scythians, Assacenians, Orietae, Memaceni—no group was too poor in means or meager in numbers to conquer. The tribes submitted to the crushing weight of Macedonian power, but only while Alexander was in the area. Time and again, once he was gone the garrisons left behind were massacred. And on each occasion, the rest of the army was never told of these losses, but left to believe in their invincibility.

Yet with each subjugation of an independent people emerged an uncomfortable truth: the Persian Empire was not what we were told it was. For years, pamphleteers like Isocrates had described a domain that was united in lucrative submission to the Persian throne. Throughout Asia, men were supposed to bow to the Great King, lavishing upon him tribute that could have gone to Greeks, if we only would agree to take it. Like a monolith hewn from rotten stone, it was only a matter of giving the empire a small push to topple it into a thousand pieces. Or so the argument went.

But the empire was no monolith. As we learned marching with Alexander, only a small part of the territory said to be under the Great King's control was actually ruled by him. These were composed of the farmlands, the habitable coastlines, and the roads that connected them. All the rest—the mountains, the deserts, the lands fit only for herding and thievery—were controlled by a myriad of petty chieftains. In many cases Darius did not even receive tribute from these chiefs, but had to pay tolls to transport his army across their territory! Alexander, as I have said, refused to do so, preferring to force them into submission. But as I have also said, the time always came when armies must move on; not even Alexander could be everywhere at once.

Please understand, I do not tell you that the empire of the Great King was poor and disunited to belittle Alexander's achievement. All told, the resources at the command of Darius were still far greater than those of all the Greeks put together. I only tell you these things for you to know the truth, to know something of what the men who marched with Alexander were thinking. Only a fool conquers the world without learning something he didn't know before.

Having humbled a continent, Alexander conceived a need to humble those who did all the work. Much has been said about the introduction of prostration among the Macedonians; my opponent even claims that I was truckling in my zeal to please the King. It seems there is no winning against Aeschines: either I defy Alexander, and I am called an obstruction, or I obey him, and I am accused of toadyism! The truth is that I understood the need to establish a conventional etiquette around the royal person. Since Macedonians and Persians would have to share responsibility, and the practices in their respective courts were very different, whatever custom the King demanded would necessarily offend someone. Rather than contribute to what I regarded as peevish resistance on the part of some Macedonians and Greeks, I showed a dutiful example. And that, gentlemen of the jury, is the extent of my sinister design in this matter!

In Greece, monarchy is preserved only in the cities with the most ancient constitutions—such as in Sparta—or as an honorific only—such as our "king archon" in Athens. Even in these cases the "king" is better understood as belonging to a class of administrator, occupying only one place in a larger arrangement by which free people govern themselves. The Persian, however, is not free, and his empire is not a city, but an agglomeration of towns, tribes, and smaller kingdoms aligned by force. To rule such a vast territory, filled with peoples who hardly agree on the principles of mortal governance, requires an authority that is more than a man.

It therefore comes as little surprise that the Persian takes his Great King as the very representative of divinity on earth. Only silk and precious metals ever touch the royal person. Suppliants at his court must dress in garments that are absolutely free of dirt or imperfection. Most are expected to abase themselves in the kingly presence by groveling on the ground; low-ranking persons are forbidden to even look upon him, but have to avert their eyes. Those of higher rank may approach, but are obliged to cover their mouths with their hands, lest the baser spirit of their breath corrupt him. Most favored attendants are permitted to kiss the king on the mouth, but under no circumstances to exhale upon him as they do so.

To Persian eyes, the way the Macedonians treated Alexander was an offense to Heaven. One does not stride up to a king in one's filthy riding clothes and slap him on the back. Nor does one smile at a king, engage him in debate, or share his drinking cup. Seeing these things in Alexander's court, his loyal Persians were disconcerted; Alexander, to his credit, understood that his legacy depended on cultivating the loyalty of Macedonian and Persian alike. In this way he transcended the teachings of Aristotle, who bid him to maintain a double standard in his treatment of Greek and barbarian. Alexander, being of far more practical mind, foresaw that Persian anger at what they took as disrespect would redound not on him, but on the other Macedonians, and manifest in rebellion as soon as his subjects were out of his immediate presence.

Aeschines has described how Alexander began to take on some of the trappings of Persian kingship. In consultation with Bagoas and Hephaestion, he adapted elements of the Persian court ritual to his purposes, such as accepting the prostration of his native ministers, and kissing them on the mouth. He also intended to inaugurate prostration among his officers. This practice, which would be fiercely resented by some, was to be introduced slowly, in stages, and never to the obsequious extreme typical of the Asians. At first, it was purely optional—those Macedonians and Greeks who went down and touched their foreheads to the floor were especially well received by Alexander, who was then disposed to look favorably on whatever they came to report or suggest. It is perhaps not surprising that the more junior of the officers understood right away what was expected of them, and prostrated themselves without outward reservation. Something similar was true of the more conniving politicians, who understood that prostration would be an easy way to gain an advantage over their court rivals. The men who loved Alexander most, such as Hephaestion, likewise strove to set an example for the others.

The greatest resistance, however, remained among Alexander's senior officers. These were the men who had fought with him since he took the throne, who had helped bind up his wounds, and had drunk with him since he was old enough to hold a cup. For them, to

risk their lives to conquer one despot, just to make another of a man they had known since he'd worn short
pants, was too much. They took no notice of subtle en-
couragements to abase themselves. Far from understanding the sensitivities of the Persian courtiers, they
were contemptuous of them.

One of these men was Cleitus, son of Dropidas. Part
of a family that had long served the Macedonian court,
he led the very cream of the Cavalry Companions, the
so-called "All Royals," and was a formidable warrior.
You recall that he saved the King's life at the Granicus,
when he struck down a Persian horseman with a bead
on Alexander's neck. More than twenty years the
King's senior, he was the sort of warhorse who was not
about to grovel before anyone. His tendency to a certain brittleness of temperament, especially while
drinking, had earned him the sobriquet of "Black Cleitus."

The mutual respect Alexander and Cleitus bore for
the other at first kept their disagreement over prostration from becoming a matter of contention. The King
had more or less publicly designated him as the new
governor of Bactria—a plum post that had the additional virtue of hustling Cleitus's stiff back out of his
court. But overindulgence in wine was a vice the men
shared, and it nearly became the undoing of both.

The quarrel began when, at the latter reaches of a
drinking party, Ptolemy suggested that Alexander
should be deified because, even at a young age, he had
already exceeded the achievements of his divine heroes—Achilles, the Dioscuri, and Heracles. Callisthenes begged to disagree.

"No man merits such honors while alive, when, for

all his miraculous feats, Heracles was not made a god until he was dead."

"The Pharaohs of Egypt are recognized in life as the divine sons of Zeus-Ammon, though all were clearly lesser men than Alexander," observed Hephaestion.

Callisthenes, who had the defect of retaining far too much sophistic skill deep into his cups, replied that a distinction must be made between divinity for purely ceremonial purposes, such as for the maintenance of the Pharaohs, and deification for the feats of some individual, as was initially proposed for Alexander.

Hephaestion shook his head. "Still, it is absurd to claim that some plump Egyptian effete is entitled to divine honors, but Alexander is not."

"And besides, I *am* Pharaoh, am I not? And I am not plump—yet!" interjected the King, making light of the dispute, so that everyone laughed with him. This seemed to close the discussion, and fortunately so, as the tender subject of prostration still hung in the air, perceived by all but unmentioned.

But Ptolemy would not let the matter drop.

"At the very least, we may all agree that Alexander has far exceeded the works of his father!"

He added that it was Alexander, after all, that had broken the hitherto undefeated Theban Sacred Band at Chaeronea, so that even at Philip's greatest victory, it was his son who merited the greater part of the glory. Alexander smiled at this, waving his hand to dismiss it, but made no clear disavowal. With that signal the more gross flatterers at the table, fearing Alexander had been insulted by arguments against his divinity, all rushed to extol the King's feats of conquest, and to declare poor old Philip's achievements as small change, really quite unremarkable. When I say "all," I include myself, though by that time I was so lubricated I would have agreed to anything.

At this point Black Cleitus slammed his drinking cup to the table. Looking first to me, he declared that foreigners who had tasted defeat at Philip's hand should be the last to belittle him. The same applied to the son who owed his very throne to his father.

"I have served with both," Cleitus went on, with stunning indiscretion, "and I can tell you that there is no comparison. Philip waged war and won against free Greeks who fought for their very homes, gods, families. Not mercenaries in the pay of painted, perfumed, pantaloon-wearing orientals!

"Alexander, besides, owes the core of his army, his tactics in melee and in siege-craft, entirely to Philip. Without the fall of Methone, there would have been no Tyre!" Indeed, Cleitus went on, such a superb army would conquer no matter who was in charge. The proof was Antipater's recent battle against the Spartan rebels at Megalopolis, which was fought around the time of Gaugamela. "Imagine that!" mocked Cleitus. "A victory that the Macedonians managed to scrape together without the divine Alexander!"

Now all understood that Black Cleitus, who favored one of those deep Spartan canteens, had drunk more than anybody. He had fallen silent, and though nobody yet dared speak, there was still time for him to make light of it all, as if his insults were mere campfire humor, or at least to dismiss himself for sickness, and have everything forgotten. Alexander, tight-lipped, did not reply to any of it, but governed his outrage, merely summoning his servant to freshen his cup. But

Ptolemy opened his baleful mouth again, and the moment for a reprieve was lost.

"Philip was no great individual warrior, while Alexander exceeds us all in his zeal for battle. Surely our friend will admit as much, will he not?"

Cleitus admitted nothing. "On the contrary," he declared, "if it had not been for this very hand—the one at the end of my arm—the great Alexander would have been dead at the Granicus, and Darius still on his throne at Susa!"

With that, Alexander leapt from his cushion to throttle Cleitus. Hephaestion, Craterus, and Ptolemy held him back, which unfortunately left the drunk to continue his tirade, boasting that perhaps Alexander should prostrate himself to him, given that he owed Cleitus his very life. Alexander was so vexed that he was literally sputtering with rage, begging for a sword to kill the man. Cleitus was rushed out of the room before he could say anything more.

But as it is so common in these kinds of confrontations—the alcoholic kind—one of the parties could not let a bad enough situation rest. The remaining symposiasts had managed to calm Alexander down, edging him away from the table to bed, when Craterus and Ptolemy returned, thinking they had delivered Cleitus to his valet. There was a commotion outside the tent, and Cleitus burst in again—this time without his tunic. Tearing off his undergarments, he commenced to show everyone his gray and sagging testicles.

"Since you prefer men without nuts, Alexander, take those of a true patriot of Macedon!"

This insult rooted everyone to their spots. Unrestrained, Alexander leapt up and took a javelin from a guard. His throw was dead on, piercing his future governor of Bactria through the chest; Cleitus collapsed with his hands still grasping his balls.

So much for the story you all know. What you may not have heard about, however, is the trouble Alexander endured from the other side—from Persians and Medes who objected violently to what they saw as the rank disrespect of their King by wine-soaked brutes like Cleitus. I am thinking in particular of a Persian noble named Rathaeshtar, who had estates in Pisidia and fought with distinction on behalf of the Great King at the Granicus. Before Issus, he switched allegiance to Alexander, albeit at great personal risk to himself. Rathaeshtar was invaluable in providing information about Persian tactics, and about the lay of the country around the Cilician Gates. At Issus, he led his armored cavalry beside Alexander's, and proved his valor by coming away with a shoulder wound. The King was very pleased with this Persian, for he had exactly the skills and the spirit Alexander would need to help his kingdom endure. That he would receive a choice governorship was a certainty.

All that ended when Rathaeshtar saw something he didn't like at court. Before witnesses, old Cleitus not only failed to prostrate himself before the Lord of Asia, but, in a fatherly but ill-timed gesture, *patted Alexander's back*. The Persian bidded his time while in the King's tent, though no doubt seething within, and confronted Cleitus when he left. Though I did not see it, I am told that Cleitus laughed and waved Rathaeshtar aside. When the Persian pressed his complaint, Cleitus shoved the man and drew his sword. At this point a fight was inevitable: the honor of Persian nobility, which was their greatest possession, could permit no other end. Rathaeshtar held his scimitar, but as his shoulder was not healed from the wound he got defending Alexander at Issus, he could not lift it. That their duel was not a fair match did not restrain Cleitus. With his opponent standing defenseless, the old general cut him down without a second thought. He then wiped his sword on the clothes of the dead man, spat on the body, and went off for a good meal in the officer's mess. At the table, he boasted and mocked the funeral rites of the Persians.

"He's as dead as Cyrus the Great! Better get the dog food!"

Alexander was furious when he heard the news. But since Rathaeshtar met his end on a dispute of honor between two officers, he could do nothing then to punish Cleitus. I leave it to you to decide whether this incident has any bearing on what occurred later.

XIII

Alexander was as sentimental a drunk as Cleitus was an angry one. Blaming himself for his quarrel with his old companion, he wept openly as they led him to his bed. Nor did his dejection lift when his head cleared: his army was unnerved to hear the bitter sobs of the King of Asia through the tent fabric for three whole days, bewailing the loss of his faithful right arm, begging the forgiveness of Cleitus's sister Lanice, who was once Alexander's wet nurse. "You lent me your sweet breast, and see how I've repaid you, with the death of your very own brother!" he cried. When gently reminded of the public duties of his kingship, he refused to appear before anyone, saying that a murderer of his friends deserved no crown.

He ate and drank nothing. Most worrying, the local tribes between the Oxus and the Jaxartes rivers were in open revolt, using raiding tactics to harass Macedonian garrisons. Informed of these attacks, which usually provoked him to immediate action, Alexander only sank into a deeper state of immobility.

Aeschines is correct to say that we all feared for his sanity. It is also true that Hephaestion was beside himself with worry, and that Bagoas attempted, but failed, to lift the King out of his funk. It was interesting to me that another person who might have helped, the divine Thais, did not make an appearance at this desperate hour. By that time she was already adorning the tent of Ptolemy, who came to me for the first time as a supplicant.

"We want you to go to him, because he has an affinity for scribblers."

"Thais might do better."

Ptolemy ignored this suggestion, but went on somewhat darkly. "We still need him. Go now."

Of the precise identity of "we," and the nature of their need, I chose not to ask, but did what I was told.

For my part, I truly believed Alexander would harm himself. For the first time, then, I built up in his mind the idea that he was not only a god, but that he partook of the prerogatives of Zeus himself. Maybe this is what Aeschines is basing his story upon—he gets it so wrong it is hard to tell—for we did not speak throughout the day, but for less than an hour, and I did not meet with him before Sisygambis did, but after.

I began by alluding to Hesiod, who describes the goddess of justice—Dike—as the companion of Alexander's divine father, Zeus. Where justice points out the crookedness in a man's heart, the Father deals out retribution. But would it not be implausible, I suggested, if the King of Heaven merely did what Dike told him to do, without expecting any service rendered to him in return? Clearly, Dike sits at Zeus's right hand not only to dictate, but to watch and heed the acts of the god. It is those acts that are the very standards by which justice is measured. It can only be agreed, then, that a king's acts must become just, simply because he has done them.

Alexander looked askance at me.

"Tell me plainly what you are saying, Machon. Do you think me entitled to murder my friends?"

"I suggest that is not the way to think of it."

"The murder?"

"Your privileges have nothing to do with who you are, personally. Think of Darius. . . . What sort of man was he? Yet to the Persians he was the pillar holding up the vault of the sky. Someone must set the limits who is not submerged by them. Otherwise . . ."

"Otherwise?"

"The men around you will drown."

Alexander sat up on the cushions. Those eyes, so wide set they seemed to be staring at me from around both sides of a corner, fixed on me with a peculiar sadness.

"I believe, my dear Machon, that you will come to regret making this argument to me."

"By my oath to my countrymen, I can offer you only the truth," I said.

"So be it then."

At the risk of seeming to magnify my influence, it did appear that from this point Alexander fought with a new ferocity. With his base at Maracanda, he waged a war of extermination against his enemies. The natives there had little taste for pitched battle, but instead bled the Macedonians white by attacking Alexander's garrisons, supply caravans, and foundations. One chieftain in particular, Spitamenes, led a clever campaign of raids that tied down a Greek army ten times the size of his own. All but the largest con-

centrations of troops were targets: in a disaster that
was never reported to the rest of the army, Spitamenes's cavalry slaughtered two thousand Foot Companions and three hundred cavalry at the Zeravshan
River. But such losses cannot be hidden for long. The
Macedonians began to whisper of a war that would
never end.

Alexander was comprehensively cruel in his
reprisals. As a matter of policy, all the males of any
town or village suspected of aiding Spitamenes were
slaughtered. The Macedonians sent out small groups
of mobile raiders who saw little success against Spitamenes, but were very good at terrifying the defenseless. Food stores were appropriated or destroyed,
fields burned, families scattered. When Alexander at
last marched for the Indus it was because he left little
intact behind him. Spitamenes himself was finally betrayed and murdered, just as Darius and Bessus had
been in their turn.

The chiefs of Sogdia were particularly contemptuous of any central authority, due in large part to their
possession of several rock-cut fortresses that had never
been taken by storm. The biggest of these was known
simply as the Rock of Sogdia—a great stone pinnacle
five stades high, with sheer walls and a snow-capped
peak. The fortress of the chief, Oxyartes, was chiseled
into the Rock, with no approach except along a narrow
ledge. It had never been attacked by the Persians,
much less taken. For this reason alone Alexander
burned to make it his.

When the Macedonians arrived, Alexander was
visited by emissaries of the Sogdian chief, cheekily demanding to know why the Greeks had violated *his*—that

is, Oxyartes's—territory. Alexander, through his interpreter, demanded the surrender of the Rock, on pain of death for all upon it. At this, the emissaries examined the backs of the Macedonians, as if assuring themselves of some fact.

"What are you doing?" the King asked them.

"You appear to have no wings," they replied, "so your threats mean nothing to us!"

This remark reminded Alexander of the arrogance of the Tyrians, before he humbled their city. He told the emissaries to prepare their defenses for a siege. They laughed at him, asking what rock ever needed preparation to resist the wind? The fortress, they pointed out, was too high to be troubled by catapults or missile weapons of any kind. It was also blessed with abundant snowmelt and enough supplies to outlast a twenty-year assault. Alexander reminded them of similar boasts at Tyre and Gaza. The emissaries' reply was a final insult, suggesting a place for the Macedonians to encamp that was sheltered from driven snow in the winter and received cool breezes in the summer—"for your pride will keep you here a very long time," they assured him.

The army made camp—but not in the place the Sogdians suggested—and Alexander rode out with his officers to scout the best point to commence the assault. They had ridden around the Rock for quite some time before realizing they had already made a complete circuit without finding a single weakness. As they stood there, they felt a tingling sensation, as if a light rain was falling on them. The sky, however, was cloudless. Looking more closely, they saw the source of the "rain"—the Sogdians had lined up on the walls of their fortress. They had their robes lifted, and they were pissing on the Macedonians below.

Riding away some distance, Alexander wiped his face with a rag. "Find me a fast way onto that Rock," he said. "Whatever it costs."

The generals conferred through the night. They considered elevating their catapults on towers, or building an enormous ramp for their battering rams. But such massive constructions would mean bringing in soil and timber from great distances, as the ground in the area was barren. The Sogdians' insults, moreover, had set Alexander in such a rage that his patience was spent.

There was time for only one solution. A call went out in the camp for those most practiced in rock climbing. To the three hundred men who responded, Alexander promised the princely sum of ten talents to each who reached the top of the Rock; once at the summit, they were to make as loud a racket as they could, so that the Macedonians and the Sogdians would know they were there. To speed their progress, Alexander made sacrifice to Hermes the Messenger, and to the mountain itself, as a precaution.

The attackers set out after dark, each equipped with sets of sharp iron stakes, hammers, rope, and two days' rations. In theory, the stakes would be driven into whatever soil or ice the men would find; in practice, as climbers rose higher, they found themselves pounding rods into solid rock. Well may we imagine their terror as they clung to the sheer wall, equally afraid to go up or down, forced to witness their comrades slipping and falling around them. As the sun set on the first day of the ascent, the survivors secured themselves by whatever method they could, some by tying ropes around themselves, others simply by wedging their arms or legs into tight places. The lucky ones were able to sleep; the unlucky, in their exhaustion and paralysis, slipped from their places and died. The cold tortured all of them, until many gave up and released their holds. The remains of some who fell were never found.

The survivors later reported that they had the same dream that desperate night: as they hugged the wall for their very lives, all were visited by a beautiful oread. The nymph, who was naked except for a sheen of the clearest ice on her body, seemed to float before them on a breeze blowing up from the base of the Rock. Using no words, she somehow communicated to each man that he should take hold of her shining hair, which fell to her waist and was garlanded with mountain flowers. Many of the climbers at first hesitated to do so, as she seemed so light as to flutter in the air before them, but were seized by such a temptation to embrace the lovely girl that they abandoned their toeholds and threw themselves upon her. Entangled in this slender form, they suddenly imagined they could sense the veins of water pounding deep in the Rock, hear the tender mosses calling to them from the hillsides, and feel themselves carried to a place much higher on the wall, where they were planted with a kiss. And when they awoke, they found themselves clinging to the exact spot where they had dreamt the oread had lifted them.

By the dawn of the second day there was a great clamor at the summit of the Rock. Looking up from their camp, the Macedonians saw that most of the climbers were now on a ledge high above the fortress, waving their arms and rejoicing. The Sogdians, for their part, were greatly disturbed by this spectacle, for in their ignorance they believed that Alexander had indeed recruited soldiers with wings, and that the flying Macedonians were not thanking the gods for their mere survival, but preparing to attack. Though the climbers had no weapons, and were pitifully few in number, the Sogdians were defeated by their fears.

The abrupt surrender of the Rock came as a great relief to us. It was also a momentous example for the neighboring chiefdoms, who might have entertained thoughts that they might hold out against Alexander. The King, hoping to discourage such ambitions with a judicious show of kindness, restrained his impulse to punish Oxyartes for his arrogance. The chief was allowed to retain nominal sovereignty over his lands. Oxyartes, in turn, invited Alexander to provision himself from the stores he had laid up in his fortress, which were so prodigious that he could supply the entire Macedonian army several times over. At this, Alexander privately savored his good fortune, for the Sogdian emissaries had not exaggerated about withstanding a twenty-year siege.

When he surrendered his redoubt, Oxyartes did it with such gracious good humor that the Macedonians were much charmed. He offered an inexhaustible supply of food, wine, and feminine companionship. Alexander, to whom gift-giving was as serious a matter as warfare itself, matched this largesse with presents of gold and silver from the treasury at Persepolis. Oxyartes took the baubles, of course, but with the slightest air of disdain for such useless things, preferring in his turn to give weapons, horses, and provisions. Alexander pretended not to need these things either, and so the competition went on for some time, with the subordinates on each side benefiting far more than either of the two leaders.

In this part of Asia it was considered proper for fathers publicly to advertise the charms of their unmarried daughters. It was on such an occasion, performing a dance for the royal Companions in the reception hall of the chief, that Alexander first saw Rohjane. With her two sisters, she wore a finer version of the formal Sogdian men's costume, with a knee-length, brocaded jacket of silk, a tightly cinched belt, and narrow trousers with the cuffs stuffed into leather boots. A cone-shaped headdress covered her head, with the tip deliberately bent forward. (The tip, it was said, had to be bent just so or the whole effect was ruined.) In their dance the girls held swords, which they swung and skipped over in unison. Rohjane's mannish clothes notwithstanding, lines of plaited blond hair swept down from the bottom of her cap, belying any possibility that she was anything but a woman. The playful Sogdians were amused at the spectacle of girls imitating warriors—a joke that was lost on the Macedonians, who had very proper ideas about this sort of thing. Alexander had eyes only for Rohjane.

In their lack of imagination, some rhapsodizers have described Rohjane as "the second most beautiful woman in Asia"—that is, the most beautiful after Stateira. For the record, I don't know if she was the second most beautiful woman in Asia, or perhaps in Sogdiana alone, or just in the Macedonian camp. What ignorance to assume that mere beauty had any influence on Alexander, who had grown up immersed in the occupations and pleasures of men! Having been there at the time, I can attest that her appearance had less to do with it than her other charms. It could have been the way she tilted her head in the dance, for instance, or the play of slight creases around her mouth when she smiled, or the way she kissed the air as she disappeared behind the curtain.

Of what the heart wants, there is no accounting. Straightaway Alexander called to Oxyartes, asking for Rohjane to join him for a drink. Surprised, the chief asked if the King did not mean her elder sister. No, replied Alexander, he meant Rohjane. At this point the chief turned white—his reluctance was obvious, though everyone assumed it had to do with disposing of his daughters in the proper order, eldest first. In retrospect, I am not so sure this was the reason. For it was not paternal propriety that showed on the face of genial Oxyartes, but apprehension, perhaps even fear for his powerful but ignorant guest. But he was in no position to refuse.

The King spent an anxious few minutes waiting for the girl to return, suffering in silence the inanity of an argument between Craterus and Perdiccas. The former argued that man always gives away the fact that he is a prostitute by the timbre of his farts. Perdiccas, showing his prudence, denied that buggery had any such effect. They went back and forth on this question for some time, until the curtain to the women's quarters rustled, and Alexander told them to shut up.

Rohjane came out in a different outfit this time. Her legs were covered by loose-fitting chintz trousers belted above her waist. Around her shoulders she had a short jacket of gold-embroidered green velvet left unfastened at the front, and a silk shawl. Her chest was entirely uncovered except for a plum-colored handkerchief that hung from her neck. This thin garment did little to conceal her shape as she moved, bewildering the otherwise delighted guests.

She strode toward Alexander on green leather shoes with built-up heels. Her every step was accompanied by the music of tinkling jewelry. When she bowed, her hair fell in curled disarray around her cheeks—a display that seemed to intrigue all the men, who rarely saw ungirt long hair among the respectable women of Macedon. There was a slight smile on her face, as if she were savoring some joke only she had heard.

Still, for all her undeniable attractions, she could not match the bounteous presences of Thais or Stateira. Her charm lay more with her quickness of mind. That, and her unaccountable confidence, for she was nothing more than a minor chief's daughter, on display at the request of the conqueror of the Persian Empire, and she showed no fear at all. In this she reminded me of someone whom I could not remember at that moment.

In trying to recall whom, I was distracted from the conversation that followed, and can only remember a few lines.

"King Alexander wishes to speak with you," Oxyartes said.

"So I supposed. Well, King Alexander, speak!" she replied, in a heavily accented Greek identical to her father's.

"Rohjane!"

"I would speak," said Alexander, "except that I am struck dumb."

"What a pair we are, then. You are struck dumb, and I am commanded to be."

Alexander looked at her with those eyes, which were not easy to withstand. Rohjane returned his stare, until he smiled, and she finally blushed, looking away. And with that, the bargain was sealed.

The next day they were married. According to Sogdian custom, Rohjane was not required to be present, but only her father. Alexander was presented with a loaf of bread, which he cut in half with a ritual sword passed down from the time of Oxyartes's earliest forebears. Half the bread went to the father, and half to the husband, and when they both ate, the union was made.

The most remarkable thing about the wedding was not the ritual, but the differing expressions on the faces of the bride's and groom's parties. The Sogdians, of course, were unanimiously delighted. The Macedonians, including Hephaestion, Craterus, Ptolemy, Perdiccas and Parmenion, could not have made their discomfort more obvious. To them, the marriage was nothing less than a disaster. Naturally, as her conqueror, Alexander had every right to take the girl into his bed in any fashion he wished. He was free to spawn a whole nest of bastards by her. But it was unthinkable that he would actually *marry* a girl of such minor status. No doubt they were also troubled by the possible implications of a "Queen Rohjane"; the powers behind the throne were crowded enough without adding a new, unpredictable player to the game. These suspicions no doubt had something to do with her cool reception among the Macedonians, as Aeschines has described. Is it any wonder, then, that I sought to

increase the Athenians' influence over the court by be-
friending her? To my mind, it would have been negli-
gent not to have taken the opportunity.

Of Alexander's thinking on this matter I can say
nothing for sure. He never discussed it with me, and
met my eyes only once during the ceremony. There
was a petulant defiance in them, as if his decision to
marry was supposed to make a point. How godlike he
was in his impetuosity, in his contempt for consequences, he seemed to be telling me. How much like
Zeus, who never let the inferiority of his mortal conquests frustrate his pleasure.

It was then, just after the wedding, after Rohjane
was led out in her semibarbarous wedding gown of
kidskin and fox fur, and presented her cheek for her
husband to kiss, that I remembered the person of
whom she most reminded me.

It was Olympias.

Speaking of his minor conquests, there is another I
must mention, though my time is short. I feel compelled to describe it because it will never appear in the
public histories, or if it does, it will only be as an un-
confirmed story that the reader may believe or not according to his prejudices. I tell you now it did happen,
in just the way I will describe it.

Just north of the Oxus river, the Macedonians came
upon a small village. As the army approached, a dep-
utation came out to greet it wearing Greek dress, and
speaking in an Ionian Greek dialect. In Alexander's
presence they declared that they were Milesians of the
clan Branchidae. At this, Callisthenes struck his head
in wonder. For these, he declared, had to be the very
descendants of the priestly clan of the Branchidae who

had once tended the sacred precincts of Apollo at Didyma. He was about to say more—but bid the King first to order the Milesians out of earshot.

When they were far enough away, he explained, "During the Ionian revolt against the Great King one hundred and fifty years ago, the priests surrendered the sanctuary to the Persians. To spare them the fate they deserved from their countrymen, Darius the Great removed the Branchidae from Ionia and allowed them to resettle in Sogdiana, far out of reach of retribution. Or so we all thought. . . ."

Alexander, not wishing to alarm his guests, called them back and told them that he would camp near their town for the night. The next day, he said, he would return to them with an announcement.

As the betrayal of the Branchidae was foremost a crime against the people of the city of Miletus, Alexander decided to put the question of punishment to them. That evening, the King called a meeting of all the Milesians in his army. These numbered less than a hundred, but came from all divisions of his force, from cavalry officers to Hypaspists to archers to quartermasters and engineers. In truth, it was quite a sight to see all these men, in their widely varying uniforms but common manner of speaking, wrestle with this dilemma. One man, a phalangite, argued for the punishment of the adult males.

"There is only one fate befitting traitors," he declared, "whether they be father, son, or grandson. What good would any sacred oath be, such as the one the Branchidae once took, if they could light out to foreign lands, and avoid all responsibility for their acts? It would be unfortunate for the women and children to lose their fathers, but their ancestors took this risk when they Medized. Any other course would invite Apollo's displeasure."

Some cheered this statement. Another man, an engineer, rose to disagree.

"One fate for traitors, of course! But these are not the traitors. They are not even the grandsons of the traitors. They are innocents one hundred and fifty years removed from the sins of another generation. The sons of many cities that Medized are with us today, including a fair number of Thessalians! Shall we punish our own comrades too?"

And the debate went on like this for some time, with a vigor that would have done credit to deliberations in our own Assembly. When the King asked for a voice vote, there was no clear majority for mercy or the sword. When the men were asked to raise their hands, the company was split down the middle.

"Damnable indecision!" cried Alexander. "You are all dismissed, then—your King will take the burden upon himself."

What he would do was not clear, as he had shown no bias toward either side in the debate. I did note a crease of agony on his face when the engineer alluded to the descendants of Persian collaborators in the army: Alexander's predecessor a century and a half earlier—also named Alexander—had sent Xerxes tokens of water and earth, emblems of Macedon's submission. Perhaps what followed had more to do with expiating this sin than any crime the Branchidae had committed.

The next morning the King went into the village with two guards. Upon arrival his small escort was surrounded by children bearing garlands for them to wear. Decorated with blooms of anemone, asphodel, and gorse, the Macedonians were led by little hands to the village elder chosen by the rest of the Branchidae to represent them. When Alexander arrived the old man was on his knees weeding his flower beds. His host gave a little cry of surprise when he looked up to see the Lord of Asia at his garden gate.

"Welcome! You were expected, but I see the children found you first. So sorry I didn't see you come . . . the hyacinths are such jealous mistresses! My name is Achilles."

Alexander could not answer at first. He was noticeably rattled by the presence of the children, and the fact that his host had the same name as one of the ancestors he so publicly revered. When he opened his mouth and nothing came out, Achilles gestured back toward his garden.

"Many of these flowers came with us from our old home. The hyacinth is sacred to Apollo. We try to keep the old ways here, but, as you must imagine, it is difficult in such a strange land!"

"Yes, one would think," the King answered.

The old man gave the king a short tour of his handiwork. The Macedonians were aloof, stone-faced, until the sweet perfume of the flowers began to work on them. The guards told me that the fragrance reminded them very much of the hills and meadows of their home near Lyncestis, northwest of Pella. Alexander, too, seemed affected by memories of home as he followed the house-proud Achilles. The weight seemed to lift from his shoulders; he began to ask gardening questions.

"You know, in my years I think I've done every kind of work there is to do in this village. But nothing gives me as much pleasure as this piece of ground," said Achilles.

To which the King made an abrupt, bizarre declaration: "If I were not Alexander, I would tend a garden!"

Achilles nodded as if this made complete sense.

"There is a story that the temple at Didyma is surrounded by great hyacinths three feet tall, and in every color! I have never seen it, so don't know whether to believe such stories."

"You should . . . though the sanctuary is not what it once was. . . ."

The talk of Didyma returned the subject to what Alexander had come to announce. His face hardened, and he turned away from Achilles' pleasant beds. Yet he could not deliver an indictment with his neck draped with flowers and the naive eyes of the children looking up at him. Instead, he bid Achilles a sudden good-bye, turned on his heel, and rushed away. When he was out of sight of the village, he tore the garlands from his neck and threw them on the ground.

At camp, he disappeared into his tent and was not seen for the rest of the day. By the evening, Peithon was summoned, and left with an impassive expression on his face. I dogged him for information, but the frigid fellow would not divulge what Alexander had ordered him to do.

Before dawn the next morning, and in complete silence, nine hundred Foot Companions encircled the village of the Branchidae. For the occasion they had left their pikes stacked outside their tents and carried only their short swords.

The killing began that day with no warning—no rebuke, no recitation of the crimes of their ancestors. Most of the people were cut down as they fled their houses, and the ones that stayed inside were driven out by fire. How can I describe the screams to you? The cries of men in agony you have all heard, in battle. But have you heard how a mother sounds when her children are murdered before her eyes? It is an inhuman thing, something between a groan and a shriek. All the Macedonians in the village, and those lying idle in the camp a short distance away, heard it for all too long, as Branchidae of all ages were pried, dug, or coaxed from their hiding places. I saw it with my own eyes as I came around to watch from the wooded side of the village. I saw fathers go down fighting against three and four assailants; I saw an entire family, parents and three children, stumble out of their burning house with the flesh melting from their bones. I saw soldiers with tears in their eyes cut the soft throats of infants and lay them down in the street, as if to sleep.

You should not suppose it was easy for the men ordered to perform this labor. Hacking and stabbing many human bodies to death takes a steady hand; for a soldier with a family at home, murdering innocents is an implicit betrayal of every rationale used to excuse a life at war. After the deed was done, these Foot Companions, all hardened veterans of the third *lochos* of Peithon's battalion, were useless for any further duty. Many of them seemed reduced to shades, with their eyes perpetually fixed on some distant place, as if they somehow might see beyond the images that appeared unbidden in their minds. Their comrades avoided the pollution that adhered to them. Alexander took pity on these men, dismissing them from Maracanda with a talent each and a personal send-off from their King. Peithon himself, I should add, showed no ill effect from leading an action that ruined so many of his men.

The bodies—more than two hundred of them—were collected and dumped into a pit in the woods. When that was done, the heavy work began: an entire battalion under Coenus was commanded to come in and remove all evidence of human habitation. This meant more than just leveling the buildings. Everything, including the foundation blocks, the fence posts, the paving stones, the roots of the trees in the orchards, was ripped from the ground. The remaining holes were filled in, and disguised with leaves and soil. Hundreds of men spent days smoothing over the plow furrows in the fields. Nothing that betrayed the existence of the Branchidae was left, whether a scrap of lumber or a single olive or a child's footprint on the ground.

The work included the destruction of several small altars to Apollo and Zeus. This task drew the most resistance, and Perdiccas was forced to apply harsh discipline to see it done. Alexander, for his part, said that his father Zeus had vouchsafed his permission for the act. He said this several weeks later, at Maracanda, when he welcomed others to drink with him again. Still thinking of what I had seen, I sat with him all night, and managed to be the last to leave when the sun came up. But he raised his hand when I opened my mouth to speak.

"I know what you want to say, Machon. But before you say anything remember what you told me after Cleitus died. Remember that I warned you."

It was true that he had warned me. But the principle of the consolation I offered was not to license any outrage at all, but only justice. To my discredit, I did not insist on this distinction, but remained silent as he rose from his cushions and dragged himself into the gloom of his apartment. Nor did I raise the issue again during any of the eventful months that followed. Perhaps it was fear that shut my mouth, perhaps ignorance of what he might do. That I kept this silence I accept as my greatest offense. If that was Aeschines's charge against me here, I would not dispute it.

Let me say this: having watched the bitter work of that day, I have impeached myself in ways none of my enemies will ever know. The nights were most difficult, after the camp had settled down. That was when, in my dreams, the wind moaning over some nameless Asian peak became the dismal plaint of the Branchidae mothers. I awoke. Fretting, I threw aside the tent flap to lose myself in chatter with the guards. Once only I longed to put the question to some low-ranking son of an Orestan farmer: should a dangerous child like Alexander be allowed to grow up? Should we all run the risk of letting him look his nature in the face? Or are we all safer keeping him as pliant as a child—or just as well, as a god? I wonder what the guard would have said. Craterus's description of Arridaeus in the temple of Heracles returned to me: He is not unhappy. He thinks he is divine.

Unwilling ever to accept defeat, Alexander raised the blighted issue of prostration again. Low-ranking functionaries were simply ordered henceforward to grovel in Alexander's presence. But prostration would never become the custom unless the superordinate

Macedonians and Greeks—the generals and philosophers and diplomats from the mainland cities—also
accepted it. Alexander, being anxious to avoid a confrontation like that with Black Cleitus—but also determined to display the kind of evenhandedness that
would ensure the loyalty of his Persian subjects—
looked to his loyal Hephaestion for help with this
problem. Together they hatched a plan that would in-
troduce the practice in a more cunning fashion.

On the occasion of a dinner party, Alexander let it
be known that those who performed prostration
would earn the privilege of receiving a kiss from the
King's mouth. This offer, to receive a special favor for
their abasement, was enough to convince the great majority of the Macedonians to succumb at last—Alexander was pleased to watch them all come before him
one by one, touch their foreheads to the carpet, and
come forward for their kisses, which the King gladly
offered on the lips. All of his Companions came—
Leonnatus, son of Anteas; Lysimachus, son of Agatho-
cles; Perdiccas, son of Orontes; Ptolemy, son of Lagus.
Of the generals, the single exception was Parmenion,
who had contrived to be off on some self-appointed
business. The Persians who were present, including
old Artabazus and Arsaces, the new satrap of Media,
were pleased by this show of respect for the traditional
custom. All was proceeding well—until it was Callisthenes's turn to approach the dais.

Taking his opportunity when Alexander was busy
talking with Hephaestion, Callisthenes sauntered up
for his kiss without prostrating himself. Alexander
would have bussed the nephew of Aristotle anyway,
until Peithon piped up that Callisthenes had not gone

down as everyone else had, and so had not earned a kiss. Alexander turned his head away from the puckered lips of the sophist, who merely shrugged and launched into a dangerous peroration, the essence of which was the following.

"I suppose I am out of a kiss. But I think it wise to keep the distinction we Greeks make between men and gods. Have we all not seen the wages of dishonoring the true divinities, as the jealousy of Dionysus led to the death of our friend Cleitus? Might mortal men, even those of the bravest and most noble character, simply wait for the sanction of the Pythian Oracle at Delphi for their divine honors, as Heracles did after he died? Indeed, it seems foolish to make a custom that the people will never follow, as we all know the Greeks back home will never bow to anyone.

"I for one think too much of this campaign to endanger it with barbarous formalities. I am too loyal to my King to render him into Darius Alexander."

With that, Callisthenes went back to his couch and took up his cup. There was consternation on the faces of the Persian nobles, and purpled rage on Alexander's. The mention of Cleitus galled him particularly, as did the name "Darius Alexander," which had the dangerous potential to stick. But Callisthenes's words were received with some sympathy by the Macedonians, including those who had already consented to prostration. Perceiving this, Alexander swallowed his anger, bidding the party to continue. But he did not forget Callisthenes's insult.

XIV

To have understood Alexander, you need to have hunted with him. This stemmed directly from his father's enthusiasm for killing all kinds of wild beasts. In Philip's time the report of a bear in the vicinity could shut the capital down for days; the mere rumor of a lion anywhere in Macedon was worth keeping peace treaties unsigned and eminent ambassadors waiting. Prince Alexander inherited his taste for the sport, and it came to dominate his thoughts in a way not even his father shared. His curiosity went to such extremes he once had six stags captured, tagged, and released. The tags ordered whomever found a dead animal to report the time and location of its discovery to the palace. In this way the Prince was in a position to turn the tables on Aristotle, lecturing his tutor on the range and longevity of the Macedonian red deer.

With all of Asia at his feet, the scope of Alexander's hunting was unprecedented. Indeed, the entire expedition might be understood as a very long, very expensive hunting trip. Alexander, it should be said, thought little of the practices of the Persian nobility, who would either use the bow on animals trapped in walled game parks, or employ armies of beaters to surround great swaths of territory. Darius was said to have "hunted" in this way, encouched in his golden pavilion while animals of all description were driven toward him. The Great King would then, at his leisure, take as much game as he had arrows to shoot. For his part, Alexander made for open country in the time-honored Macedonian fashion—riding bareback, naked except for a sun hat, armed with a single thrusting spear.

His first challenge was the wild asses of the high plateau of Cappadocia. These were blazingly fast animals, easily able to outrun any horse, with the teasing habit of stopping every few miles to allow hunters to get close before racing out of sight again. After hobbling a number of good mounts chasing them, Alexander noticed that the asses tended to run in great, sweeping circles. This suggested the trick of sending out his men one at a time, with each hunter keeping his quarry on the run until he was replaced by a fresh rider. After just a few stages of these relays the animals collapsed from exhaustion.

On the plains of Arabia were vast numbers of wild ostrich. These were not as fast as the asses, yet far more difficult to catch. They ran in straight lines, holding their wings out as they ran, their feet sending up a blinding trail of dust behind them. Some writers, such as Xenophon, have suggested that they use their wings like ships under sail, but Alexander thought this idea must be wrong, since the birds used their wings irrespective of the strength of the wind. In any case, only a lucky bowshot ever brought one down, and on these rare occasions the meat was red and very tasty, much like the better parts of beef cattle. Some of the men also collected the eggs, using the contents for nourishment and the shells as canteens.

The King found more sport on the riverbanks of Assyria. Though that ancient land was full of people and farms, the population of lions in the southern part of the kingdom had lately been on the rise. The cats achieved this by a degree of organized hunting that defied the natives' attempts to control them. As the new Lord of All Asia, Alexander took it as his personal business to defend his kingdom from all invaders, two-legged or four.

The lions were tracked to their lair in an abandoned estate beside the Tigris. Leading a party of thirty cavalry, Alexander planned his attack as he would against any other hostile tribe. The female cats, who were defending several litters of cubs, made a desperate stand. The lions easily snapped the hunters' cornel-wood spears with their jaws or forelegs; two riders were killed when the cats leaped on the backs of their horses. After some hard fighting with javelins, Alexander and his men carried the field. All the cats were killed, except for two of the males, who made a fine show of their cowardice by swimming the river to escape.

There were other expeditions against exotic game of all kinds. Under the wild pistachios and tamarisks of central Persia they roused giant bustards with wingspans wider than a small temple. By the Indus they stalked wild elephants and hippo. As the army crossed the pass over the Paropamisus, his men starving, Alexander could not resist having a go at the great twirl-horned goats of those mountains. In almost all cases these adventures served to bolster the morale of the men who shared the trail with the King.

The sole and sad exception to this was the instance—during a boar hunt—when the page Hermolaus was foolish enough to deprive Alexander of the final kill. Alexander was furious at this impertinence. Right there in front of the party, he ordered Hermolaus dismounted, stripped of his clothes, and whipped. He even took the crop himself, administering the blows as the Companions, the guides, and the other pages looked on with great embarrassment. All were disturbed both for the humiliated Hermolaus, and for Alexander, who never before treated his pages with anything less than tender forbearance. Yet there he was, wearing a barbarian riding cloak, Persian diadem on his head, horsewhipping one of his countrymen.

Telling Hermolaus that he had lost his privilege to ride a horse, Alexander confiscated his mount for the return to camp. Abandoned, naked in the wilderness, the page was set upon by parties unknown, and his manhood insulted in a way on which I need not elaborate. When he arrived back among the other pages, Hermolaus was hobbled, bloodied, and outraged at what he thought to be Alexander's injustice. No one, however, foresaw the extremities to which the boy's resentment drove him.

In the King's defense, everyone knew that taking the prize in the hunt was serious business. Since their days in Pella, Alexander and Cleitus had waged a running competition on who could accumulate the most kills. The difference this time, I believe, was not that Hermolaus was a lowly page, but that Alexander's patience had greatly diminished since the death of Darius. With every unfamiliar mile, from every new kind of nettle that cut his feet and every drink from a torpid stream that made him sick, the humor drained out of him. This was something the men close to him could see happening by the day. Hermolaus should have seen it, but he had the kind of proud temperament that, in cases like this, lowly pages could not afford.

It was the privilege of the corps of young pages to guard the King's bedchamber as he slept. Often, when indulgence in wine prevented Alexander from reaching his pillow, they physically placed him in his bed. Hermolaus convinced certain of the other boys—namely, Sostratos, son of Amyntas, and Epimenes, son of Arseus—to join him in a plot. At an agreed signal, after the King had gone to bed drunk, they would gather around him when he was most vulnerable, and set upon him with daggers.

Now it so happened that the night they agreed to do the deed Alexander drank very late, coming to bed with the first gray of the morning. It was Hermolaus's turn to sleep at the King's door. Rising, the boy was pleased to see Alexander too intoxicated to walk—but with Bagoas at his side, supporting him with his arm. As he passed Hermolaus, Alexander called to the page, telling him that he was a good lad after all, and that he had been wrong to take his horse from him. Then the King winked at him, and patted him on the cheek, saying that his mount was restored, as long as he didn't "hog the boar" next time. And Alexander proceeded to chuckle at his own feeble pun as Bagoas led him to bed.

This apology took Hermolaus quite by surprise, so that he failed to take Alexander from the eunuch. Instead, he gave the signal belatedly, and the three conspirators were left standing outside the bedchamber, waiting for Bagoas to leave. After an hour of this, they grew nervous that their gathering would attract suspicion, and gave it up.

It was the conspirators' intention to try again the next night, and the next one after that, until their goal was achieved. It was thanks only to the indiscretion of one of their own that the plot was uncovered: Epimenes disclosed it to his bedmate Charicles, son of Menander, who thought the secret would be safe with Eurylochus, son of Arseus, who happened to be Epimenes's brother. He was mistaken, for Eurylochus went straight to the King.

Under torture, certain others were implicated in the plot, most notably including Philotas, son of Parmenion. When Alexander went to the prisoners to demand an explanation for their treachery, none would speak at first. The King promised a merciful death to anyone who would enlighten him, for he was greatly puzzled that those in whom he had placed such trust would cravenly betray him. At this, Hermolaus rose to denounce the King's naivete in posing such a question, when it was clear to all that he had become a tyrant.

"A tyrant? How?" Alexander asked.

Hermolaus described the general outrage at the King's arrogance, his imposition of barbarous customs, and the endless campaign, which shed Greek blood for the sake of one man's bottomless vanity.

"And what have you suffered personally, that you would hate me so?" asked Alexander, with some sadness.

"You are a fool to ask me that," replied Hermolaus.

"Better that you beg Cleitus's pardon, when you see him in Hades."

With that, the other pages were executed by having all their bones broken with stones. What was left of them was then hanged. Aeschines is wrong, however, to tell you that Hermolaus died with them. His end came much later, as I will describe in due course.

Philotas's guilt lay not in taking any active part in the plot, but a tacit one. For it so happened that another of the pages—Anticles, son of Theocritus—had earlier approached him with important news for the King, but that Philotas did not act to secure the boy an audience with Alexander. Though Anticles had not specified that his news involved a plot against Alexander, Philotas's inaction hinted strongly at his complicity. Armed men went to Philotas's tent, placed a bag over his head, and led him away into the night.

Suspicion next fell on Philotas's father, Parmenion. No direct evidence existed against him, yet the execution of his son, and his position in command of his own troops, made him suspect. He had also been heard to make some intemperate remarks that had gotten back to the King. Indeed, the old general was all too honest in his appraisal of Alexander's value to the campaign.

"Arridaeus is responsible for all the generalship," he declared to his staff of yes-men, "while the wisdom and experience of others"—meaning himself—"is the real glue that holds the army together. The time was past for kings to expose themselves to danger in vain cavalry charges. Real soldiers didn't mind if a young king gets all the credit, as long as the boy doesn't believe his own publicity!"

Instead of braggadocio, Parmenion should have had the wisdom of his years. But it was not Alexander who held him to account, but the troika of Ptolemy, Craterus, and Perdiccas. That Parmenion claimed credit for Gaugamela was bad enough. The old man's disclosures about Arridaeus, however, were potentially fatal to all the elaborate legend they had built around the King. If Parmenion got away with it, perhaps Coenus or Peithon or Nearchus might become indiscreet. Worst of all, Callisthenes and Machon might be emboldened to write the truth into their histories!

Even when informed of Parmenion's arrogance, the King was initially reluctant to act against him. Craterus convinced him, however, by playing on his dread of assassination.

"It may be true that Parmenion is innocent so far. But he is proud, and he is popular, and his position is too close to you to take such a risk. You only have this moment to judge him now, but if you pardon him, he will have the rest of his days to conspire against you!"

These and similar absurdities took their toll on Alexander's resolve, until he took refuge in his divine right to wash his hands of all consequences.

Armed messengers went out straightaway, before the news of Philotas's death could reach Parmenion by other means. Alexander had written a dispatch to divert the old general's attention; he was killed as he bent under a lamp to read it.

Parmenion's execution shook the Greek camp. He had, after all, served both Philip and Alexander faithfully for many years. Among other critical tasks, it was he who had overseen the passage of the army across the Hellespont, and anchored the Macedonian left wing at Issus and Gaugamela. His sad end sent reverberations all the way back to Macedon, where old Antipater must have wondered if he was due similar recompense for his long service.

Even Callisthenes was shaken by it. I sincerely believe that he did serve an inspirational role for the pages, though it is a lie to claim that I instigated the charge against him. And what a feat of mendacity to insinuate that I sought to remove a rival by condemning him! Callisthenes's history, after all, is already for sale all over the world, while as Aeschines has so clearly said, I have so far published nothing. So in what way did I benefit from his death?

The prime instigator of Callisthenes's fall was Callisthenes himself. The story went that Hermolaus, before he hatched his plot against the King, came to Callisthenes with a question: which were the heroes esteemed most by the Athenians?

"That would be the Tyrannicides—Harmodius and Aristogeiton."

"And why are the Tyrannicides honored most?" the boy asked.

Callisthenes replied, "Because they freed the people from the state of their oppression."

"And would similar men be welcomed by the Athenians today, and given refuge in their city?"

"They would be given refuge in any city where Greeks dwell," answered Callisthenes, "but most gladly in Athens. For she has always opposed tyranny, from the end of Eurystheus's domination of Greece, when he pursued the children of Heracles into Attica and was defeated there, until recent times."

"Until . . . today?"

"Recent times," said Callisthenes, smiling and saying nothing more.

More serious than the substance of this exchange, Callisthenes had failed to report Hermolaus's sudden interest in tyrant-killers to anyone. On this basis alone, Alexander was prepared to accept his guilt, for the King defined loyalty as much in terms of what was omitted as what was done. Callisthenes's record of public statements against prostration, and against Alexander's divinity, also came back to haunt him, for these insults did not dispose anyone to give him the benefit of the doubt.

Upon his arrest, Callisthenes was brought before the King. Echoing his question to Bessus, Alexander asked, "Why have you betrayed me?"

To which Callisthenes charged, "Why are you betraying history? Do you believe that the boasts of Olympias will assure your fame, Alexander? It is only because of the writings of Callisthenes that the world will know about you!"

After this, the historian disappeared. Some say he was hanged right away, some say stabbed. Still others swear he was clapped in irons and died much later, of despair. But no one is sure.

The weight of endless campaigning, massacre, and deceit began to have its effect on the morale of the men. Those who shared Alexander's symposium likewise faced narrowing options. As the King's wife, Rohjane could not substitute for the unabashed Thais, who was by then more or less a fixture in Ptolemy's tent. The army was by then approaching the Indus—too far for most entertainers to come out from Corinth or Athens. Alexander's pretensions to divinity would not allow him to condescend to the usual subjects of conversation, namely prostitutes, wine, and buggery delivered or received. Instead, his purview shrank to arcana having to do with battlefield equipment, and feats of horsemanship. In other words, he became a bore. Nor, of course, was Callisthenes around to elevate the topics. Matters became so desperate, at last, that the Macedonians were reduced to louche drinking games, such as flinging the dregs of their wine at targets on the floor. The party was desperately ready for something new.

The solution came from the prisoners' stockade. He was an old priest of Zoroaster with an unpronounceable name that we took to sound like "Gobares." He was not a Persian or a Mede, but came from the Hyrcanian region, south of the Caspian Sea. The guards had been surprised to see him proselytize among the enemy prisoners, having wrongly believed that since Darius was Zoroastrian, all the Persians must already have been so. Great crowds formed around him as he disputed with his doctrinal adversaries, with the debates becoming so impassioned that the Macedonians took notice, though few of them spoke Persian, Aramaic, or any of Gobares's other languages. Upon his interrogation and punishment for this troublemaking, it was learned that he had been active in Ionia in years past, and could also speak Greek. This earned him an interview with Alexander, who was curious about the beliefs of the lands he conquered.

He came to the symposium in a simple white cloak with a rude rope tied around his waist. This rope, we learned, was only removed during the act of worship, when it was loosed and tied again to symbolize the

conquest of order over chaos. Of these practices Gobares was eager to speak, as if he expected to convert
some general or even the King himself.

"Our prophet was Zarathustra, son of Pourushaspa,
or 'Zoroaster' to you Greeks. No one knows exactly
when he lived, or where, except that it was at a time
before men worked metals, and in the east. As a young
man he was a priest of the cult of his people. One day,
after he had reached his maturity, he was collecting
haoma-water from the center of a pure running
stream. As he turned to go back to dry ground, he saw
a messenger of Ahura Mazda waiting for him there.
This messenger, whom we call Vohu Manah-the-well-
intended, had the appearance of a mortal man, except
that a pure light like the dawn through a keyhole em-
anated from his eyes and mouth. The messenger led
Zarathustra to the Creator, who told him that because
he was a man of *asha,* or righteousness, he was chosen
to bring the truth of Ahura Mazda to all men. And
Ahura Mazda also informed him of the proper way to
honor Him with prayer, about the ways men of faith
may remain pure, and about the observances the Creator desired men to make throughout the year, so that
they may help Him in his great struggle. . . ."

Though we never asked him to, Gobares then went
into the details of his ritual. The proper observance, he
said, is made five times a day, at midnight, sunrise,
noon, afternoon, and sunset. Most commonly, it is
made by standing before the flame and reciting a short
prayer handed down from the prophet himself. The
prayer is an affirmation of the Creator's power that,
Gobares said, will aid Him in his struggle with the
Hostile Spirit, Angra Mainyu-may-his-name-be-

forever-accursed. It is not recited out of any vain desire
to satisfy the worshipper's needs, but to do the work
of driving evil from Creation, until the day when the
work of the Hostile Spirit has been expunged utterly,
and what he called the "Third Time" begins. As Gobares explained this, he pretended to untie his rope, and
as he spoke of the Hostile Spirit, he snapped the ends
of it, as if he was lashing Angra Mainyu.

His people had many other strange beliefs. They attributed to that single god, Ahura Mazda, the creation
of both the spiritual and physical world. They held
that men would be judged after death for the rightness
of their actions by a great weighing of all they had
said, done, and thought. That is because, according to
the Zoroastrians, good words, deeds, and thoughts are
not the mere private business of individuals, but all
have influence on the universal struggle against disor-
der. If the good side of the scale was heavier the de-
ceased proceeded to a kind of Persian garden, or
pairi-daeza in the old tongue of their prophet. If the bad
side prevailed, the dead person was cast into a chasm
that was like Hades, only worse, where Angra Mainyu
ruled.

At some future time there would come an ultimate
triumph over evil when the bones of the interred dead
would rise up and be reunited with their souls. The
last battle against the minions of the Hostile Spirit
would then be led by the savior named Saoshyant. He
would be a mortal man, but would be born of a virgin
mother after she bathed in a blessed lake containing
Zoroaster's seed. Upon his victory would commence a
Final Judgment, where the resurrected bodies of all
who had ever lived would be forced to swim a river of

molten iron. To the righteous this ordeal would seem like bathing in mother's milk, while the not-so-good would suffer the flesh seared from their bones. The torrent would then wash the rejects down to Hell where they, Angra Mainyu, and all his *daevas* would be finally annihilated. With their destruction would commence the "Third Time," when all the mortals of the earth would consume haoma for the last time, attain immortality, and realize eternal happiness.

Gobares continued: "Zarathustra did not have great success at first in enlightening his neighbors. After years invested in teaching them, all except one rejected the truth. His single success, the first Zoroastrian besides the prophet, was Zarathustra's own cousin. The prophet made many more converts later, when he preached among strangers. Today his truth has been accepted by men from Africa to India and, if I might say, in your country as well."

Craterus was fuming before Gobares was finished.

"Are these the beliefs of adult men, or of children? Really, do you honestly believe that your prayers, personally, will affect the planets in their courses? What arrogance! And do you believe that the gods care for the individual fates of such insignificant creatures as ourselves? What do we care for the fates of ants, though ants are far closer to us than we are to your omnipotent Creator! Really, I'm surprised even Zoroaster's cousin believed him!"

"I have heard these beliefs before, among the Jews in Syria," observed Ptolemy.

"The Jews," replied the unflappable Gobares, "imbibed the teachings of Zoroaster during their captivity in Babylon. When Cyrus the Great allowed them to return to their homelands, they took this wisdom to the west with them."

"Let the Jews and other slaves delude themselves with tales of virgin births and lakes of fire and dead souls rising!" Craterus scoffed.

Alexander took his chin from his hand, where it had been resting as he pondered the implications of what he had heard. We all looked at him when he spoke.

"There is nobility in believing in a just god. Our Olympians are too much reflections of ourselves, are they not? They do not compel us to be good."

"Is compelled good any good at all?" asked Hephaestion.

"Perhaps not. But that does not concern me as much as this: there is no place for my father Ammon in your story, Gobares."

The old man nodded as if to agree. But he was not done.

"Perhaps, O King, you will see something of yourselves in the truth of the Creation. The world began as a thought in the mind of Ahura Mazda, the eternal and uncreated one, and the first manifestation of this thought was a spiritual world. With this stage appeared the spirits of all the beings that would later appear as material things: the spirits of the air and the earth, of the Single Plant and the Single Animal, and of First Man. And because the spirits were not yet admixed with their physical forms, Ahura Mazda's first creation was not subject to flaw. Yet he was not satisfied by the spiritual world, splendid as it was, because in its perfection there could be no change, and without change there could be no virtue. And so Ahura Mazda with his will gave birth to Time, and his son Time, in his turn, begat the Amesha Spentas, the Sacred Immortals.

"Each of these Immortals was responsible for one of the seven lesser Creations. Sky appeared as a great stone sphere into which the second Creation, Water, was poured. And floating upon Water, like the froth strung upon the sea, appeared the Earth. The fourth, fifth, and sixth lesser Creations were the physical manifestations of Single Plant, Single Animal, and First Man, who lived on the earth, and with the blessing of Time, ramified into all the types and tribes we see today. The last and most important Creation was Fire, for it is the link between the two worlds of the Great Creation, through which the spirits may animate the physical bodies while they live."

"And does this wisdom explain why you all wash in cow piss?" interjected Craterus, laughing.

"Upon the completion of Second Creation it was perfect," said Gobares. "But it was also subject to imperfection because it existed as a physical thing. In that instant, before First Man took a single breath, the Hostile Spirit, likewise uncreated, launched his attack. He burst through the stone sphere of the Sky, making the hole we see at those times when the Sun or Moon disappear from view. Plunging down, he landed in the sea, and churned it up with storms, and turned it bitter to taste with the salt of his sweat. And striding out on the Earth, he plucked the Sun from the sky and grazed the land with it, scorching all the many forms of Single Plant. These places are now desert. And places that were not scorched were afflicted by swarms of insects, or the brown of withering, so that the principle of Fire could no longer hold spirit and matter together, or only for a short time in each case. Thus mortality appeared in the world."

"And so," asked Alexander, "may we say that Ahura Mazda ran a risk when he decided to make a material world, because his creation could be attacked?"

"Yes, that is true. Among some *herbads*, or priests, Ahura Mazda is called 'the god who risked.' Yet witness the wonder of His handiwork, as the people of the Good Faith take every one of the Seven Creations to be holy. All water is holy, all metals, all plants and animals, all fire, all men—not just this one plant here, or that one man there. All merit our reverence, and in accord with His revealed word, we take all the world as our temple."

Listening to Gobares, this seemed to me a naive way of thinking, to take everyone and everything to be sacred. If all is worthy of worship then nothing is, I thought. But later I came to observe the basic gentleness of these so-called people of the Good Faith. Their discipline and humility is remarked all around the lands of the Great King. In Babylon I heard a saying that attested to the trust they earned: "Fight by the side of a Greek, eat in the house of a Jew, but sleep under the roof of a Zoroastrian." Their decency is obvious to anyone walking through the narrow alleys of a Persian village. Where in Greek towns we must dodge sewage dumped from windows, Zoroastrian women set pans of embers sprinkled with marjoram on their doorsteps, to perfume the air for all who must breathe it.

"The Great Enemy then visited his predations on First Animal, slaying the Uniquely-created Bull. Angra Mainyu then sought out First Man. He found him sit-

ting in a garden, completely unafraid because he had
never known harm in the unmixed Creation. 'Who are
you?' asked First Man, in his innocence. 'I am a teacher
of a different kind,' replied the Hostile Spirit. And with
that he set upon First Man as his corrupter, appearing
to him as a beautiful woman. First Man, who was curious, approached Woman as a child might, without
fear, as the Hostile Spirit afflicted him with temptation
beyond his experience. Stirred in that way for the first
time, he pushed inside the womb of Angra Mainyu.
The Hostile Spirit made First Man's progress inside
him smooth, like a woman who was willing, but cold
and hard, as if he lay with a figure of polished marble.
In that instant fear was born in First Man. With fear
came doubt. With further generations, doubt feasted
on the minds of men, making them forget the truth of
Ahura Mazda's supremacy. Some of these doubters
became the agents of the Hostile Spirit. Corrupted,
they are what we call the *daevas*."

"The *daevas*—we've heard of them already."

"You've heard of them and seen them. For the
daevas are everywhere, in every form. In ancient times,
and in ignorant lands today, they are worshipped as
gods. They exist only to thwart wisdom. Where there
is peace, they bring tumult. Where there is order, they
bring caprice. You may know them by their fires, for
smoke is the degradation of fire, and the haze that follows in their train. They are the soldiers of Angra
Mainyu."

A different expression appeared on Gobares's face
as he described these acolytes of ruin. For the first
time, his tranquility abandoned him, and he stared in-

tently downward, as if trying in vain to temper the force of his condemnation.

"Gentlemen, I think we've been insulted!" I said.

"I know we have been," agreed Ptolemy.

"Eminences, I assure you I meant no offense."

Craterus, rising on uncertain legs, glowered over the priest.

"This is a dog that must be beaten!"

With that, he called for a riding crop. But as a slave went out to fetch one, Bagoas seized his chance to speak up, appealing to Alexander:

"Lord, let me be the one to thrash the priest! I have had the privilege before, in the garden of the Medan palace of Ecbatana, after the *dahmobed* of the temple breathed his rue-smelling breath on the Great King!"

"This is a job for a whole man," replied Craterus.

But Bagoas pressed his appeal, training his petulant eyes on Alexander, telling him again that Darius had once been liberal enough to grant him this honor. Against this argument Alexander had no reply, determined as he was to outdo Darius both in the breadth of his mercy and the depth of his wrath.

And so the party was treated to the spectacle of the smooth-cheeked, smooth-bottomed Bagoas putting the crop to the naked back of the priest. It rounded out an evening of Macedonian conviviality very well. The humiliation of a beating from the nutless one so tickled the symposiasts that they either wet themselves with laughter or did a little healthy vomiting. Gobares was the only one who kept his silence, even as Bagoas kept swinging hard; his sole request was to ensure that any crop that touched his body was free of impurities.

That the old man took his punishment well impressed his hosts. They would therefore have occasion to take him out of the stockade again from time to time, when they lacked for amusement. He enters my story again when Alexander is on his return from India.

XV

One of the more charming tales attached to Alexander involves his relationship with his horse, Bucephalus. Aeschines has done his part to perpetuate this myth. And it is true that the King had a special connection to this animal, which had begun when he was a boy in Macedon and lasted beyond the battle at the Hydaspes. Little Bucephalus would suffer no one else but little Alexander to ride him, and as the years and the distance accumulated, the King took care to lighten his burden as much as possible, to prolong his life.

What is less often remarked, however, is that Bucephalus was a cantankerous nag. Being the royal favorite, the animal seemed to believe that he himself was King. No other horses could be grazed with him, even ones much larger in size, because Bucephalus would pick fights. He would usually lose against bigger, stronger cavalry mounts, but the risk of injury to Bucephalus always resulted in the other horse being removed or killed. The grooms swore that the horse seemed to know this, and actively schemed to destroy his rivals. Even the people obliged to care for him grew to fear him. To care for the King's mount became dangerous duty, as a long line of grooms were attacked or stepped upon. One boy, a Persian of long experience at the stables at Susa, was kicked fatally in the chest by Bucephalus.

Perhaps all this had something to do with the horse's disappearance one day, when the army was camped several parasangs east of the Swat river. That horses died or vanished on campaign was not unusual: the Bactrians and Sogdians were accomplished rustlers, and wolves and lions lived in the more remote places. Difficult animals had a way of coming up lame or tied up when they injured the wrong person. Though ordinary cavalrymen were free to keep a close eye on their own horses, the King naturally could do no such thing.

Alexander flew into a rage at the loss of his horse. Where in other cases wild replacements could be captured out on the hoof, or found among reinforcements from home, Bucephalus himself could not be replaced. The King therefore summoned Peithon, who in turn called a meeting of all cavalry officers down to the tetrarchs. They were given a message to distribute to the natives: if Bucephalus was not returned alive by noon the next day, all their villages would be put to the torch, their men killed, and their women and children sold into slavery.

Bucephalus reappeared the next morning. He was hungry and muddy-flanked, but otherwise his old miserable self. The mystery of his disappearance and reappearance was never solved. That the King would make such a threat, however, said much about his precarious state of mind. I have no doubt he would have made good on it. At the very least, thousands of innocent people living over hundreds of square miles had been driven into panic—all for the sake of a horse. When the detestible creature did die, shortly after the battle at the Hydaspes river, there was quiet rejoicing all over the Macedonian camp.

Yes, I was to blame for encouraging Alexander in these whims because I wanted to save him from his despair over Cleitus. My goal was to save his sanity, but I discovered that his apotheosis had only bought us all time. In the end, his new, grand proportions only seemed to make his fallibilities more grand.

As it happened I did get one last glimpse of a younger, less encumbered Alexander. We had camped some miles west of the Indus on some high ground, when the wind came in from the northern wastelands. The sudden cold sent the men scrambling for supplies of firewood, which was scarce at that altitude. We were fortunate, however, to find a good supply of cedar-wood boxes scattered over the slope, each filled with what we took to be flammable rags. After burning several hundred of these, the Macedonians were comfortable, but the people of the nearby town were in an uproar. It seems that we had burned the ancestors of these natives, who had a custom of leaving their coffins above ground.

Armed men sallied up from the valley. There was a brief clash; the attackers retired, and Alexander prepared to lay siege to their town. It was at this point that the townspeople sought a parley, and in a haunting repetition of our encounter with the Branchidae, they addressed us in Greek. Indeed, their dialect was an archaic one that was much closer to the Macedonian argot. Unlike the Branchidae, however, they did not request Alexander to spare their town, but demanded it. For it seems the founder of their city was Dionysus himself!

Fittingly, the name of the place was Nysa. In a bygone age the god of wine and ecstasy had passed this way, on his return journey from India. A number of the god's followers, on seeing how appropriate the place was for cultivating the grape, decided to stay. Dionysus blessed their endeavor with prosperity. And indeed, all around them the Macedonians found reminders of home: vineyards, of course, but also clematis, ivy, laurel, oak, poplar, acanthus and myrtle. None of these had been seen in such profusion since we had crossed the Hellespont. As a final proof, the Nysans said that the mountain above their town was called Meron, "the thigh." To the Macedonians, this name was a clear reference to Dionysus's birth out of the thigh of Zeus.

So instead of laying siege, Alexander made sacrifices to Dionysus and Zeus-Ammon. The Nysans, pleased, invited the King and his officers to sample the hospitality of the god. Craterus, Perdiccas and the rest thought themselves above such frivolity, however. Hephaestion was off managing the construction of a bridge over the Indus. So our party on the mountain was therefore a small one: just Alexander, myself, Rohjane, and Bagoas.

If there is one truth in life, it is that we remember every moment of a dull party but all too little of a good one. Our day and night on the slopes of Mount Meron exists in my mind now as images only, savored to be sure, but without a story to put them to. I do know that we began by drinking wine neat from silver cups.

Somehow, as the god took hold, Alexander ended up in women's clothes, with fawn-skin tunic, fennel garland, and rouge smeared on his cheeks. Looking down, I saw I was dressed the same way, though I must have made a very ugly woman! Then we were running under the pines, on the soft grass, leaping and laughing like delighted children. As our intoxication deepened, we were encouraged by attributes of Dionysus that seemed miraculously placed for our use: musical instruments hanging from boughs, more wine, figs out of season. At the base of the bay tree, Bagoas found a thyrsus wound with ivy, and for reasons known only to himself, used it to strike the ground there. From where the thyrsus struck the earth flowed a stream of thick goat's milk. We fell to our knees and elbows, lapping up the milk as Dionysus seemed to stand over us, a tinkle of cymbals like laughter wafting down from unseen branches. Bagoas, his mouth and jaw lathered in cream, looked up at Alexander and kissed him on the lips. Then he did the same to me as Rohjane sat back against the trunk, caressing herself down the neck and between the breasts in beastly, contented remoteness.

I think there must have been something in the milk, for my recollections get more indistinct from there. There was more running, and calling of the Bacchic refrain, *"Euoi saboi, euoi saboi."* A nest of fat snakes appeared in our path. The snakes seemed drugged, sluggish; Rohjane tore into one of them with her teeth, ripped off the living flesh, and swallowed the chunks. Alexander, pleased, took the head for himself, while Bagoas performed a sinuous, serpentlike dance. Much aroused by this, the King grasped him by the flanks and buggered him in the sight of Heaven. Yet not even this seemed strange to me, as Rohjane and I shared a winking glance, and the Queen lay back in my arms with my hand intwined in her thin, blood-caked fingers.

Through our frenzy we became conscious of an urgent sensation in our throats. We had to come upon a cold, clear stream before we realized that this sensation was thirst, and that we were parched from what must have been hours of exertion. We bowed and drank like things of the forest, stopping only when our bellies were full and we could barely turn our backs to the smooth creekside rocks warmed by the sun. Lulled by the song of the cicada, we fell into a deep, untroubled sleep.

When we awoke the sun was down near the shoulder of Meron. My head was a bit clearer, and I could see the evidence Bagoas and Rohjane bore of their experience: cuts on their feet, burrs in their hair, blood and milk on their chins. Alexander was standing some distance away, looking through the trees down to the valley below.

Evening shadow had fallen on the Macedonian camp. Torches winked in the distance, arranged along the ranks of tents. The King had an odd expression on his face, both curious and wistful, as if he were regarding evidence of an ancestor's life. I plucked the half-crushed garland from his head and tossed it aside.

"The sundown watch must be coming on," he told me. "Look—the Third Battalion of footmen still can't pitch a straight line of tents."

"Shall we get back?"

He sighed, and putting his weight on my shoulder,

remarked, "It's always there, is it not? Somewhere around me like the Furies. Jealousy, Blood Avenger, Unceasing Pursuit! Other men have gone abroad, explored foreign lands. I must take an army with me to see new places! The original blunt instrument! I love them so much I would run away right now. I wonder if you understand, dear Machon."

I thought it best to say I did not. But he continued to walk with me as we descended the mountain, Bagoas and Rohjane stumbling behind us in the twilight. As we proceeded it became clear that we had waited too long to start back: the light was failing, and the path was little more than a deer track. Soon we lost our way, but pressed on down the slope. Finally the ground leveled, and we came upon the outskirts of a village we hadn't passed on the way up. Alexander called for the little column to halt.

"Is this Nysa?" he asked.

"I doubt it," I answered, "but I may not have seen it from this side."

"There—someone's coming." Bagoas pointed.

Three women appeared. They were neither girls, nor particularly old—young mothers, perhaps. Their heads were covered with particolored cloths, their hands hidden behind the folds of their dresses. They were approaching a flat stone scattered with flowers and spice leaves. Spreading a cloth on the ground there, one of the women dumped a handful of small objects in the center—in the gloom it was hard to see what, but they appeared to be either chickpeas or some kind of nut. As the woman in the middle set about picking chaff out of her nuts or peas, the other two looked reverently at the flat rock. It occurred to me then that they may have come together to a village shrine for some kind of observance. To be watching them secretly therefore seemed to be something of a transgression, though of what faith I had no idea. I swallowed my qualms, though, when it was clear that the others would not move on.

The woman in the center began to speak in a language I couldn't understand. Cocking her ear, Rohjane gave a little gasp, then a smile of recognition. We all looked to her.

"She is not speaking Sogdian, but I understand some of it. They are performing the rite we call 'Miserable Peas.' It is done by women only, in times of trouble in the family. I used to see it done by my grandmother. We also used chickpeas."

As the woman spoke, the others knelt by her, giving affirmations now and then, though they did it somewhat perfunctorily, as if they had heard her words many times before.

"What's going on now?" asked Bagoas.

"There is a tale that must be told before the peas are purified and given away. In my father's kingdom the story is about the wise daughter of a goatherd. There was a drought, and there was no food for the girl, her father, or the goats. The goatherd prayed to Ameretat for aid; the Yazata appeared to them with the gift of a handful of chickpeas. The Shining One said: 'Purify these as you know how, and after the rite give them away as best serves the good.' The father gave thanks, but when Ameretat was gone he complained that the Spenta had given no help at all, for they had been given only a few miserable chickpeas. And he was about to share them with his daughter for eating, when she begged him to purify them first. 'Foolish girl!' her father said. 'Purified or not, these miserable peas will not save us.' But her piety shamed him, and he relented, saying the words that consecrated them in the sight of Ahura Mazda. Again, he was about to eat them, when his daughter objected, saying she wanted to give her share to the goats. 'Foolish child!' the goatherd chided her. 'What good will a few miserable peas do for our whole flock?' The wise daughter replied: 'I know not, father, but I cannot eat while others suffer, even if they are animals.' At these words the goatherd was proud of his daughter's sense of duty to *asha*, and ashamed at having indulged his despair. He bid her to eat her share of the peas and give his to the goats instead. When she threw her father's peas among the flock, a miracle happened: where each pea hit the ground a beautiful green tree sprouted, grew, and ripened before her eyes, until she was standing in a grove of myrtle trees, each with boughs groaning under the weight of berries.

"In this way the goats, the father, and the daughter ate, and were saved from the drought. Soon the prince of the kingdom came by, and seeing a grove of myrtle more splendid than in any of his father's gardens, came to the door to congratulate the owner. There he saw the goatherd's daughter, and fell in love. When she came of age, he married her, and in due course she became Queen. But for the rest of her life, in trouble or not, she was sure to perform this rite of the chickpeas, to protect her family from harm."

Rohjane finished the tale long before the other did. When the village woman was finished she said a short prayer over the chickpeas in a different tongue I took to be Avestan, the language of Zarathustra's revelation. When that was done, the three women solemnly scattered some of the chickpeas on the shrine, and threw others on the roofs of the houses around them.

"This land is not in drought," Alexander remarked in too loud a voice. The women looked in his direction, and seeing us crouching there, turned away in fear. Alexander stepped into the open to appeal to them.

"Maids, stop! You have nothing but compassion to expect from the hand of your King!"

His words had the opposite effect. Instead of simply running away, the women began to shriek *"Daeva! Daeva!"* When he followed them through the narrow lanes of the village, the people scattered. Women dropped their baskets and ran into their houses; little children fled into their mothers' arms, crying *"Daeva! Daeva!"* Alexander, still convinced he could soothe their fears, went from door to door as they slammed in his face. And though he was oblivious to it, he was a frightful sight, with his face rouged with snake blood and his woman's dress caked in mud. Persistent, he chased them all, holding out his arms in a supplicatory gesture that promised to swallow them up.

At last he relented, sitting against a wall. We caught up to him as he slumped there.

"I take it, then, that we are not in Nysa," said Bagoas.

Not in Nysa indeed. For it was clear that the Macedonian foraging parties had already visited this place, and their exactions had caused the hunger that the 'Miserable Peas' were supposed to remedy. More than mere thievery seemed involved: I had seen the same headlong flight, the same abject terror among the women of a small village before, in Doris, north of Amphissa, after Philip's army had come through in the maneuvers that led to Chaeronea. It must have been much the same in Thebes, or Attica during the Persian occupation, or in Ionia after the revolt failed. Places where men once lived, worked, made love, became haunted places; the presence of those missing was still palpable, and every pair of eyes, including the children's, seemed to contain a story that they would sooner forget, but would tell for the rest of their lives.

I should add that Alexander, like Philip before him, expressly forbade disrespect of women, the elderly, or children. In Bactria there had been a man in my battalion, the Second Hypaspists, who had been given the rather arbitrary-sounding punishment of one hundred and eighty-two strokes of the lash. The number was based on an estimate of the number of women he had raped in the lands of Persia, Hyrcania, and Bactria. The man did not survive the putrefaction of the wounds he received during the scourging. Yet not even this example had brought safety, it seemed, to the people of that village at the foot of Mount Meron.

"I think . . ." said Alexander very deliberately, "that I shall be glad when this is all over."

XVI

The army pressed on to the Indus. The huge bridge of boats assembled by Hephaestion was sturdy enough for eighty thousand Macedonians and twenty thousand horses, but still failed to inspire any respect for him. As usual, the way was smoothed by the surrender of the next kingdom to the east, in this case that of a character named Aambhi (or "Omphis," as Aeschines called him). A more self-interested climber we had not encountered in eight years of campaigning in Asia. Already under severe pressure from the two Indian kings to his east—Abisares of Kashmir and Porus of the Pauravas—Aambhi made a profound gesture of surrendering what was barely his in the first place. Moreover, Aambhi overdid his show in nearly disastrous fashion: by assembling his entire army before the gates of Taxila, his capital, he so alarmed the Macedonians that they rushed to organize a defense. The confusion was only resolved when Aambhi came out to surrender personally. Alexander met him in the center, both men now a picture of fraternal goodwill, both smiling, both unable to understand a word the other said.

As expected, the toady was confirmed in his kingship by Alexander, whereupon he changed his name to "Taxiles." This struck me as odd, something like Alexander styling himself as "King Pella." In any case, the Macedonians made such an impression that Taxiles's enemy, Abisares, sent tokens of submission. This left only King Porus to oppose their invasion of the Gangetic Plain. Beyond that, the Macedonians expected only to find the eastern limit of the continent, washed by the waters of unending Ocean.

Each time the corporation known as "Alexander" called upon the skills of Arridaeus, it took a risk. Accordingly, it made a number of sincere efforts to persuade, overawe, threaten, and otherwise motivate Porus to give up his enmity against Taxiles. But this Porus was a stiff-necked fellow, repeatedly sending back the Macedonian envoys. The final time he added a promise: Porus would indeed greet Alexander at the Hydaspes river, but only at the head of his army. "And when Porus takes the field," the message read, "it is not to stage a pageant like Aambhi, but to make war."

So war it was. Aambhi warned the King that Porus was a formidable foe, with a well-trained army and a large corps of war elephants. Far from giving Alexander pause, this news delighted him, for he was tired of petty conflicts with brigands and hill tribes, and longed for a good, pitched, set-piece battle.

The Hydaspes is only a tributary of the Indus, but no trickle like the Granicus. It was deep and fast enough to prevent a crossing in all but a few well-known places. Porus blocked them all with an army of thirty thousand infantry, four thousand horses, and two hundred elephants. Except for the elephants, the Pauravas' force was smaller than Alexander's, but had

the advantage of the best ground, and the knowledge
that they were fighting for their homes and children;
the Macedonians were exhausted, ignorant of the territory, and far from home. For these reasons, it would
seem, Porus believed he had a chance to stop the man
who had toppled the empire at his doorstep.

Porus was clearly not a man to be panicked by a
quick offensive thrust. Instead, Alexander opened the
battle with a series of cavalry feints up and down the
river. In response, the Pauravas' elephants and horsemen went out to shadow the Macedonians, massing at
the points where Alexander's cavalry bluffed a crossing. The Macedonians kept this up for several nights,
whooping and carousing as they galloped, more or
less telling the Indians exactly where they were. With
this tactic Alexander so exhausted the enemy that they
ceased to respond to these moves in force—for it is not
an easy thing to get a corps of elephants on the march!
Instead, Porus convinced himself that Alexander
would not attack at all that season, but would wait for
the late summer, when the water level would be more
suited to an attack.

Having lulled the Pauravas into complacence,
Alexander slipped out of camp and surveyed a crossing Aambhi had pointed out to him, some distance to
the north. The river was deep there, but narrower.
Judging the ford to be manageable, he ordered his men
to construct rafts as they had on the Danube and the
Oxus, and also to bring forward one of the large gal-
leys he had disassembled at the Indus and portaged to
the Hydaspes. Though no enemy scouts had appeared
on the opposite bank that far north, Alexander felt
obliged to wait for the most opportune moment to

cross, for the Macedonian reputation of invincibility was at stake.

His moment came two nights later, when a great rainstorm broke over the battlefield. With storm clouds blocking the moon, and the rain and thunder muffling their manuevers, Alexander moved the bulk of his army to the crossing place. Craterus was left opposing Porus with a small force that kept up a large number of campfires, to fool the enemy into believing the Macedonians had not moved. An officer named Attalus, who was about Alexander's height and coloring, was dressed in the King's clothes and diadem, so the Indians would not think the King had left the camp. Finally, Craterus was given orders to cross the river when Porus decamped, and to follow the sound of the battle wherever it might be.

The crossing was accomplished before dawn without the loss of a single man. Alexander drew his men into formation, expecting to receive a counterattack at any moment. His scouts then returned with disturbing news: the Macedonians had not landed on the opposite bank of the Hydaspes, but on an island in the stream! An additional crossing would be needed before he could engage the enemy. His men were now stranded uselessly, while back at the main Macedonian camp the diminished size of Craterus's holding force would become obvious as the sun rose.

It was not in Alexander's character to rage at Aambhi's bad advice, but only to apply himself with greater resolution. The island had at least shielded his army from the eyes of Porus's scouts. His men proceeded across the arm of the Hydaspes without delay, sinking up to their necks in raging snowmelt.

Weapons disappeared in the current; horses and men lost their footing and floated away. The bulk of the Macedonian forces completed their second crossing of the morning just as a mounted detachment of Indians finally sighted them. The horsemen attacked, but upon seeing that the phalanx was safely across and deployed, turned and fled. There was a skirmish as the Cavalry Companions intercepted the Indians. One of Porus's sons was killed after a brave struggle, but the bulk of his force escaped.

From across the river, Craterus witnessed riders arrive in Porus's camp with news of Alexander's appearance on the east bank. The King of the Pauravas ordered his men to march north, leaving only a token force to prevent Craterus from following him. The last of his elephants departed just as the bodies and *sarissas* of the drowned Macedonians floated past the Indian camp.

The armies met on flat ground. Hoping to nullify Alexander's skill at wide cavalry sweeps, and knowing that the horses of the Macedonians were terrified of the elephants, Porus pushed the larger creatures far forward. Aambhi, however, had told Alexander that the Indian mahouts had never faced an army of well-drilled pikemen. Alexander sent word to his infantry to be ready as he feinted with his cavalry. The Pauravas took the bait, sending out their horsemen to chase away the Macedonians. Just as the Indian army split in two, Alexander ordered the Foot Companions forward, brandishing their *sarissas* under the snouts of the elephants.

For a few moments, the battle hung in the balance as Porus's infantry held firm against the Macedonian attack. His elephants, tusks raised, charged into the Macedonian ranks, snorting and trampling, plucking unlucky phalangites out of the ranks with their trunks. The victims were suspended helplessly by their legs before the Indians dispatched them. Archers stationed on the elephant's backs fired into the phalanxes from above, doing great damage.

The Macedonians tried to use their pikes against the eyes of the elephants. The elephants were most sensitive about wounds to their trunks, which they held out of reach of the soldiers. The Pauravas' mahouts were much more skilled than those hired by the Persians at Gaugamela. Porus's elephant corps did its job very well, keeping the Macedonians away from the Indian center just as it was ordered to do. The heads of the creatures were armored, so it was difficult work to damage them. The Pauravas sallied out against the phalanx several times, their tuskers working terrible carnage against the Foot Companions, who often could not generate enough force behind their *sarissas* to pierce their thick hides. The Macedonians finally used their war axes against the elephants, chopping at their trunks until they were severed or too mangled for use. In agony, their eyes put out, the giants soon went out of control, thrashing at anything in their reach, including their Indian masters.

The Pauravas' cavalry, having made no headway against the mounted Companions and Thessalians, added to the chaos by returning to the center. The Indians' fate was sealed when Craterus appeared at their rear, charging on the double upon them. Porus tried to organize his army into a defensive square, but as Arridaeus had envisioned, his elephants could not turn around quickly enough. With the luxury to charge the Indians at a run, the Macedonians put their lances right through the shields and leather armor of the enemy. This triggered the final panic, and sealed the victory for the Macedonians.

Surrounded, Porus's army became a bloody, mud-spattered confusion of men, horses, and elephants, all doing as much damage to each other as to the Macedonians. Alexander ordered the phalanx on his left to withdraw, opening a path for the survivors to escape. For it seems that already, before the battle was over, Alexander had plans for Porus and his gallant fighters.

To my mind this victory came as hard as any fought by the Macedonians in Asia. Alexander's infantry was the most demoralized after this battle than after any other. The thousand men lost at the Hydaspes, and the way many of them had been crushed to death, made the Macedonians very reluctant to meet any more elephants in the future. And India, as everyone knows, is the wrong place to go if you fear these animals!

Alexander sent his ally to solicit Porus's surrender. But when Aambhi rode before the Indian King and addressed him in his own tongue, Porus turned his elephant to attack, declaring "A crown yields only to a crown, not a dog!" Aambhi escaped, telling Alexander a story that the Pauravas' monarch preferred death to capture. But Alexander saw through this, having a better understanding of the proud King's mind. He then obliged Aambhi to return with him as his translator.

Confronting Porus, Alexander dismounted and made such signals as to indicate he wished to parley. Porus, staring down on his adversary from the biggest war elephant on the field, halted. While he was not out of his mind as Aambhi suggested, he must have been troubled by the nine wounds he had received that day, and the ordeal of witnessing all three of his grown sons killed. He might have tried to run his enemy down right then, but with his army destroyed and his kingdom's fate sealed, such spite would have gained him nothing. Instead, he stepped onto his elephant's bent front leg. The beast gently lowered its master to the ground before Alexander.

The Pauravas' King was a giant nearly eight feet tall, with a crest on his helmet that made him seem taller still. His posture there was unbowed and unafraid, though he had no fewer than three arrows still stuck in his body. Alexander seemed little more than a child standing before his father—except that it had been the Macedonian who had come to give the lesson that day.

"Tell me why you fought me," Alexander asked him, "when you see your rival here has profited by forswearing the sword?"

Porus answered, "If you had come to me in friendship, it is you who would have profited."

"I can ask for no worthier opponent. Therefore tell me how you should be treated, and it shall be so."

"As a king. No more, no less."

"It shall be as you wish for your kingdom. And for yourself, whatever you desire is yours. What may I give you?"

"I have given you my answer. Give to a king as a king ought."

And give Alexander did. Perhaps because he was angry at the poor intelligence on the river crossing, or perhaps because Porus presented the kind of ally he trusted more at his back, he did not give the Pauravas' kingdom to Aambhi. Instead, he confirmed Porus as ruler for all lands between the Hydaspes and the Acesines, and went on to enlarge his kingdom with lands around the Hydraotes. In return, he stipulated that Porus would contribute as many garrison troops and all the elephants he could spare to the Macedonian army. Porus, for his part, accepted his responsibility, and discharged it faithfully in the campaigns that followed against the Cathaei tribe, so that Alexander's realm ran to the west bank of the Hyphasis. Beyond that river beckoned the great Gangetic Plain.

There is one other detail Aeschines failed to mention in his account of this time: in the chaos of the end of the battle, a crazed, blinded elephant veered into the Macedonian line. Undeterred by lances or arrows, this elephant charged through a phalanx sixteen shields deep, turned left, and ran right over Arridaeus and his screen of protectors. All the guards on the exposed side were crushed; Arridaeus was thrown when his horse panicked, and kicked by a hoof as his mount escaped.

This was the worst sort of disaster for the Macedonians. Alexander abandoned his chivalrous interview with Porus the second he got the news. The royal doctor was summoned, and a tent thrown up over Arridaeus's body to conceal the incident. Soon Alexander and his staff learned the diagnosis: his brother had been struck in the side of his head. The all-enclosing Corinthian helmet had not protected him, but added to the injury by shattering with the impact. Lacerations had caused him to lose much blood. He was alive, but unconscious in a way that did not promise he would ever recover.

And so the campaign was both literally and figuratively at a crossroads. Among the generals who ran the army, there seemed a real possibility that all of Asia would bow to a Macedonian master, and consequently to governors selected from among themselves. Yet without Arridaeus how would they ever defeat the Great King of India? For surely the wealthy lands around the Ganges must support a powerful kingdom. No one knew for sure what lay ahead, but imagination filled in the details: the Indian monarch must have an army of half a million men, with elephants twice as large and ten times more numerous than those of Porus.

Not knowing what to do, the Macedonians did what they'd always done: march east. By then they were suffering from the almost constant rain of that part of the world. The heavens opened every day, letting down a streaming torrent that rusted armor and rotted wounds. Spoiled food and contaminated water fouled the stomachs of the men, and the stench of widespread diarrhea gave away the army's position to anyone with a nose. To give his men some relief from the heat, Alexander took care to march in the shadow of whatever high ground was available, but this was meager in the region.

These and other miserable conditions conspired to make a crossing of the Acesines River an expensive proposition. The river was almost two miles wide in the spring, and the natives, by now aware that the Macedonians would seize any vessels they found, hid or scuttled all their boats. Alexander therefore had to dig deeply into the huge fortune he had raided from Persia to purchase the transport he needed.

There were two deaths around this time that did not come on the battlefield, but that each affected Alexander in its own way. First, Bucephalus at last passed on from old age. Alexander grieved for him as he would for a close comrade, and erected a shrine for him on the hillside where his ashes were buried. He also founded a city in the place where he had crossed the Hydaspes on that stormy night, and called it Bucephala, so that the animal's name would forever be on the lips of men. There he settled soldiers who had grown too old to serve him, and those who had married Indian women and wished to stay, with his blessing, in the lands they had conquered.

The other death was of Darius's mother, Sisygambis. She had been ailing for some time, and had long expressed through intermediaries that she preferred to return to Persia. But Alexander, perhaps out of affection for the kind of mother Olympias never was, kept the old woman close to him. In any case, the heat and constant rain of India in that season wore her down, until at last she stopped eating, and called for Alexander from her deathbed.

The latter, coming into her presence, was shocked and saddened by her wasted appearance. Kneeling at her side, he begged that she might live to see the shore of the great Eastern Ocean with him. At this, she laughed at him.

"You are a fool. Neither of us will live to see the Eastern Ocean!"

"Why not?"

"Because Asia is not little Europe, my dear boy! Its

vastness exceeds your imagining, with kingdoms beyond India you cannot conquer in five lifetimes. For your happiness, be content with what you have accomplished. Make an heir with that half-wild woman of yours! That is my testament to you."

And with that she allowed him to kiss her hand, and ordered him to leave her, for she wished to die with the survivors of her royal household around her, as she was attended in happier times. And when word came that she was gone, Alexander mourned, putting off eating and washing for three days. He sent her body home unburned, so that she might be buried whole, in accord with the Persian custom.

XVII

Alexander forgot his grief by attacking a hostile tribe called the Cathaei. These people were under the influence of a priestly class called the Brahmins, who were known both for their wisdom and their pride. Alexander's informants told him that these Brahmins had been fomenting resistance to the "unclean" Macedonians up and down the Indus valley. The King was therefore keen to confront this enemy head on.

Hephaestion took it upon himself to go to Taxila to observe the Brahmins there. When he returned, he reported that they lived together in the woods like wild animals. The young ones went completely naked, letting their hair grow long. At the age of thirty-seven they were allowed to shave their heads and wear linen robes. Despite their poverty the Brahmins were held in highest esteem by the people, for only they were permitted to make prayers, conduct sacrifices, or entreat the gods in any way. For this reason they had no need of material wealth: if they became hungry they went to the markets and received supplies from the merchants without needing to ask. But because the Brahmins believed it polluting for anyone of a lesser class to touch their food, their meals could only be prepared by other Brahmins. Similarly, when the unguent sellers saw one of these sages in the marketplace, they would do them conspicuous honor by covering them with expensive oils. To go about so annointed therefore became something of a badge of Brahmin virtue.

Hephaestion approached a beautiful young Brahmin who was standing by a stream. His hair was divided into two queues, one draped over each shoulder, and his skin was shining with oil as I have described. The young man was standing on one foot, arms outstretched, with logs two feet long in each hand. He kept this excruciating position, staring straight ahead, never wavering, for the entire time Hephaestion watched him.

As he did so an older Brahmin approached to ask about the philosophy of the Greeks. Hephaestion obliged by telling him something of the teachings of Pythagoras, Socrates, and Diogenes.

"You Greeks have some wisdom," the old Brahmin finally said. "But all in all you concern yourselves too much with politics. There's nothing less worth the time of a mature mind than the ways men contrive their social relations."

"It surprises me to learn that," replied Hephaestion, "because it is said that you Brahmins advise your kings on all matters of state."

"The wise man must raise his children, but does not confine his thinking to childish questions. Would you like to learn the proper objects of serious thought . . . ? Good! First, take off your clothes."

Hephaestion declined.

"Then let that be your first lesson: if you cannot put

off your clothes, you cannot lay aside the more profound burdens. Remember what I have told you."

With that the old Brahmin walked away. The young
one was still holding up his logs; as Hephaestion was
conversing with the elder, he had slowly switched
from standing on the left leg to the right, but had otherwise stayed motionless.

The capital of the Cathaei, Sangala, stood twenty
parasangs beyond the river Acesines. The natives defended the place with a triple line of wagons around
the town. Although the Macedonians had the advantage of massive numbers, the Cathaei retreated in
good order as their enemies took each line of defense.
At length, after many casualties on both sides, the
Cathaei were shut up inside the walls. Facing the unpleasant prospect of assault by Alexander's siege engines, thousands of enemy fighters tried to sneak out
of Sangala during the night. Peithon was waiting for
them.

The prisoners were then given a choice: execution, or
a place among Alexander's auxiliaries. They all chose
the latter. But it seemed a peculiarity of the men of Asia
that such promises were taken lightly. The following
night all of them tried to escape yet again. This time the
Macedonians showed no mercy: by the time the work
was done, they had hacked to death more than seven
thousand of the deserters. Another ten thousand were
killed in the siege. Upon seeing all these bodies littering
the ground, I could not restrain myself from a reproving
look at Alexander. To my surprise, he tossed his head
with a smile.

"Don't worry, Machon! I shall be gone soon enough!"

The King ordered Peithon to spare ten Brahmins

from the general slaughter. Knowing their reputation for virtue, and still assuming they belonged to a kind of Asiatic school of sophists, Alexander had these specimens brought before him. It was his intention to host a debate, and perhaps in this way revive the spirit of inquiry that had steadily been snuffed out by the brutality of the war.

But he was destined to be disappointed. When he posed a series of philosophical puzzles to them, believing he might learn how they think, none of the prisoners answered. On pain of death, he repeated his questions:

"Which are more numerous, those now alive or those who have died? Where do more creatures live, in the ocean or on the land? Which came first, day or night? How shall a man make others love him?"

Yet even under the most dire threats, the Brahmins stayed silent. In this way Alexander learned that they were not sages at all, but a class of haughty nobles who needed to learn humility.

"I had asked once for you to speak," he said. "A god does not ask twice."

The penalty was severe: for their silence, Alexander had their mouths sewn shut. The Brahmins were then left to languish in full view of the camp. For the most part they did so bravely, except for three who somehow managed to drink through their noses. These were killed as the army decamped to cross the next river to their east, the Hyphasis.

This was another muddy, roiling torrent that was bigger than any river in Greece. Faced with the prospect of another laborious crossing, and the need to cross it again on the way home, a change abruptly came over the hearts of the rank-and-file soldiers. Where before everyone simply went along with the rest of the mass, it suddenly became thinkable to demand an end to the misery. In the tents, around the cookfires, in the latrines, the talk was quite open about it. Their immediate superiors, moreover, stopped punishing such chatter.

Alexander's position on this was far less clear than Aeschines represents. Idle curiosity to see what lay on the other side of the next hill was part of his nature, to be sure. The prospect of returning to Babylon to become a mere administrator, or worse yet to Pella and inevitable assassination, held little attraction. Better to die in battle, spear leveled against the elephants of the Great King of India! But on the other hand, without Arridaeus or Parmenion, the prospect of victory against superior forces was remote. As resigned to death as Alexander was, he still preferred to die as the victor than as the vanquished. Nor was he blind to the suffering of his men.

You have heard the prosecution relate the substance of a speech the King gave on the shores of the Hyphasis. In this speech, Alexander is supposed to have argued for a continuation of the war to the farthest shores of Asia. When this wish was defied by his men, he railed against the cowards around him, and stripped off his clothes to show his scars. Then he supposedly retreated to his tent, to sulk like Achilles.

That speech did occur. What my opponent misses, though, is everything the speaker really meant. The simpleminded heroism of Aeschines's version serves the purpose of Ptolemy and Antipater, to burnish the legend of the god-hero who assures their authority. The real story is a great deal more interesting—it was the subtlest speech Alexander ever produced. For at the same time, he had to encourage his men to fight on, but also to make sure that his appeal was denied. And once it was denied, he had to convince everyone that he was disappointed! It was a short, shrewd performance from a man more used to giving orders than working persuasion.

He gathered his officers irrespective of rank in a field outside the camp. Just as the setting sun broke through under the storm clouds, he mounted a wagon and raised his hands for quiet. The late sunshine cast a golden light on him that made him seem like his own commemorative bronze.

"My friends, I have been knocked about a fair amount these last years. My ears have rung as much as yours, but rest assured I am not deaf yet. It comes to my attention that some of you want to go home. And I must say I understand, for we now know why there are so many big rivers in India—Zeus never stops the rain!"

It was a well-timed joke, but drew only grimaces. Rain in India is not a laughing matter.

"It is still only a short time since we met the Pauravas in battle. We fought that morning as the superior force, overmatching our enemy in men and horses and, in the end, in valor. Even so, a thousand of our companions will not see home after that test. A thousand more have claimed their rest in the time since, of wounds and sickness. You are wrong if you believe I have not noticed these losses.

"Now we march toward the lands of the Great King of India, whose domains encompass the balance of Asia. I have been as immersed in rumors of what we will find there as I have been in this fetid air, and I must say they are just as unhealthy! So if you want to know what you will find at the Ganges, don't ask your tent-mate—ask me! Go ahead, ask!"

There was a pause before the officers took his invitation. "What will we find, O King?" they cried.

"Death," Alexander said. "And victory. Exactly what you found everywhere else. For have we not learned that the butt of a sword feels the same in every land? Or its edge, for that matter? Whence this morbid curiosity, my friends? Have we not found the same reward everywhere—death to some, victory for the rest, and another river to cross? Comrades deserve the truth from comrades. From me you should expect no fairy tales, no rosy scenarios. To civilize the world is hard work.

"But here's another dose of honesty, boys: I won't go on without you. I've got more treasure than Croesus, and I could hire ten times your number in mercenaries, but I won't. We've come this far together, and on the strength of your loyalty this campaign will live or die. I want to go east; some of you want to go home, the job only half-done. Some say leave something of the world for our sons to conquer. I say leave our sons a world at peace, under the rule of a king who knows how much you bled to win it.

"You all have misgivings, I know. You have questions I haven't begun to answer. Where does Asia end? Are the elephants in India twice as large as those of Porus? Will we all stray so far from home that we will return more barbarian than Greek? Of these matters, I can only tell you I don't know yet. But I want us to find the answers together. I await your reply."

As you recall, the response came from Coenus, son of Polemocrates. This man was a competent infantry commander—his role in defeating Spitamenes and pressing the Indians at the Hydaspes were decisive—but as an orator his talents were decidedly modest. I was there when delivered his rambling argument for withdrawal, and it is a wonder how it has been built up into the tearjerker it has been by Ptolemy and his followers. But the reason is simple enough: given that Alexander's professed wish to go on was defied, only a brilliant oration would motivate the retreat without diminishing the King.

Coming forward, Coenus said, "I address you reluctantly, as the humble must naturally be in the face of the Lord of All Asia. For who would dispute that you already bear that title, now ruling lands greater in extent than the Great King himself? My King, hear the words of a man who has been with you since before the Granicus. Hear one who was there before the Hellespont, the Danube, or Thebes. Hear one who first rode during the first campaign against the Triballians, and yes, who shed his share of tears at the funeral of your father.

"For eight years, you have led and we have followed. We have been privileged to do so, for it is ever a blessing to serve in the company of greatness. Let none of us here forget who we were but a generation ago, when we fled to the hills at the mere sight of Illyrians and Thracians, and were the butt of jokes from fancy city-dwellers from the south. Now the primitives fear us, and the cities compete to flatter us. You have shown us what men are capable of when their honor is awakened. For that, for your wisdom and leadership, we are ever in your debt.

"Today we count on that wisdom again. You see us standing before you, and you must know that there are no gods here. Men stand here broken, their every step made in agony by wounds that won't heal in this infernal heat. They stand here naked, or in the garb of barbarians, for they have gone beyond the limits of resupply from home. And they stand here dispirited, for all of them have wives they can barely recall, and children they scarcely know.

"O King, remember your beloved Bucephalus, who rests now among those hills behind us! Even he, your most faithful companion, was allowed to find his stall at last. All of us witnessed the tenderness with which you handled him in his final months. And yet, do not your men deserve the compassion you displayed to your horse? Like him, there are limits to how far and how hard an army may be ridden. On this, I don't pretend to tell you what you must already know.

"Our plea is not made in contempt of your ambitions. Not at all! We advance your plan, because the conquest of India is a job we leave to the next generation. Your next army already awaits you, at home. It tends flocks on the plains of Emathia; it waters its cattle in the swift, sweet Axios. With wooden swords it drills in earnest, fondly imagining the celebration that will attend the return of divine Alexander, so long absent from the land of his countrymen! And that youthful army yearns to give you India, Africa, Europe. We who have shared some modest part of your glory beg you not to deprive our sons of this privilege.

"Please know that I say nothing of hubris, or pride,

or any of the sins whispered by those who take a darker view. Personally, I don't believe such talk. I know that a mind so keen on the timing of things, when to encamp, march, or attack, can also know when it is time to stop. Wisdom knows when to push away from the table, to retire for the night. In truth, even the gods must take account of Fortune, and the bitter way she may turn on even the most successful. So much more so, then, mere mortals like us. And that is all I have to say."

As it was, many were surprised that Alexander perceived his case so devastated by Coenus's arguments. What really happened, I suspect, was that after the King pretended to have been defeated in the debate, weeping and rending his clothes, he went back to his tent and enjoyed a three-day bender. Then he came out and made the "concession" he intended all along: the army would turn south, to the sea, and after that march for home.

Coenus was as desperate in his sincerity as Alexander was not. Believing himself to have defied a god, his anguish drove him to illness. Immediately after the King left, he could not breathe; within a day he was bedridden, unable to eat or sleep. Some suspected he had been poisoned for opposing Alexander, but as I have said, Alexander only pretended to oppose withdrawal. Coenus was only thirty-six when they put him on the pyre.

Indeed, Ptolemy, Perdiccas, and Craterus had better grounds than Alexander for wishing Coenus had kept his mouth shut. Though they never communicated their preferences to me—not in any overt way—it would have better served their purposes for the King to have found a gallant death in battle. Afterward they could lead the beleaguered Macedonians on an epic retreat—like Chirisophus leading the Ten Thousand—dispose of the ailing Arridaeus, and divide the empire between them. Of course, I can offer no evidence that my story should be preferred over Aeschines's. No evidence at all—except the minor fact that I spent more than a decade observing the characters of these men, and Aeschines was not there at all.

I will not hide my own preference from you on this question: I supported an Indian campaign. For as I watched the King change over the months and years, I came to believe that if he survived to see his old domains again he would not rule them the same enlightened way. For the sake of his life, I helped convince him of his divinity, but at the cost of making him half-mad with godly demands. He now expected not only his subordinates to grovel before him, but kings and chiefs. How much more a tyrant would he have become if emissaries from all the Greek cities came to him with all manner of gross flatteries? Would the free men of Athens be obliged to prostrate themselves at the feet of the universal conqueror? The thought revolted me. If I indict myself with this admission, so be it. One way or another, Alexander was bound to be assassinated like every other Macedonian king in his line. Better that he find his reward in far India, fighting in the manner that he loved, than have his reign collapse on our heads here.

XVIII

That Aeschines accuses me of plotting against Alexander is not surprising. What is unexpected is that he indicts me for my association with Rohjane, when in fact this was one of the great services I did for the King! There was a desperate need to civilize the girl, and the oafs and thugs who surrounded Alexander were useless for this work. That I was a Greek and an Athenian seemed further to recommend me for the job. The Macedonians, after all, prided themselves on knowing more about horses than women, and what was a "Greekling" to them, anyway, but a particularly useless kind of woman?

After the breaking of bread with Oxyartes, the honeymoon lasted just a few days. Divine Alexander's side of what happened has gone with him to Olympus, but for Rohjane's part it was a peculiar induction into the ways of men and women. She came to him, of course, as a maiden. For those unfamiliar with the customs of royalty, her virginity meant she had experience only with her handmaids, and that restricted to what may be indulged away from spying eyes. Her curiosity about men was therefore strong, and she could be excused for expecting that the Lord of All Asia would be unequivocally a man. She found herself instead cast in a much more complex role than simple receptacle for the royal seed. Unprepared, confused, she plied me with questions that gave more information than they got.

Though some would call her lucky, Rohjane did not have many natural allies in her husband's retinue. There was a growing number of noblewomen attached to his camp as hostages to their families' loyalty, but few of these saw her as their equal. She had no friends among his other companions, the rough-hewn Crateruses or Ptolemies or Parmenions, and certainly not the best wishes of Hephaestion or Bagoas. Certainly because she was a barbarian, but possibly because she was beautiful, Callisthenes the historian had treated her with deliberate contempt.

Sogdian nobles educate all their children, male and female. Their native language is impossible for outsiders to learn, so full of such arbitrary complexities that it makes every other language seem easy by comparison. Rohjane therefore had knowledge of Persian and Greek, could recite the names of important historical figures, and even knew something of Hellenic and Indian philosophies. Of the skills that are more immediately useful to a Macedonian wife she knew nothing—not how to dress, nor how to display the appropriate courtesies, nor how to be silent. I decided to start at the beginning: to wean her away from her trousers, furs, and animal skins, and into appropriate clothes.

There were garments of all kinds for trade among the merchants and thieves who followed Alexander through Asia. Bearing a simple chiton of Ionic type, made of good linen, I arrived at Rohjane's tent and asked to be admitted. Inside, I found her with Youtab, the sole handmaid permitted to follow her to her new life. The two women were sitting around a small fire, turning a wild piglet on a spit. Rohjane had a hunting knife on her hip. She had apparently used this to cut an impromptu smoke-hole in the roof.

"Machon! You are just in time to eat with us—"

I explained that my purpose had to do with gentler arts than the roasting of meat.

"That is your loss," said Youtab as she extracted one of the piglet's eyes with her knife and offered it to the Queen.

"You have Greek clothes . . ." Rohjane said to me with her mouth full of eyeball. ". . . I have those too."

She rose and threw open a cedar chest. Inside was a large woolen garment. Inspecting it, I saw it was a peplos of Doric cut, with no armholes or neckhole. The dress was meant to be fastened at the shoulder with fibulae.

"This won't do," I told her.

"The wool is good. It was bought in Sardis."

"Dresses like this have been out of favor in Athens for many years."

"I like the hardware," she said, showing me a pair of long, sharp pins that might have served as daggers.

As this was a good opportunity to begin her education in Greek history, I told her the myth of why Athenian women were forbidden to wear dresses of Doric style. Once, in the city's distant past, the army had been humiliated by the Aeginetans in battle. A single soldier returned home to report the disaster. The women of Athens, outraged by the loss of their husbands, pulled the stickpins from their dresses and flayed the messenger on the spot. Needless to say, the elders of the city were disturbed by this incident. From that day Athenian women were forbidden to fasten their dresses with pins. Or so says Herodotus.

"The Athenian men would have done better to win their battles than to tell their women what to wear!" Rohjane cried.

It took much coaxing to get her to try the dress I brought for her. As she went behind a screen to change, I found myself awkwardly confronted by Youtab, who was as delicate as a Bactrian camel and possibly less attractive.

"Wanna go?" she asked me. Then she held up the two long fingers of her left hand, with knuckles pressed together and slightly flexed. In the moment, I had no idea what this signified. She laughed at me.

"Oh, don't play the fool! I've heard all about you Greeks and your pleasures . . . ." she said, inclining her head toward her mistress. "But she also tells me you never use your mouths *down there* on a woman. Is that true?"

If what she meant by "down there" was what I thought she meant, then I told her that the very thought would revolt any man.

"Don't be so sure. The Persians make quite a practice of it."

"That explains their performance on the battlefield," I replied. Yet Youtab's impertinence made me wonder about something else. Greek soldiers had a name for the Persians—"carpet-munchers"—that I had thought referred to their habit of bowing their heads at the feet of their masters. Perhaps, I thought, it referred to their bedroom perversities instead.

Rohjane came out with her head and arms in the right places, but with no sense of how to gather the chiton properly to make it drape. I helped the Queen as best I could without touching her, leaving it to Youtab to tie and retie the girdle around her hips. The result was very pleasing. It took some effort not to stare at the sheerness of the fabric, which clung in ways that would have given Praxiteles much to ponder.

"Not bad, but I can improve it. Youtab, my knife!"

Before I could utter a word, Rohjane cut the dress to make a rude opening for her breasts to show through. She then covered them with a small square of silk, tied in Sogdian fashion at the neck.

"Better, no?" she asked me.

In most respects this was the kind of problem I faced. Asia now had a barbarian Queen with a weaker sense of decorum than a small girl. Not only did she feel herself entitled to appear at drinking parties, speak her mind, and show her body as readily as any man, but she assumed that any other arrangement was inconceivable. To correct her was nothing less than a Sisyphean task. No sooner had I convinced her that the casual display of her breasts was shameful, than she took to walking around with her chiton hiked up to her thighs. When I got her legs covered, down came her hair. Not even the finest of golden fillets would convince her to restrain that wild coif. Faced with whatever other little rebellions she could conceive, I decided to grant her that impropriety.

Where was Alexander in all this? At best, he was ab-

sent; at worst, drunk. As the weeks passed, the novelty
of his new bride wore off. By the end he spent no more
than one night in five in her bed. Bagoas, on the other
hand, was either a fixed presence around the King, or
always close enough to come running. When Alexander left to do the duty of a husband, the eunuch would
jeer or groan. In this I believe he was encouraged by
Perdiccas, Ptolemy, and Craterus, who had little interest in the production of a legitimate heir. If Youtab's
testimony is any guide, they had little grounds for fear
in this regard.

Along with the unconstraint Rohjane displayed
about her person went other strange habits. The Sogdians, like many people of Asia, had a particular dread
of women at the time of their monthly flow. The
Zoroastrian custom was not only complete separation
of the "unclean" female from her family, but separation from all aspects of the Seven Creations. Their handling of food, drink, water, animals, and fire was
forbidden. Since ordinary clothes were ruined by contact with the woman's body, she was required to wear
special garments reserved for that time. For a menstruating woman even to breathe on another person
was an assault that demanded vigorous ablutions. The
same applied to her gaze, which was reputed to have
the power to stifle the generative power of men. Many
of the humble women of Asia therefore spend their
days of corruption in small, dark, stifling hovels where
their opportunities to pollute the cosmos—and therefore to aid the Hostile Spirit—were restricted.

Now I am aware that certain Greeks have queer beliefs about these matters. In Ionia, the influence of
menstruating women is thought to be noxious enough

to kill agricultural pests. Wives and daughters are sent in their vulnerable times to walk the fields, their dresses above their waists, to control beetles and worms. Even in Attica it is thought that the inception of flow at a time of lunar eclipse is bad luck. I have heard doctors debate over the dangers of sharing bathwater with women, menstruating or not. But even these beliefs are a far cry from utter segregation from the course of life, as is the custom in much of Asia.

A hovel would not do for a Queen in her indisposition. Rohjane refused to spend those times in her usual tent either, claiming that it had too many corners.

"And what is wrong with corners?" I asked.

"Corners, O ignorant one, are places where the evil influences released by the menses may hide."

Rohjane therefore required a special round tent be prepared for her use. She also could not touch the earth with her bare feet, or use utensils to eat. If she happened to touch any metal tools, Youtab took them outside and washed them first with cow urine, then sand, then water. It was essential to observe the correct order of ablutions, or else some deity or another would be weakened in the struggle against the *daevas*—

"The defendant is warned again to confine his remarks to topics relevant to his defense," Polycleitus interjected.

"I beg the magistrate's indulgence, due to the breadth of the prosecution's indictment. My intention is to show what difficulties the management of Rohjane presented for the Macedonians, and how my presence was beneficial to Alexander. I also believe it essential to my defense to establish the nature of my relationship with the Queen. If you recall, I was accused of using her in a plot against the King."

"It is nothing to me if you squander your time, Machon,"

said Polycleitus, waving his hand. "Only be aware that you will get no further indulgence from me."

It would not be true to say that Rohjane was the most observant of Zoroastrians. How could she be, if she was obliged to spend her life in the company of unbelievers? Still, her customs raised so much curiosity around the camp that Alexander brought out Gobares to render some explanation. The question of cow urine was again raised, albeit in a less obviously dismissive way.

"What you Greeks don't grasp is the comprehensiveness of the prophet's vision," he told us. "For when he tells us that Ahura Mazda created the six Amesha Spentas, and they in turn made the elements of the world, and that Angra Mainyu seeks the ultimate corruption of all those elements, the revelation means what it implies. The corruption of fire is smoke; of living beings, death and decay. Water may also be polluted by contact with the things of the Hostile Spirit—dirt, blood, the dead. Therefore, we may not defile water by washing certain things with it, such as that which a menstruating woman has touched, gazed, or breathed upon.

"The effluent of the cow is holy to us, as it is to the Indians. It has special power to cleanse other substances without corruption adhering to it. So when we wish to purify something, we use the cow first, before exposing it to water."

"And so you may refresh yourselves by standing under a pissing cow?" asked Perdiccas.

"More or less. Those with certain scruples may opt to strain it through muslin into a clean vessel."

"Show us," ordered Alexander.

We all went out to the stock pens. Since it was dark, we bore torches. The eyes of the animals shone back at us as we waited at the gate for the telltale sound of divinity manifesting itself upon the ground.

"It is not usual to wait for the *pajow* to appear, but to take it as a blessing when it does," said Gobares.

"I feel the same about wine," Craterus remarked. "Hand over that jug!"

At last Gobares heard what he was listening for. As he ran out into the yard with a basin in his outstretched hands, I looked to Alexander. Despite his drunkenness—or perhaps because of it—he had the look of a man who was hopeless to comprehend what he was seeing. In that moment I felt sympathy for him, for as the new Great King, he took upon himself obligations as well as palaces. Everything in his character compelled him to understand the people he would rule. Yet as he watched Gobares at his strange lustrations it was clear that, despite his new Persian diadem and tunic, he feared that he would never succeed. When he went back to his tent that night, it was without Bagoas or Rohjane.

Alexander turned away from India, but that didn't mean he wanted to go home. That left the alternatives of proceeding north, where there was nothing but savages and wasteland, or south, to the Indus delta. The choice was obvious: the entire army, the King decided, would sail down the great river to the sea, with the double objects of exploring this unknown territory and rounding out the limits of his empire. The plan was to go south along the Hydaspes just above the confluence with the Acesines. From there the other tributaries—the Hydraotes and the Hyphasis—would add to the great stream until they joined the Indus proper for the unknown distance to the ocean.

In the center would proceed a fleet of boats under the immediate command of Nearchus of Crete. This man had been with Alexander since the beginning, but not being a Macedonian had limited his prospects for advancement. On the water, however, Nearchus's value was undeniable. In many respects he was the sort of man that complimented the best aspects of Alexander's character: loyal, resourceful, possessed of a fervent curiosity.

The floating contingent was made up of Alexander's court, the lighter auxiliaries, a few select units of cavalry, and most of the supplies. The heavy infantry and cavalry marched on the right bank of the river with Craterus, while the elephants, siege train, and Hypaspists went on the left, under Hephaestion.

When all was prepared, Aristander the soothsayer conducted a sacrifice in the center of the Hydaspes. The blood of the bull was poured into the river to honor it, and also the deities of the Indus and all her tributaries, as well as father Zeus-Ammon, uncle Poseidon, brother Heracles, and Ocean. Afterward the Persian allies held rites in honor of Ahura Mazda and Haurvatat, Zoroastrian god of water. Their libations did not use blood, but cow's milk sprinkled with marjoram leaves, ladled into the river with a copper spoon. Alexander presided with equal reverence over both ceremonies, and for a moment the confluence of these rites, and therefore their peoples, seemed more propitious than ever before.

Many armies have come and gone in the eternal history of the Indus. Yet the river had probably never seen anything like the Macedonians who passed that way. On the stream were almost a thousand boats, their oars stroking the water to matched drumbeats, the colored flags of each unit snapping on their staffs. Along the banks marched one hundred thousand men, fifty thousand followers, and two hundred elephants, spread along columns that covered miles on both shores. The dust raised by their feet was visible as twin plumes towering and mingling as they rose into the sky. Villages surrendered days before they were glimpsed; saffron-robed natives, awed by the spectacle, gaped from beaches and hilltops.

It was remarkable that anyone would dare resist such a force. Yet the Brahmins persisted in their defiance, convincing two of the local kings to oppose Alexander. The first, King Musicanus, first pretended to submit, then killed all the Macedonians left in his kingdom after Alexander had passed. Peithon was sent back to deal with him, assaulting his city walls with siege equipment the Indians had never seen before. The Indians died by the thousands, with the survivors sold as slaves under the auspices of Oxyartes, Rohjane's father. Musicanus was brought before Alexander in chains and hung next to the Brahmins who provoked his treachery. But before the last Brahmin was killed, he cried out to Alexander.

"Beware, O Alexander, lest you lose all!"

"What do you mean?" the King asked the man.

"The only ground any man truly owns," he replied, "is that under his own feet."

This advice, exclaimed Alexander, reminded him

something Diogenes the Cynic might say. He therefore let this last Brahmin go free.

The other defiant kingdom was that of the Mallians. I was not present at the conquest of Multan, their capital, so I cannot appraise Aeschines's account of what happened there. What is certain is that during his attack on the mud-brick wall of the town, Alexander somehow contrived to be inside the city with his guards outside. Alone among the Mallians, he drove off repeated attacks as he was heard to cry out, in a voice full of joy, random phrases that verged on nonsense, such as "There it is!" and "Upon the color of it!" He was finally pierced by a lance, falling backward with only the shield of Achilles to protect him. Though almost a thousand years old, the relic warded off all blows until the outraged Macedonians broke in to his rescue. Alexander's men, seeing the King fall, focused their wrath on the survivors. Every single Mallian in the town was slaughtered that day, down to the youths, the infants, and the unborn babes inside the womb.

Alexander suffered a deep chest wound in the brawl. His condition deteriorating to the point where it seemed he would die, he was carried in stages back to the river. There he hovered near death for a week.

Aeschines says his men kept up a constant vigil, but my memory is different. With each day that passed without sign of Alexander, more of his men were convinced that he had already died. Few protested when, with the necessary connivance of Perdiccas, Ptolemy, and Craterus, Peithon began to issue orders in his place.

His first act was to separate the allied Persians from the Macedonian units they had joined. This was a pop-

ular order among the Macedonians, but divided the
army against itself, bringing the camp to the brink of
hostilities between the new imperial "partners." After
a few more days passed, Peithon was emboldened
enough to put a golden fillet around his head. One day
more, and he ordered a final inventory of the contents
of Alexander's tent. Objects of the Persian style—furniture, lamps, native clothing adopted by the King—
were collected in a pile outside the tent, apparently
waiting only for Peithon's order to set them ablaze.

I was not alone in being concerned at this arrogance. Nearchus shared my feelings, but dared not
defy the usurper or those backing him. We agreed that
someone should get word to Hephaestion. To this end
Nearchus lent me a few Cretan archers. Our party left
early the next morning, just before the changing of the
dawn watch.

It was just a few miles to the little camp upstream
where Alexander lay. We arrived just as the sun rose on
our right shoulders, illuminating the tent and wagons
on a little knoll above the Hydaspes. Forming my men
into two columns of sixteen each, we approached the
place guardedly, not knowing what we would find.

The first movement we saw in the camp was the
bent figure of the King's doctor, Critobulus. From a
distance I could see he held a water jug in his hands,
and he turned his head toward us as I hailed him. With
the sound of the stream so close to me I could not understand his replies. He began to point fretfully in the
direction opposite to us, jumping up and down.

"On the run now, boys!" I ordered my archers, understanding his warning at last.

XIX

The dark-haired Mallian horsemen arrived just as we did, at dawn. They were riding in hard from the flat-lands, blades raised, eyes blazing with vengeance for the massacre of their people at Multan. My men sur-rounded Alexander's tent just in time to set them-selves, each draw an arrow, and let fly. The Cretan reputation for bowmanship was fulfilled: five of the Mallians went down right away. The other ten reached us before we could get off another shot. At that point we took the worst of it, since only I had a proper sword, the archers being equipped only with daggers. We made a fighting retreat with our backs to the tent, a few of us forming a screen for the rest to use their bows. Three more Mallians dropped as our legs brushed the tent cords.

It took some time before I realized a short-limbed demon was fighting beside me. It was Alexander, his sword flashing, clad only in his own bloody dressings. The appearance of the great Alexander took the heart out of the Mallians. They began to give ground until the arrows flew again. Then, with a final, undecipherable curse, the last one wrenched his horse around and rode away.

The King said nothing during the fight. When it was over he just stood there on uncertain feet, smiled, and collapsed where he stood. Critobulus reappeared from his hiding place in the bushes.

"Help me get him inside!"

Fresh bleeding had soaked through the linen wrappings around Alexander's chest. Cutting the dressing away, the doctor washed off the old and new blood, the poultice of sea salt, and exposed the wound. It was an arrow hole in his left side, surgically enlarged to extract the head. The scab had been ripped in two, no doubt during the exertions of the fight, and the wound issued blood-red foam.

"There is air mixed with the blood, so the lung has not healed," said the doctor. "But the bleeding is our concern now. Lay this on with your whole weight . . . use both hands."

I stood leaning on Alexander with a wine-soaked cloth until Critobulus was ready with another styptic. When it was applied, and we had the King wrapped in fresh bandages, I finally asked the doctor the question I had meant to ask him since I had arrived.

"What happened to your guards?"

"I don't know. When I got up to check the wound before dawn they were already gone."

"Where is Hephaestion?"

"I told him to sleep in his own tent last night. He was accomplishing nothing here."

I dared not leave the King during the day and the night he slept after this near-disaster. That his guards had been withdrawn, and the Mallians made aware of his location, suggested a level of Macedonian duplicity that I had not suspected. For this reason I could not even risk sending word of the attack back to camp, lest it invite another attempt. For this precaution Hephaestion would be furious with me.

Fortunately, there was a lot of work to divert me from these troubling thoughts. Twelve of the Cretan archers had died in the raid, with three surviving their immediate injuries. Despite our best efforts, one of these men died from loss of blood. The others lost an arm and an eye, respectively. I heard the survivors boasting hopefully among themselves during the night.

"If those fools in Sogdia got ten talents for climbing a rock, we should get a thousand for saving his life!"

Alexander awoke with no memory of the raid. When I reminded him, and added that his guards had vanished just before the attack, he laughed. He relished the irony of it, that a battle with consequences as momentous as Gaugamela had been fought and won for him by an Athenian and handful of bowmen.

"So if it wasn't for you my torment would be over, Machon! Do you expect to be rewarded for this cruelty?" he asked, indicating the tent, the sky—in short, life itself—in his conception of "cruelty." His attitude changed, however, when I told him that Peithon was rifling through the royal tent.

"Peithon . . ." he said, weariness creeping into his voice. "Why do you force me to act this role? Where is Hephaestion?"

"Exhausted. Shall I send for him?"

"No. I'll go."

The physician laid a restraining hand on his shoulder. "You must not rise," he said.

"I have no intention of rising, dear Critobulus! But we can't leave our friend here to Peithon's tender mercies."

A boat was brought in secret to a place below the knoll. The doctor oversaw the rigging of a stretcher between the wales. In this way, we floated Alexander downstream to the Macedonian camp. The sentries saw him first as he approached, shouting out that Alexander's funeral barge was on the water. Alexander lay still as his men gathered on the bank, some wet-eyed with grief, some in wonder. Then, at exactly the most opportune moment, the King opened his eyes and raised his fist, proving to all that he still lived.

Aeschines described the scene in his statement. But my opponent is wrong to claim that the King did this simply to prove he had lived. When he raised his arm, the finger on the end of it was pointing straight at Peithon. The officers around the usurper stepped away, leaving him standing alone in his glad silks and golden fillet. He was arrested by Perdiccas's men, and after a short trial, disappeared. Some say he spent his last days in whatever hole that contained Callisthenes before he died.

Despite hints that verged on outright denunciation, I could not convince Alexander that Craterus, Perdiccas, or Ptolemy had a hand in Peithon's crimes. His resistance to this idea seemed to have a practical purpose: with Arridaeus still incapacitated, and Philotas, Parmenion, Cleitus, and now Peithon gone, the King's circle of experienced commanders was shrinking. But I also believe there was the usual strand of Euripidean fatalism in his attitude—a conviction that his time was short, and someone strong needed to be left to pick up the reins. For their part, then, Perdiccas, Ptolemy, and Craterus suffered nothing from allowing Peithon to overplay his hand. A potential rival was removed, and they had an opportunity to make a display of their loyalty to the King.

Aeschines, you are mistaken in another way. You say that all the Macedonians rejoiced when they saw Alexander alive, throwing blossoms and money at him. In fact, while some cheered his appearance, the response was not overwhelming. The ambivalence showed painfully on many faces, for Alexander to have survived his wound would mean there would be much more fighting and dying before they reached home. Many of these deaths would be against petty tribes like the Mallians. After the stupendous achievement of conquering the Persian Empire, to risk themselves that way, pacifying primitives in marginal places, seemed a task less than worth their lives.

Pushing south, we watched the Indus grow wider, and its waters rougher, until many of the boats were forced to find shelter along the banks. But when the men returned to where they had beached their craft, they found that the river's level had risen while they were away, and their boats had floated off. Moreover, the Macedonians were confounded to watch the great river do an about-face and flow north. This inspired great unease among them, for they thought nothing mortal could make such a large river reverse its current. Some whispered that it was a signal of the gods' displeasure that the army had pressed so far into unknown lands.

Alexander sacrificed a spotless white heifer to Poseidon and to the Indus. Upon the performance of the ceremony, the Indus slackened and reversed her current again, so that the Macedonians believed the sacrifice had pleased these gods. But the complete cycle of flooding and ebbing happened again the same day; the flood, moreover, was composed of salt water, which could only have come from the sea. This phenomenon of the tides is known only on the shores of Ocean. Proceeding a few miles south, the Macedonians saw at last the great mouth of the river, and the infinite waters beyond. To commemorate their safe arrival, Alexander ordered a great trophy to be built of square-cut blocks, and more sacrifices. A hecatomb of Aambhi's gift oxen were slaughtered offshore and the meat distributed to the men on the beach; so much blood was poured into the waters that the sea's foam washed up red at the men's feet.

Aristander reported the auspices to be favorable for the King's next project: a voyage of exploration along the southern coast of Asia to the Persian Gulf, under the command of Nearchus. To prepare the way for this journey, Alexander sent parties of men into the eastern desert to stockpile supplies and dig wells for the sailors. When a number of these parties did not return, the King blamed the natives for their disappearance. Punitive action brought these people—principally the Arabitae and the Oreitae—into line; as penance, he ordered the tribes to bring all the stores they could gather to the coast. Though the people had little to spare, they obeyed, so that Alexander gave permission for Nearchus to proceed when his fleet was ready.

He ordered the bulk of the army, including all the

Foot Companions, half the Hypaspists, the elephants corps, and all the native auxiliaries, to follow Craterus to Carmania along the safe route west, through Gedrosia. The rest of his men, amounting to about six thousand infantry and one thousand horses, plunged with him into the Gedrosian desert. Alexander had heard that entire armies of Persians and Babylonians had been swallowed up there; in former crossings, an army of the Babylonians had been reduced to twenty men, while another of the Great King had lost all but seven. Naturally, it became Alexander's intention to succeed where these others had failed, and become the first to lead a force through the desert intact.

I went with Craterus, so I did not witness the ordeal that was in store for Alexander and his men. The outlines are clear, though: for two months the expedition struggled through such infernal wastes as to make the trip to Siwah in Egypt seem easy. Though they were never far from the ocean, they found little fresh water except deep underground, and that only after expending more sweat and effort than the meager flows would replenish. They found no animals, and no plants except a kind of nettle that, for all the sustenance it provided, might have been made of bone. Though Alexander had intended to lay up supplies for Nearchus, he could spare none, and feared that the desolation of the coast would doom his fleet as well. Autumn came but the sun did not relent, forcing them to travel at night. This further confused his guides, who already contended with the disappearance of their landmarks under the shifting sands. Days and weeks were added to the march as the expedition drifted on and off the trail.

Alarmed, Alexander sent scouts to seek the help of the native people of the area. His riders returned with discouraging news: the barbarians of the coast were too backward to possess towns, weapons, or buildings of any kind. The natives, whom the Persians called the "Fish-Eaters," went about mostly naked, with hair and nails left uncut over their whole lives. They lived in holes dug in the sand, roofed over with fish bones and seaweed. The only moisture to pass their lips was dew collected on sealskins they left unfurled by night, or the blood of the creatures that swam in those waters. They had no word for "rain" in their language.

"Have the barbarians acknowledged our sovereignty over them as the Lord of All Asia?" asked the King.

"My lord, the Fish-Eaters lack knowledge even of chiefs, let alone of kings that might reign over them from afar. We did not think to demand their submission."

"Ignorance is no excuse for their disrespect."

Alexander sent a force of cavalry to demonstrate his authority. The troops returned without suffering any losses, and bearing the finest tribute the Fish-Eaters had to offer: a handful of seashells. This gift Alexander accepted as gladly as any from the wealthiest of his subjects, for he was not unreasonable, and could only expect the things thought most precious in the lands he conquered. The King returned their gift with a dozen javelins, for use in fishing or any other purpose they wished.

The real dying began when the guides lost the trail again. With hopelessness spreading through the ranks, men straggled, fell behind the pace, and disappeared into the night. They went by twos and threes, until Alexander had lost more men than to any human enemy. There was a look of despair on his face, they say, that had never been seen there before; no doubt he took pity on the faithful Macedonians who had followed him, and received only death for their trouble. This expression worried his men as much as the desert, for if the indomitable Alexander lost heart they were certainly doomed.

That Alexander understood this is clear from a famous story most of you already know. Some of his men had dug a deep pit and managed to collect a helmetful of fresh water from the bottom of it. When they brought the water to their King, he was tempted, but in the end refused to drink, pouring it on the ground. His men were comforted by this, knowing that Alexander expected no more of them than he was willing to suffer himself. Many of the survivors attest that this gesture gave them the will to go on. Alexander had therefore worked a kind of miracle: he had rendered a single helmetful of water enough to satisfy an entire army.

At length Craterus, who was waiting for them on the borders of Carmania, saw a party of burnt skeletons emerge from the desert. When Alexander joined him, he had the appearance of a dust-covered reptile, but a smiling one: the Persians had lost all but seven men, and the Babylonian Queen Semiramis all but twenty, but Alexander saved more than three thousand, or about half his force. Thus the King triumphed over history, if not over the desert itself.

Thanks to Peithon's example no one was willing to assume Alexander was dead until they laid eyes on his corpse. Craterus, instead of taking the diadem for himself when the King was overdue, just followed orders. Indeed, he led the army more sensibly than Alexander himself, for in his lack of imagination he simply took us from point A to point B, without turning aside every few miles to overawe every feathered native he saw.

Harpalus was unique in failing to share in this good sense. As Aeschines has said, he was a personal friend of the King's, his treasurer at Ecbatana. In the end, in a fit of what may have been grief at Alexander's death in the desert, but was probably just greed, Harpalus abandoned his post and fled to this city with a fortune of six thousand talents. My opponent misleads you, however, when he makes wild accusations based on some moneylender's records of one thousand *darics* due for my collection. That money was not a bribe from Harpalus, but Alexander's reward to me for saving his life in the Mallian raid.

Nor is there much significance to the fact that the payment was made in *darics*: a great deal of the Great King's fortune, out of which Alexander issued all his rewards, was minted in that coin. This is not a secret. If Aeschines had bothered to check with any of the other Greeks who have come home with money from Alexander, he would have found many of them were paid in *darics*. Aeschines furthermore neglects to mention that Harpalus was expelled from the city on the order of the Assembly, and then murdered at the instigation of his own bodyguard, Thibron the Lacedaemonian. Yet wasn't Harpalus supposed to be allied with . . . dare I say his name . . . *Demosthenes?* So much for the vaunted influence of Aeschines's personal bugaboo!

XX

When I saw the King again he posed a question to me that had preoccupied him during long night-marches in Gedrosia: what does it mean to be Persian? When he first asked this I thought it was a joke. But he was serious, and by asking it he meant more than simply the fact that a man was born in Persian territory.

"Are you asking about the customs of the Persians?"

"I'm asking about customs," he replied, "and clothing, and the way they think, and everything in their history that makes them what they are."

What reply to make? As Greeks, we have insults for the Persians like "carpet-munchers," "runaways," and "spear-droppers." And we have words to describe the Persians that flatter us more than they describe them: words like arrogance, decadence, slavishness, obsequiousness, cowardliness. These are venerable notions, handed down to us from the men who fought at Marathon, Salamis, and Plataea. But no one who saw the Persians take the field against the Macedonians, pitting their leather armor against the *sarissa*, could say they were cowardly. No one who has seen the splendor of their architecture, art, or gardens can doubt their ingenuity. And no one who has worked beside Persian administrators or fought beside their nobles, as we came to do, has any grounds to doubt their basic decency.

What is a Persian? It was easier to speak of individual Persians, and the qualities that blighted or recommended them. Pressed by the King, I suggested he look to the beliefs that most of the Persians had accepted—that is, the odd philosophy of Zoroaster, who taught that our sins each have cosmic consequences, that judgment awaits us all, and that all life is worthy of reverence. Yet how can a soldier believe such a thing, objected Alexander, if it is his duty to destroy life? They may believe it, I replied, but at the cost of fearing death, which as every Greek knows makes a man useless in the phalanx.

"So the Persians run from the field," he asked, "because Zoroaster teaches that life is superior to victory?"

"One might suppose so; in any case, no philosophy can be entirely bad that holds the dog in such high esteem!"

We posed our questions to Gobares, who said the following: "A Persian is not a Greek in pantaloons. He is still a creature of the open steppe, taking the sky as the roof of his lawful abode. He cares less for abstractions than you Greeks, and for that he belongs to a far, far happier race. You would all do well to give back the lands you took, for the Persian wears the responsibility more lightly than you. Mark my words—in Greek hands, this monstrosity of an empire you've built will not survive. Indeed, you all should have let yourselves be conquered by Xerxes. A distant, contented overlord would have been a far better neighbor to you than you have been to each other!"

This reply was not satisfying, and it did not settle the issue. For Alexander, resolving this question promised a way to square the political circle: to escape the squalid end of every Macedonian king, it would be necessary for him to become something else. Yet at no point did his exact goal seem clear in his mind—he didn't want to become Persian, nor did he wish to remain no more than the semi-Greek monarch his father had been. Could he, by some contortion of his character, make himself the measure of all the people he undertook to rule? Or were Persians and Greeks fated to lack a common factor, but forever remain, like the side and diagonal of the square, incommensurable? On this proof, more than geometry was at stake.

Gods and children demand that the world reflect their preferences. Alexander, who was both, attempted to force the fusion he couldn't realize in himself by mongrelizing his army. For some years he had financed the training of thirty thousand Persian boys in Macedonian customs and tactics. As these recruits came of age, he marched these "Inheritors" out in front of his troops with a conspicuous and tenderly paternal smile on his face. What good he was expecting from this display was difficult to understand, but among the Macedonians it produced nothing but hard feelings.

Their resentment was aggravated further when his "Inheritors" began to take positions in the phalanx vacated by his aging veterans. Watching the Persians ape the ways of their betters on the parade ground is one thing, but having a barbarian recruit behind you in the ranks holding a sharp pike at your back is quite another. Exactly how Alexander expected his men to trust these newcomers, when the Macedonians' entire experience consisted of watching Persians run from the battlefield, was beyond my understanding. And I keep hearing that Alexander always had a deft way of handling his troops!

The King also invited many of his officers to take Persian wives. These sorts of "invitations" were, of course, not meant to be declined. Hephaestion therefore took Drypetis, a daughter of Darius; Craterus drew Amastrine, Darius's niece; and Ptolemy a girl of noble birth named Artacama. Nearchus, newly returned from his explorations at sea, got a new wife, as did Perdiccas and Seleucus and Peucestas. Alexander himself added two wives to the one he already had: Barsine, Darius's eldest daughter, and Parysatis, daughter of Artaxerxes III. The King's double nuptials were meant to legitimize his sons through both Darius's line and that of Artaxerxes, whom Darius had overthrown.

The banquet was held at the palace in Susa. In the forecourt he built a gilded loggia draped with garland and perfumed by aromatic woods, lined with ninety-two nuptial couches each carved from single trunks of Lebanese cedar. The loggia surrounded a tented close centered on the golden couch of the royal couple. Pennants trimmed with tiny bells tinkled in the breeze as peacocks strutted across the great orchestra, each one followed by an attendant to assure no bird would soil the blessed event. The brides, who were delivered from the hands of their fathers according to their

ranks, presented themselves in veiled finery to the re-
clining grooms. Each was married as she was pulled to
a sitting position on the cushions.

For this event Alexander costumed himself as
Dionysus triumphant, complete with leopard skin,
golden fillet, and thyrsus of cornel wood and ivy
arranged in the shape of a pine cone. Like the god,
Alexander had invaded India, and was not a stranger
to wine. We may imagine the ivy leaves also concealed
an iron spear point, as the stories tell of Dionysus in
his warrior aspect. The god's theatrical patronage was
honored by troupes of actors, dancers and musicians
who had come out from Ionia and Athens to liven the
proceedings.

The splendor of these ceremonies notwithstanding,
I don't think many of the Macedonians took these marriages to heart. Many of them already had wives back
home that they never renounced. Ptolemy's marriage
to Artacama, for instance, did not compel him to turn
Thais out of his tent. In fact, taking native women was
a common practice on long campaigns—wives, concubines, or other varieties of female companionship
could be obtained in the camp market like any other
commodity.

I say "I believe" the banquets went splendidly because I was not there. Instead, I drew the task of handling Rohjane. The Queen was—no surprise—not
invited. I had had some success in getting her to
change her wardrobe and habits, but the insult of
Alexander's betrayal undid all the progress I had
made. Now everything Macedonian was shameful,
odious. This reversal was ill-timed because by some

perversity of the Fates she was at last pregnant with Alexander's child.

Rohjane herself would not speak to me, preferring to lie on her couch and nurse her injury in silence. Youtab presented herself as an intermediary.

"Do you Greeks know anything about women? Do your queens suffer themselves to be made foolish in your country?"

"The Macedonians are not Greeks," I said, changing the subject. "And very few kings or queens rule over us."

"You're all fools, whatever you are! Does your King, who barely serves my lady as a man, imagine that his acts have no consequences? Don't insult us by pretending you don't know what we mean!"

"I don't know what you mean."

"The Queen carries his heir," Youtab pointed. "Don't doubt it is a boy."

"She is only two months pregnant."

"It is a boy," Rohjane interjected from the other room.

"If you were not all fools, you would know that the sex can be told from the way the child lies within!" Youtab hectored me. "But as easily as that may be told, there may be problems. . . ."

I shook my head at this impossible woman.

"Yes, you know what I am saying," she said. "It took that kinglet four years to do his duty by the Queen. Perhaps we should let him try again with that chubby Barsine. If he is lucky he may get a son in ten years!"

I stuck my finger in Youtab's face. "That kind of talk

should not be idly made, for as you say, there may be consequences."

"Don't show me your cock's comb, Machon! It is far too late for that!"

"Youtab, that's enough," commanded Rohjane. She was suddenly standing at the door, wearing the woolen peplos I had forbidden her. Her hair had escaped its clasps, and there was a puffiness around her eyes that showed she had been crying. This was the first evidence I'd had that she possessed any sort of feeling regarding Alexander. Whether her tears were out of jealousy or damaged pride or both was impossible to say.

Youtab shot to her feet, and Rohjane took her place opposite me. The Queen's manner was calm, even sage, as she began to speak.

"You must excuse Youtab, for she is upset. She does not understand the matters that oblige kings to do what they must. Honestly, I expected something like this, though I confess my guard went down when our son was conceived. I therefore have one question for you, as our friend, which I hope you might answer the best you can. . . ."

She proceeded to ask about the history of the Macedonian throne, and specifically the fates of those mothers and children who ended up on the losing side of succession disputes. As the daughter of a king, she must have suspected that the picture was a grim one. I was therefore in no way free to make up any story I wished, as Aeschines claims. What would have been the point, when she could have gotten the truth from any number of other sources? Perdiccas and Ptolemy, to take just two, would not have hesitated to describe in detail what end awaited her and her son! If I had lied, all I would have accomplished would have been to discredit myself.

"I thank you for your honesty, Machon," she finally said. "We will not speak of this matter again."

The speaker was interrupted by a noise from the floor. It was Swallow, scratching one of his uncut toenails against the planks. When Machon looked at him, Swallow pointed at the water clock. The flow from the reservoir had slowed to a trickle.

Yes, I see that my time is almost up. I suppose I had flattered myself to think I had the same skill as Aeschines in sensing when his water has run low. And to think I haven't even killed Alexander yet—so to speak! Relax, Aeschines . . . that was a joke, not a confession! So I must conclude. . . .

As he alienated his wife, Alexander made additional trouble for himself with his veteran soldiers. It had now been ten years since the Greeks had crossed into Asia. Since many of Alexander's men were then too old or too weak to serve him further, he ordered ten thousand Greeks cashiered from the army, albeit with a fortune of one talent each as a bonus for their service. Craterus was given the task of leading these veterans home.

The veterans, having already seen their commanders take Persian wives, and their positions taken by barbarian levies, were in no mood to accept dismissal. As Alexander took the rostrum to praise them, the men responded with jeers, performing mock prostrations, asking him if he would prefer an army full of Persians and, yes, calling him "Darius Alexander." The King did not perceive these things at first, speaking as if in a dream from which he was reluctant to awake. When he did notice them, however, his face flashed a deep red, and he looked directly at those who insulted him.

"What injustice have I done you," he asked, "that you dishonor this leave-taking? Speak out like men, not children, for after our service together you owe me as much!"

"The dishonor is done upon us," said a voice from the crowd. "For Alexander has forgotten the men who gave him the land of Asia, and thinks they may be bought off for mere gold."

"Maybe he thinks he will invade Africa by himself!" cried another.

This remark made the rest of the men laugh. Alexander did not laugh, however, but instead called his Agrianian guards. The instigators were arrested in a dead silence, as King and army eyed each other. Their mutual hostility was strange in light of all they had accomplished together. It was as if the mortal body resented its divine head, and the divine head spurned its body. Alexander moved to speak, but was seized by a violent coughing fit that lasted a long time; as he convulsed, he grasped his side, over the place where the Mallian spear had punctured his lung.

"This is a fine day, my Companions. For this is the day I found out your true estimation of me. You gave me Asia, you say? I gave you respect! I took a race of cowardly, dung-smeared vagabonds and forged an army! I gave you lifetimes of memories to grace the heritage of your families. For you will return to Macedonia with much more than a talent of gold in your hands. You return with the kind of esteem that is unassailable for the rest of your days! And for what have I asked in return? A bit of purple to wear, and the kisses of my dear companions! Beyond these, I have demanded no special privileges—I have known the rigors of the camp and the march as well as any of you. In the Gedrosian desert, I could have taken water, but did not, because there was not enough for us to share—can any of you deny it? So what will you say now, when people remind you that you consigned me to our enemies? How will you explain the end of Alexander? Go then! Go back to your small lives, your ordinariness! Sustain yourselves with wisecracks instead of honor! I have nothing more to say to you."

Thereupon he spat on the ground and retreated to his tent. As he had done before, on the death of Cleitus and when he was forced back from India, he took no food and saw no visitors for the next day. For a good number of the men this temper had a too-familiar ring, and they did not respond to it. Yet for others, particularly those of weak or compliant minds, the King's upset was intolerable. Alexander increased their discomfort by issuing new commissions for officers: most of the names on the list were Persian ones, and some of the nicknames of the regiments had been transferred to their Persian counterparts.

Again, for those who had set their hearts against him, who considered their divorce to be final, the commissions only confirmed their suspicions. But for some, this estrangement had gone too far—abandoning their pride, they surrounded Alexander's tent and called for his forgiveness. When he did not answer, they broke down entirely, making such a riot of pitiful wailing that the King's heart softened. Appearing before them, he honored all by receiving their kisses, and wept tears of good fellowship with them, saying— without irony this time—that it was indeed a good day.

Of course, not all the ten thousand veterans came to Alexander's tent that night, or even most of them. But instead of dwelling on the absence of their comrades, the King chose to recognize the humility of the few hundred who did come, and in so doing to excuse the lot. The incident perfectly typifies the dilemma of his leadership. Among his veterans, as in this city, his hegemony did provoke bitter and, in some respects, unjustified hostility. To both challenges Alexander responded wisely, choosing not to force his will when a simple declaration of victory would do.

The other important part of this incident was that Perdiccas and Ptolemy managed to maneuver Craterus into leading the veterans home. Alexander presented it as an honor to his old comrade, and under other circumstances it would have been. I am suspicious, though, that this honor absented Craterus from the scene just as Alexander fell sick at Babylon. When the veterans marched at last, I saw Craterus embrace Alexander for what seemed like a long time. Then the King kissed him, and brushing away a tear, Craterus barked an order to the men, who also had tears flowing down their cheeks. And so the weeping army departed for Cilicia, where they would construct a fleet to sail home. None of them would see Alexander alive again.

But it is late in our story. After years on campaign, Alexander's exhaustion manifested at every level a man may show it—physical, intellectual, emotional.

Since his latest injury, he leaned on suppliants who came to receive the royal kiss, and seemed to cling to his horse instead of ride it. For those with eyes to look for them, the signs of his end were increasingly at hand.

At that time the King, who was on his way to Ecbatana, paused in Media to inspect the stock of wild horses in that country. He was entertained there by the governor, Atropates, son of Attalus, in an unusual way: into his camp, they say, marched ten files of armored, spear-bearing Amazons. Their leader, who called herself Queen Hyster, was presented to Alexander. After the obligatory prostration, she thereafter addressed him as an equal, declaring that those in her faraway country had heard something of his prowess, and that she wished to take her pleasure with him. If their joining produced a daughter, she would be fit to rule her tribe; if a son, he would be delivered to his father to be raised, for—as we all know—the Amazons do not nurture their sons but expose them.

By all accounts this Queen Hyster was most beautiful, her charms revealed by her short tunic and the tightness of her leather girdle, which showed to best advantage the surprising prodigiousness of Amazon breasts. These were exposed and utterly complete, in contradiction of the legends that one breast was always removed. This fact, along with the high heels on their boots, suggested to some that Hyster's company were not real Amazons at all, but devised as a joke by Atropates. Yet Alexander, for his part, accepted Hyster as a genuine Queen. He acceded to a political alliance with her, but declined any further entanglement, noting that he was already married more than once. This excuse was received with regret by Hyster, who led her pendulous sisters away from the baying worship of the Macedonian soldiers. It seemed clear to other witnesses, however, that the tired, wheezing Alexander refused her invitation because he was simply unfit to take it up. And indeed, hers was the only challenge from which the conqueror of Tyre and the Rock of Sogdia had ever shrunk.

It is a truism that men enjoying good luck turn skeptical of prophecies. Tyche's graces are understood as the fruits of hard work, wise planning, or whatever virtues men like to attribute to themselves, and not the whims of the gods. Since the news for Alexander had been very good for a long time, he lately had little use for the services of the soothsayer Aristander. The King attended the regular morning sacrifices as a duty, though his face showed his mind was elsewhere, and the seer seemed to take the hint, producing auguries that provoked little comment one way or the other. It was therefore something of a surprise when, during the reading of a ram's entrails at the palace at Ecbatana, Aristander paused over the liver. The King asked what troubled him.

"This liver has but two lobes—and look here, how the vein is distended."

Alexander looked. He was no judge of such things, but knew very well that it portended an event of significance. Euripides wrote of a similar sign in *Electra*, when Aegisthus sacrificed a calf with a lobeless liver just before Orestes killed him with an axe.

"It could be an ill omen, or just as well not," said Aristander, evidently not sure what the King wanted to hear. "It suggests a disappearance of some kind. But what shall disappear is not evident."

Alexander was preoccupied with the planning of a naval expedition through the Caspian Sea. That his whole fleet might disappear was worrisome, but Aristander found nothing inauspicious about the King's relations with Poseidon. For lack of a specific sign, Alexander contented himself with the usual precautions—extra dedications to all the gods—and instructed Aristander to sacrifice again. When the second try showed nothing amiss, Alexander seemed to put the incident out of his mind.

At this time his relations with Hephaestion had lapsed into a kind of tense formality. With the arrival of Bagoas, then Rohjane, then Barsine and Parysatis, the King's intimacies became increasingly subordinate to the rule of his empire. His old companion was assigned a series of important but distant tasks—to build a bridge here, to settle some provincial dispute there—which kept him away from the Greek court for longer and longer periods. To be sure, Hephaestion relished these opportunities to show his competence: no doubt he was sensitive to insinuations that he was little more than Alexander's bedfellow. In any other army, beside a leader of merely human brilliance, Hephaestion would have been a formidable presence. However, on campaign with Alexander, whom he never ceased to love, this uncommon man understood the greater virtue of serving the throne before himself.

Nevertheless, what mortal would not resent being supplanted in the familiarity of a god by eunuchs and barbarians? When he did come to attend the court, Hephaestion said little, and when he did speak his voice was laced with sarcasm. Perceiving his jealousy, Alexander would spare his feelings by sending him away again, until the next time he would come, and his hostility was still deeper. Witnesses say that even strangers became uncomfortable around them, so palpable was the strain.

But Alexander's continued affection was clear when his old companion was suddenly taken ill at Ecbatana. When his fever stretched into a second and then a third day, the King sent his own personal doctor to tend to him. Hephaestion rallied, his appetite returning. Alexander, meanwhile, was obliged to attend athletic games he had organized for Persian boys, whom he had observed lacked civilized pursuits. It was while he presided over these games that word came that Hephaestion had relapsed.

Abandoning the event he had worked so hard to organize, Alexander rushed back to his friend's side, but he was too late. Hephaestion was gone, the dregs of a pitcher of wine he had ill-advisedly taken with lunch still at his side.

Alexander behaved at first as if he would not believe it. He carried on with talking to the dead man, breaking his monologue only to snarl at anyone who approached the body. After some hours this banter lapsed into inconsolable despair. Casting himself on the corpse, Alexander wept without shame, crying out his regret at this or that disagreement going back to their boyhood. At length he bellowed for a knife, and those around him became genuinely fearful that he would do harm to himself. But instead Alexander sliced off all the hair on his head, including his eyebrows, and retreated, crazed and bloody, to his bed-chamber.

Alexander and Hephaestion had not been close in their final years. It took all of us by surprise, then, that the King went so entirely to pieces over his loss. He ceased to wash. His skin again became covered with the spots I had first seen on him years before, at Chaeronea. In that time he passed just two orders: first, the doctor who tended Hephaestion, Glaucias, was to be executed. This suggests that the King at best suspected incompetence in the manner of his lover's death, and at the worst actual malice. For all were agreed that despite his illness the victim was sound of body, very much in his prime, and for such a man to descend so acutely was most suspicious. The dregs of the wine pitcher were examined with no conclusion reached one way or the other. Yet there are many known poisons that would leave no obvious trace.

His second order was for all the fires in Babylon's temples to be snuffed out in Hephaestion's honor. Despite invasions, earthquakes, and every other kind of disaster, many of these fires had not been allowed to go out in a thousand years. This decree, which was made with no apparent concern for the Babylonians, was alone enough to put the natives in a deadly mood.

When he emerged at last, Alexander seemed to have aged ten years. His cheeks were sunken, and he held his side as if his Mallian wound was not months old, but fresh. Resuming something of his old decisiveness, he ordered the court moved back to Babylon, where he intended the funeral to be held. He also sent messengers to the sanctuary of Ammon at Siwah, with the request that Hephaestion be deified in death. The

King did not wait for the god's answer, however, of-fering immediate sacrifice to the memory of his de-parted friend, and speaking to him in the old, easy style they had known in happier times together.

It is some three hundred miles as the crow flies be-tween Ecbatana and Babylon. Alexander walked the entire distance in his bare feet, with just an old cloak over his head to protect him from the late-spring sun. For the journey, Alexander had, according to the ad-vice of his Egyptian ambassadors, placed his compan-ion in a series of five nested sarcophagi, with a golden one closest to the body and a lead vessel outermost. The Egyptians are known masters of the embalmer's art. When the sarcophagi were cracked open some weeks later all were amazed to see that Hephaestion's body was utterly free of corruption. This preservation did not mean that Alexander had abandoned the rites we recognize as Greeks—Hephaestion would have his cremation. The pyre Alexander had in mind, however, would be unique in the history of the world.

But before the King reached the gates of the city an-other portent darkened his path. A party of Babylon-ian magi—priests of the Temple of the High Head, whose reconstruction had not yet begun in the seven-and-a-half years since Alexander promised to restore it—approached him with a warning. Their god Bel had revealed to them that Alexander would meet his death if he entered their city. Instead of marching west, they said, the great Alexander should go to the east, where nothing but victory and good health would be his for the rest of his days.

Still in the depth of his grief, the King had little pa-tience for diversions of any kind. He understood that the Babylonians, whom he had freed, would prefer to enjoy their autonomy without their liberator's actual presence. Yet the lands through which his army had marched were already stripped of usable stores—gods notwithstanding, he could not turn east. Hephaestion's spirit, moreover, was destined to depart this Earth from its very capital. No other place would do.

Alexander did his best to accommodate Bel by marching beyond the city and entering from the east, by the Adad Gate. In this way it could not be exactly said that he entered Babylon by marching west. The magi seemed unmoved by this logic, until the King facilitated the release of funds for work on their temple— after which they endorsed his acts without reservation. We might even suspect that this was the object of their embassy to him all along, if subsequent events did not prove the worth of their original warning after all.

Other than assuring Hephaestion's commemoration, few other matters preoccupied the King's attention in his last days at Babylon. The only blemish on what he considered his ideal capital was her dilapidation under Persian rule; where the Great Kings kept the city a backwater, Alexander planned to bind it to his empire with a massive dredging and enlargement of her harbor. The new facilities would be filled with warships that would carry his rule to Africa and, ultimately, to Carthage and Rome. To these ends he ordered further exploration of the lower reaches of the Euphrates river and beyond, to the coast of Arabia.

The dredging and shipbuilding paled in comparison to the titanic construction under way near the west sector of the city's ring wall. There, Alexander ordered the erection of a pyre as massive as a Gizan pyramid, consisting entirely of the most precious offerings imaginable. Troops swept through the city to accept—or in some cases to compel—donations of rare furniture, statues, vehicles. These were assembled on a series of platforms increasingly set back as they soared to the summit, where Hephaestion would lie on a gilded couch set inside a gilded room within an entire gilded house.

When it was completed the pyre was more than two hundred feet tall; the commissioned elements alone, including the wood and the gilded giants and faux ships' rams and centauromachies, cost ten thousand talents. This figure does not include the value of all the private donations, or the cost of the funerary games the King held, which included thousands of athletes from as far as Sicily. All these together made Hephaestion's funeral the most lavish dedication to fraternity in the history of the world.

The time finally came when Hephaestion, dressed in his armor and still as beautiful as the day he died, was borne up to his bier. Four regiments of Inheritors armed with bows were arrayed opposite each face of the pyramid. At a signal, the archers loosed flaming arrows; the sight of the blazing bolts simultaneously rising to ignite the pyre was unforgettable. The mass of wood, ivory, silver, and gold erupted on all sides like a volcano, with a heat so intense it melted the bronze bosses on the wheels of the chariots parked a hundred feet away. The flames reached high enough to daub passing clouds the color of blood.

The historians will forever report that Alexander constructed a pyre the size of Cheops's pyramid to honor his dead friend, but that is only half the truth.

The King made the pyre to honor himself too. Recall that he was fond of saying that "Hephaestion is also Alexander"; the vast, burning museum of treasure that he made for his friend was, in some sense, a way for him to stage-manage his own funeral.

The manner of Hephaestion's death called for an investigation. Yet there had to have been as many suspects as grains of sand on the beach. The nature of Hephaestion's relationship with Alexander, which by its nature was difficult to rival, had made him many enemies. That Alexander insisted on placing older, more capable men under the command of his lover built up resentment against him. Hephaestion's personal qualities, his loyalty, his good looks, had always attracted envious eyes.

Gossips spoke of a feud between him and Eumenes, Alexander's personal secretary. But would even a secretary be foolish enough to take action for such a public spat? Others said that Bagoas wanted him dead. Yet Bagoas had long before stolen Alexander's intimacy, so what more did he have to gain by murder? I would have suspected Perdiccas and Ptolemy had a hand in it, to further assure the succession of either one of them to power. Which is to say, I would have suspected those two, if an incident had not occurred that convinced me, in this case, of their innocence.

On the night the great pyre burned I was standing next to Rohjane. Her mood was as buoyant as I'd seen in months. With the rest of us, she watched as the lights were extinguished in the temples, and the stars appeared with a brilliance rarely glimpsed by the citified Babylonians. I heard her gasp with delight as the conflagration wafted Hephaestion's spirit to Heaven.

But just as the athletic games were about to begin, the Queen excused herself. She complained of a headache. Yet after spending more hours with the woman than her husband, I could sense her insincerity.

"Yes, you should retire," the King told her with fraternal warmth. "I will come and see you after."

"Yes, you will," she replied, the tartness in her voice entirely escaping him.

I followed an hour later. Her apartment was in a remote wing of the palace, as far as possible from the nuptial beds of Barsine and Parysatis. When I found Rohjane, she was lying on a drinking couch opposite Youtab. There was an open brazier beside them, and bread and eel on a table between them; they held drinking cups in their hands.

"Is this some barbarian custom, to make a celebration at the time of a funeral?" I asked.

"*Pah!* Who invited sourpuss?" cried Youtab.

The Queen laughed, stretched her arms. "We are having a symposium! Or haven't you ever seen a drinking party just for women?"

"The premise, my lady, is absurd."

"Oh, stop being the tutor! Yes, there is a funeral, and yes, Hephaestion was a fine fellow. But the innocent suffer all the time, don't they Youtab?"

"They suffer particularly."

"Yes, particle . . . partickle . . . particularey . . . by the gods, what *is* in these cups?"

Then the women laughed in that way I had seen so often among Alexander and his companions, when the craters were running low and there was nothing very funny to laugh at. I crossed my arms and waited for their attention.

"It has always been my intent to help the Queen understand her responsibilities in the Greek style," I said. "And so I must tell you now that this behavior is entirely inappropriate. To retire to your tent is perhaps understandable . . . but to carouse in this way? I think not."

"Isn't it funny how he speaks of what a wife should do, but never the responsibilities of the husband?" Rohjane asked Youtab, as if I was not standing there.

"Maybe he means that you should consider yourself lucky to be dishonored by a husband like the great Alexander," answered Youtab.

"You mean, dishonored by a god?"

"Reduced to an ass!"

"Ravished by a swan!"

"Seduced and abandoned!"

"On a beach on Naxos!"

"The very son of Zeus!"

"Lord of the mountaintops!"

"Master of the backcountry!"

They leaned into their pillows in their hysterics, until Youtab raised her head and cried through her laughter, "Oh, that's too much. Too much! I've wet myself!"

I turned to leave them. Rohjane called after me.

"Machon, only friend, come drink with us!"

"Yes, come back! Just watch what you drink from around here!"

I again call your attention to Youtab's words: "watch what you drink from." This seemed rather a morbid thing to say, given the circumstances of Hephaestion's death. Of course, it doesn't constitute evidence that Rohjane or her servant was responsible. It may have just been a bad joke. Nor was any poison ever found, in the dead man or anywhere in the palace. But I can tell you that Rohjane was not over the insult of Alexander's other marriages, which occurred just a few months before Hephaestion's death. Youtab's choice of humor—and the poor timing of their "women's symposium"—were suspicious.

It is true that Alexander sent a request to the Ammon temple in Siwah that Hephaestion be accepted as a god in his own right. All of us—his advisors, his family, the priests of Ammon—indulged him this, taking it as a harmless, if somewhat indiscreet, testament to his love. What was not so easy to excuse, though, is a letter the King sent to Cleomenes, his governor in Egypt. Remember that this was the same Cleomenes who, upon taking control of Egypt in Alexander's name, cornered the grain market in that country. I am told this raised the price of bread tenfold here in Athens. I submit a copy of this letter into evidence, with the magistrate's permission.

"The clerk will read the letter," said Polycleitus. When the recitation was done, Swallow, Deuteros and the rest of the jury were stunned.

This is the exact text of Alexander's letter. I was there when he dictated it, and obtained my copy from Eumenes. Yes, Alexander orders Cleomenes to construct a marble monument to Hephaestion in Alexandria, and promises that if the construction pleases him, he will pardon all of the governor's past malfeasance—his expropriation from the temples, his looting of the public treasury . . . and the famine he caused here and elsewhere in Greece. What is more, Alexander also promises to ignore *any future crimes.*

You heard that right. Can you imagine such a promise coming from a man you all agreed to take as a god? Indeed, that it could be bestowed on a creature so villainous, so reprobate, that not even Ptolemy could stand him? The latter, as you recall, had Cleomenes killed soon after he arrived in Egypt.

I will say no more about Alexander's letter. There is no need to gild that lily—memories of the pain in your empty stomachs, and the cries of your underfed children—shall be testimony enough. But out of curiosity, how high did the price of wheat go in the market just a few feet from where we sit here, Aeschines? Three drachmas for a *capithe*? Four?

"Higher!" someone cried from the back of the room.

Higher still! But we must forgive Aeschines his ignorance, for he was not here to suffer with you. Nor was I, for that matter. The difference, I submit to you, is that I am not here extolling the virtues of the man— I mean, the *god*—who offered pardon to a man who brought famine to this city, or promised to look the other way when a villain like Cleomenes committed any other crimes that might have entered his head.

As deep as his grief was for Hephaestion, there should be no doubt that Alexander did recover from it. At last he resumed work on his many projects; it was at this time, for instance, that he undertook a detailed examination of the shipping channels downstream from Babylon, thinking he would instruct the engineers on the best route by which deep-draught vessels might enter his harbor. As he often did, the King took the helm of his boat himself, showing as much skill afloat as he did directing armies on land. It so happened, however, that he rode up on an obstruction in the shallows, which knocked everyone on the deck to their knees. After his sojourn in the Gedrosian desert, Alexander had taken to wearing a hat to protect his neck and shoulders from the sun. With the shock of running aground, this hat flew off his head and landed in the water some distance away. Before the current carried the hat too far, a slave on board took it upon himself to swim after it.

This man's initiative was especially welcome, as the hat was fixed with a royal coronet of gold. Allowing this emblem of universal kingship to wash up on some dung-strewn shore would have been awkward indeed. Yet all were equally appalled when the slave plucked the hat from the water and, perhaps thinking he would keep it from further damage, put it on his own head for the swim back. The Macedonians were murmuring, and the Persians gesticulating at him to remove it, but he came on and climbed up anyway, conscious of nothing but his pride. He was oblivious, that is, until he saw the circle of frowning faces around him.

Now I know that it has been a long time since we Athenians have had kings. It has not been too long, however, for you all to imagine the magnitude of this disaster: for this slave to put the royal device on his head was just as ominous a sign as a servant taking the throne, or walking on the royal carpet. Nor was Alexander immune from such concerns, for it was now obvious in his mind that Hephaestion's death was connected to the discovery of the ram with the deformed liver. So where as before he would have forbidden the presumptuous slave to be punished, this time he allowed him to be severely beaten; the hat was then tossed back into the water, where it was retrieved properly by a sailor with a better grasp of the side-stroke. Later Alexander regretted the beating, and rewarded the slave's good intentions with a fortune of thirty minas in silver. That particular coronet, however, was locked away, never to be worn again.

As I have spoken to you here, friends, I realize I have asked much of your credulity. You have all heard what you believed to be the truth about Alexander, have even sat your sons upon your knees and told them these same stories to fill their hearts with pride at the exploits of the Greeks. So it is with some trepidation that I speak to you now of the death of Alexander. Though you may find what I say difficult to believe, I assure you it is what Perdiccas in Babylon knows, and Ptolemy in Alexandria, and the handful of others who witnessed the events I am about to describe. By the gods, I swear it.

Alexander, believing himself abandoned by both friends and fortune, sought comfort in wine and conversation, as his sociable nature had always been accustomed. He was sharing the cup with Peucestas, Ptolemy, and myself when the first signs of fever came over him. Thinking perhaps that he would nip his sickness in the bud, the King took a last drink from a great Spartan canteen before going to bed. As he downed the wine, we saw a strange expression come over his face—an expression that did not necessarily show pain, but a kind of dejection, as if he was reminded of some inescapably dispiriting thought. Then, in a voice so small none of us could recognize it, he bid us a good night.

The testimonies of his servants give us some hint of what happened next. Alexander spent the next hours in fitful sleep, and rose with his fever worse than before. Unwilling to skip his obligations, the King presided over the morning sacrifice, then reviewed two regiments of troops newly arrived from Macedon. He then bathed and withdrew early, perhaps still convinced that his illness would pass. When he awoke the following morning his fever was worse; though his chamberlain had ordered all the windows in his chamber to be left open, so the breeze over the great palace would sweep over him, his bedclothes were soaked. Nevertheless, he again insisted on presiding over the morning sacrifice, then met with Nearchus about his plans for the exploration of the Caspian Sea. And again, he bathed and retired before sunset.

There began to be real concern in court for Alexander's health. In fact, the execution of Glaucias had left him without a regular doctor, and the death of Hephaestion had left him suspicious of the care of anyone unfamiliar. By the third day he failed to rise for the sacrifice and was not seen at all. On the fourth, the servants were barred from the royal chamber.

The King began to drift in and out of consciousness, at times barking out bizarre commands, or violently stripping his bedclothes from his body, then lapsing into a trembling stupor. The foremost Babylonian physicians were brought in to attend him; his bedroom was transformed as they forbade certain fabrics and substances from his proximity, brought in braziers burning medicinal incense, and applied ointments to him that no Greek doctor could recognize. His officers, meanwhile, gathered in the forecourt of the palace, each insisting he had some essential business to discuss with the King, but—we may assume—wishing instead only to have a last look at Alexander before he was gone.

The next day, to the surprise of everyone except perhaps the Babylonians, the patient rallied. The fever broke at last, and Alexander was able to sit up and take food. As he did during his recovery from the fight with the Mallians, his thoughts turned to settling the apprehensions of his men by making an appearance before them. With servants supporting both shoulders (for he was still quite weak) he came out on the balcony of the palace and looked down on a sea of faces. Upon seeing Alexander, the troops erupted in joy, begging him to lead them again, and promising that they would follow him to the shores of the great Ocean if he so wished it. The King raised his hand to acknowledge them all, and opened his mouth to speak, but could produce only a whisper. In their thousands the soldiers all leaned forward, as if they might discern the invalid's faint words from hundreds of feet away. Of what Alexander actually said, none could be sure, except that his statement twice included the word "duty." Exhausted, he then had to be carried back to his room.

It was at this point that a peculiar thing happened. Rohjane, who had been standing behind the King as he appeared on the balcony, attended him as he settled back on his bed. It was the first time she had stood at his side since the illness had struck. She then insisted on helping her husband drink some water, which she professed to have fetched herself from the cistern. The Babylonians, who were not unfamiliar with the art of poisoning, examined the contents of the cup and could find nothing suspicious about it. Nevertheless, they brought in a taster. Rohjane professed great annoyance at the doctors' impertinence, demanding by what power they could so insult their Queen. When the taster did not drop dead, they begged her forgiveness, and thereupon left the patient to his wife's tender ministrations.

Alexander took the water and slept peacefully. The next morning Rohjane was gone, and the doctors were confounded to find the King in the grip of a fever and new symptoms. These included sharp pains in his abdomen, and a fierce thirst that propelled him into a frenzy. The latter would not let him rest, so that Alexander could not conserve his strength at all. By the evening both his heartbeat and his breathing were faint. The doctors, perhaps with Glaucias's example in their minds, brought to bear every art at their disposal to save him. By early the next morning, they managed to wake him for what all expected would be the last time. His generals were brought in, and he was asked if there was anything he wished to tell them. Perdiccas leaned down to hear his answer, which was but a single word: "water."

Hours later, the messengers to Ammon in Egypt returned with an answer to Alexander's request for Hephaestion to receive divine honors. The god said that all such men, including Heracles and Achilles, merit worship as demigods. It was an answer that would have pleased Alexander very much.

XXI

Notice, gentlemen, that unlike Aeschines I did not tell you he died on that occasion. To be sure, Alexander very nearly did succumb to poison—as my opponent has told you, by the fourth day of his illness matters were desperate. What Aeschines does not know is that, in fact, the efforts of the King's Babylonian doctors met with complete success. Now that I see I have your attention, and though I know I am racing the clock, I will try to tell you the real circumstances of Alexander's death.

Thanks to the arts of the Babylonians, the King's fever broke within two days; before the end of the week he was able to hold down his food. As it happened, then, this incident seemed like yet another of the King's victories over mortality. Rumors spread that Alexander had rallied; the world, having held its breath, took ease at last. On orders of the King, however, no official announcement was made of his recovery. While it seemed odd that he wanted to withhold this information, I presumed he wished only to test the loyalty of those satraps who might revolt. On this, as on several other matters that day, I was wrong.

For Alexander was not pleased with his recovery. Instead of launching himself into fresh plans for building or conquest, he sat with a dejected look on his face. No one—not his friends, his new wives, nor Bagoas could rouse him. As for me, he tolerated my presence in the room, but would not speak. When he looked at me, it was with accusation in his eyes, as if I had been responsible for the undue extension of his life.

Rohjane gave the entirely appropriate reaction to his improvement. For the very first time, she had followed my directives on dress and comportment to the letter, looking very much like the dutiful Greek wife.

"My lord, I rejoice at your recovery!" she exclaimed, approaching to give him a kiss.

But Alexander turned his face away from her. She soldiered on, smacking him on the cheek, going on about the growth of the child within her. Alexander was silent, regarding her coldly. He only seemed to relent when she held up a piece of woven cloth for him to see.

"I've had Youtab begin the swaddling clothes for our son. I've made her swear to finish before he comes. . . ."

The King's brow softened a bit as he looked at this naive bit of handiwork. He was filled, no doubt, with that ambivalence particular to new fathers, as yet unsure they are up to the demands of the role. In Alexander's case, the uncertainty must have been deeper still, convinced as he was that his wife had a hand in his poisoning. And yet, while she carried his heir, there was nothing he could do about it. Knowing Rohjane, I am also sure that everything she did in that meeting was contrived to remind him of this fact.

"If I may serve you in any way, please call me."

"If I call for anything," he finally said, "it will not be for the water you brought. Do you remember?"

"I remember."

"Good. And do you remember Hephaestion, too?"

"Of course," she said, keeping up her denial. "Who could forget such a noble captain?"

"Very well," he replied, waving her away.

After she was gone the King grew tired, and slept for three hours in the middle of the afternoon. When he woke up, he called for all his personal companions to attend him. Perdiccas was there, and Ptolemy, Nearchus, Eumenes, and myself. Pulling himself to a sitting position, the King asked a strange question:

"Eumenes, is Hermolaus still with us?"

"You mean, Hermolaus, son of Sopolis? The page?"

"Yes."

"He lives, though in what condition I cannot—"

"Good. Bring him."

And so I learned that Hermolaus, the main instigator of the pages' plot against the King's life, had not been executed yet. It was a peculiarity of the Macedonians, I saw, that certain important prisoners were not killed right away, but imprisoned for as long as it took to wear down their defiance. For particularly stubborn characters, this process might take years. There were still rumors about the camp that Callisthenes was not dead, but languishing in some hole until he earned a kiss with his prostration. Only then would he be allowed to die.

None of us had seen Hermolaus for some years. In his confinement he had grown into a man, albeit a thin, pale, unkempt one, so unused to daylight that he could not keep his eyes open. He was naked as he was brought in, bearded to his breastbone, shackled by his feet.

"Do you know where you are, boy?" Alexander asked.

"By the stench of oppression, I would say I am before Alexander."

"It is the stink of sickness you smell, and your own rot."

"Rot, sickness, tyranny—all the same."

Alexander laughed. "A clever answer from a ghost! What a man you might have become, O Hermolaus. Now peevish retorts are all you have left. Or are they?"

The page's eyes cracked open a bit. "The Alexander I once loved did not waste time with riddles."

The King rose to his feet, stretched his arms, and grimaced in pain from the Mallian wound. "Fair enough. The day of execution is at hand! Eumenes, bring him arms. Meet me under the east wall, near the Marduk Gate. Hermolaus, once during the hunt you stole the boar from me. I give you an opportunity now for the biggest game of all. Don't disappoint me!"

With that, the King left. The rest of us, including Hermolaus, stood dumbfounded. Perdiccas came out of it first. "You heard him! Arms for the prisoner!"

Alexander waited for Hermolaus outside the Marduk Gate. He had only his chamberlain with him; on his back and legs he wore the cuirass and greaves of divine Achilles. He left the ancient sword leaning against the pitch-clad bricks, and the great Gorgon's-head shield next to it, still marked from the ordeal at Multan. As we all met there, it seemed we were all on stage, with the scene lit only by torches set in the theatrical backdrop of the Babylonian wall. Like distant stagehands, the tiny, helmeted heads of two guards looked down on us from hundreds of feet above. They were, as it was, the only other audience for the night's drama.

Still in shackles, Hermolaus had a peaked Phrygian helmet with the cheek-guards down, a leather corslet, and a hoplite shield. He was standing straighter now, his eyes wide open, but he still had the look of a man who expected at any moment to wake up from his dream.

Alexander took up Achilles's shield. "Give him a javelin," he ordered.

"If the King permits it, we might execute the prisoner in the usual fashion," suggested Perdiccas.

Alexander answered with these verses, from the twenty-second book of the poem:

> *The running is over, Achilles! No more.*
> *Three times around the city of Priam I ran*
> *Unable to face your assault.*
> *But courage anew I feel in my heart*
> *To face what must be faced. . . .*

As you all may recognize, it is Hector's last challenge to Achilles before their duel at the walls of Troy. And though I had heard him quote the Poet before, this was the first time he had cast himself not as his ancestor, Achilles-the-Swift-Runner, but as Hector-Breaker-of-Horses.

Ptolemy gave Hermolaus a javelin. The latter looked at Alexander, then the weapon, holding it in front of him as if he'd never seen one before.

"Do you expect me to kill you with this?"

"I expect you," replied the King, "to accomplish what you swore with your comrades. There was a time when you stood before me and called me a tyrant. Well now, here I am, boy! Strike me down! Fix my arrogance! I promise no one will stop you."

Perdiccas looked to Ptolemy, who looked to me in amazement. It was the first time I had seen either man in such dire confusion. I suppose they would have said the same of me.

Hermolaus shrugged, seized the javelin with an overhand grip, and cocked it above his head. Then he sang:

You beyond forgiveness should not speak of pacts
Can there be deals between men and beasts?
Between wolf and sheep there is no common ground,
Born as they are to live in undying hatred.
So it is between us, no love lost, no peace
Until you or I may strike the dust and sate Ares,
Shielded scourge of men, with our blood.
Come to me, then, with what courage you have left
Death or victory! Show me your skill,
As a daring man of war!

He made his throw. The javelin flew from his hand and straight for Alexander's head, only to lodge in the soft brick of the wall. The King had ducked.

Missed, have you! Now look at the divine Achilles!
So sure you were that Zeus decreed my death!
You were bluster only, trying to strike fear in me,
Make my legs shake, lose my nerve!

And so the King, taking his turn, lofted his spear. With the same unerring skill that had killed Cleitus, Alexander made a dead-center shot. This time, however, his opponent was armed with more than a drinking cup. The metal tip bounced off Hermolaus's shield, leaving only a small dimple in the surface.

"I see you have no spear in reserve," said the King.

"Only this sword," replied the other.

"As do I."

They closed on each other with blades unsheathed. Alexander seemed to be moving at half-speed, not yet at full strength after his illness. Hermolaus likewise had none of his former quickness, having spent much of his youth in a cell. Yet the slowness with which the duel unfolded only made it seem more terrible, as we could all anticipate and feel every blow. Alexander was on the attack, striking at his opponent as he grasped his wounded side. Hermolaus parried, backed up, counterattacked. The King stumbled and fell, his sword clanking to the dirt beside him. Perdiccas moved to intercede, but Ptolemy held him back. It had not taken long for the latter to realize how he could benefit from these incomprehensible events.

Hermolaus, perhaps overwhelmed by the prospect that briefly opened before him, did not kill Alexander right then. Instead, the King had time to take his sword again and ward off the final blow. As Hermolaus lost his balance, Alexander tried to get to his feet—but froze with the torment of his Mallian wound, his face and neck contorted with the agony of it. In that second, with Alexander's hesitation, Hermolaus saw his chance: he put the point of his sword right through the cleft at the King's throat, just above the top of

Achilles's cuirass. The blade cut with appalling ease through the soft flesh, exposing the white surface of his windpipe. Then the blood rose and covered everything—the windpipe, the blade, the hand that held the blade, the ground—

"*Defendant, stop speaking,*" said the judge. "*You have run out of time.*"

XXII

Machon stood with his mouth open. The water had stopped. For a professional speaker to be interrupted like this would be very bad form—the jurors were left hanging just at the moment of Alexander's death. Yet Swallow didn't think this blunder would count too much against Machon. He was, after all, an acknowledged amateur, defending himself against one of the most formidable orators. To show his inexperience was to make himself sympathetic, for if there was anything Athenian jurors hated more than a bad show in the courtroom, it was a career litigant.

Machon sat down. At that point in the procedure there was an unofficial recess as the magistrates conferred and the clock was reset. The jurors stretched their legs, and although any sort of discussion or politicking was forbidden before the verdict was read, deliberation was already under way by other means. Experienced jurors could always gauge sentiments by exchanging glances with the men around him. Arguments could be joined by raising an eyebrow, and resolved by a downward flicking of the eyes. Swallow looked at Deuteros, who concurred with a nod. Matters were not looking good for Aeschines. Though it came only near the end of Machon's testimony, and was only one incident in Alexan-

der's eventful life, the pardon of Cleomenes finally seemed to turn most of the jury against Aeschines and the appeasement faction.

"The parties will have one measure of time each for disputation. Prosecution, do you wish to ask questions of the defendant, or make a statement?"

Aeschines didn't answer but simply manifested, bright-robed and full-throated, from his seat.

Athenians, we meet on a sad day, for what we have heard from the defendant represents a challenge to all of us who believe in the truth. Where to begin to unravel this Gordion Knot the defendant has spun for us? To be sure, the events that I have narrated and Machon has distorted took place years ago and far away, and are already passing from the vale of living memory. Yet I say that their passing should not be an occasion for self-serving revision. I say that what the mass of observers believe to be true should command respect, and the subjectivities of certain others less so, no matter how well placed they may have been. I say that *something* happened in the past, and those happenings stand as facts regardless of insinuation or anecdote.

For my part, I am not afraid to tell you that I take these proceedings seriously. I spent a considerable time preparing my presentation, which was gleaned from the reminiscences of numerous witnesses. Based on those testimonies, I learned much about my subject, and I must tell you that the Alexander I came to know in no way resembles the person Machon has described. According to the defendant, the Lord of All Asia was little more than a quailing, querulous child. He was afraid of the future, afraid of his enemy, and afraid of battle—imagine that—Alexander afraid of battle! Machon tries to exploit unkind rumors about Alexander's friendships with men to portray him as some kind of womanly chimera. We should all reject anyone's claims to know what the King and Hephaestion did in private, and it is nothing less than rank slander to claim, as Machon does, that Alexander let himself be used like a common prostitute! For that outrage alone he deserves conviction!

Perhaps Machon thinks so little of us as to think we can be fooled by his strategy. To defend himself, he must try to pull down Alexander. What a curious defense, to deny his impiety by denying the god! Meanwhile, he insults all Greeks with his malicious "recollections" of Alexander's doubts. Could a man full of doubt have led an army for twelve years against the largest, most populous empire the world has ever seen? How does a general in constant fear of assassination so inspire his men as to leave behind an unparalleled legacy of peace and esteem? Could a mere drunk simply fall onto the throne of the Great King?

As he maligns Alexander, Machon slanders the characters of his most trusted lieutenants. Perdiccas and Ptolemy are made out to be craven opportunists who plotted and schemed for their own benefit while Alexander still lived. Craterus and Cleitus are, in Machon's own words, "thugs." Hephaestion was somehow reviled by everyone, though every scrap of evidence attests to the admiration he inspired in all men. How fortunate for you, Machon, that these men are not here to make you answer for your lies!

In these proceedings, we must be content to note that events since the King's death do not bear out Machon's version: it is not true, for instance, that Perdiccas or Ptolemy seized authority upon Alexander's passing. Perdiccas, by all accounts, was most reluctant to pick up the King's ring, and now rules by consent only as regent to Rohjane's infant son and the half-wit Arridaeus. Ptolemy did not claim the throne at all, most obviously because his rank did not merit it, and also because he is a man of unimpeachable integrity. He is only the governor of Egypt now, not her king! How Machon can profess to know that Ptolemy has intentions to be Pharaoh is beyond my understanding.

Distortions of this kind at least have the virtue of referring to actual persons, and therefore having some root in reality. Tales of massacres of nonexistent people, such as "the Branchidae," deserve no refutation. That Alexander died in a fight with Hermolaus is accepted by no one. Nor should we be detained by Machon's claims that it was Arridaeus, not Alexander, who generaled the victories of the Greeks. Machon presents no evidence to support this contemptible assertion for one simple reason: it is nonsense. I myself glimpsed Arridaeus during an embassy to Pella some years ago. I assume my impression of him still holds. He is a fool, completely unable to care for himself, much less command an army. That a man may somehow be a drooling idiot at one instance and a dashing strategist at another is absurd. There is no such thing as a half-time half-wit.

The felicity of this phrase earned Aeschines murmurs of assent. He seemed to absorb this encouragement and magnify it, becoming still more compelling as he went on.

Though Machon is an uncommon liar, he cannot help but ensnare himself as any liar must. Note that several times in his narrative he esteems himself as a skilled warrior. Yet in his account of Chaeronea he clearly states that he was "in the sixth rank of a phalanx eight shields deep." As we all know, veterans are never placed in the middle of the phalanx! They are either in front, to inspire the rest with their valor, or in the last rank, to prevent cowards from fleeing. So which is it, Machon—are you not such a doughty fighter after all, that you were stuck in the middle? Or was your account of the battle a fiction after all? See how he sits there, having sought so vainly to disrupt me before!

All these matters distract us from the real issue. To my mind, these are and always have been the specific charges against Machon: that he violated his oath to the Assembly, and that he showed impiety. That he failed in his service is proven by his own testimony. By his own admission he was in charge of "managing" Rohjane, yet he also suggests that the woman had a hand in Hephaestion's death. Once a poisoner, always a poisoner: I have argued myself that this same person slipped the fatal dose to Alexander. So on this count the effect of Machon's work was far less than negligible—his gentle instruction was the very incubator of her crimes.

Regarding his other claims of service, such as repelling a Mallian raid on the King's tent, no one else corroborates his story. Yet he admits that he tried to twist Alexander's mind in an effort to "help" him. What arrogance! As if anything poor Machon would have to say would affect the fate the gods had in store for noble Alexander! It is interesting, though, that Machon admits wishing for the King's death, and therefore the failure of Greek arms, during the invasion of India. By the gods, what sort of patriotism is that?

I must address the issue of the alleged letter to the governor of Egypt. Gentlemen of the jury, I will not stand here and claim that Cleomenes was a virtuous man, or that he did not deserve the end he found under Ptolemy. He was indeed rapacious, grasping, despicable—any adjective you choose! But to claim that he alone caused the famine in Attica is to engage in irresponsible exaggeration, for the truth is that the shortages began as early as the archonship of Aristophanes, which was almost exactly the time Cleomenes was first appointed tax collector. So unless we are prepared to believe that this man seized control of the grain trade instantaneously, it cannot be true that he caused the famine. Ships carrying grain from the Black Sea were sailed through a war zone during those years; anyone may go down to Piraeus and talk to the captains there, who will speak of massive disruptions in this trade.

Again, I excuse nothing. That Cleomenes's greed may have worsened the crisis deserves our contempt. But that is a far different proposition than suggesting Alexander turned a blind eye to crimes that caused hunger in Greece. The letter Machon bandies about, therefore, is a transparent forgery. That Eumenes would even share such a letter, if it had indeed come from Alexander, beggars belief.

Machon's impiety requires no proof from me, for it festers in the open, in every word that he utters. It lies not only in his contempt for Alexander, and his lack of respect for the beliefs of his elders, and his inordinate fascination with the ravings of Zoroastrians, Brahmins, and other aliens. You may hear it in the way he speaks of Macedon, where great Olympus stands, as if it were foreign territory—or in his eloquence when he describes the charms of notorious courtesans! This last we possibly excuse, as his mother was a whore. But what we cannot excuse is his mendacity, Athenians, for his is the type of thinking that has always placed our city in danger. His affinity for ambiguities of his own making, his championing of the weaker argument over the stronger—these are the legacies of men like Machon. Hearing his testimony, is it any surprise that strumpets, pacifism, and sophistry have become our leading exports? For this reason, for his presumption, for his failure, indeed for every reason in the world, I ask you to take the only just course—conviction. Only with that may we begin to redeem the damage he has caused to us all.

For the final time, Aeschines brought his statement to a close just as his time expired. Deuteros nudged his friend, and Swallow nodded in response. Aeschines had made a strong response to Machon, and had been clever in linking the defendant to that class of professional obfuscators who had been in ill repute since Athens had first lost her empire. True, only yokels still believed the agora to be crawling with sophists. Philosophy had run out its string, having long since been domesticated, professionalized, and packaged for the consumption of rich men's sons. Yet nobody was ever disappointed who counted on the votes of ignoramuses.

It was hard to tell now which advocate had the advantage. It was beyond dispute that Machon had an interest in blackening Alexander's name, and as the orator said, men don't just fall into such fabulous success. Yet Aeschines could not allay concerns over the pardon of Cleomenes quite so easily. Claims of forgery were easy to make, and could not erase a few simple facts: before Alexander, no hunger—after Alexander, hunger. If it wasn't by his encouragement of Cleomenes, Alexander had to be responsible for the famine in some other way.

Swallow looked at the sky through the window—daylight was fading. More than for the fate of Machon, he feared he would lose his sleeping spot by the shrine if the trial went on much longer. With a shudder, he realized he might even be forced to go home to sleep with his wife.

Polycleitus indicated to Machon that it was his turn. The defendant took his feet with none of Aeschines's élan. Instead, he seemed exhausted.

I must tell you that I was not expecting to have to speak again. Never in my life have I had to keep my mouth running for so long! Really, Aeschines, I have new respect for those in your profession. In war, we try to have at it and settle the issue as quickly as possible. In the courts I see it is the longest-winded set of lungs that carries the day.

Before I rest, I must tell you a few more things. First, although Aeschines tries to put the best face on it, he cannot excuse Alexander's letter to Cleomenes. The argument that Cleomenes was not so bad because he only aggravated your misery is just too subtle for a simple soldier like me to understand. Alexander did not just pardon the man's past crimes, though that is bad enough. He also forgave in advance any others he would see fit to commit in the future. It therefore follows that if Cleomenes did take it upon himself to starve the Greeks at some later time, that would have been fine with Alexander. I say this without taking any satisfaction in it—had he lived beyond his grief, the

King himself would probably have regretted his action. Didn't he always regret the awful things he did? As it was, the letter was written and delivered, and the offer was never rescinded. These are the facts.

Nor does the mere assertion that the letter is a forgery necessarily make it so. The clerk has the original, and originals of other letters the King sent to the Athenians—I invite the clerk to make a comparison of the documents. Does the seal match? Is the style comparable? I have nothing at all to lose from giving back my time for this purpose.

The clerk just sat staring, doing nothing, while Polycleitus glanced at the clock.

I see the magistrates are late for dinner, so I will not insist. And so on to my second point, which is this: I do not now bear, nor have I ever borne, any ill will toward Alexander. To say that I try to save my skin by harming his reputation is nothing but a handy supposition by my accuser. Against Aeschines's word I have almost twelve years of continuous service, which is a long time to serve under someone one supposedly hates! The truth is the very opposite of what my opponent says: as time passed, I grew to esteem Alexander more, for no man had ever faced the challenges he did. To conquer an empire, to become the target of universal flattery, envy, and hope—these would try the sanity of any man. For suffering these assaults who can despise him? I could not have done half as well as he.

Indeed, if I truly wanted to disparage Alexander I could do no better than to repeat the stories that have persisted here in Athens. I could have said he was nothing but a brat, a drunk, a barbarian, a sodomite, a lunatic, or best of all, an illusion! For at one time or another I have heard it claimed that Alexander died at the Granicus, Issus, Gaugamela, and Multan, and that the Macedonians had concealed this truth from the world for their own purposes. I have also heard that he is alive right now, in this city, preparing to succeed where Xerxes failed by annexing Attica to his mongrel empire! Beside these rumors, my tale is tame stuff.

Nor have I criticized him for the edict that raised the most protest in all the years he lived. I'm talking about his decree to all the cities of the Corinthian League that they must take back their exiles. That this measure was a selfish one on Alexander's part is beyond question: Asia was full of banished citizens from all the Greek cities, many all too eager to hire themselves out as mercenaries. Darius employed many; Agis of Sparta got his hands on no less than eight thousand of them for his revolt in the Peloponnese. For the stability of his empire, this pool of dangerous labor had to be dried up.

His reasoning has done nothing to make the order popular among the landed classes here. Naturally, many of them have become comfortable on the estates of their exiled rivals. But I am here to defend myself, not the interests of the five-hundred-bushel men of Attica or the Samian colonies. If you have lost your farm to a returnee, or been forced to tolerate the presence of a political rival, or of the man who killed your ox or diverted the water from your stream, perhaps you will find sympathy with me. But I count on nothing.

It is my own fault that I did not leave time enough to complete my account of Alexander's death. As it was, I did not see him when he was most ill, so there's not much for me to add to that sad succession of bad omens and sickness. I did have access to Rohjane, though, and offer the following incident, if only to show that I have told you all that I know.

It was on the third night of Alexander's illness that Rohjane, who had become an insomniac since the onset of her pregnancy, heard someone walking through the royal apartments. She rose, and seeing that it was the King, followed him on a circuitous route through the building. At last he came to a back door of the palace. Puzzled, she called to her husband.

"My King, can that be you? May we celebrate your recovery?"

The sound of her voice startled him. Drawing up his exhausted self, he replied in a voice so dry it testified to every mouthful of dust in every desert he had ever crossed.

"You would do better not to interfere."

"Interfere in what?" she asked.

"Barbarians and sycophants! How can you understand?"

"My lord, let me help you—"

"You may help me by allowing me the end my Father expects of me! Instead you delay me at the last minute with your foolishness."

"If I delay you, I do so only for the sake of your people, and your son who you would never meet."

"My son would thank me for my disappearance!"

By this time their conversation had roused the servants, who gathered around them in collective incomprehension. The King, knowing he had missed his chance to escape, allowed himself to be carried to bed.

If this story is true—and I see no profit for Rohjane in fabricating it—then it suggests Alexander accepted that his end was near. Instead of making a spectacle of his mortal end, he planned simply to vanish into the desert. No doubt such a disappearance would have served his legend well, like that of a god on loan to mankind, making his return to Heaven.

I cannot believe, though, that it was the exit he most wanted. He preferred the taste of metal on his tongue as an arrow shattered in his throat—the fatal fall from a speeding horse on a rutted field. Any death in action would have been better than some second-rate apotheosis, this stealing away in the dead of night from a bed of stinking nightclothes. Taking a knife from a skulking assassin, like his father, would not have been much better. At last, with the help of Hermolaus, he found a better way.

We all went to him as he fell. The wound in his throat did not penetrate his voicebox, but it was still painful for him to speak. Asked to whom he left his throne, he breathed, "To the strongest." We swooned in disbelief as he faded. This was, after all, Alexander, encased moreover in the armor of matchless Achilles. It seemed impossible that he could die so splendidly armed—until I remembered Hector's death. He was also wearing the armor of Achilles, having stripped it from the dead body of Patroclus.

Most of you will probably not accept my story without further evidence. This was exactly the thinking of Perdiccas and Ptolemy when they sought to cover up the manner of the King's death. Hermolaus, of course, was executed straightaway. The two witnesses on the top of the wall were likewise ordered down and killed. I would have joined them, except that I still had use as recorder of Alexander's greatness, and would not be believed anyway if I tried to spread the baseless story that he died in a duel with a minor prisoner!

The story went out that he died of sickness. The response of his men was no surprise, given that Alexander had killed many of them, had tried the patience of the rest, and had driven them all as ruthlessly as he drove himself. The survivors mourned him out of genuine respect, yet also embraced each other out of relief that he was finally gone, as if they had collectively survived some great storm. The Persians grieved too. In their case it was less in their esteem for him than because they were about to exchange the known sins of Alexander for those of someone unknown. Their uncertainty has still not ended even to this day—as it also hangs over us.

Aeschines asks how I know the characters of men like Perdiccas and Ptolemy. I must say I find his case laughable, for as he questions the experience I report after years in their company, he bases his whole prosecution on the written hearsay of absent witnesses! Aeschines, don't insult these gentlemen by overstating your case! Fine turns of phrase cannot hide your ignorance: if you had been there, for instance, you would know that the head injury Arridaeus received at the Hydaspes has done him some positive good—that he talks more, has taken up the wearing of clothes, and all in all seems ready to reign in his brother's place. It only serves the purpose of Perdiccas, that fine fellow, to keep Arridaeus from ruling outright.

From the sound of the water it seems I have a little more time, so I will help you to understand the man you have come to judge today. Aeschines says I lack zeal for the Greek cause. He is wrong—I have fought for that cause all my life, in ways and to extremes far beyond mere talk. I was not only at Chaeronea, but carried a spear against Philip on the island of Euboea, and Acarnanian Argos, and Cardia in the Chersonese and in Thrace. This was while our friend Aeschines took his sinecure on sunny Rhodes. And when I was sent to Alexander to fight for him, and the Fates abruptly decreed that the nature of my help must change, I did my best, though I knew little of diplomacy or of educating barbarous females. Never once have I said that if the Athenians wanted the skills of a diplomat or tutor, they should not have sent a soldier. I wonder if Aeschines had been there, would he have done better? Certainly his skills have served the Macedonians well in the past. But I don't think his golden throat would have done him much good against the Mallian raiders that morning on the Hydaspes!

It is in your hands to determine whether I will take part in the coming fight with Antipater. For my part, I hope never to pick up a weapon again. A man can see enough war to understand that it is an exceptional opportunity for the triumph of mediocrities. Mediocre men—who ordinarily stand tongue-tied on the dais, who fight half heartedly for their city, who make affordable sacrifices to the gods instead of genuine ones—can, with the benefit of arms, snuff brilliant minds, rape graceful women, destroy the greatest art, murder children. Mediocrity always triumphs, no matter how lofty the ideal by which we begin, no matter how great the leader. Neither great evil nor great virtue can be around all the time, can see everything. Yet mediocrity flies on horseback all over the battlefield, shouting "On to Pella, boys!"; it is living it up

right now on native labor, on the estates owned by
Greek barons in Sogdia and Bactria. Foundations
crumble, fame fades. All hail the middling—so ubiquitous and eternal!

*The defendant took his seat with water still running
through the clock. Polycleitus let it flow for a few awkward
moments as the courtroom absorbed Machon's strange outburst. To Swallow, this incoherence was the inevitable result
of an unschooled speaker forced to defend himself beyond his
means. After all, this was no Demosthenes who had shared
the floor with Aeschines all day; where Machon had begun
his trial with a face of polished calm, he finished with his
manner perturbed, his voice trembling. Whether the jury
read his attitude as presumptuous, or as the outrage of a
man unjustly accused, might figure yet in the verdict.*

"The jury will vote," *pronounced the archon. Then, leaning forward with his voice full of significance, he added,*
"The city expects you all to fulfill your oaths."

*Two boxes were set out in front of the dais. Each juror had
been issued two bronze disks: one disk with a hole in the center, signifying a vote of "guilty," and one without a hole.
The votes went into the first box, the discards into the second. As each man filed up to deliver his token, he was
obliged to conceal his choice by putting thumb and forefinger over the center of the disk.*

*The Scythian bailiffs were watching, lest anyone tried to
influence the verdict by speaking, or by bandying his token
uncovered. To defeat this, jurors over the years had hit on a
simple convention: votes for conviction were dropped in the
box with the left hand, ones for acquittal with the right.
When this ploy became too well known, the magistrates decreed that tokens would always be handled with the right
hand. The jurors answered with a variation: if voting guilty,*

the center of the disk was covered with thumb and forefinger, if not guilty, with thumb and middle finger. So far the authorities had devised no response to this.

The first vote was on the charge that the defendant had violated his oath. The citizens came up by rows, with Swallow and Deuteros among the first. Swallow delivered his token by thumb and middle finger, as did his friend. As the box filled with votes, the sound each bronze made as it hit the bottom passed from a wooden thud to a bright clink. Aeschines sat with his back straight and his legs together, looking more anxious than at any point in the trial. Machon slouched, his ankles crossed ahead of him as he looked out the window.

The vote seemed to be closely divided. When the next to last row filed out, the rube who had brought livestock to the courtroom finally woke up. Rubbing his head, he turned to Polycleitus.

"Magistrate, I appear to have fallen asleep. Where is my lamb?"

The archon signaled to a bailiff, who shoved the man toward the tally boxes. Bewildered, the hayseed collected his tokens and went forward, though he couldn't have heard a word of either presentation. Swallow watched when he dropped his disk: he used his thumb and all four fingers to handle the token, and so his vote was a mystery.

The last vote was cast. The clerk and his assistant emptied the box and began to count as another set of tokens was handed out to each juror. The voting began on the second charge, impiety, as the counting for the first proceeded. Swallow watched with curiosity as the clerk finished the tally, frowned, and decided they should count again. Because of this, the jurors sat for an unusually long time as *their stomachs growled and the full moon dipped into view through the windows.*

At last the clerk handed Polycleitus a lead tablet with the count for both charges. The archon looked to the clerk as if to assure himself of the numbers. The clerk tossed his head in the affirmative. Polycleitus faced Machon.

"The defendant will stand."

XXIII

Machon hauled himself to his feet. With the possible exception of the archon, he appeared to be the most dejected man in the room.

"Regarding the first charge, failure to fulfill his oath to the Assembly, the jury finds the defendant, Machon, son of Agathon, not guilty. The votes are 251 to 249—"

The room erupted as the jurors turned on each other. Accusations were met with counteraccusations, hands raised in denial, fingers jabbed in every chest. Deuteros was almost pushed off his bench as a juror leapt to his feet behind him, screaming that the vote had been fixed. Another raised his arms toward heaven beseechingly, crying, "May the gods protect us from the fury of the Macedonians!" Soon the bailiff's truncheons were swinging, men were hitting the floor, and two citizens dueled with knives. It took some time before order was restored.

Swallow was silent throughout the riot. In fact, this was only the second most even tally he had seen in his time. Machon was acquitted by a margin of two. Five years earlier Swallow participated in a corruption trial that ended 251 to 250, with the tie-breaking vote for conviction cast by the archon.

"*Whatever we do, we must talk to that shepherd!*" he told Deuteros.

"On the matter of the second charge, of impiety," Polycleitus announced at last, "the jury finds the defendant not guilty. The votes are 309 to 191. Clerk, release the jurors."

The five hundred poured out in the alley in front of the courthouse. The jurors were each clutching their jury-pay—seven newly minted obols—in their hands. Despite the lateness of the hour a number of vendors on the agora stayed open for business. A man went around selling fresh water from a spigoted skin on his back. Another hawked flatbread from an oily sack, while a handful of women of various ages haunted the half-shadows around the crowd, murmuring to whomever was nearby.

Some of the jurors went off right away to taverns specializing in the law-court trade. The rest surrounded the bewildered Machon, pounding him on the shoulders, pumping his hand, begging to drink with him.

"Tell us, were those your own words?" someone asked.

"Did Demosthenes write the speech?"

"Demosthenes," Machon replied, "would not have been so inept."

"Has anybody seen Aeschines?"

"Gone through the back door, I'd think! With his reputation, after so many trials, to be so thoroughly beaten by an amateur . . ."

Searching the mob, Swallow caught sight of the shepherd. Someone had left his lamb tied to a stake outside the courthouse; the man had already spent some of his pay on water for the sick thing. Swallow poked the man with his walking stick as the lamb lapped the water from his cupped palms.

"Friend, tell us—did you hear anything of the case?"

"Can't see as it's any business of yours, friend."

Swallow tossed an obol on the ground. The other looked at the coin, gathered it under himself with his foot.

"In case you didn't see, I was . . . out . . . the entire day."

"So how did you vote?"

Silence. Swallow showed him another coin.

"Are you sure you want to pay him again?" asked Deuteros.

"There's another case to be tried tomorrow . . . and the day after that. For now I must know his answer."

The lamb having finished its drink, the shepherd dried his hands on his ragged tunic. "I would love to take your money," he said, "but no one explained the rules to me. I can't remember which token I dropped. I can't remember at all."

XXIV

After his acquittal, Machon was seen carousing with well-wishers. Such good business followed him that the tavern stayed open until dawn. The barkeep had a pretty daughter who poured out the jugs, and kept the roast eel and pork womb coming in a way that made everyone forget the privation of the trial. Swallow and Deuteros found the party soon after it started, the former buying the jurors several rounds of Thasian black from some seemingly inexhaustible source of silver.

"So where do you keep all that cash, Swallow, that you can treat us all so generously?"

"You don't want to know where he keeps his money," warned Deuteros.

"From the fact that you are here," asked another juror, "may we suppose that you were in accord with the final verdict?"

Swallow smiled. "If you knew me personally, my friend, you would not suppose that at all! But in this case, you are right—I had something to do with the happiness of this occasion."

"But did you have a verdict in mind when you

came into the courtroom—or was it something Machon said that convinced you?"

Again, Swallow found himself obliged to make some meaning of what they had heard that day. This time, however, the defendant himself was among those staring at him. Confronted with the question of what verdict he originally favored, he glanced to Deuteros, who was engrossed in skimming the sediment from his wine to the edge of his cup.

"I will not lie to you—knowing the nature of the charges, and the stakes of the trial, Deuteros and I came to court today intending to vote 'guilty.' In this, we had only in mind the necessity of giving the Macedonians no excuse to attack the city. Of the wisdom of this view, we shall all learn in the near future. In any case, the credit for forcing me to look more deeply into the questions at hand, into the problem Alexander presented to us all, belongs to Machon alone. It was nothing in particular that he said. Instead, he convinced me that the fate of men like him and the fate of the city are not distinguishable. Athens is men like Machon."

Drinks were raised all around, and murmurs made in solemn agreement. Machon's cup stayed up longer than anyone's, though, as he stared into the fleshy crevices that contained the eyes of Swallow. The latter, feeling some modesty was in order, then took to emulating Deuteros's fascination with the debris in his wine.

"But what of Alexander himself? Now that you have heard what Aeschines has said, and then Machon, which do you think better captured the truth of the man?"

Swallow frowned. "If I foolishly professed to know

the answer to that question, I would scarcely deserve
the puzzling interest you all share in my view!"

"Oh, come now!" groaned the juror. "Though we
know you only in the courtroom, that you have an
opinion about everything is public knowledge."

"Fair enough. If you want to hear me say something
of him—though it can only be part of the truth, and
something of a truism—here it is: in times such as
these, when everything seems diminished, the Greeks
yearn for the straightforward heroism of Achilles. To
his credit, Alexander tried to fulfill that need. But not
even Achilles could provide himself with a worthy
enemy to overcome and seal his fame. That is, instead,
a gift of Fortune. Alexander was not so lucky. He was
forced to march through half the world to find his Hector. This foolish lionizing of Darius, of Porus, of dead
competitors like Cyrus and Xerxes, is evidence of his
failure. If events had not intervened, he'd still be looking today, I wager."

At this, no one raised a cup, and Machon kept his
eyes on the table. This response, far more than their previous eager agreement, compelled Swallow to go on.

"But if you want to hear something I do know for
certain," he said, "understand this: the Macedonians
will never accept a court verdict with which they so
strongly disagree. It is not in their experience."

Swallow directed this warning at Machon. The latter, however, made no other response but to lead his
entourage through the rest of the Chian wines, and
then the Lesbian. They had moved on to a local vin-
tage when someone began to sing the paean the soldiers gave before Chaeronea. At this, Machon's eyes
filled with tears, and he joined in the singing three

times over until his voice gave out, worn down after his day of speechifying. The singing done, the party smashed their drinking cups against the wall. The taverner smiled, added the cost of the cups to their bill, and ordered up another amphora from the basement.

Idling outside were the two Macedonians who had watched the trial from the spectators' gallery. Another man was with them but stayed in the shadows. As gray light filled the eastern sky, they looked up to the Acropolis to see the night lamps snuffed out on the Propylaea. When the drinkers staggered out of the tavern at last, they lofted borrowed torches above their heads. The Macedonians stayed out of sight as they pointed out the figure of Machon to their hatchet-faced companion. He nodded, then stayed behind as the Macedonians disappeared into the warren of the Kerameikos.

Decent lodging houses were not common in the center of Athens. There was one good place near the law courts, run by a Corinthian medic. It was beyond the west end of the Painted Stoa, just a little way toward the Dipylon Gate. A man of Machon's importance would only be found there.

The leader of the assassins was moving up in the world: it would be his first job for the Macedonians. As Machon was reputed to be a tough old soldier, and Hatchet Face was by and large risk-averse, he invited a pair of friends with him to do the deed. The freelancers were of the kind of common hooligan usually seen on the roads out of town. They had all killed people before, though this was most often a side effect of stealing a good overcloak or a pair of lace-up boots. The three of them agreed to show up dressed the same way—wide-brimmed hats pulled down close to their eyes, tunics covered with leather butchers' aprons. If they timed their escape well enough, they would exit through the tannery quarter just as the market day began. By then almost everyone would be wearing a bloody apron.

No one stopped them at the door of the lodging house. Expecting that Machon would be in one of the better rooms away from the street, they proceeded down the hall with their knives still sheathed. As they approached the last door on the corridor, they heard someone chanting in an unfamiliar language. That room no doubt housed a foreigner. They knocked instead at the room adjacent, taking out their blades and holding them behind their backs.

A man opened the door. He was young, no more than twenty, with rouged cheeks and a dressing gown that hung off one shoulder.

"Yes?" he asked.

"We want to talk to Machon," said Hatchet Face.

"Who?"

He pushed his way past the boy. Inside, a figure was cowering under a blanket. Hatchet Face signaled his men to surround the couch. Drawing the blanket aside with the point of his dagger, he found the boy's terrified, gray-bearded patron.

The old man lay there pale and trembling. He looked up without saying anything, his breathing becoming more audible each time he exhaled.

"Machon?"

"Not Machon."

Just then Hatchet Face realized that the chanting in the next room had stopped. Cursing his luck, he led his men to the next door. Finding it locked, they forced it off its flimsy hinges. What they saw inside brought them up short.

The room was redolent of perfume. Peering into the smoke, they saw a small, round brazier with its flame still burning. Hatchet Face came in and looked down on the table where the fire danced: beside the brazier was a dish of ground spice that looked like frankincense, and fine twigs stripped of bark.

"This stick smells like apricot," one of the hirelings, a dispossessed farmer, said. "And this one is pistachio."

Hatchet Face made a perfunctory search of the place, but it was obvious that their quarry was gone. The window curtain was pushed aside; there was no sign of a heavy cloak, so Machon must have taken that with him. He came back to the table, noticing for the first time that there was a rag of pure white cotton lying on the floor. He picked it up. The rag had two strings attached to it, as if it was meant to be tied around the face or the neck.

"What is all this?"

"I don't know," said Hatchet Face. "Get a sack for the spice."

After bagging the frankincense and stripping anything else of worth in the room, the assassins stored their loot under their aprons. With their knives hidden and hats pulled down on their faces, they slipped away. Machon's abandoned little clay amulet of the winged disk—his symbol of Ahura Mazda—they left behind as worthless. His thanksgiving fire was left to burn itself out.

AUTHOR'S AFTERWORD

In this portrayal of Alexander and his world, I have attempted to remain faithful to the better-known facts. These facts, however, don't always address the most interesting questions about his extraordinary life. Historical fabulists tend to be attracted to the lacunae and the mysteries of their subjects, where the truth may be lost, forgotten, or suppressed. It has therefore been necessary, at times, to aim not for the literal truth, but for the ring of it.

A number of the events in Alexander's life have therefore been deliberately relocated in time and place. Many of these elements have bases in fact, but have been fleshed out beyond the rather telegraphic versions reported by the ancient sources; others did not, in fact, happen at all, but should have. Certain events, (such as the siege of Aornos) were left out because the themes they illustrate are adequately covered elsewhere. Readers hungering for the full story (as far as it is known) are encouraged to consult the original sources or scholarly biographies.

In addition to the ancient texts (the histories of Arrian, Curtius Rufus, and Plutarch; Xenophon's *Anabasis*; the forensic speeches of Demosthenes and

Aeschines; accounts of legal proceedings in Lycias, Antiphon, and Apollodorus; numerous tidbits of ancient knowledge from Herodotus, Athenaeus, Strabo, Diodorus, Pliny, et al.), a number of modern sources were useful in researching this story. These included, but were not limited to, Alexander monographs by Robin Lane Fox, Mary Renault, and Michael Wood, and treatments of ancient Greek life such as those by Robert Flaceliere (via Peter Green's translation), Robert Garland, Sarah Pomeroy, and James Davidson (whose delectable *Courtesans and Fishcakes* is much recommended). Whatever is accurate about my portrayal of the Zoroastrians should be credited to Mary Boyce's scholarship; whatever is inaccurate is my fault. The works of J. K. Anderson and Victor Davis Hanson were invaluable for envisioning infantry battle in the fourth century. Early modern accounts of travel in the near East (such as Charles Masson's 1842 *Narrative of Various Journeys in Balochistan, Afghanistan, and the Panjab*) were helpful in envisioning Alexander's route as it was in ancient times. Profuse thanks as well to Professor Ioannis Akamatis of the Aristotelian University in Thessaloniki, for an enlightening afternoon at his excavations in Pella, and to Professor David Hollander of Iowa State University for his feedback on the manuscript.

Some may be interested to know what really happened to Athens after Alexander died. In fact, the anti-Macedonian faction, powered by the indefatigable Demosthenes, did rouse the city to resist the Macedonian regent in Greece, Antipater. The result was a bitter affair called the Lamian War. Things went well for Athens at first: having at last found capable leaders who had fully absorbed the lessons of Chaeronea, the Athenians and their allies compelled the formerly undefeated Macedonians to retreat. The regent holed himself up in the city of Lamia, and faced being overrun there—until some of Alexander's veterans from the Persian war returned to break the siege. The Greeks fought on, defeating the Macedonians yet again, until Antipater brought them to battle for the last time near the Thessalian city of Krannon. The immediate result was the Macedonians owned the field, though the allied army was still not destroyed. What finally ended the revolt was the age-old Greek problem—failure to hang together in the face of a common adversary. Demoralized, facing an enemy that was unchallenged at sea and getting stronger on land, the Greek allies melted away. At that moment, for all practical purposes, Athens ceased to exist as an independent power.

The book suffers from its share of blunders. But just as all who wander are not lost, not all inaccuracies are mistakes. Purists may object, for instance, that I oversimplify the state of Athenian politics in many ways, including by making the historical Aeschines (390–circa 314 B.C.), into an undisguised Macedonian apologist. The most relevant question here, though, is whether the man was capable of playing the toady, if it suited his purpose. The answer is yes.

Readers of forensic bent will note that the court procedure described here does not resemble current practice. Indeed, moderns first encountering the courtroom literature of classical Athens are often surprised that rumor, hearsay, irrelevancies and character assassination were rampant in the incubator of Western rationalism. Orators had common recourse to insults, such as during a public prosecution of Timarchus in 346, when Aeschines accused the defendant's political sponsor, Demosthenes, of favoring girlish underwear. In the popular court I describe, the Heliaia, standards of evidence, discovery, and examination of witnesses were all strikingly casual. When the prosecution and the defense had finished their statements, jurors were indeed called upon to render their judgment immediately, with no deliberation or politicking allowed. While I cannot claim that every detail of this procedure I describe is accurate (for much is unknown), it is likely that Athenians of the time would have recognized the procedure depicted here as typical of their courts.

Could there be any truth to Machon's story of Arridaeus as the "secret weapon" of the Macedonians? Though it is known that Alexander's half-brother was present on the march, the sources are notably silent on what, if anything, he did during the entire twelve years of the Asian campaign. My guess is that he impinged on events more than the official historians acknowledge. The precise nature of his mental deficiency would of course be nice to know. This side of the story, unfortunately, may never be recoverable. Given the substantially different developmental environment that existed in antiquity, it is not altogether clear to me that the kinds of illness seen then (or the kinds of sanity, for that matter) are exactly the same as the ones observed among modern people. The truth about Arridaeus may be far stranger than the autism I suggest for him here.

From the structure of the novel it should be clear

that I see little profit in attempting to find the "real" Alexander. Alexander has been a perennially popular subject for classical scholarship, yet his study suffers from the fact that the man himself left relatively scant direct evidence for archaeology to uncover about him. New developments in our understanding of Alexander is largely restricted to rereadings and re-rereadings of the ancient texts, all of which are secondary, late, and ideologically driven in one way or another.

Those looking for the key to Alexander's fall will likewise be disappointed. To my mind, what stopped him is not as interesting as what kept him going. While Alexander clearly relished building and administering things, it was the opiate of conquest, of taming the new, that came to dominate his short life. One can only imagine what he might have accomplished had he engaged his other talents.

Authorities will long debate the significance of the achievements ascribed to Alexander, including his military innovations, the founding of Alexandria, the spread of Greek culture over a vast area, the model of divine kingship he bequeathed to Hellenistic, Roman, and later rulers, dreams of a transethnic empire, etc. Perhaps the most unappreciated implication of his career, however, was the realization—dawning somewhere deep in the ancient mind—that such mythic accomplishments need not be the works of a god at all, but of the ingenuity, persistence, and vision of a flawed human being. In this sense, his story is a modern one.

Classics from
Ancient Greece

THE ILIAD
By Homer *trans. W.H.D. Rouse*   527372
This very readable prose translation tells the tale of Achilles,
Hector, Agamemnon, Paris, Helen, and all Troy besieged by the
mighty Greeks. It is a tale of glory and honor, of pride and
pettiness, of friendship and sacrifice, of anger and revenge. In
short, it is the quintessential western tale of men at war.

THE ODYSSEY
By Homer *trans. W.H.D. Rouse*   527364
Kept away from his home and family for 20 years by war and
malevolent gods, Odysseus returns to find his house in disarray.
This is the story of his adventurous travels and his battle to
reclaim what is rightfully his.

THE AENEID
By Virgil *trans. Patric Dickinson*   528638
After the destruction of Troy by the Greeks, Aeneas leads the
Trojans to Italy where, according to Virgil, he re-founds the city
of Rome. And begins a dynasty to last 1,000 years. This, Virgil's
greatest triumph, was seen by many Medieval thinkers as linking
Rome's ancient past to its Christian future.

THE GREAT DIALOGUES OF PLATO
trans. W.H.D. Rouse   527453
Here are some of the most influential texts in Western Literature.
From Classical times till now, these have been considered funda-
mental texts that every learned person should have read. This
volume includes the complete texts of *The Republic, The Apology,
Crito, Phaedro, Ion, Meno, Euthydemus,* and *Symposium* in a widely-
acclaimed translation.

Available wherever books are sold or at
www.penguin.com

Penguin Group (USA) Inc. Online

What will you be reading tomorrow?

Tom Clancy, Patricia Cornwell, W.E.B. Griffin,
Nora Roberts, William Gibson, Robin Cook,
Brian Jacques, Catherine Coulter, Stephen King,
Dean Koontz, Ken Follett, Clive Cussler,
Eric Jerome Dickey, John Sandford,
Terry McMillan…

You'll find them all at
http://www.penguin.com

*Read excerpts and newsletters, find tour
schedules, and enter contest.*

Subscribe to Penguin Group (USA) Inc. Newsletters
and get an exclusive inside look
at exciting new titles and the authors you love
long before everyone else does.

PENGUIN GROUP (USA) INC. NEWS
http://www.penguin.com/news